Redeemer of the Dead

A LitRPG Apocalypse

Book 2 of The System Apocalypse

By

Tao Wong

Copyright

This is a work of fiction. Names, characters, businesses, places, events, and incidents are either the products of the author's imagination or used in a fictitious manner. Any resemblance to actual persons, living or dead, or actual events is purely coincidental.

This book is licensed for your personal enjoyment only. This book may not be re-sold or given away to other people. If you would like to share this book with another person, please purchase an additional copy for each recipient. If you're reading this book and did not purchase it, or it was not purchased for your use only, then please return to your favorite book retailer and purchase your own copy. Thank you for respecting the hard work of this author.

A Starlit Publishing Book

Published by Starlit Publishing

PO Box 30035

High Park PO

Toronto, ON

M6P 3K0

Canada

www.starlitpublishing.com

Ebook ISBN: 9781775058700

Paperback ISBN: 9781775058748

Hardcover ISBN: 9781989458457

Books in

The System Apocalypse Universe

Main Storyline

Life in the North

Redeemer of the Dead

The Cost of Survival

Cities in Chains

Coast on Fire

World Unbound

Stars Awoken

Rebel Star

Stars Asunder

Broken Council

Forbidden Zone

System Finale

System Apocalypse - Relentless

A Fist Full of Credits

System Apocalypse - Australia

Town Under

Flat Out

Anthologies & Shorts

Comic Series

Contents

Chapter 1

"This is a bad idea." Ali, my two-foot-tall Spirit Companion floats next to me, staring at the cave entrance cut into the river canyon's side.

I crouch, glacial water flowing past my armored legs, summer sun highlighting the emerald greens and clear blues of the river. "Of course. What exactly in the last four months has been a good idea? Taunting a Salamander? Hunting a Drake? Clearing a monster lair? Ever since the damn System came into place, it's all been one bad idea after the next. It's just a question of how bad we want to make it."

I check the readings from Sabre, my Personal Assault Vehicle (PAV). Normal humans would just call it powered armor, or maybe a mecha. After all, a half-hour ago it was a bike. I got it nearly at the start when the System, the over-arching mechanism put into place by the Galactic Council, came into being. According to them, since "Mana" had finally reached significant levels on Earth, the System could now be put in place. Along with the System and Mana saturation came the destruction of all our electronics and the mutation of Earth's ecosystem and spawning of monsters from lore. Cue the Apocalypse as civilization fell.

In the end, what Ali and I are arguing about is the blue floating System window dominating my vision.

Dungeon Located!

Warning! The current dungeon has not been categorized at this time due to System limitations. All XP rewards are doubled. Successful completion of the dungeon by a System-registered individual will generate increased rewards.

"You said it. These kinds of rewards can be quite good." I stare into the darkness and heft my armored right arm, where I recently integrated a projectile weapon. While I love my beam rifle, good old solid projectile weaponry has certain advantages, including the option of using multiple ammo types to suit the situation.

"Still a bad idea, boy-o. Could be a bunch of really high-level monsters in there," Ali says as he spins around in agitation.

"Yeah, yeah. Then we run. We still have a full charge on the QSM."

The Quantum State Manipulator, or QSM, is one of the first toys I acquired when the System kicked into play four months ago, bringing an apocalypse to Earth and shutting down all our higher-end electronics. When activated, the QSM phases me into another dimension, which makes it incredibly useful for running away. It has drawbacks, including a long recharge time and a short use period, as well as allowing high energy states—read explosions—to pass through, but it's saved my life more times than I care to count.

"Fine, fine. Light her up," Ali mutters and I grin, pointing the barrel down the cave entrance.

I cycle the ammunition in the barrel then open fire, embedding three glowing light sources into the cave walls. I learned my lesson about going into a dark cave a month ago. Even if Sabre and my helmet give me enhanced low-light vision, it's still a better idea to light things up.

The cave entrance shows me nothing new, but better to be cautious. I launch one of my drones to check things out, sending it to the ceiling to scan for potential threats, before I send it deeper and lock it in place a couple dozen meters ahead of me. Once that's done, I walk in while shrinking the feed enough that I can watch it and my surroundings at the same time. I keep an eye on the mini-map that my Spirit and my Skill Greater Detection updates even as I do my best to stay hidden. I'm a pretty good sneak, if I do say so myself, though announcing myself with a bunch of lights probably takes away from the surprise factor. Can't win it all.

The first cave I find has nothing more dangerous than some mutated fungus. Fungi. Whatever. It shoots out spores that are probably poisonous, but I'm in a fully sealed armored suit with an independent oxygen supply so John 1, Dungeon 0. Sweat runs down my back as I walk farther in—cold sweat that even the environmental controls in Sabre can't fix. Fear courses through me, but along with it comes excitement.

Yeah, I'm screwed up in the head. I was before this started, and now I'm probably even more twisted. I actually like this—risking my life, dancing along the knife's edge of danger. It wakes me up, thrills me in a way that nothing else ever has, and I'll admit I take risks no one else would. That moment when everything tilts, when I could live or die, is when I finally feel truly alive. No more walls, no more compartmentalized and contained emotions, just moments of perfect control amidst the chaos.

Crazy. Told you.

"Picking up two. Nope. Three," Ali mutters.

A moment later, I feel them myself. Damn, even now he's better than I am. Then again, if the Spirit wasn't, I'd feel as though I wasn't getting my money's worth. Not that I pay him—not exactly, at least. He's a Perk I gained for being in the wrong place at the wrong time, and the System pays for his upkeep. If it didn't, I'd have slowed my Mana regeneration down even further and I've got enough Skills that do that already.

I send a slew of new commands to the drone, launching it toward a higher point in the ceiling to check out the new threats while I lay down more light orbs. I wonder what I'll find this time?

The answer is ugly, ugly monsters. Quadrupedal creatures with faces like a mutated rat's, spiked bodies, and whip-like tails that drip with acid. The creatures are dark green with blotches of black across their bodies, providing them an effective camouflage in the darkness of the cave.

Kongorad (Level 28)

HP: 480/480

Status Effects: None

I watch them for a few minutes in my feed, the creatures not noticing the drone. They don't do much beyond strolling around in curious circles in the cave ahead of me, occasionally bumping into each other and play fighting. After I've watched them long enough, I sneak in and launch a single light orb into the cave.

As they startle, twisting to stare at the orb, I take the opportunity to put a few rounds into them. I've staggered the rounds in the loading chamber, so I shoot high explosive, armor piercing, and normal in order. I then put a single round into each of my opponents. The high explosive projectile blows up the spine of the targeted Kongorad, the armor piercing drills all the way through, and my normal round smashes into but doesn't pierce the monster I targeted. Armor piercing it is.

Even as I make the adjustments to my ammo lineup, the surviving Kongorads are returning fire with their barbed spines. I duck behind a nearby outcropping, but the launched spines move so fast and cover such a wide area, I get caught by a few. They drill through the nearby walls, the outcropping, and my armor with ease, carrying their Mana-imbued barbed poison into my body. I grunt at the notification that lets me know I've been poisoned. There is no pain though, just a comforting numbness that slowly spreads.

A light chime lets me know the gun is ready, and I twist around the corner of the outcropping to open fire, concentrating on slamming three bullets into one monster. Each bullet smashes through its body, splattering blood around it before I duck back behind the measly cover provided by the rock. Thankfully, after drilling through all the rock, the spines can't completely penetrate my armor.

"Can't touch this," Ali chants and literally dances as he floats in front of the Kongorad attempting to kill him. He might be visible, but he's not corporeal, which means he's a very good distraction.

Grinning in my helmet, I charge the distracted Kongorad and slice down with the sword I conjure into my hand. My personal weapon might not look like much, but with my Advanced Class skills, I cut through the monster's head with ease, killing it.

Level 28 monsters are a cakewalk for me. While my own Level might be a measly 23, because I have an Advanced Class, my "true" level is about double that. *About*, since as Ali points out, the math gets fuzzy. Jumping directly to an Advanced Class without a Basic Class has given me a bunch of side benefits, including a higher resistance to most effects—like poison.

Monsters dead, I scan for any further surprises before slowly sinking down. My body shudders slightly as it fights off the poison, heat washing over the numbness. I lick my lips, tasting the salt from my sweat while I wait for the effects to go away. It doesn't take long at all, then I'm standing, walking over to the bodies, and putting the System-generated loot into my inventory before dropping the bodies into my Altered Space. The Altered Space Skill creates a dimensional pocket I can store objects in, a nifty little Class Skill that lets me store more loot and corpses than most parties can as a whole.

Right, that wasn't so bad. If that's all I'm facing, this should be simple.

***

"Ali, this cave seems huge," I mutter, kicking the latest victim off my blade. I've been down here for a good hour, walking through caves and killing Kongorads, and there is no way this canyon holds such an extensive cave system. It makes no physical sense. If I'm going to be walking around here for much longer, I better get started recharging my beam rifle, since I've switched to using it as my primary ranged weapon.

"Dungeon," Ali answers.

"That isn't an answer."

"Yes, it is. The System designated this a dungeon, so it altered the physical space. It's now bigger on the inside." Ali pauses, awaiting a reaction. When he gets none, he mutters, "Goddamn muggle."

"I think I liked it better when you were watching reality TV," I grumble while walking the cave.

Normally my Skill gives me more of a heads-up about potential problems, but the increased Mana density in this dungeon is screwing with my Skill, reducing my ability to scan for threats to a bare ten meters. Ali's got it better, but it still means we have to move carefully.

The bat drops from the ceiling and I sense it just a moment before it hits. I twist, spinning around and conjuring my sword as I cut the Noxious Bat in two. Not its real name, but after my first encounter and a quick briefing, I had to turn off my oxygen tank. They're extremely good at hiding, but they smell like the seven heavens—so much so that even through the environmental filtering, my best method of locating them is my sense of smell. Of course, considering how powerful the environmental filtering is supposed to be, the fact that I can even smell them makes no sense. Then again, it doesn't have to make sense if the System decides to break the rules. Again.

I loot the Noxious Bat's corpse but don't stick the body in my Altered Space, not wanting to contaminate my other goods. Then again, I'm not entirely sure the Bat would contaminate things. I have a theory that the System breaks many of the rules of physics because it's trying to balance technology, magic, and skills. So if it gives a monster an environmental advantage, it wants that to mean something. Thus, the System breaks other rules to make it work. On the other hand, I can punch through walls without breaking the ground while doing so, so I'll take the occasional weirdness. Not that I have a choice. The System is the System.

After another half hour of walking, I finally come to the end of the first floor. And I say floor since I find a straight chute going down, leading to what I can only assume is another level. Arse.

"How many floors do Dungeons have?" I frown. I'm confident, but if I'm looking at a dozen…

"How long's the Ether Serpent's tail?"

I point the gun down, firing another light orb, then call back my first drone so it can recharge while I send my second down. Hopefully it's only these two floors—I only have two drones and their batteries take forever to recharge.

***

Down, down, down we go. Wherever we go, that's where we kill. That doesn't work, does it? Fine, you put together a rhyme while fighting off spine monsters in packs. Here, I'll wait. Actually, no, I won't, because I'm fighting Kongorads.

Ducking low, I grab a Kongorad and pick it up, power armor assisting the lift, and I use the creature to block the spines from its friends. I poke my rifle barrel around the twitching body, using the camera mounted on the barrel to target and fire. As I hear a distressed beep, I send the rifle back into my inventory and throw my improvised shield, following it to the last of the still-living monsters, which I stab in the head.

Monsters dead, I squat as my head swims, my body shuddering as it fights off the poison and gives me back full control of my body. Casting a Minor Heal helps a little, so I do it again.

The second level is taking forever. The Kongorads move in larger packs down here and they have a friend, a tripedal creature that skitters along the ground and releases beams of light that I have to dodge. Luckily, they aren't that common, but between dealing with increasing amounts of poison and greater swarms, I've been having to take longer and longer breaks between each encounter.

"John, you sure you can do this?" Ali asks again.

I nod firmly, slowly standing and rotating my shoulders and knees as I check how far I've recovered. I check my projectile ammunition next, noting I'm down to less than two dozen armor piercing bullets. I queue up high explosives next, but I never bought that many of them—I'm a bit of a cheapskate and high explosive rounds are expensive. I kind of regret cheaping out now. Just another thing to lay at my father's door.

Tackling these monsters head-on isn't going to work. I need to think of a new idea or pull back. I frown as another shudder crosses through me. I can't snipe the monsters—I don't have the line of sights. The monsters work in packs, so trying to drag them out to kill one by one doesn't seem to work. So...

***

"This is degrading!" Ali grouses.

I chuckle, looking over the cavern I've altered. If I can't kill them one by one, I'll pull them into a kill zone and force them to fight me in smaller numbers. I've torn down some stalagmites and stalactites and piled them up to create a bottleneck by using some of the insta-cement grenades I carry these days. On the improvised wall, I've got a small perch that has a little extra padding to slow down spines, enough that I can shoot at the monsters in relative safety. I've also added light orbs as far as I can see to give me as much visibility as possible. After that, well, it's all up to Ali to play bait.

"Yeah, yeah, suck it up, buttercup." I grin, leaning back and checking the map again.

"Asshole." Ali heads toward the nearest group on the map, fully visible and glowing ever so slightly.

The kill zone works almost too well—pulling monsters to a fixed position and firing on them as they near me ensures I take out one or two before the swarm arrives. After that, most initially try a long-range duel. When that fails, they charge the opening I've left. It's so tight that the monsters have to scramble and push to get through it, giving me more than enough time to whittle them down. The monsters are so blindly aggressive and stupid, they keep coming because they've got just that little chance to end me.

After each group, Ali gives me a few minutes to rest and loot before we start the process again. Each break takes longer as he searches farther and farther afield, drawing the monsters to me. The T'kichik are the most difficult, since they actually understand a bit about cover and sniping at long-range. Unfortunately for them, I can use magic and I'm more than happy to spam my Improved Mana Dart (II) at them till they fall over and die.

I almost feel bad for the Kongorad Alpha when Ali finally locates it. It comes rushing forward, flanked by its guards, and I greet them with a pair of plasma grenades, one after the other. The explosions rip apart most of my improvised walls, but between the grenades and my Lightning Strike spell, the guards are so much crispy meat. Facing the Alpha, who's just a bigger version of the Kongorads, after that is simple. Outside of the numbness in my body that slows me down and makes me feel as though I'm running through water, killing it isn't difficult at all. I just have to keep ducking, cutting, and shooting the monster till it falls over. When I'm done, I finally get what I'm looking for.

Congratulations! Dungeon Cleared

+5,000 XP

First Clear Bonus

Having cleared the dungeon for the first time, you have been rewarded an additional +5,000XP +1,000 Credits. Bonus for being the first explorer +5,000 XP +5,000 Credits.

Ingles Canyon Dungeon classified as Level 20+ and above

Damn. That was a good haul. That's a huge experience increase, especially at my level. Between the two bonuses, I'm nearly halfway to a new level. I loot the last body and drop it into my Altered Space.

Pursing my lips, I consider the room around me. I always knew we'd be facing more and more dungeons—after all, we are designated a "Dungeon World" by the Galactic Council and System. Having finally run one, I'm thinking these will be a real problem. Running something that's half my "real" level has me nearly out of ammo, tired, and just a little nauseated. Overall, I think it's time to call it a day and head home. Home is good.

Chapter 2

Home is a two-story log house set at the turn-off on the Klondike Highway that leads to either Carcross or Teslin. A former restaurant and grocery store, the Cutoff has clear fields of fire up to fifty meters around its gravel parking lot and System cleared trees. In the past few weeks, I've paid to add reinforced System walls, windows, and doors to the building to increase its security, along with a simple Command Center that provides me with a System-enabled sentient tracking system and System-compatible utilities. The once-abandoned building is quite livable, if lonely.

I had a house in Whitehorse proper. Okay, in Riverdale, but that's a fifteen-minute walk to downtown for a slow walker. I still have it really, though I've not really been back for a bit. Being out here, a good thirty minutes away by bike, has been peaceful. When the System came, it destroyed anything with electronics or delicate mechanisms. Since then, mechanics in Whitehorse have been fixing up cars and trucks to make sure they're System-enabled, but it's still rare to see a vehicle on the road. Certainly no one is taking joy rides anymore.

I might return to Whitehorse proper one day, but for now, my ex-party is staying at my house, taking care of the upkeep and ensuring monsters don't move in. Whitehorse still hasn't reached the threshold required to become a safe zone, which would stabilize the Mana flow around the city and stop monster evolution and spawning within the city limits. Last I heard, about thirty percent of the buildings in the city still need to be purchased. I can't even imagine the time it'd take to get a place like New York completely stabilized.

As I pull up on Sabre, I find myself groaning and stretching slightly. I can't help but think about the hot shower waiting for me inside the building. It's why I don't even see the giant armored hand that hauls me into the air before it's too late to stop it. Reflexes honed through hours of battle kick in immediately and I'm jabbing forward, calling forth my sword. Before I can hit anything, my hand is locked to my side in an iron grip. I don't stand a chance of breaking out of it so I don't even try, curling my body up around the arm holding me and kicking at the body with everything I've got. The impact is enough to rip me away from the arm, my body rolling and coming up by reflex even as my brain finally catches up to wonder what the hell is happening.

"Stop!"

I freeze as my brain points out the many, many guns pointed at me. I'm surrounded by armored attackers slowly shimmering into reality, cloaking deactivating. All of them are large, tusked, and fully armored in black-and-green futuristic combat armor.

Hakarta Lieutenant (Level 31 Burning Scar)

HP: 4890/4890

Status Effects: None

"Gremlin's balls! It's a full Elite platoon, John. This isn't even the right lineup!" Ali almost screams as he pulls up the information, displaying data above each of my attackers.

Lieutenant, a pair of sergeants, four privates, and a major. The lowest levels come from the privates, and they're Level 17 Advanced Classes.

I've never heard Ali sound panicked before, not even when I was taunting and kiting a Salamander across kilometers of forested terrain. His fear opens up a cold pit of dread in my stomach, one that I forcibly compartmentalize. I'm so out-leveled it's not funny. The Cutoff is a System-designated fort, which means it has certain importance in terms of location and placement. When I first drove past it months ago, I was shot at by these guys—the Hakarta. Space mercenaries, most closely resembling our version of an Orc but with sci-fi armor, tactics, and laser weapons. Not to say they aren't armed with a series of nasty-looking melee weapons either.

"Are you the owner of this fort?" the major asks, making me turn slightly to look at him.

I keep an eye on my original attacker, noticing how he's leaning forward, hands opening and closing. Trouble is going to come from there. The major's voice is low, a growl more than a phrase, but it's tinged with an upper-class British accent that reminds me of my popular Victorian TV shows. The idiosyncrasies of learning a language from the System can be particularly amusing, I've realized. I'd laugh, but I don't think they'd get the joke.

"Yes," I reply, my hands twitching slightly as one of the Hakarta picks up the sword I dropped when I was blocked.

As a private grabs my pistol, I tense up slightly then force myself to relax as the rifle barrels shift, following even that slightest of motions. Arse. They don't bother touching Sabre, probably realizing it won't work for them without significant hacking. They do take my energy rifle from its holster on her though.

"What happened to my men?" the major says.

"Uhh…"

As I hesitate, the lieutenant steps forward and throws a punch at me. I see it coming, in time perhaps to dodge it, but under their guns, I take the punch. It slams into my stomach, forcing me to bow slightly in pain and exhale. Of course I'm wearing an undersuit of armor, but the son of a bitch hits like Mike Tyson. Or what I figure Tyson hits like.

"Remove your helmet. And do not hesitate again," the major says.

I comply, removing the helmet to look around me. "*Ali, glitter ball special on my command,*" I think to him while answering the major. "They're dead."

"You are their killer?" the major asks.

I can't for the life of me read him. It's not just the alien body language or the armor covering his body; it's that he isn't giving away anything. I consider, very briefly and very quickly, lying, but reject the idea. The Yerick and Roxley both have ways of telling if someone is lying, and I am willing to bet so does the major.

"Yes. They attacked me first," I answer, ready to let Ali know and trigger my QSM. The last time I fought these guys, they had quantum grenades that ripped through me even while I was in in my phased state, but any chance is better than none.

The major looks at me for a time then nods to the lieutenant, who steps back, away from me. "Explain the incident to me. In detail."

I cough, rubbing at my stomach. As the lieutenant moves to hit me again, I start explaining, in detail, how I was looking for survivors after the System came into place, how I was attacked while driving here, my tactics, and finally, how I finished the matter. When I'm done, the silence lingers for a time.

The major makes his helmet disappear, an act that is copied by all his men. "They hid in the command room?"

I nod, fear slowly replaced with burning anger. I flex my hand, letting my gaze wander once more as I try to think of a survivable way of fighting back. I come up with nothing even as the major's face twists and he spits on the ground. A few moments later, the other Hakarta follow his example. Interesting fact—Hakarta spit is green.

"I am Labashi Ruka, Major of the Sixty-Third Division. It is a pleasure to meet you, warrior," Labashi says, deadpan.

The lieutenant twitches again, his purple eyes narrowing in displeasure.

I stare at the lieutenant for a moment before turning to Labashi. First they attack me, then they beat me, then they introduce themselves? Well, I guess Orc manners are just a little different. Or insane, if you will. So fine, insane it is. "John Lee. This means you decided not to kill me?"

"Haven't decided yet," the major answers. "Your actions have cost the Sixty-Third Division a decent supplementary bonus."

I feel my grin widening as he so casually mentions my death. Well, okay then. I keep my voice level as I buy time to figure a way out. "Supplementary bonus?"

"Information about the city of Whitehorse was requested. As the information was not part of the original contract, the bonus is supplementary. It was, however, substantial." Labashi just stands there, staring at me.

"Right…" I stare at him then flick my glance to Ali. "*Is he hinting I should give him that information?*"

"*YES!*" Ali bounces up and down, nodding. "*If you don't, I will!*"

"Well, perhaps I can help with that." My smile widens, becoming all teeth. All right, let's see how this dance goes. "What do you need to know?"

Labashi returns my smile, all toothy grin, then flicks his gaze over to the lieutenant. The lieutenant makes a slight motion and a blue screen appears in front of me, detailing the information they wish. Current owner, political situation, individuals in power, notable parties, defenses…

I shake my head, looking the list over. "I know some of this, but I've not really been plugged in for the last few weeks."

"Plugged in?" Labashi snorts slightly, large green nose flaring around his tusks.

"Uhh… been in touch. I moved out here a few weeks ago and haven't been talking to people as much," I explain.

Labashi nods. "That is acceptable. Tell us what you know."

"Right, let's see. Lord Roxley is the current landowner. There's a Human City Council that sort of, but not really, works with him about running the city. Some Yerick arrived a few months ago and moved in too. No one truly notable beyond Lord Roxley and the Yerick First Fist. Everyone else is low level compared to you guys. The city still doesn't have a stable Mana flow, so safe zones are limited to buildings. The human population is just above four thousand, if I recall correctly." Down from a population of nearly thirty thousand before the Apocalypse.

As Labashi nods, I continue to speak, digging through my brain for the information he wants. I give him a list of facts, things he could purchase off the System if he really gave a damn to. None of this is "secret," so none of it would be expensive. Hell, with their Stealth capabilities, it'd only take them a few days at most to figure this out.

"Security includes gate guards, a stone wall, and I believe technological shielding on the walls, though I've not seen them in play. Guards are, of course, Lord Roxley's men and some humans."

"Good. Tell me of these Lord Roxley's men," Labashi says.

I grimace but settle in, detailing who I recall seeing. The only thing I leave out are levels. No reason for him to know that I can read them, and I'm not offering that information up. For what seems like hours, the questioning continues. Once they realize I'm willing to talk, the guards relax slightly and we end up on my porch, drinking and snacking. I introduce the major to chocolate, which he seems highly appreciative of. He in turn introduces me to a fruit drink from his home world.

It's a friendly interrogation, but it's an interrogation nonetheless and he pulls a ton of information from me. I let him lead the questioning, never offering more information than what he asks for, but he's good, very good, at getting what he wants. All the while, the lieutenant stands directly behind me, and if looks could kill, I'd be a laser-riddled corpse.

The flow of information isn't just one way though. Being able to talk to them in a more relaxed setting means I can ask questions too. Carefully. I learn why it took them so long to come check on the fort. It seems their employer is a bit of a cheapskate and since each confirmed death of a Hakarta had a blood price, so long as the Hakarta were marked as "missing," he didn't need to make final payment. This little journey is actually off-the-books and completely on Labashi's time.

"I do like these Belgian chocolates best." Labashi pops one last piece into his mouth before he stands. "However, I must return to my division. Would you prefer the blade or the beam?"

I stand too, offering my hand once again. When my brain catches up, I freeze, staring at the hulking brute before me. Shit…

"John?" Labashi asks again, his voice calm.

In my peripheral vision, I see the Lieutenant has already drawn his blade. I shake my head then slowly speak. "Why?"

"Blood must pay in blood," Labashi answers, and I gulp.

"Bullshit!" Ali pops into existence, glaring at him. He's been quiet, invisible the whole time, and working furiously on his own screens while we talked.

"Ah, the Spirit makes his appearance." Labashi's lips pull apart, widening into what could charitably be called a grin. "And why would I shit with a bull?"

"Bugger that, you're just angling for something with boy-o here. Why don't you just say it?" Ali taps his foot. "You boys aren't that bloodthirsty, and the fight was fair, so there's no blood debt."

Labashi continues to grin, staring at Ali before he laughs then nods. "Very well, Spirit. I shall stop pulling the leg of the Adventurer. We stand to gain additional Credits for continued information about this Whitehorse. I desire John to provide that information."

I grunt. Now that my heart isn't thundering, that makes a lot of sense. In fact, from the way he was speaking during our interrogation, I was pretty sure he was going to ask me to do that, though I didn't expect him to threaten me. Then again, I guess this is what they call blackmail. That word, that thought sets off the slow kindling flame of anger in me again, the one that's been trying to get out since I got attacked in my own home. I really, really don't like getting pushed around. "Can do."

Labashi grins again, clapping me on the shoulder and gesturing for his people to get together. "We will provide you a list of what is required."

I nod and wait till they're gathered and have walked away a bit before I call out, "So what am I getting paid?"

They turn as a group, and even Ali spins to stare at me.

Labashi opens his mouth and I continue. "Don't bother with threats. If you kill me, you get nothing, so that doesn't work out for you. Of course, I'd be dead, but it still doesn't help you."

The lieutenant shifts, stepping toward me, and I shake my head. "Last warning, don't try it."

"Kyroc," Labashi says, and the lieutenant steps back. Good discipline. "Do you believe you can beat us?"

"No, but I'm really good at running. I just need a little head start." I smile slightly, gesturing to where they are, and let just a little of my anger reach my eyes. "That's about enough."

"I see... and what do you desire?" Labashi answers, sharp teeth beginning to show as he looks at me.

"Payment of course. You want me to be a spy? Well, spies get paid." I shrug. "We'll call it, oh... twenty percent of the System price. And a guarantee we don't ever have this conversation again."

"Impossible! Twenty percent is too high."

I glance at Ali, who doesn't make a move. "What's your number?"

"Ten percent."

"Twenty-five."

"That is not how you negotiate," Labashi replies, eyes narrowing.

"It is when you give a too low number to begin with." This is stupid, but that's okay. I'm about fifty percent sure I can get away before they can kill me. And if not... well, fuck it. I was dead as of three months ago anyway. "Shall we try for higher?"

"Twenty-five," Labashi answers, nodding.

"And a guarantee of immunity from prosecution from the Hakarta," I add.

"I can only guarantee for my division," Labashi says.

"That'll do."

"Then the deal is done."

"One thing—I don't guarantee I'll be able to get all the information you want," I add.

"The deal will be voided if you do not treat fairly with us and attempt to learn the requested information," Labashi adds, then his grin widens. "And I will find you and show you how we feel about deal-breakers."

"Fair enough." I smile back at him, the pit of anger still burning away.

"Then the deal is done," Labashi repeats again.

The way he says it makes me think it is ritual, so I repeat it myself.

Contract Initiated and Agreed Upon by Labashi Ruka and John Lee.

Further Details? (Y/N)

I blink and my eyes narrow slightly at the Orc. He just flashes me another toothy grin before pulling on his helmet as the group turns and walks away. I watch them leave before I retrieve my weapons and dismiss my sword. I have a feeling I somehow got played…

***

"Well, that was fun." I slump down next to the door, letting out a long exhalation when I finally decide that they really are gone.

"What the hell!" Ali mutters, shaking his head. "You had to challenge him?"

"Didn't like being pushed around."

"Idiot! And he got you into a contract. You sure you up to this, boy-o?"

"Why not? Aren't you the one who's always saying everything has a price in the System? If they really wanted to know, they could just buy it. I might as well get paid," I say a bit bitterly. "Anyway, I never said I wasn't going to tell the others about this."

"Playing both sides?" Ali says, and I shrug.

"Possibly. This way, at least we know what they want to know. Better to control the flow of information than not." I rub my temples before I tilt my head toward Ali. "I wonder who their employer is."

"You could find out."

I consider it before shake my head. I'm not that interested in wasting good Credit. I look down at my hands, seeing that they've stopped shaking and somehow a chocolate piece is in one. I finish unwrapping it and pop it into my mouth, leaning back against the wall and savoring the taste. Gods, that was close.

"Could I have escaped?" I wonder aloud.

"No idea. Probably not," Ali adds, shaking his head. "You don't become a major without at least a few tricks up your sleeve."

"Yeah…" I shut my eyes, shaking my head. At least for now, the Hakarta are a known threat. I'll have to figure out what, if anything, to do about them later. "So, care to explain contracts?"

"It's a Skill." Ali's brows furrow. "I guess it's not surprising Mercenaries have it, but I should have warned you. I just didn't realize he had it. The Skill binds the user and other parties into the deal they agreed upon. If you fail to live up to your side, it not only notifies him, but the System will also impose a penalty upon you. Mostly a Mana tax and the ability for the user to track you. Which can be transferred. Bounty hunters make most of their living off contract breakers."

I nod slowly, grimacing. Great. And the deal's open-ended. The only advantage is that like any permanent alteration in the System, the major's got to be paying for the contract through his Mana, so it's not something he'd want to keep forever.

"All right, boy-o, up and at them. You need a bath," Ali says after I've been sitting there for a bit.

"I…" I frown then shake my head. "No. Let's head in. I think… I think I need some company."

I slowly stand up and look back at the fort. Company, safety, perhaps a place to put my head down. The Hakarta aren't likely to come back, but… tonight I'll sleep in my house in Whitehorse.

Chapter 3

"John!" Xev chitters, hunched over and waving its claws in my face.

I plaster on a smile for Xev, looking it over. With six legs and a pair of three-fingered hands on a black, hairy body with a bulbous abdomen and front, Xev looks like a giant black spider with hands. It's a little disconcerting, and the first time I saw it, I had to work really hard at not shooting it and I'm not even scared of spiders. It's no wonder Xev mostly hides in its store.

"Is Sabre good?"

"Not bad, just some minor structural damage." I gesture at the bike as I turn it off in the parking space outside Xev's workshop.

Xev chitters angrily, waving me away before it starts prodding at Sabre. As Xev scrambles around the bike, fitting a variety of wires into various slots, it pokes at one of the armor points and peels the point away with its tools, staring at the insides of the bike. "This is old! You should bring it in faster next time. Even if your nanite upgrades fix the armor, the structural damage is still there."

"Sorry," I say automatically.

Really, the structural damage was so minor it didn't seem to matter. Putting all that money into the *Omnitron Class II Nanite Armor Upgrade* has saved me a ton in repairs, even if the armor class didn't go up. As Xev mutters to itself, I have to clear my throat to get its attention.

After a quick discussion, I leave Sabre with it for the evening and head for the butchering yard. The butchering yard is what used to be the old fire hall, a single-story sprawling building with wide barn doors that face onto the old prospector train tracks. The train tracks aren't connected to anything anymore, and before the Apocalypse, they were mostly used to gouge tourists during the summer. The entire area from the fire hall to the old train station is part of the yard now, with the newly made compost piles making up the third portion of their rather smelly triangle next to the river.

Thankfully, low-level enchantments keep the wind blowing into the river, keeping the smells of butchered and rotting carcasses away from downtown Whitehorse. Occasionally a mage will come along and cast a Purge Disease spell to keep things sanitary. Or as sanitary as anything can be around here. Of course, sending all those lovely smells out across the river brings its own problems. They've recently had to add guards on the other side of the river to deal with the increased monster presence.

At the yard, I follow directions and watch as the bodies from my Altered Space are pulled apart, weighed, and portions of the body separated for both Sally, the town's leading Alchemist, and Xev. As usual, I get a Quest completion with a small amount of experience and Credit bonus for turning in the meat, which is partly why I do so. The other reason is that while we're doing well with food for now, come winter, food will be significantly more difficult to acquire. Even now, the city is desperately attempting to stock up for winter since we aren't getting deliveries from down south anymore. I wonder how they're doing down there?

Shaking my head, I dismiss the thought. Not really my problem. I watch the men and women swarm the bodies, harvesting the body parts and dumping them into carts, moving with grace and strength that would have been impossible even a few months ago. As I turn away, my eye is drawn to the futuristic, towering monstrosity of an office building that sits smack dab in the center of the city, its mirrored silvery appearance at odds with the quaint two-and three-story 1920s era commercial buildings of the town. That tower is one I know well—it's where the Shop is, and where Lord Roxley resides and reigns over us all. Once upon a time I was a regular visitor there, till things fell apart. Once upon a time…

I shake my head, dismissing the matter. As I walk up Main Street, I notice that more and more buildings are coming back to life. We have a grocery store with handmade local luxuries, an armorer with locally crafted low-level armor pieces, a couple of competing alchemists, a trio of clothing stores, the Guild, the hotels that have been purchased, and of course, the only open pub in the city.

As always, the pub is noisy and busy. What kind of Adventurers would we be without a pub? It's not as if the Yukon led Canada in the highest alcohol consumption per person. Or that our local brewing company was set up two weeks ago as one of the first major private enterprises.

I feel my lips twist as I stare at it, wry humor and irritation sparking alongside one another in my mind. I don't even know why I'm angry… I shove it aside, bottling up the anger once again as I step into the establishment. The inside of the Nugget is all dark faux wood and worn, mismatched furniture. The Apocalypse came on fast, and rampaging monsters and panicked humans destroyed the old furniture sets. Now, it's catch as catch can.

At eight in the evening, the Nugget is busy and noisy, filled with people resting, eating, and drinking after a long day's work. Hunting parties sit together and dominate the room. A few craftsmen sit in their own groups. Skimpily dressed young women do most of the serving, dropping off beer, steaks, and fish and chips in large quantities. As I survey the inside, a waving hand catches my attention. Jason, a thin, weedy-looking teenager who looks way too young to be in here.

For a moment, I consider not going over. However, Jason hasn't done anything to me and I do want to check up on the kid. I walk over, letting my gaze slide over the group with him. Richard, redheaded and dashing with a new young lady on his arm and Shadow, a pony-sized husky, curled up beside his feet. Mikito, her ever-present naginata resting against the wall behind her, a look of strained patience plastered on her face. Constable Mike Gadsby with his metal arm and tired eyes. The first two were my former party members; the last was one of the leaders of Carcross.

Jason Cope (Level 38 Elementalist)

HP: 230/230

Constable Mike Gadsby (Level 37 Guardian)

HP: 940/940

Mikito Sato (Level 32 Samurai)

HP: 530/530

Richard Pearson (Level 31 Beast Tamer)

HP: 250/250

I look around, spotting Rachel with the Brothers of the Wolf, the First Nation's exclusive group of teenagers, and my eyes narrow. Did she quit to join them or…?

I shake my head as Jason pulls a chair to the table for me, squeezing it in so I can take a seat. My back is to the door, which makes me twitch slightly, but I'm the last to arrive, so beggars can't be choosers. "Evening."

"John, we wanted to ask Ali about something," Jason says immediately, not even bothering to greet me.

A passing waitress drops a pint of beer on the table for me, assuming I'll be drinking. No need for questions of what I'll drink—it's either water or beer here and I'm not drinking water.

"Questions are five Credits, answers are ten," Ali says as he floats after one of the waitresses. "Toots, I need a drink too."

I see the quick flash of irritation before the waitress's face smooths out. She returns to drop a glass from her tray before she heads back to the bar, where the bartender works feverishly to keep up with the nonstop flow of orders.

"You drink?" I stare as Ali picks up the pint glass before chugging it down.

"I do now." Ali smirks, clearly proud of himself.

Jason blinks at Ali before he shakes his head. "It's about Stats, man. We've been talking about it and I've been charting the growth. It just doesn't make sense. Like, I've got a Strength of 20 now. So that should mean I'm, like, twice as strong as a normal human, or maybe double the peak? And I sure aren't.

"Even dumber? The non-physical ones don't even make sense. I'm smarter than before, but I'm not, you know, making physics breakthroughs. Richard's all kinds of sexy and he's getting laid like crazy, but so's Mike. No offense, old man. But for the level of his Stats, I should be wanting to sleep with Richard and I ain't. No offense."

"None taken. I don't do kids," Richard replies, and the pixie-haired blonde next to him frowns, looking at Richard then Jason.

"So what the hell? I don't get this shit," Jason says.

"*Ali, I got this,*" I think to my friend. As the waitress comes up, I point at the chalkboard menu. "One of everything."

Having delayed it long enough, I turn to Jason and grin, a little cruel streak popping up. "First, stop swearing. Your mom would be angry. Second, you sure you're old enough to be drinking here?"

"Har, har. Funny. I was talking to Ali." Jason prods at his nose in an attempt to adjust non-existent glasses.

I chuckle, leaning back, and pull a chocolate piece from my inventory. "Seriously though, I can answer this. It's very simple—it's the System."

Richard groans and Mikito snorts, sipping on her beer. The others just look puzzled at the inside joke.

I elaborate. "The System's the System. No use trying to figure it out. It doesn't make sense."

"Oh, come on! I know you said this isn't a game, but we still need to understand!"

I grimace then glance at Ali, who sighs, putting his third pint down half-finished. He lets out a large burp before he waggles his fingers, a glowing blue screen appearing. It's filled with symbols, circles, dashes, and dots that combine in distinct groupings much like Egyptian hieroglyphs. "Right, System basics 101. One hundred Credits. And I won't ever give this talk again."

"A hundred!" Jason sputters, glaring at Ali, who nods before Jason relents, sending over the payment.

"Good man. You see that? That's what it actually says for 'Strength.' That's in System," Ali points. "That gets translated to this"—the screen shifts, the language changing to a series of scrawls now—"which is Galactic Script. That then gets translated to your respective human language. As you can guess, the translation is actually a lot more complex.

"When you increase your Strength attribute, you're adjusting all of that. The change actually adjusts the way you manage Mana via the System. For example—Gadsby. You should have shattered the table and your pint glass by being that rough. After all, you probably could punch through steel right now. However, your Strength comes from the System. So the System alters the density and strength of things you interact with, thus, non-breaking tables and ground that can handle movement at speed. Hell, Mikito even bends beam weapons ever so slightly around her as she dodges. The System 'helps' all of you without you consciously knowing it."

Jason opens his mouth then shuts it while Gadsby and the blonde look on in interest. Richard and Mikito look bored, having heard this before. Me? I just get to eating as the first plate arrives. Funny thing about adventuring—you end up eating a ton.

"So your points aren't a straight line. They literally are a kind-of-approximate tool to let you understand the System better. The Council cobbled it together from the way you guys understand the System and what it'd bring about.

"As for Intelligence and the other intangibles, well, as I told John a long time ago, Intelligence increases don't necessarily make you smarter. Physically, your brain has been altered a bit. But you can't do higher physics because you never learnt the basics. You have faster neural processes, but if all you've done is fight, those new neural connections might help you think and react faster in a fight but that's it. Also, don't forget that much of those increases and changes are going to help you control and manipulate Mana itself." Ali shrugs. "I've heard of a few people who have managed to become super-geniuses from increasing their intelligence, but most of them were already on the borderline anyway."

Jason shakes his head, trying to put it together. "What are you saying? That Intelligence isn't intelligence? That it's more Mana pool?"

"Yes. No. Maybe," Ali answers. "Look, think of it like your Earth computers. You got a motherboard—your body. Intelligence increases help adjust the motherboard and the RAM, increasing both. Sometimes it upgrades your motherboard, sometimes it upgrades the RAM. Sometimes it adds a new graphics card or new slots so you can plug in more things, like Psionic powers. However, you still need to run the right programs to make your computer work. That means getting the right Skills. Doesn't matter how good a computer you have, if you're doing 1+1, it's still 1+1."

Jason frowns then opens his mouth before shutting it. Kid's trying to game the System again, just like he did when he started. Still, the fact that he's filled out a bit and doesn't look like a stiff breeze will send him over probably means he's been putting points into something other than Intelligence. Which is good.

"How about Charisma? Am I sleeping with Richard because I want to or because he wants me to or because the System does?" the blonde queries, brow furrowed.

I push my plate aside and tackle the next one—a plate of cross-hatched ribs stewed in a really tasty barbecue sauce. Even as I dig in, I make sure to listen to this answer. I know I have... issues with that ability. It's part of why I turned down Roxley. And Lana. I don't like the idea of being told to like someone.

"Sort of." Ali shrugs and opens his hand. "It's the same answer. Yes, his Charisma trait makes him look better to you, makes his pheromones more powerful and enticing. No, it's not directly affecting your emotions or thoughts. You need to use a Skill for that." Left unsaid is the fact that a successful Skill use would leave no traces when it came to Social skills like that. "Maybe the System is affecting things to some degree. Then again, if Claudia Schiffer came along, I wouldn't say no."

The girl opens her mouth then shuts it, looking at Richard then back at Ali. Unconsciously, she edges away from Richard, putting space between them.

Richard rolls his eyes at Ali, mouthing, "Thank you," as he leans back and folds his arms.

Mike, on the other hand, is frowning, rubbing his chin. I guess the question of consent really bites considering his former profession. Must be tough being one of two living constables in a couple of hundred kilometers.

I push my other plate aside, grabbing the third and last one, a bowl of stew. Not much choice yet, but what there is is good. As the others devolve into discussing details, forcing Ali to pull up descriptions and going into them line by line, I turn back to my own thoughts. One thing I don't add is that it's quite likely whoever created the System is purposely nerfing Intelligence. I'd lay good money down that whoever built this didn't want a bunch of super-intelligences running around. After all, if we get too smart, we might figure out a way to survive without the System and that, I know, is something the creators don't want. I've called the entire System a scam, and the more I read and learn, the more certain I am that it is. It's like one of those multi-level marketing schemes where the moment you buy in, you have to keep buying in.

"Coming tomorrow?" Mikito says when she manages to catch my eye.

I blink, raising an eyebrow and she sighs.

"The Boss attacks?"

"I don't know what you're talking about," I say.

She frowns, shooting a look at Richard, who has joined in the discussion. "That's why Jason and Mike are here. We're grouping up to take on some of the Bosses. You should have been invited." Concern tinges her voice.

"I'm not exactly Mr. Popular around here."

"I don't care. Are you coming?"

I shrug. "No idea." I lean back as I push the stew aside, wiping my face before sipping on my drink. "Maybe. You guys probably can handle it."

"It'd be good for you. For us." She sighs. "Fine, you baka."

Yeah, well… I don't really see a point. I don't owe the city anything, not anymore. And whatever she thinks, my presence might cause more problems than I fix. As she falls silent, shrinking back into her seat, I listen in on the conversation. It's moved on, thankfully, from the System to town gossip, and I make sure to pay attention. After all, you never know what I might learn, and I'm getting paid now. I think.

***

"Lana," I greet the redheaded stunner as I walk into my house.

She's tucked away in the kitchen, waving at screens only she can see. Richard and Mikito left the pub hours ago, both of them heading home to get some rest for their big day tomorrow. I have to admit, I was kind of glad to see them go. While I might not hold much animosity toward them, the camaraderie we had is now strained. By the time I decided to leave, I was getting more than a few dirty looks from the tired bar staff as they worked to clear up for the evening.

Lana looks up, and Richard's sister, as always, takes my breath away. Piercing bright blue eyes that turn green and violet in certain lights, and her version of a uniform—a simple blouse and pair of jeans—does nothing to hide her ample curves. There are people in this life who, if you're real lucky, you have that inexplicable "it" with. Call it chemistry, call it a biological urge, some even call it love, but there's an instantaneous attraction. As Lana smiles at me, I can't help but think it only took the end of the world for me to meet not one but two such individuals at the same damn time. Of course, it would require the end of the world to meet a Truinnar like Roxley. All in all, it's about about par for the course with my luck.

Flicking her hand to dismiss her System screens, she says, "John."

"Up late?" I step into the kitchen, drawn like a moth to a flame. Closer, I see slight bags under her eyes and a tension in her shoulders that I've never seen before.

"Just work." Her eyes flick over my form too in silent assessment. "What's wrong?"

"Isn't that my line?"

"Har! I'm not the one who runs into trouble all the time. I'm just a paper pusher," she says, shaking her head. "Seriously, John, what's wrong?"

"Nothing much." I keep my hands on the table, mostly to make sure I know where they are as I sit down across her. I have to admit, it bothers me a little that she can read me so well—even my father never seemed to be able to do that. Not that he ever paid that much attention to me… I push the old bitter thoughts aside.

"John…" Lana's voice changes, growing stern.

"I just had some visitors. The Hakarta." I shrug, and at her puzzled expression, I add, "The Space Orcs."

"Oh." Her lips tighten, then she shakes her head, drawing her own conclusions. Probably violent ones.

"So what papers are you pushing?"

"The usual. Business proposals. Loan extension requests. Reports and cashflow projections." She shakes her head before rubbing her temples.

Lana runs the biggest investment fund in Whitehorse, initially funded through my killings, but these days it's pretty self-sufficient. From what I recall, she basically has a hand in every significant private enterprise since the System came into play. Not that I've seen a Credit in return—every single

Credit of profit has been plowed right back into the City and the fund. Still, it's nice to know I've got a nest egg growing somewhere.

"Get an AI, toots," Ali says, appearing on the table next to her and flashing her a grin.

"Ali."

The smile Lana gives the Spirit sends a spike of anger through me, and I quell it. Just because the two have gotten closer since they saved my ass a month ago is no reason for me to get jealous. None at all.

"Aren't those expensive?" she asks.

"Only if you get them as a Companion. If you get an off-the-rack one, they'll be pretty cheap. A basic one shouldn't cost you much at all. Just make sure to get the heavy security models. Definitely don't get a Spirit. No self-respecting Spirit wants to be a glorified personal assistant."

Lana nods, rubbing her chin. "I don't know, I don't have a lot of Credits left…"

"Use the Fund," I chime in. "It's a business expense."

"I don't think it works that way," Lana says, frowning at me.

"Says who?" I smirk then wave. "Not as if the CRA are coming after you for taxes. So long as you buy it through the Shop, Roxley gets his cut. Way I see it, you're all good."

"I guess…" She rubs her temples again before her voice drops lower. "John, we should talk…"

"Yes." I blink, tilting my head. I quell the urge to flee, sensible as it may be.

"Mikito says you won't be with us tomorrow," Lana says.

My brain jerks to a stop as thoughts rearrange. Oh, we're not having The Talk. Just a talk. Right, I can deal with that. "Yeah, I wasn't… wait. Us?" I lean forward, my voice tight.

"I'm going too. The Bosses, they need to be killed."

"Of course they do. Why are you going?"

"Because it needs to be done," she replies, frowning.

"Sure, sure. But you're…" I open my mouth then clamp it shut as Ali shakes his head at me. Oh crap.

"I'm what, John?" Her voice rising, Lana glares at me. "A paper pusher? A girl?"

"No, not that. You just, you know, haven't really been…"

She snorts. "If you've forgotten, I walked here with Mikito and Richard. I still go out with them once in a while." Lana gets to her feet. "I saved your ungrateful ass a month ago. I can take care of myself."

I open my mouth, wanting to point out that, if I knew her at all, she was just about to ask me to keep her higher-Leveled brother safe, but I snap it shut at Ali's screamed, mental, "*NO.*"

Right, right. Not the way to win an argument. While I'm working that all out, Lana stomps right out and I watch her back, grimacing.

"Well done, boy-o." Ali golf-claps from his seat on the table.

"Bite me."

***

Late at night, I stare at the ceiling, trying to figure out what went wrong. I spent weeks away from them all, trying to come to terms with who and what I am. With the anger that sits in me, the world that we live in. And within hours of coming back, I'm fighting with Lana and confused once again.

I don't know what they want from me, not really, and the gods know I definitely don't know what I want. To survive, sure. To get through another day, get a little stronger, get a little better. To fight, because I can? Saying it, thinking it out loud, it seems so stupid.

I slowly exhale, focusing on just breathing for a few moments. I don't know what I want for myself or for Lana. I just know that I don't want her to die. I don't want anyone else I could save to die. Truth be told, as much as I said otherwise to Mikito, I probably would have gone and kept an eye on the group anyway. Now that Lana's going, I'm definitely going. I don't need another ghost haunting my conscience—I have enough already.

Chapter 4

"What did you do?" Richard mutters as he grabs my arm, dragging me aside the next morning.

The hunting groups had gathered around the sternwheeler near Rotary Park. When I drove in, late, Richard immediately spotted me and stalked over.

"My sister's been on the warpath all morning!" Richard growls, gripping my arm tightly. "She's insisting on being part of the main teams instead of the reserve."

"What makes you think I did anything?" I ask innocently, giving him big eyes behind my helmet.

"Because she only ever gets that angry when it comes to you!" Richard lets go of my arm, glaring at me. "If she gets hurt…"

"You'll get your puppies to tear me limb from limb. Got it," I reply wryly and shake my head. Those two…

As Richard opens his mouth to say something else, he's cut off by a short, angry man in a suit. A suit in this day and age. And in Whitehorse too, where formal attire is your best plaid shirt and a pair of clean jeans.

His voice rising as he speaks, shorty says, "What is he doing here?"

I grin at Eric Roth, aka Minion. "Just ambling along. How you doing?"

"You! Get out of here. This is official Whitehorse City Council business and you are not invited," Minion snarls, stepping forward and vibrating.

I'm reminded of a tiny yappy dog. I feel one side of my lips tug up at the thought, and he stops and steps back.

"Trust me, I'm not here for you," I drawl then raise a hand. Minion flinches slightly, probably remembering my hand wrapped around his throat, and I flick it, shooing him away. "Go do your thing."

Minion glares at me, opening his mouth to say something else before he's cut off by a low rumble.

"Are we to begin, Councilor Roth? I am being paid by the hour." The speaker is a nine-foot-tall bull-man hybrid, a full-on Minotaur from legends, in sci-fi battle armor. The Minotaur even has an axe, though the barrel shape in the center lends credence to the idea that it's more than just a melee weapon.

The Yerick—the real name for the Minotaurs—is the only group of immigrants to Whitehorse thus far. They haven't had the best of receptions and there's a large degree of animosity toward them. Led by Capstan Ulrik, their First Fist—whatever that means—the Yerick are a tribe of career Adventurers. When the Yerick are invited and I'm not, that shows you how low I am on the totem pole of popularity.

Minion's face twists again in a sneer before he hurries over to the group leaders, where Lana and Mikito stand. Lana shoots me a glare that could freeze water solid.

Richard mutters next to me, "You have got to stop antagonizing that man."

"Better to twit him than kill him," I reply, flexing my hand by my side.

"Sometimes I'm not entirely sure if you're joking," Richard says.

I don't let him know that I'm not sure either. Minion almost literally admitted to burning down the Yerick's buildings, but here he is, walking around free and clear and organizing everyone, and I'm persona non grata. Okay, fine, choking him out in broad daylight might have been a bit of an overreaction to losing face in front of Roxley and Capstan, but even now, I feel my blood boil at the betrayal. I exhale, forcing myself to let it go. The past is past, after all. Time to stop bitching about it. What is, is.

I shake my head slightly, realizing that Richard left while I was caught up in my thoughts. As much as I believe Minion was the mastermind behind the fire, there's no evidence. He never directly admitted to anything, and the actual culprits have been caught and tried. They're working off their debts in the compound that the Yerick built on their burnt-out plots of land, and as far as the city is concerned, the case is closed. Tensions between the races are high still, but between the increased surveillance drones and a few very public and nasty beatdowns by the Yerick, direct attacks have stopped.

As I stand by myself and idly watch Minion speak to the groups, I read lips and pick out where he's sending everyone. Ali helps by hacking his System window and displaying it for me, adding annotations as each group is directed to a different Boss. I wonder where Fred, our erstwhile mayor, is before I remember he prefers to let his minions do the actual work.

If I have to say one good thing about Minion, it's that he's highly organized. Ten minutes later, the groups are disappearing and that's even after time to answer any questions. My gaze wanders over each group once more, watching as Capstan splits a few of his men off to join different groups. It's not a horrible setup, other than the fact that Minion only intends to keep a single reserve team—the Chaos Hands. I check their levels again, see that nothing is over 25, and wince. We're all still under-leveled for this area.

My gaze sweeps over the group again and I realize that gathered here are the careful, the lucky, and the crazy. The brave, the rational, and the unlucky are dead, murdered in the first few days of the System for the most part. First responders, the RCMP, the burgeoning heroes all died in the opening scenes of the Apocalypse, fighting creatures that out-leveled them. It's only through the mercy of the gods and Lord Roxley's presence that we've survived as long as we have.

"So, boy-o, we following the girl?" Ali sends to me mentally, and I nod. *"You know she's going to be pissed, right?"*

"Better pissed than dead. We'll hang back a bit though."

***

Ever since Mana flooded the world and the System came, monsters have been appearing all over Earth. There are two kinds: the ones that have evolved from Earth and the ones that have been 'imported' into the world via the System. Occasionally those monsters are particularly nasty—a System-designated Boss. Or maybe they're already Bosses and the System just tags them. Either way, they're strong and tough and their presence means that particular monster group will populate faster than normal. Leave them alone long enough and you get monster swarms and they become a mainstay in a region, flooding outward. If you're really unlucky, they find a location with a high Mana density and stay there, eventually creating a dungeon.

Since the entire world has been designated a Dungeon World and we're getting the overflow of Mana from every other System-controlled world, it's pretty much a given we're going to get a ton of Dungeons and Bosses. The goal today is simple though—just like we used to manage the wildlife, we're going to manage the monster population. Just like you kill the bulls to reduce the herd, we kill the Bosses. Of course, along the way we'll be killing a ton of normal monsters too, but that's the way it works.

Loping along far behind Lana's group, I have a lot of time to think. The occasional monsters they miss and the ones that try to sneak up on them aren't even a challenge. I have Ali patched into their communications channel as he floats alongside me, listening in just in case something important comes up. Mostly though, the two of us are along for the ride. If we're real lucky, I won't even need to get involved.

An hour later, I come to a stop as Lana's group hits the boundary of their target's area. I pull up my minimap, focusing on the green dots.

Knight Beetle (Level 29)

HP: 180/180

Ali pulls up some information for me, flicking over the System window. As I read the monster information, I relax. Each beetle is purple and gray, about two and a half feet in length and a foot tall, with armored carapaces that give them their name. Tough and they have a tendency to swarm. However, Lana's group of five humans is augmented by her three oversized huskies and a mutated fox. While Lana might not go out as often, she certainly knows how to control her animals and the way the red dots of the low level enemies she fights keep disappearing on my minimap tell me they're doing well.

I rub my neck, fingers hitting armor as I do so and I grimace. Armor is all nice and good but try giving yourself a massage while wearing it. I sigh, giving up on trying to get rid of the tension that way, and just pull out some chocolate to chew on while I wait. Ali's head is tilted as he obviously listens to something before he grunts.

"John… how much do you like Jim?"

"What's wrong?" I look for where Jim should be and realize he's only a few kilometers away.

"Nothing yet, but I don't think his group can deal with what he's going to be fighting," Ali says. "So we going?"

I hesitate, looking back at where Lana fights. She hasn't hit the Boss yet and those things can change the flow of a battle. On the other hand… I bite my lip, twisting to where Jim's Boss marker is and take off running. I hope I'm doing the right thing.

"What's so bad Jim can't handle?" I ask as I pound through the dirt, the powered armor covering the ground at a good pace. I shatter rock and the occasional fallen tree, knowing that I don't have a lot of time. His Boss wasn't that much farther out than Lana's. Still, Jim's a big boy—he's the most senior of the City's Hunters and a tough old coot.

"Lightning Squirrels." Ali floats alongside me with ease as I activate Thousand Steps, a skill that lets me move faster. "They're mutations of your ground squirrels. Individually, they're really low level. However, they swarm. Each of them feeds off the other and there's a *lot* more of them than Minion knows about."

Even as we talk, my map updates with little gray dots. Low level indeed. I watch as the dots disappear in front of the friendly blue dots of Jim's group. No surprise that they're taking them out at range—his entire group is composed of rifle users. Unfortunately, what they can't see is the swarm of gray dots that have begun to converge on them.

As the swarm closes in, I spot a blue dot flicker and disappear. I grit my teeth as the blue dots pull back in a somewhat orderly fashion, but they can't keep ahead. I can see flashes of electricity with my eyes now. The never-ending arcs have lit the undergrowth on fire. Beam weaponry stabs out from the embattled group, along with the crack of projectile fire, each shot killing individual Squirrels. There's even the occasional explosion, but that doesn't really seem to change my map.

I've opened fire myself, keeping to normal projectiles as I unload on the Squirrels. Each shot disintegrates a small creature, turning it into red mist, and I even occasionally manage to get more than one with a shot.

"This isn't working!" I yell, bouncing forward.

The occasional lightning arc at this distance feels like a static electricity discharge through the armor, but we're going right into the center of the swarm and I know it's going to get worse. I draw a deep breath, letting the shooting and running go on autopilot as I reach into myself for my own link to the Elemental Affinity and push it out of me, letting it envelop me. When the next lightning strike hits, I use the Gift to reroute the arc around me and Sabre rather than through us. Once that's established, it takes me a moment to cast my next spell. Greater Regeneration increases my natural healing rate so that I can deal with the bleed-through. A thought lets me review the damage I'm receiving from each blast.

-13 HP (78% resisted)

"I've got a plan," Ali shouts as I keep firing. "Just follow the bouncing ball!"

I snarl, running ahead and following the bouncing ball that appears in my display as I keep shooting. Occasionally my path intersects an unlucky squirrel and I either stab or stomp it. Electricity keeps building around me and we're almost constantly wreathed in lightning now. Ali isn't speaking, his face set in grim concentration as he floats alongside me. My jaw hurts from clenching it so tight as the lightning shudders through me even as it slowly drives my health down. A slow ticking down in the corner of my vision tells me Sabre's not doing great either.

"Okay, boy-o. Grab me when you reach me and lend me your Mana and strength!" Ali says as he darts ahead, right to where the bouncing ball lands. He appears for a second, his hands raised as the lightning flows through him.

I extend my sense, my Affinity, and I see what Ali's doing. Everything that hits him, he attaches a thread to, sliding it into the bodies of the squirrels. I place a hand on Ali's and make the connection, feeling the lightning rip through me and pull Mana alongside the flow.

Pain fills my world, consuming me, and all I can do is go along for the ride. Muscles clench and spasm, my heart beats erratically, and I'm pretty sure I void my bowels at some point, but I keep holding on to Ali, refusing to let go. Pain, anger, and stubbornness—linchpins of my life.

A part of me watches as Ali threads all of it together, faster and faster until everything around is attached to him. Ali snarls, twisting with his hands, and I feel the change as the threads of Mana he has connected via the lightning tug on the Squirrels. It's just a little, a small alteration in their atoms, but at the speed of well, light, the change happens. Electrons slip free, loosened from their moorings. A small change to each atom multiplied thousands, millions of times.

The lightning explodes. Lightning Squirrels are no longer able to contain and direct the overflow, so it heats them up—heats us up—and I know I'm screaming. One second we're in the middle of a maelstrom, and the next, it disappears. Stray arcs jump and skip all around us, the ground molten glass. I stumble away, brute forcing Sabre to move because it's still rerouting from all the damage. I fall on my face on smoking, ashen ground as Ali slowly floats down, his eyes sparkling.

"What a rush!" Ali says, holding up a hand and waggling olive-colored fingers that dance with electricity. "Woah! That's a ton of notifications—wait one second!"

I stare into the sky, my muscles twitching occasionally from the after-effects. Eventually, I reach out with one of my Shop-purchased Skills and dump Sabre directly into my inventory. Quite a useful Skill to have, being able to put anything that the System registers directly into my inventory just by being in contact with it. My body drops onto the scorched earth and I groan, rolling up as the heat cuts through my skin-tight armored coveralls. I don't even want to know how much it's going to cost to fix Sabre. The remains of Jim's party, with an added golden-brown Minotaur, stumble over, staring at the smoking squirrel corpses around me, their eyes wide.

I look around for a moment, taking in the smoking grass, the occasional glassy spot, and the hundreds of corpses, as well as the occasional burning trees, and realize I'm having one of those post-apocalyptic moments in real life. Hell, I can't even be blamed for this one.

"John?" Jim, the big First Nation Elder, stammers as he limps up to me.

"Yeah?" I look at Ali, who continues to float, muttering to himself. "I thought you might need some help."

"Shit, you got that right." Jim's voice rises and falls as he tries to stay calm. "It was supposed to be a relatively easy kill, just a bunch of ground squirrels. I lost half my men…"

"Sorry." I looked around then sighed. "That's a hell of a lot of looting."

The group jerkily nods, each of them moving to their respective glowing corpses. Lovely System, only allowing us to loot our own kills. At least if you aren't in a party and I never did formally join theirs. Not that I really want to share – it's going to be expensive enough fixing Sabre.

I start looting after a few minutes, when I can handle standing up, after eying Lana's group in the map. Seems like they survived without me. A short while later, Ali finally perks up and waves, flicking a series of System windows to me.

Level Up!

You have reached Level 22 as an Erethran Honor Guard. Stat Points automatically distributed. You have 3 Free Attribute Points and 4 Class Skills to distribute.

Resistance Improved: Electricity +10% (50% Total)

Well, that was interesting. I'm grateful I don't have to wade through all the text about how many monsters I killed. Looking at Ali, I point at the bodies while I pull up my information to take a closer look at my Status. I can hear him muttering about being given the scut work as he does the looting for me but I ignore him. If he didn't complain, I'd be worried he was sick. Can Spirits get sick?

Status Screen			
Name	John Lee	Class	Erethran Honor Guard
Race	Human (Male)	Level	22
Titles			
Monster's Bane, Redeemer of the Dead			
Health	1070	Stamina	1070
Mana	840	Mana Regeneration	70 / minute
Attributes			
Strength	66	Agility	102

Constitution	107	Perception	42
Intelligence	84	Willpower	90
Charisma	16	Luck	20
Class Skills			
Mana Blade	1	Blade Strike	2
Thousand Steps	1	Altered Space	1
Two are One	1	The Body's Resolve	1
Greater Detection	1	Instantaneous Inventory*	1
Cleave*	1		
Spells			
Improved Minor Healing (II)		Greater Regeneration	
Improved Mana Dart (IV)		Tinder	
Enhanced Lightning Strike			

I nod slightly, glancing over the basic screen. Got to let Ali know to add a section about Resistances to this, but it looks a heck of a lot neater without my Skills. They were cluttering it up, and like Ali said, what's the point of listing them? I can either do it or not.

Mental note—time to purchase another area effect spell that isn't Lightning. Maybe a Fireball or something like that, though maybe there's a Skill. Then again, all the really useful Skills are expensive. Not that Spells aren't either, but didn't I come along just to watch out for Lana? How the hell did I end up in this situation again?

I glare at Ali who, at least, is helping with the looting and storage of bodies. This is going to take forever, but every single Credit counts.

Chapter 5

It takes me hours to get everything collected and shoved away. Hours of collecting dead bodies and scanning the map to ensure the others are fine. Only once does Ali stop, frowning before he shakes his head. He lets me know, later, that it was just the reserve team being called out to help another group with a larger monster mob than expected. Since the initial party had scouted it out before engaging, it all went pretty smoothly.

By the time I get back, most of the groups have already reported in and the day is coming to an end. Walking without power armor sucks, but at least that gives me time to kill more monsters. I drop Sabre off with Xev, who promises to give me the estimate later. The way Xev says it, I make sure to head to the Shop and the butchers immediately. A few hundred Squirrel corpses and fur and assorted loot drops later, I might have enough for a few days of meals. Gods, that sucked.

As I exit the Shop, I find a golden yellow Yerick waiting for me, the same one that was in Jim's unfortunate team. Standing just under nine feet tall, he wears a bulky armored vest along with a simple, reinforced jumpsuit. Slung over his shoulder is a rifle, and another pistol is strapped to his legs. A series of grenades hang off his belt. Other than the lack of a melee weapon, it's a pretty typical setup for the Yerick from what I can see.

Aron Hauser (Level 38 Axe Brother)
HP: 1240 / 1240

"Monster's Bane Lee," he greets me, bowing slightly. "I am Aron Hauser. I wish to thank you for your aid this day."

"Not at all." I flash him a grin then tilt my head. "Jim and the rest okay?"

"Elder Calbery is speaking with Councilor Roth. He requested I pass on his thanks as well."

"You're welcome." I grunt, walking past him.

Aron just nods slightly, watching me stomp off. Thanks. Har. Thanks doesn't pay my bill with Xev or get me a new bike. Stomping back to the city, I glare around me, headed back to my house.

Grumbling to myself, I find myself staring at my house. No Sabre, not enough Credits to fix her up properly, and no transportation means I'm stuck in Whitehorse for the next few weeks. As much as I love the mecha, getting her fixed is becoming a real drain on my resources each time she gets damaged.

"John! Everything okay?" Richard asks, watching me and the floating, silent Ali.

"Fine. Just fine," I snarl, not bothering to stop as I head downstairs.

I shut the door, forcing myself not to slam it, before I flop onto my bed. Why the hell did I help them? I glare at the ceiling. Every time I think I've contained one problem—the Yerick, the Hakarta, my anger—something else crops up and bites me in the ass.

***

"Morning, John," Lana says as I crawl up the stairs the next day.

Mikito and Richard nod to me, tension filling the room. When I choked Minion in public, it was Mikito and Richard who stopped me, rather forcefully. Let's just say I wasn't exactly in a listening mood. Since then, I've been staying away, hiding out in the fort while they lived in my house. I needed time to sort out my brain, my emotions. While we've interacted in passing since then, things just haven't been the same.

"Where's Rachel?" I tilt my head as I look around the kitchen.

"She, well… she's with the Brothers of the Wolf," Richard answers.

Mikito nods, adding another piece of fried fish to her bowl of rice. I sigh and take a seat at the setting that has been laid for me. I nod in thanks as Lana drops a stack of pancakes on my plate before taking a seat herself.

Lana smiles slightly, stretching and making my gaze shift to her ample rack before she continues. "I heard you had some trouble yesterday."

"Not me. Jim," I reply around a mouthful.

"Really? I heard you had to walk home," Lana replies, her face perfectly serene.

"Sabre was damaged." My eyes narrow as I dump more maple syrup on the pancakes. I could almost feel bad about how well we eat compared to the general population, but we do pay for this food ourselves. Most of us spend our days working to get additional food and Credits for the city—so spending our own money on luxuries shouldn't feel wrong, right? Right.

"Mmmm… so, trouble." Lana sips on juice before she continues. "And someone was worried about me."

I sigh, finally catching on. "All this was to say 'I told you so'?"

Lana smiles innocently, slowly cutting apart her own pancake. "I never said those words."

"Uh huh." I grunt, and a part of me wants to point out she'd have been in as much trouble as Jim was if she had been the one fighting the Lightning Squirrels. A wiser part of me makes me focus on my own breakfast. Some things, you just don't say.

As I chew my next bite, I see Mikito smiling slightly while Richard pays way too much attention to Shadow. I sigh, deciding to not engage further as Lana finishes her breakfast.

As I finally finish eating, Ali pops into existence next to me. "So, boy-o, where to next?"

"John?" Richard butts in, leaning forward. "We could use your help. There's a monster lair we'd like to clear out."

I grunt and shake my head. "No. I'll be fine."

Mikito opens her mouth then shuts it, staring at me before she sighs and grabs her naginata. Richard nods as well, following Mikito out. I watch them leave, a part of me wondering if they're going to try to take on a lair all by themselves.

"You going to cold-shoulder them forever?" Lana asks as she puts the plates away, leaning against the counter.

"What?"

"You know what." She points at me. "You need a ride and you're refusing to go with them? For what? Your pride?"

"I'd rather hunt by myself," I mutter, not meeting her eyes. "They're doing well enough without me. I like hunting alone."

Lana uncrosses her arms, shaking her head. "Well enough? Rachel left because of you. Richard and Mikito have been grabbing whoever is free whenever they can, working what they can, when they can. They aren't leveling up that well because of that." I keep staring at my empty plate and Lana sighs, shaking her head. "You could just admit you're still pissed at them you know."

"I'm not," I protest, looking at her again, my anger flaring.

"Really?" Lana crosses her arms, staring at me before shaking her head. "Fine. You stubborn idiot."

"I am not." I watch her leave, and I sigh. At some point, there's a conversation we have to have. But I think we both know it's one that can't be taken back. I shake my head, dismissing the thought, and I look at Ali. "I'm not being stubborn. I like hunting alone."

"Uh huh. Right. Sure." Ali nods. "Let's head south. Records indicate that it hasn't been swept in a few weeks. If we move fast, we should be able to break out into a higher-level zone too."

"Gotcha."

***

The first couple of hours are easy. I turn on Thousand Steps the moment I break into the tree line at the back of the house, moving from one blip to the next. None of the monsters are hard; in fact, they're so easy it's trivial. Alpine forest filled with aspen, pine, and fir has mutated under the influence of Mana. Some just grew stronger and harder. Other trees grew new defenses— a silvery sheen on one, spikes on another, pollen that's acidic or toxic, fruits that are now edible. I dodge the dangers I know of, breathe deeply when I can, and make note of new changes absently. The forest changes, just like the rest of the Territory, and all that we can do is wait for everything to settle and change with it.

Moving in a zig-zag pattern, I end up spending more time than I'd prefer in the lower level zone around Whitehorse. I'll have to ask Ali to run the numbers later and see if it's worth the time compared to what I can get dealing with higher-level monsters.

Monster zones aren't particularly steady, especially in a burgeoning Dungeon World. They're more a guide than a rule, which is why when I hit the Level 30+ zone, I slow down. You never know when you'll run into a truly nasty monster out here, and without Sabre, I'm not entirely confident I can take on anything above Level 50 without getting seriously hurt. Sure, we heal after a few minutes, but you try having your guts torn out repeatedly and tell me you want to sign up for it on an on-going basis.

Without Sabre, all I've got for protection is a simple armored coveralls that might soak up incidental damage but not much else. That means that when I fight, I can't just bullrush into danger and let the mecha soak up the damage while I hammer away at the monsters. Instead, I have to fight like Mikito—working on positions, dodging, and striking only when it's safe to do so. It slows down fights and forces me to use a lot more Mana to heal when I inevitably get hit. Worst, since I'm fighting alone, I can't afford to let my Mana drain completely in case I run into something nasty, so I end up doing more rest stops.

Funny thing is that the drop in mobility is the least of my concerns. Sure, in mecha mode I could run through the forest at a slightly higher speed due to the increased attributes, but it's not that much different these days. When I first bought the personal assault vehicle, the boost in attributes by itself made the purchase well worth it. At that time, it added anywhere from a third to half again to my physical stats, making me stronger and faster when I desperately needed every edge I could get. These days, the boost is much less, though even a ten percent increase is nothing to sneeze at. And while in bike mode, I can cover a lot more ground a lot faster. I long ago stopped working easily accessible hiking trails, preferring to head into the untamed wilderness. Lots more monsters out there since there are fewer hunters.

In the end, all my concerns about dangerous monsters are for nothing. I don't run into anything out of my level, and while today's hunt is slower than previous ones, I don't run into anything that gives me too much trouble. I admit, it's a bit of a cheat when you can sense and track monsters before they can see you, especially when you can take them out at range.

When I get back, it's around four in the afternoon and the only reason I've called it a day is because I'm out of space. I have trouble just leaving corpses around and not dragging the bodies back for processing. It's not as if the many, many, many new bugs, pests, and other vermin don't clean up those bodies within days, but just leaving the bodies seems wasteful. It's not an entirely rational viewpoint since the Credits I gain from doing so won't make a dent, but there it is.

In Whitehorse, I head straight to the butchering yard, then I go to the Shop to sell my System Loot. As I exit the Shop, I find myself overtaken by a man dressed in clothing two sizes too large. The man is hunched over, his fists curled up and his face scrunched as he strides right past me. I have to jerk to a stop so that I don't run him over, and I almost call out to berate him when something makes me stop. I frown, staring after him as a sixth sense nags at me. Something. Something is wrong and I work on pinning what it is down.

I look closer as he walks right down the street to a new store finally realizing what it is. His right hand—it's larger than his left because it's curled up around a grenade.

I shout at him, but he's already throwing the grenade into the store, screaming, *"I warned you!"*

I flick on a Thousand Steps as I sprint toward him, my head turning to see who is within the store. I see the storekeeper, and without thought, I activate my other Skill—Two are One. She's staring with a dumbfounded expression when the grenade explodes, cutting off my line of sight in an explosion of flame and glass. My body feels as though it's being roasted alive in a sudden flash of heat that cuts right through my coveralls before the explosion itself reaches me, throwing me back.

I have to pick myself off the ground, my pain already receding. The attacker is rolling on the ground from the backblast, and the storekeeper, despite my Two are One skill, is dead. I force myself to take in the injured who were caught in the explosion, and I stagger over to the first injured body I can reach, casting my Minor Healing Spell.

It takes a surprisingly short time for things to calm down. A nearby mage throws a raincloud into the burning store while her neighbors fix the walls leading to their stores by purchasing upgrades in the Shop itself. Bodies are either healed by spells or mend on their own, and the survivors stagger away. The attacker is hustled off into Roxley's domain by a pair of silver-and-gray-clad guards. Fred Curteneau, our erstwhile mayor, pops out of the Council building to talk to people for a few minutes, walking around and glad-handing people with that big, oily smile of his. Somehow, people find it comforting. They set to work sweeping up the mess of glass and steel from the road, then it's over. At least for most people.

"Amelia?" I walk over as one of the guards bags the storekeeper's body under her directions.

"John." The ex-constable nods to me, a hand on a wide hip. She's wearing her RCMP uniform again, though it looks to have been let out to accommodate growth in her shoulders. Amelia's voice is cool and professional, but there's a tightness in her eyes. I don't envy her. She's the only human in Roxley's guard and as such, takes all the flack that we throw at him on her shoulders.

"What the hell happened?" I look into the remains of the store, shaking my head.

She purses her lips, shaking it after a moment. "I cannot comment on an on-going investigation."

"What investigation? I saw it. A whole group of us saw him throw the grenade. He murdered her!" I snap, temper flaring.

"John, I can't talk about it," she snaps, and Vir materializes at my side.

The entire "looming to intimidate" thing never really worked on me, not even pre-System when I was a good four inches shorter than most Westerners. Now that we're nearly the same height, it really doesn't work. I return the black-skinned, white-haired dark Elf's glare.

Amelia snaps, "There are rules, damn it. I know all of you people think there aren't, but the rules are in place for a reason."

"All of us people?" I snarl, my hand clenching. Sure, ever since I got the genome treatment I look more Keanu Reeves than Jet Li, but that doesn't mean that I've forgotten the barbs and screamed insults over the course of my life. Not that I've forgotten being told to go home to China, even if I grew up in Vancouver.

"Hunters," Amelia says, pointing a finger at me. "All of you, walking around with your weapons and powers, thinking you've got it all figured out. There are rules, and I'll be damned if I'm bending them to just satisfy your curiosity."

"Give it up, boy-o, she's got a job to do," Ali interjects.

I grit my teeth and look between the pair before finally jerkily nodding acceptance. What can I do? Beat them up for not answering my question? I walk away, snarling to myself, questions unanswered. What the hell was that all about?

***

"He wanted his store back," Lana fills me in later that evening. I caught her in the backyard, playing with her furry friends, and prodded her for information while children laughed and played in the living room. "His family owned the store pre-System. Then, well, Holly bought the store from the System and set up shop. He wanted her out, said she didn't have the right to it. She refused. The guards had been called in before and sided with her..."

"And he killed her for that?" I mutter.

Lana snorts, burying her face in the dog. "You tried to kill Eric."

Rufus whines slightly, feeling Lana's tension, and the puppy turns in her hands to lick at her face.

"I... I might have," I admit, shaking my head slowly. I had my reasons, but so had he probably. We're all under so much stress, and everything that we knew is gone. "Shit."

"Yes," Lana replies and hugs Rufus. She lets the silence linger as I stew on the parallels. In the end, she speaks again, her voice low. "It's not the only case like this. Not like this, like this, but similar. People moving into houses that aren't theirs. People taking cars from lots and having them fixed up. The workers at the brewery getting upset because we don't hire them because we don't need them."

"I didn't know it was that bad."

"Bad? That's the easy stuff. Who owns what, that's easy!" She laughs, slightly hysterically. "We have kids who don't have parents, parents who don't have kids. We have fathers who won't pay or help take care of their kids. We've got assholes who decide that because they've got combat classes, they're important now. They start throwing their weight around, acting like big shots. And because everyone—*everyone*—who is important is out hunting, they are big shots.

"You know why we opened the brewery? Do you?" She twists her hand slightly, pulling out a small ampule that she hands to me. "Aarak Blood. The best high in the System for us humans. Better than meth supposedly. We had people buying this and giving it out because there was no more alcohol. And they took it because they needed something to get their minds off this life. So instead we opened up the brewery and let them get drunk. That was a fun conversation to have with Jim."

"What's Roxley doing about all this?" I say, frowning.

"Roxley? Nothing. He's letting us humans sort out human problems, or so says Vir. Except when someone gets his guards involved. And then the troublemakers end up getting fined. Fined!" She shakes her head. "It's as if everything is about Credits to him."

I shake my head, trying to understand why Roxley would do that. It didn't mesh with the man I remembered. Not knowing what else to say, I murmur, "Sorry."

"No, I am. You don't need this. It's not your job, not your thing, right?" Lana rubs her face, wiping away the tears.

"Lana…"

"It's okay. This isn't your city. It isn't your problem. Just… thank you for listening." She stands, pulling Rufus with her as she walks away.

I open my mouth then shut it again, watching her leave. She's right—I left. I purposely chose not to get involved, not to be part of this. Hell, I'm playing both sides of the equation with the Hakarta just to see what the hell might happen. It was a choice, so now I don't get to bitch about it.

***

"Ali?" I stare into the distance, absently stroking one of the huskies, who has taken to lying next to me.

"Yeah, boy-o?"

"Is it all like this?"

"Mmmm… you mean the other cities?" He shakes his head, holding up a hand. "No. You guys are lucky. For definitions of luck. Most places don't have enough people to have a functioning government, never mind worrying about things like who owns what. The big cities were hit harder than anyone else. No one got Perks or any other bonuses, so they had no way to fight back. They also got a slew of higher-level monsters. And you know that monsters level up too? Yeah, guess what killing hundreds, thousands of humans did to even low-level monsters.

"You guys were lucky Roxley came along and brought his guards. Lucky that the System decided to put a Shop right here. You might be losing a few people here and there, but it's a hell of a lot better than the tens or hundreds you have."

I grimace, nodding slowly. "Are we the only big organized group left?"

"Get over yourself, will you? Of course not." Ali rolls his eyes. "There were a few armies that were out in the field, training or fighting with their weapons fully loaded. There are towns that have managed to survive and hold on, like Carcross. And Roxley isn't unique either. Quite a few others jumped on the chance to buy up small towns and villages and play lord.

"Truth is, take a city like New York, add all the survivors together, and you'd still have a bigger population than you have here. Just that, so far, they're scattered. Give them a bit of time and you guys will just be another small, remote group."

I grunt, smiling slightly. That's good. That's very good. "Do you have a number?"

"Of?"

"Survivors."

"Twelve percent or so." I flinch, and Ali sighs. "Some places, some cities, they weren't that lucky when the System hit. Santiago disappeared when an Air Elemental sucked up all the Mana and air in the region. Bangalore had a swarm of Liminir Locusts, flesh-eating insects that get into everything. New Orleans was flooded when a Leviathan surfaced nearby and got shot at by the navy. As I said, you got lucky."

I twitch, eyes going glassy as I imagine what it'd be like in any of those cities. Gods. "Lucky."

Chapter 6

I hold up the claw I took from a mutated wolverine and another from a Crilik shifter, comparing them and my soulbound sword laid out before me. I extend my senses to feel the Mana they contain, staring at them in silence. I've been doing this for the last few hours and I can finally, finally sense the differences, the way the Mana changes.

I slowly put down the Crilik shifter's claw and pick up a discarded armor plate from Sabre, one that had a hole punched through it earlier. Gently, I feel for the Mana that imbues it, then I bring the wolverine claw into contact.

There. Right there. Just at the edges of my senses, where the two make contact, I can feel the way the claw's Mana and the armor's interact, pushing against one another instead of melding. I shove harder, feeling the minute changes until the claw cracks, splintering under the pressure. I grunt, discarding the broken claw and picking up the shifters.

Again, I work slowly, adding pressure, but almost immediately, I can feel the difference. The Crilik shifter's claw has a significantly denser Mana signature, and as I press it into the armor, it punches a hole almost immediately, the denser Mana signature pushing against the weaker signature in the armor.

At the same time, I feel the electromagnetic force of the armor change. Mana that is absorbed by the claw directly weakens the bonds of the armor, making it easier for the claw to punch through. When I repeat the experiment with my sword, it slides through the armor the easiest, shaving off bits with almost no effort.

When I'm finally done, I stand up and stretch out of pure habit. I hate to say it, but Manbun—Aiden—had a point. It's all about perception, and that damn hipster/hippy wannabe has a better idea of it than anyone else in the city. Everyone, everything around us is permeated with Mana. The higher the level of a creature or thing, the higher the density of Mana it carries. We all interact with Mana regularly, shaping it to our wills even when we aren't actively thinking about it. It's why we don't break doorknobs with a touch, why a giant can walk across a wooden bridge that isn't rated for its weight, or why when I run, I can gain the speeds I do without tearing giant divots in the ground.

We reshape the Mana around us and use it to make the world fit our preconceived notions. The Classes and Skills we use are just a shortcut that the System offers, a set of buttons for the monkeys to press to make Mana work for them—but if you want, if you put the work in, you can directly influence Mana itself. That's what most Class-enabled, non-affinity mages do, even if they don't realize it. The ones with an elemental affinity manipulate the element itself instead, which is a whole different can of worms. I haven't figured that one out yet properly, though I'm making slow gains.

Grinning, I stretch and pull up my notifications, which I've had minimized till now.

Skill Increase
Mana Manipulation Level 4!

Skill Acquired
Mana Sense (Level 1)

The ability to sense Mana in people and objects is extremely important for mages and Mana users. Current range is limited to touch and will expand on training.

Quest Update—the System
You've taken another step in understanding the secrets of the System by expanding on your ability to sense Mana.

Reward: +500 XP

All right, enough lounging about staring at my abilities. Even if the Hakarta aren't expecting me to provide anything new anytime soon, I'm going to have to come up with something. I'm not entirely sure "humans are being humans and hurting one another" is going to cut it. At the very least, I should be out hunting.

***

Not that I'm going to be hunting, at least not today. Jogging over the bridge that connects the suburb of Riverdale to Whitehorse, I glance at the clock in my peripheral vision and put on a little burst of speed. I'm late. Not that I've ever seen them leave on time, but it's still unprofessional.

Unsurprisingly, when I get to Main Street, the trucks and cars that make up the caravan to Carcross is still getting itself put together. I'm not the only one who's late. Jason spots me almost immediately, waving me to the front, and I jog over to him, nodding a greeting.

"You can relax, they're still in the meeting." Jason waves toward the Elijah Smith Building that the remainder of our local government has moved into. The squat, gray building stares onto Main Street itself, opposite the towering monstrosity that makes up the System-designated City Center and Roxley's offices.

"Morning, squirt," Ali greets Jason, who snorts.

"Morning, jumpsuit," Jason retorts then offers me a piece of dried fruit.

Taking the fruit, I take a seat next to the teenager. "You got kicked out?"

"Never invited." Jason rolls his eyes. "I'm too young to be of use in the negotiations. It's fine for me to fight monsters, train the adults, and walk the walls, but sit in a negotiation about our city? Too young!"

"Isn't that the way," I sympathize, glancing back at the building. "What were you guys negotiating anyway? I never got the full story."

"Huh," Jason says. "As I understand it, Whitehorse wants us to stop taking in so many immigrants. Particularly their crafters. They've also been pretty unhappy with the loot we're purchasing from their hunters direct. Or the goods we're bringing in for resale."

I frown, noting how it's all things that Whitehorse wants. "What do you get for this?"

"Food. Credits. More security." Jason shrugs. "Whitehorse has an actual working farm, something we don't. We're still importing a bunch of food to keep everyone fed, so getting a surplus would be good. And we wouldn't mind more hunters working the area around Carcross. We've still got to keep half of our hunters on the wall."

I nod slightly, sighing. "You guys still intent on sticking it out?"

"Uh huh." Jason lowers his voice, murmuring, "I don't get how you people live here without a safe zone. At least when I'm home, I know I'm safe. I keep looking over my shoulder for trouble when I'm in Whitehorse."

I chuckle, shaking my head. "It's not so bad. The guards are always dispatched to potential spawns before they actually come through, so we just have to worry about the spontaneous evolutions."

"Still, gives me the creeps," Jason replies. "Anyway, they've been talking about it for the last few days, but they should have been done already. I guess there's always something new."

"Old. Something old in this case," Elder Andrea Badger replies, stomping forward. The old First Nation's lady and titular Mayor of Carcross walks up to us, greeting Ali and me with a smile. "Bureaucracy kept us up. However, the forms are all signed now."

Jason shrugs before jumping up and waving to everyone. Once he gets their attention, he points at the cars before clambering into his car without waiting for the others. Behind him, the constable rolls his eyes, calling out orders to get everyone moving. I open the door for the elder before heading to my seat in the front. Time to babysit the children.

The trip back is relatively uneventful. More monsters than normal—six groups to be exact, but Jason, Mike, and I tear through them like hot knife through butter. Gadsby still likes getting in close and pounding on them with his truncheon, though he seems to have picked up an upgrade that fires bolts of pure Mana into bigger and nastier monsters. Jason keeps things simple, casting bolts of plasma and ice to rip holes into monsters. Myself? I switch tactics, of course—beam rifle for soft, simple targets and the sword for harder things.

I'm not entirely sure why they even bothered to hire me—the pair of them are more than enough for the monsters we meet, and the additional hunters aren't exactly sitting around doing crossword puzzles. Unfortunately, I'm not seated next to the elder or else I'd ask her why they bothered.

When we roll into the city, I get a quick notification that the quest is completed. Carcross hasn't changed much since I last came here—the improvised wall is now less improvised and an actual constructed wall with watchtowers and automated sensors set up throughout. I know the wall is just the most visible of the town's defenses—multiple shield defenses are active and ready, protecting against ground and air infiltration. There are numerous pits and even a few automated gun stands, all waiting to be activated. In fact, I'd say Carcross is better defended than Whitehorse. They certainly have more firepower packed in than we do.

Every single-story building in Carcross is System-enabled by now, and the elder waves goodbye to me before heading for the Cultural Center and headquarters. Gadsby follows her to report in, and Jason gets dragged away by a cute blonde almost immediately, leaving me alone among strangers. Except the citizens of Carcross aren't exactly strangers, not anymore. A fact that I'm reminded of as I'm dragged into the mess hall for a late lunch.

As Ali and I sit around, drinking and eating and chatting with the locals, I wonder if this is Andrea's play. Reminding me that the people of Carcross are still here, still around, still friends. I laugh at a joke as I finish off my latest bowl of stew and glance at Ali then at the time. Well, it's only three o'clock and Jason did say they had a problem with monsters around the city. No reason not to do a little hunting out here.

Waving goodbye to the group and declining offers of help, I get Ali to show me the latest known monster groups on the map. Time to go kill something. I'll head back to Whitehorse tomorrow.

***

Life has fallen into a routine since my talk with Lana—I wake up, I meditate, I train for a few hours, sometimes by myself, sometimes with Mikito or Richard and his pets. Training together, we're slowly breaking down that wall we put up between us. It's not perfect, but it's better than nothing and holding a grudge over the fact that I nearly killed Minion is just silly.

After training, it's always hunting, working to keep the monster population down and gain further experience and Credits to fix Sabre. Putting the mecha back together—or better than it was—is expensive. Without Sabre, I spend a portion of each day just getting to appropriately leveled locations, but at least I'm getting a decent Skill in running. I keep going till late at night or my Altered Space is filled, whichever comes first, then I head into Whitehorse and do a quick dump. If it's still early enough, I'm out again to hunt.

Being in Whitehorse, I start seeing the things Lana spoke of and some that she didn't. The bulletin board of the missing always seems to have just a few new faces as people disappear into the woods. Or the corpses of those who don't even bother going that far, leaving their bodies in the shelters for others to dispose of. People who have just given up, who can no longer handle this new world.

Then there's the lazy, the incompetent, and the cheats who refuse to help out, living off the largesse of everyone else. I see the occasional fist fights, the shouting matches that Amelia and the other guards have to put a stop to. No surprise there's more than a little resentment over the lack of help.

The City Council has even gone as far as creating their own court system, overseen by one over-worked ex-judge. He does his best to mediate issues among the population. He tackles everything from ownership and living arrangements, custody battles between families, to figuring out foster care situations for those who need it. Once in a while, he even has to deal with real crimes—theft, a few rapes, beatings, and shakedowns that escape the attention of Roxley's guards or are just never brought to their attention.

Most of all, worst of all, is the way those with combat classes and everyone else are segregating into the haves and have-nots. The tensions just get worse and worse as the stores that open cater mostly to the combat classers. No big surprise, they're the only ones with any Credit. Everyone else is busy saving up to buy their own place to live, to get a little bit more food or other necessities. That doesn't stop people from resenting the combat classers or their fortune.

There's nothing I can do about it. Not really. So I just go out and do my thing—fighting and killing and attempting to save enough Credits to finally fix up Sabre. Which means killing this ugly bastard.

Mountain Troll (Level 52)
HP: 3580/3580

This monster is over ten feet tall, rocky gray, and covered with warts. An extra-long nose and a hunched back, along with a rocky club, complete the ensemble. After hunting them for the last few days, I now know more about Troll physiology than I ever want to —including why they're so angry all the time. I'd be angry too if I was that lacking in that department.

My first shot takes it in the right knee, the second its left. I keep crouched after crippling the creature, my beam rifle blasting open and searing wounds closed as I get to work killing it. The monster is tough though, its resistances to energy significantly reducing the damage I'm dishing out, and its natural regeneration fixes my initial onslaught.

As the troll lurches toward me on all fours, it picks up real speed and I flick the rifle back into my inventory. Hands free, I cast my Improved Mana Dart spell, creating four glowing blue darts that shoot forward as I flick my hand at the creature. I grin wolfishly as the Troll staggers, its resistances utterly useless against the Mana Darts.

I summon another four and repeat the process, doing so two more times before I charge to meet it face to face. As we close, I use Blade Strike to catch the monster before he can reach me, then I duck beneath the first swing, slicing upward with my sword and shearing through muscle. I spin around as we cross each other's path, laying its back open before the Troll can turn, then I kick it away from me. Now with enough space, I focus on

Cleave and swing down with full force, the sword picking up a red-and-blue glow that sheathes the blade. The cut takes the creature straight on, opening it from shoulder to hip. Before it can recover, I swing again and trigger Cleave once more, leaving a giant bloody X on the Troll's body.

It's not enough to kill it though, and the Troll swings its club, using the momentum from my attack to smash into my leg. Only a last-minute move keeps my knee from shattering, but I end up on the ground, kicking up dirt as I slide a good ten feet. I bite my lip, a rush of pure adrenaline shooting through my body. Gods, but I love fighting.

When the Troll closes in on me and starts its swing down, I call forth my sword and make sure it's right where the Troll's arm will be, letting it impale itself on my sword. I leave the blade in its arm, kicking on its knee to push myself away and give me momentum. I roll to my feet just before I charge it.

Our next clash is very different since I stop trying to overpower it, instead dancing around the creature. All those hours training and fighting has helped me develop an innate understanding of combat that the System download didn't impart. I turn aside blows, dodge under or around them, and always, always chip away at its health. Whenever I have a moment, I throw another set of Mana Darts into its face. In the end, the Troll falls over, dead as can be.

Breathing hard, I chop the head off the monster just in case and kick the body once more. I loot it then dump the body back into my Altered Space before slowly stretching and waiting for the broken ribs to heal fully. Pain and adrenaline, my constant companions these days. I find myself grinning, knowing that this Troll finished the Quest I've been running for Sally. Seems like Troll Blood is in high-demand among alchemists.

In the distance, I see something white against the clear blue sky. At first I think it's just a cloud, but something tells me to look closer.

Ali, drawn by my focused attention, follows my gaze then yelps. "Hide!"

I move, months of constant danger making me duck toward the nearest tree and shrink down as tight as I can get. When I'm as hidden as I'm going to get, I ask, "*What's wrong?*"

"*Dragon.*"

"*Shit.*" I reach out mentally for the QSM before Ali growls at me.

"*Don't. It'll attract his attention. They can see between dimensions.*"

My eyes widen. That's the first I've ever heard of something being able to do that naturally. I slowly poke my head around the corner as I hit the magnification in my helmet. The dragon jumps in size, pure white with an elongated neck and wings that triple its width. Above its head floats its status bar.

Dragon (Level ???)

HP: ???/???

"*Ali? Shouldn't it be a winter dragon or something?*"

"*That's all the information I have, boy-o. Way too high level for me to extract information from the System.*"

"*What's it doing here?*" Hell, I knew we were in a high-level zone, but this area isn't that bad…

"*Best guess? It's probably hunting. I doubt the Kluane Icefields are that populated yet.*"

I wince, nodding slowly. It makes sense that the Icefields would have something truly nasty there—it was the largest icefield in the world outside of the poles. But does it have to go hunting while I'm around?

I curl down further and get ready to wait. At least it's not likely to have seen me, being as far away as it is. It does remind me how big a gap there is, between the true Powers of this world and piddly little beginners like me.

***

Hours later, the dragon has gone and I'm jogging back from the east on the other side of the river, having decided to take the long way round just in case. I shake my head as I consider how easy it would be for the monsters to run into Riverdale itself. As a suburb of Whitehorse, there's no wall, no good way to stop anyone from just walking in. It's why there are checkpoints at the bridges and the roads entering the city. Still, if we ever got hit by a swarm, those who live in Riverdale would be in real trouble.

Crossing the bridge, I absently nod to the fishermen who line the path to Sally's. At her shop, I find an attendant watching over the front, and when I make myself known, I'm ushered into the backroom where Sally keeps her workshop. It only takes a few seconds for the four-foot-tall Gnome to string up the entire Troll and plug in various tubes to begin the draining process. When that's done, she flashes me a grin and I get my notification.

Quest Complete (Troll's Blood)

Retrieve 40 Liters of Troll's Blood for Sally

Rewards: 2 Tier II Health Regeneration Potions, 2 Tier II Mana Regeneration Potions, 2,000 XP

"Thank you. Any other requests?" I ask.

She snorts, shaking her head. "Not until you upgrade your herb lore, you big lug." Sally waggles her finger at me, eyes twinkling. "I still don't believe you brought back Jarsik Weed."

"It looked exactly like what you asked for!" I protest.

"If you are blind and stupid, sure."

I roll my eyes and admit defeat. Seriously, it looked exactly the same. Though truth be told, I'm okay not playing gardener. The one day I spent poking around looking for herbs for Sally was an utter waste of time. Nearly ninety percent of what I brought back was useless, which meant I didn't even get halfway to completing her Quest. I could buy the skill in the Shop, but really, I'd rather just kill something. "Fine. Call me if you need anything killed."

She grins, pushing me out. "Out, I got work to do!"

My next stop is the butchering yard, where I drop the last of my day's earnings. As I make my way down the street afterward, I notice a commotion at the entrance to the city council's offices. I push my way through the crowd, picking up scattered words. Luthien's back.

I almost walk away when I hear my ex's name, but after a moment's hesitation, I push forward. I might not want to see her, but the Raven's Circle was our highest leveled group before they left for Dawson. Something had happened on the trip there and what should have been a couple of days away had become weeks.

"Jim?" I catch the eye of the hunter as he glares at everyone milling around, his presence sufficient to keep most back.

The older First Nation gentleman's face is lined even further than normal, his dark eyes filled with worry as he shifts, still clad in his hunting gear. It's a mix of old and new, a simple one-piece nano-woven jumpsuit with armor plating at appropriate locations, covered by a gray hunting vest for additional weaponry and gear, and his favored rifle and knife at his side. Pretty standard fare for the combat classes these days.

"John," the elder answers, and at my raised eyebrow, he beckons me over.

I see a few people glare at me, but I ignore it. It's good to have a few favors owed. "Luthien's back?"

"Yes." Jim frowns at the group that surrounds us, waiting to hear something. He seems to debate saying more before he continues. "Seven people came back. Four strangers and three of the Circle."

"Who?" I say softly, knowing that at least Nic is dead. His house stopped being a Safe Zone about three days after they left, which is when we knew for sure something had gone wrong.

"Luthien, Kevin, and Tim." Before I can ask, he adds. "The other four, that's all that's left of Dawson."

The words are like a punch to the gut of those who hear him. Those in the front of the group fall silent, only answering those behind after repeated requests. The words spread like wildfire, reactions wild and varied. Some nod, accepting what they probably feared. Others deny the words and get angry, while others break down crying.

Including the Circle, eleven people left to visit Dawson and see what good they could do. The Circle had asked for volunteers and some—the brave and the desperate—joined them. Eleven people left and only three of ours came back. My lips purse and Jim meets my gaze, obviously having done the math himself. This is the kind of trade-off we feared. Worst, we had lost two of our highest level fighters in this stupid expedition, all because the damn woman wanted to show off again.

As I draw in a deep breath, forcing down the anger, the door opens. I turn to look and spot a man I've never seen before stride out as if he owns it all. A good 6'4", middle-aged with a strong jaw and a brown, crewcut hairstyle, he's handsome in a "human" way, someone you'd see walking down the street rather than in the movies. Ali frowns slightly, twitching his hand as the man appears, and information blooms above his head.

Bill Cross (Level 46 Enforcer)
HP: 1400/1400

Interesting Class. Behind him, a familiar face. Luthien—my ex—walks behind him, just a little too close. Tall, thin, blond, and pretty with pointy ears, she strides out and I spot more than one admiring gaze roam over her body. I almost want to wave and shout "Run, run for your life," but that's a touch too dramatic. And petty. Luthien's clad in tight leather pants and a corset-like armor piece that covers her upper body quite well.

Luthien Celbrindal (Level 38 Sorceress)
HP: 540/540

My eyes narrow, lips tightening as I scan the rest of the group as they come out. People make way, pushing back to let the newcomers exit while Jim and I are forgotten. The entire group has incredibly high levels, all in the high 30s or low 40s. As Kevin and Tim bring up the back of the line, I can't help but notice their slumped shoulders, tight lips, and hangdog expressions, along with the slight hesitation in their steps. There's a distance between Kevin and Luthien that wasn't there before they left. I almost think the man might be smarting up enough to realize how dangerous a relationship with her is. Almost. As Tim clears the doorway, I hear more than a few drawn breaths as people spot his half-dragon form. I'd almost forgotten he had his race changed—he's been gone so long.

"Where's everyone else?" a voice calls out from the crowd when no more people exit.

The crowd stills for an answer, hoping against hope.

"I'm sorry. We're all that's left of Dawson," Bill says, his voice clear and loud. "We're all that survived, and if the Circle hadn't come, we'd be dead too."

Murmurs run through the crowd, a few people peeling away.

"I don't believe you! My son was in Dawson. He wouldn't die," a woman screams, pushing to the front of the crowd.

"I don't lie. There's no one left alive in Dawson." Bill glares at the woman for a moment before he shakes his head, the glare disappearing. "I'm sorry, but they're all dead. The monsters, we couldn't fight them all."

The woman screams a denial then launches herself at Bill, fingers curled into claws that she swings at his face. Before she can reach him, Luthien raises a hand and bonds of air grip the woman, holding her in place as she screams and struggles. Ugly sounds come from the crowd before the guards led by Amelia arrive.

"That's it, everyone. Show's over. Time to get going." Amelia grabs and pushes people away, as do the other guards, all of them radiating a subtle menace that I recognize as a Skill.

Many of the people grabbed protest then see the look in the Truinnar guards' eyes and shudder before moving off. The crowd disperses quickly with the guards there. Jim taps Luthien's arm, gesturing to the distraught mother. Sniffing in disdain, Luthien flicks her hand and the woman collapses into Jim's waiting hands. She struggles for a moment, but as he continues to hug her, she stills, finally just crying.

"Nice town," Bill drawls softly to his group, probably thinking no one can hear him in the commotion.

Standing next to the wall, unmoving and forgotten, I do. A few of the group titter while Tim shifts uncomfortably before he pushes away to walk up the street.

"Tim!" Kevin says, moving to grab his friend.

"Let him go," Bill barks, shaking his head. "We don't need weaklings like him."

Luthien nods firmly when Kevin hesitates, biting his lip. When her boyfriend finally turns aside, Bill smiles at Luthien, who preens slightly. It's so subtle, someone who wasn't watching for it and who didn't know her would never see.

Oh, you poor bastard. For a moment, I almost pity Kevin. Almost. When the crowd has dispersed enough, Bill leads the group off, stopping only long enough to speak with Amelia to thank her before they head out.

Well, this is going to be interesting.

Chapter 7

As momentous as the news about Dawson City was, life settled back into the norm soon enough. Bill and his group moved into the Circle's old house, repurchasing the house from the System with little fanfare. Since then, they've made themselves scarce in terms of their interaction with the local population. Outside of hitting the Shops and occasionally the Nugget, the group seems to be focused on hunting and leveling. Of course, I hear there's a little tension there since they refuse to bring back food for the pot and deal directly with the low-level Alchemists and Sally when they have parts to sell. As I understand it, Fred was rebuffed when he tried to talk to them about helping out the City. Seems like the time it takes to drag back corpses isn't worth the payout. That does at least explain their levels somewhat. If they're focusing only on leveling, it's no surprise that they're slightly higher than most of us.

Truth be told, I can see the appeal. Go out, kill, level. It's the only way to stay safe, to be safe. Strength is power and safety in this world, and strength comes from Credits and Levels. At least, that's what more and more hunters are saying. Goodwill gets you only so far, and the hunters under Jim have started fracturing, some following the Circle's example and refusing to hunt for the pot anymore. Many point out that there's more than enough food these days, pointing to the stores of meat and vegetables as the farms come in. The Council's charts and explanations get thrown by the wayside—the simple fact that they can see the stores are more convincing proof to them. Anyway, they know the City could just buy more food from the Shop directly if they needed it.

When I see the Council individually or in a group, I almost pity them. The strain is beginning to show, the pressures of keeping the city together beginning to pull them apart. More and more people are blaming the Council as monsters continue to spawn in the town, even if we aren't losing people to those attacks anymore. More and more people are wondering why they're being asked to contribute Credits when they see so little results.

Through all this, Roxley stays hidden in his offices. No one sees him, no one speaks to him. The Yerick and his guards bear the brunt of the growing animosity, the glares and the whispered insults. Still, no one takes direct action as the threat of being sold into debt slavery keeps people in line. For now, anyway.

***

As I enter the Nugget, I find it filled with Adventurers and Crafters kicking back after a hard day's work. Looking around, I spot Lana, Mikito, Amelia, and a few others sitting together. Ali floats alongside me, ogling the waitresses, as I walk up to the table.

"John," Lana says, flashing me a smile.

"Ladies…" I blink, realizing that the entire group is made up of women. Oh. Right, not joining them then. "Just thought I'd say hi."

"Good evening," Mikito adds as I beat a hasty retreat.

There's only a single table left, way too big for me alone, but what the hell, it is what it is. I grab a seat facing the doorway, and Ali plops down next to me. Out of idle curiosity, I glance over the group again.

"*So, Lana, you … sleeping together yet?*" Amelia says, her head turned just enough that I can lipread her. I almost feel guilty about intruding, but curiosity keeps me looking.

"*No.*" Lana shakes her head, emphasizing her answer. "*I told you, we're not like that.*"

"Why not? We all know you … the hots for him. Not … it. I mean, he's … looking but he's so angry all the …" Amelia says, her hair occasionally sliding across her face and blocking my line of sight.

"Is he ever," Mikito mutters. *"I think he likes being angry."*

"There's no future for us. One day he's going to leave, even if he doesn't realize it yet," Lana says, shaking her head.

"…" another girl interjects and the group laughs.

My eyes narrow as I wonder what was said, and when Lana begins to speak, my line of sight is blocked by a large armored form. I snarl slightly, looking up and up and up before I meet the placid gaze of the ten-foot-tall Yerick leader.

"First Fist," I say, plastering a smile on my face.

"Redeemer. Will you allow us to join you?" He gestures to the table and benches and I look around, realizing that there are no seats anywhere else.

I nod, and Capstan takes a seat in front of me, permanently blocking my view of the ladies. His party mates join him, and I suddenly feel rather crowded among the large and slightly musty-smelling aliens.

"First Fist, I didn't expect to see you here." Ali hugs his beer mug to his body.

"We are celebrating this day and were informed that the Nugget carries a passable alcohol for our purposes." Capstan glances at his companions before waving to them. "Redeemer, may I introduce my companions—Aron Hauser, Nelia Renar, and Tahar Ocasio."

Aron, of course, is the Minotaur fighter who was with Jim. Nelia I've seen before, a Level 48 Shaman Truthseeker—whatever that is—and Tahar seems to be another generic Yerick Adventurer.

I greet them in turn before I ask the obvious question, "What celebration?"

"What drink?" Ali adds.

Ali's question is answered when the waitress comes over with a dark, almost black liquid in mugs the size of a pitcher. Even from my seat, I can smell the alcohol in them.

"Good gods," I mutter, leaning back a bit. Sure, the beer I drink really doesn't do anything for me with my Constitution, but that's for the best. Being drunk in an unsecure city seems like a bad, bad idea. "What is that?"

"Your brewery calls it Apocalypse Ale," Capstan says, pushing a mug to each of his companions. "It is decently strong."

"And the celebration?" I ask as Ali floats over to a waitress to order an ale for himself. I watch the waitress nod before letting my gaze flick to the other tables. We're getting more than one nasty look, but no one feels the need to start a fight they'll lose.

"We completed a dungeon!" Aron butts in, grinning as he leans forward. "Level 35 and up!"

Capstan nods while keeping a straight face, though I can tell he's quite proud of the group. The robed and hooded Nelia nods as well.

As Ali floats back with his mug in hand, I pick up my own. "Well, congratulations then!" They stare at my glass that I hold in the air before I chuckle a bit awkwardly. Right, culture. "Uhh… humans normally drink after the congratulations."

The Yerick look at one another then simultaneously pick up their drinks, quaffing them without hesitation, followed by Ali and myself.

"A strange custom. Yerick prefer to enjoy their drink," Tahar speaks for once, looking morosely at his empty glass.

"I'll remember that." I'm saved from more embarrassment as the waitresses bring dinner out at last. Capstan makes a face at the food laid out before me. "Problem?"

"No," Capstan replies immediately, shaking his head while Tahar keeps his head down.

"Yerick don't eat meat, boy-o." Ali shakes his head. "You'd think you'd know that, what with them looking like cows."

"We are not cows," Aron snarls. He immediately subsides when Capstan gives him a look.

"Ali didn't mean that." I glare at the Spirit stealing a fry from one of my plates.

"Yeah, yeah. So you guys cleared a dungeon, eh? We did one too, a month and a half back. Boy-o lost his mojo though when he lost his bike," Ali adds, and I grunt, shaking my head.

"You cleared a dungeon by yourself?" Capstan says.

"Just a Level 20 one," I say. "I've run into a few locations since then, but I got run out of one and another, well, I figured I'd test it out soon."

"Really?" Capstan leans forward. "Would you care to trade on the locations? Unexplored Dungeons are quite important."

I stare at them for a moment, my lip pulling up slightly into a smile. "Well, now that you mention it…"

***

"This is the dungeon you cleared, eh?" I look at the large building in the abandoned village the next day, frowning. Unlike most of the other buildings around here, this one looks to be in pretty good repair. "It doesn't look that big."

"It isn't out here," Capstan answers me, rotating broad shoulders as he adjusts his gear. "You stay in the back. Use your Spells and rifle and watch our backs. Nelia is our mage and healer, so she'll be ahead of you and backing us all up. The three of us, well, we'll be in front."

I nod and turn to look for Ali. The Spirit floats in mid-air, staring at the abandoned buildings. I let my gaze wander over the remnants of the small community, a place where a hundred or so might have lived before the System. Happily, I guess, or at least as happily as you could be in a place like this. There aren't that many corpses around, just a few scattered bones, broken-down houses and cars. All of it abandoned and slowly being overrun. A part of me wonders if I could find more corpses if I looked for them. Most of me decides against looking.

"You good, boy-o?" Ali asks and points toward where the others are already entering.

"Let's go," I reply, following the Yerick.

***

When you think dungeon, you think stone walls or caverns or maybe a castle. What you don't expect is an old office building that stretches on and on, hallways that lead to rooms that loop around back to the hallway, never seeming to end. Off-white walls with fluorescent lights that work without electricity, lighting everything just a little off. It's a weird reminder that the System doesn't necessarily line up with our expectations.

No traps in this dungeon but golems, lots and lots of golems. Humanoid, bipedal constructs that totter forward, raining energy beams and fire on us, occasionally interspersing the attacks with more exotic weaponry like sonic grenades or ice darts.

The Yerick plow forward through the attacks using portable shields, firing from under the cover of the glowing blue domes. Aron and Tahar lead the charge with wrist-mounted beam weaponry till they're close enough to engage the creatures in melee. Capstan uses a rifle behind them, ignoring the occasional shot that gets past the shields and picking off those behind us. Nelia in her robes does little, occasionally casting a healing spell or a weird web-spell that constricts and slows the monsters. The team is a well-oiled machine, each of them covering for the other with a minimum of words and confusion. I don't even bother attempting to shoot past them, knowing that I'm as likely to hit a friendly as a monster.

Instead, I keep an eye on the back and deal with the occasional Golem that pops up behind us. Blade, rifle, and spells are more than enough to deal with the threats, especially since their flanking attacks are limited.

I have more than enough time to muse, being safely ensconced in the back as I am. More than enough time to think about the peculiarities of character builds and team tactics. In a "traditional" multi-player game, every character gets a Class and that Class generally has a role. Tank, damage dealer, healer, crowd control. More complicated pen-and-paper role-playing games added less direct combat-oriented Classes like the Bard. Everyone specialized because you had to, that's what the game required.

Of course, most of those games were set in a fantasy world. Modern-day combat stopped having people carry around melee weapons because a spear isn't much use against cannonballs and muskets smashing into your ranks, killing and wounding before you could near your opponent. Machine guns that threw hundreds of rounds a second meant that rushing an entrenched position led to thousands of casualties.

All that reasoning seems to kind of go out the window in System reality, as I told Jason months ago. Classes are given, and at first glance, it seems you should specialize and become a fighter, a healer, a mage. But none of that matters since you can purchase nearly anything in the System, including Class

Skills. You can and probably should become a jack-of-all-trades with a minor specialization in your original Class. Watching the Yerick fight, that seems to be the preferred method among them at least. Probably a good idea to have everyone dabble a little bit. After all, you don't want to get caught out if your only healer goes down or your only ranged fighter dies.

On the other hand, armor and shields soak up a bunch of ranged attack damage in the System, even if they don't stop the damage entirely. Every single person is a moving tank with the right kind of equipment and Skills. The Yerick cover ground quickly, ensuring that they bring their physical strength to bear in any encounter, using melee weapons that deal as much, if not more, damage as beam weaponry. Take the shots, deal a little damage on the way in, then get close and rip them apart while the healer/mage keeps your health up and ensures you aren't too overworked. I do wonder what it'd be like if they met a sentient group willing to run away as much as they were willing to charge. Would it just be a giant running battle?

***

Hours later, Capstan holds up a hand as the last Golem falls in the room we're exploring. The others turn to him, and he makes a few gestures with the same hand. The group quickly splits up and sets small boxes in front of the doorways. After a moment, the boxes glow green and the Yerick relax, grinning.

"Portable shield generators. More powerful than the personal ones the Yerick use but with a lot less time on the clock. They have an in-built alarm and scanner, so if something tries to come through, they'll activate." Ali yawns. "You bored as I am?"

"No." I join the Yerick as they sit on the floor, pulling cubes of green and brown paste from their inventory. "Lunch?"

"Yes. We are two thirds of the way through the dungeon, I believe," Capstan replies, nodding. "Single floor, but long, as you can tell."

"Yeah." I grimace and sit down, tapping my helmet to make it fold down and free me to breathe unencumbered. "Where do the Golems come from? They aren't evolutions from Earth for sure."

"Probably a template somewhere. Maybe in the ground, maybe in a wall. The System diverts the Mana in the dungeon to the template to create the golems. Each golem birthed this way requires Mana, which is the main reason dungeons are created." Capstan pops open the cap of his green paste. "Leave it alone long enough and they'll spill out, but most dungeon-born monsters prefer to stay in the dungeons they were created in."

"That's the prevailing theory of dungeons anyway," Ali sends to me as he fishes out some soggy fish and chips from my Altered Space. My nose wrinkles slightly at the smell, but he doesn't seem to care about it.

I nod slowly as I suck on the all-in-one meal I brought for my lunch. It's edible—sort of like apple sauce, just a little grainier. I figured the Yerick would prefer if I kept my meat eating down around them, though Ali of course doesn't give a damn. "So what about the Alphas? The Bosses?"

"If a monster group has an Alpha, the System creates an Alpha because that's what the monster group should have," Aron answers, looking at me as if I'm stupid. "Why would the System change what works?"

I open my mouth to retort, but Ali adds, "It's a safeguard too. Alphas and Bosses require more Mana, so in a golem dungeon like this, the Boss is just a monster that's had more Mana diverted into it. You can't do that too much to normal monsters or they go pop, so only a few special ones can be

Bosses. The System has to do it because the Mana flow isn't even. It's more like waves in the ocean. If there's a surge, it needs a place to dump."

"That… makes sense." I switch over to some juice, staring at the doorway as the group continues to chew placidly on their food. "I don't understand why the System wants to deal with Mana that way though."

"8Ink," Nelia says.

"Gesundheit."

"It's an old story, idiot," Ali says.

"Sad story," Capstan says.

"Stupid," Aron adds.

"Still not explaining," I grumble.

"When the System came to 8Ink, the ambassador let the inhabitants of the world know. The inhabitants were supposedly a psionic race, an empathic one. They decided, as a world, to reject the System. When the System came, none chose to interact with it. No one leveled, no one used Mana. So the Mana kept pooling and pooling and pooling. The Council tried to divert the Mana elsewhere, but back then, we only had four Dungeon Worlds. It wasn't possible to get rid of enough of it," Capstan says. "Eventually, well, the Mana density became too much and even the sentient inhabitants started transforming, evolving. Still, they refused to interact. Eventually, the entire world evolved."

"So's Earth," I point out, tossing my used meal into my inventory.

"Not like… the entire world evolved. 8Ink became a World Titan," Nelia clarifies.

I wince. Oh, shit. "What…?"

"It got up and flew away. Records of where it went and what it's doing have been lost. Some say hidden," Tahar says, sudden passion entering his voice. "8Ink's return is quite a popular branch of fiction. If you want, I have a few books on me."

Aron rolls his eyes while Ali actually nods in excitement. Aron lets out a low huff of exasperation while Nelia and Capstan go back to eating, waiting for me to continue.

"Let me get this straight. Too much Mana means giant Elementals. To stop that, the System puts Mana into monsters it stores away? Isn't killing a monster then releasing the Mana?" I ask.

"No." Nelia shakes her head, glitter-decorated horns flashing in fluorescent light. "Some Mana goes back into the environment, but... the System uses a lot. Mana is necessary for the Loot, for our experience, for running the...?"

"System," Capstan finishes for Nelia absently, filling in when the mage falls silent.

Brows furrowed, I puzzle through it. "If you could do all that, why bother with all the intervening steps? Why not just convert the Mana straight away?"

"Why do you think it's a Quest, John? If we had the answer to that, the Quest would have been complete," Ali says mockingly.

Capstan and the others nod as Capstan stands. "Do not chase that Quest, Redeemer. It leads nowhere and the rewards decrease as you journey along the path. Gravity pulls you down, the axe hungers for blood, and the System is the System."

As the group gets ready to get going, Aron and Tahar grabbing the portal shield generators, I sigh and put that question away again. Ali smirks at me then flicks a finger, sending a window to fill my vision.

Quest Update—the System

The creation of Dungeons and Mana are important for the Quest, but why? You have found some answers, but more questions.

Reward: +200 XP

Yeah, yeah, I got it. What is, is. Better to go and kill something.

"Uhh… was he that big before?" I whisper to the Yerick as we huddle around the corner from the doorway.

"No. This might be… interesting," Capstan says and I stare at him. Really?

I poke my head around the corner again, getting a hiss from Nelia as I do so, but I need to see our opponent again to get my head around this. The Golem boss doesn't look any different from its brethren really. Bipedal with two heads and four arms, each wielding a combination rifle and fist with a metallic exterior. Sure, it's green, which is rather unique, but the bigger surprise is that it's twenty-five feet tall.

Golem Arcana (Boss Level 42)

HP: 7420/7420

"Also, boy-o, it's an It," Ali adds. "You're such a misogynist."

"Ali," I snarl, temper flaring.

Capstan claps me on the shoulder, hissing at me. I blush slightly, somewhat embarrassed at my outburst. Right, we're trying to come up with a plan.

"Spirit, is the creature vulnerable to anything?" Capstan asks.

Ali stares into space, his little fingers waggling. "Water."

Aron whispers to Nelia, "Told you you should have gotten another Ice spell. No, you had to go with Fireball."

Nelia growls at Aron while Capstan and Tahar look at me.

I open my hands, shaking my head. "Nothing useful. I could hit it with Lightning, but that jumps around. I have Mana Dart…"

Aron rolls his eyes, and Tahar snorts dismissively. Fine, fine. It's the lowest-level combat spell out there, and even improved, it's still not particularly impressive. Personally, I think if I can improve it to send out dozens of those darts, it'd be amazing.

Capstan stays silent, scratching his arm as he stares into the distance. "We will need to stay close. The fists are dangerous, but the beam weapons are more so. Nelia will attempt to disable the upper left arm. I shall take the upper right. Redeemer, you must take the lower left. Aron and Tahar will take the last. Disable, then help the others. And then we kill it."

The three Yerick twist and jerk their heads in unison in their traditional yes while I nod.

"Nelia, you will begin. May the herd watch over us." Capstan stands, unslinging his axe for once.

The other pair get ready, their breathing increasing in speed slightly as they pump themselves up. I quietly activate Thousand Steps, figuring we could use the extra speed, and call forth my sword.

Nelia steps out past the door as she calls her spell into being. It takes longer than it usually does, a giant ritual circle of glowing blue lines and symbols appearing behind her as she builds and shapes her spell, Glacial Wall. Unfortunately, the Golem isn't waiting for her to finish and is already turning, raising its arms.

The boys dash off to the right, opening up their beam weapons while Capstan steps up to Nelia's side. I'm running to the left, cutting outward with my Skill and sending a Blade Slash directly to my assigned arm, watching as the glowing blue curl of Mana impact and create a small diagonal tear in the metal. Crap—the damage from my attack doesn't even budge its health meter.

As the Golem lets loose with all four of its beam weapons aimed at Nelia, Capstan raises his axe, which bursts into flames. As he swings down, the flames erupt and spiral forward to meet the beams. Defying logic, they clash with the incoming energy and stop it. A part of me is sitting in a corner of my mind, pointing out that energy does not get stopped by shooting flames! Physics does *not* work that way. The rest of me is too busy lashing out with the Blade Strike in an attempt to disable the cannon.

When the beams stop firing, so does Capstan. In the brief moment of silence, Nelia finishes her spell and it comes into existence in a stream of cold energy from the symbol, enveloping the monster's arm and coating it in ice. The monster attempts to raise its arm, and with a creak, the entire arm breaks off, falling to the floor and shattering.

Unfortunately, I'm running right into that mess. I have to spend the next few seconds ducking and covering up from the shards of metal and ice that fly all around me. The Yerick throw up their force shields, taking the shards directly to close in on their arm. When I've got a moment, I throw up my hand and throw a few Mana Darts at the creature as I regain my footing, swearing under my breath.

"Can you see this? Or this? Or this?" Ali taunts the Golem, ducking back and forth in front of the creature as he partly blocks the monster's view.

That lasts only long enough for the Golem Boss to decide to do something about Ali, its eyes glowing and sending a pair of blasts. Ali yelps when he gets caught by the edge of one of those blasts, his body smoking. After that, he pays more attention, but his distraction lets us get in close.

For the next few minutes, things are hectic. I catch glimpses of what's happening on the other side—Capstan jumping into the air and bringing his axe down on an arm, shearing halfway through it, Aron grabbing the attacking arm that misses him by inches and holding it steady as Tahar takes his Warhammer to the elbow joint. The damn Golem has no problem focusing on multiple attackers at the same time, so we're all fighting our own battles. I find myself with little time to worry about the others though. The problem isn't that the target is hard to hit, it's that it's so big and well-armored, I need to keep hitting the same location in the hope of cutting through.

Capstan takes his arm down next, then a short while later, the third one the boys are dealing with goes. As I finally lodge my sword in a joint and get ready to trigger Blade Strike, I find myself staggering at a sudden change of direction. The blade gets pulled down with the rest of the arm, the Golem having ejected its arms as it retreats. A few minutes later, its body opens and dozens of beam weapons appear across its torso before it opens fire again.

Caught in mid-charge, we're taken by surprise. Capstan is targeted by over half of the beams and is blown into the ground, flesh sizzling and hair burning. The other Yerick get their shields up in time, but they have to hunch over to protect themselves. As for me, I manage to get out of the main line of fire and only eat about a third of what it aims at me. Flesh cooks off, bones heat up, and most of my armor gets chewed through. I grit my teeth, pain shooting through my body as I roll on the ground to get away.

"John, Nelia!" Ali shouts.

I stagger to my feet facing her and see the woman on the ground, whimpering with smoke rising from her body. Even as I watch, another beam targets her prone body, intent on ending her. Not again!

I snap a hand out, casting Two are One on her and taking a portion of her damage. Unfortunately, getting distracted in the middle of the fight means I get shot too. Beams that initially missed me find their target now. I sink to the ground, pain filling my existence as the damage accumulates even through my resistances. I focus, casting Greater Regeneration on myself to buy Nelia and me some more time.

The shots cut off suddenly as a bestial roar and a resounding clang occur in short order. The clanging happens again and again, and I slowly force myself to stand up as the Golem is knocked off its feet.

"Heal Nelia!" Capstan barks at me as he runs forward, smoke still rising from his body.

He jumps into the air, fire enveloping his entire body as he accelerates down onto the prone Golem. At its feet, Tahar is swinging away at a joint. That's all I have time to see before my lurching, smoking form reaches Nelia's still body, a Healing Spell ready in my hand.

Even as the spell wraps around Nelia's body, I'm stabbing a syringe filled with an immediate healing potion into her neck. Her health bar inches up under both effects and I drag her into the hallway and out of the battle. Safe, I inject her with a health regeneration potion that will heal her over time before I duck back in just enough to see what's happening inside.

The battle is nearly over. Capstan is halfway into the Golem's body, tearing larger and larger holes in its torso, still filled with that boiling red mist, with his axe. Crouched next to him is the blond fur of Aron as he leans into the open cavity, pulling out gears and cogs with his bare hands. Beneath, at the Boss's feet, Tahar has pulverized a knee and is working on the other one. With a final ear-wrenching squeal, the Golem stops moving. I exhale in relief, turning back to make sure Nelia is alive.

Gods, that was close. I can't help the smile that plasters itself on my face as the adrenaline slowly subsides and I help Nelia slowly make her way into the cavern. There's nothing like fighting for your life. Seeing Aron stand on the body of the fallen Golem and crowing about his victory and seeing Tahar's wide grin, I can't help but think I'm not the only one. The Yerick look worse for wear, their armor burnt and torn, flesh devoid of fur, and giant holes in the body showcasing slowly regenerating wounds.

"Thank you," Nelia murmurs to me as she slowly pulls herself straight. "What was that you cast?"

"Skill." I flash her a grin. "It's called Two are One. Lets me take some of the damage."

"Can you split it across multiple people?" Nelia asks, her eyes gleaming.

I pause, thinking about it. "Not sure. I've never tried it actually."

"Well, if you can..."

I wait for a moment before realizing that she's forgotten about what she had to say. I shrug, dismissing it as I just can't be bothered with that train of thought right now.

"So what's the loot?" I ask when we finally reach the rest of the group.

Ali is silent, floating above the Boss and frowning before he twitches a hand, making the Golem's entire body flash. When the flash subsides, parts of it glow. Oooh, that's a new trick.

Capstan flashes me a smile, his prodigious regeneration already replacing burnt and damaged skin and fur as he walks to the body. "Let's see."

***

Hauling the Golems' bodies back to town is a bitch of a job. It takes hours to grab and drag all the various pieces and parts to the hover-truck. I get more than one jealous glance as I make entire Golem bodies drop into my Altered Space. I still grab and haul bodies of course, though the Yerick boys generally haul about half of what I do. Pretty damn impressive considering my own Strength stat.

When we get back into Whitehorse, we catch more than a few curious looks. Not every day you see Yerick with a bunch of their fur burnt off and missing most of their armor. Xev chitters angrily when we arrive, staring at the giant mess of metal and wires that we drop in its yard before it skitters around the pile, muttering to itself. After a time, it looks at us and orders us out, promising to send a full accounting later. None of us feel particularly up to arguing, so we do as it says.

After a quick visit to the Shop to split our profits, we convene in the Nugget for dinner and drinks. Thus far, I've yet to be invited into their compound, but I can live with that. The Nugget's more my speed, even if the Yerick find it slightly small for their taste.

We're mostly done dinner, the pub filled to bursting, when trouble starts. An inebriated hunter stalks over to us, stopping a short distance away to glare at the group. The Yerick ignore him so I do too.

He shouts, "Get out!"

I tilt my head, shifting in my chair as I consider the slightly weaving, plaid-wearing xenophobe. The Yerick continue to ignore him, sipping on their drinks, though they've stopped discussing the dungeon run.

"You deaf as well as ugly? I said get out. We don't want you fucking aliens here. This is a good human establishment," the man shouts again.

My hand clenches slightly, but Capstan just shakes his head.

"You—"

"You will get out," Lana says, her voice cutting across his, perfectly calm and quiet but somehow piercing. Stupid looks at her, mouth opening, before she continues. "Henry, you're not welcome here anymore."

"Lana." Stupid's voice is ugly, filled with hate, as he steps into her space. Lana doesn't back down, though her nose wrinkles as his spittle and hot breath blows in her face. "You meddling bitch. You've got no place telling me what to do."

"Actually, I do. I'm the owner here, and you're not welcome. Now go," Lana says again, her gaze turning even colder.

Stupid snarls, grabbing Lana's upper arm to make his point. Instead of reacting physically, Lana's face flushes slightly. Something changes in the blink of an eye as the friendly, personable, and beautiful young woman disappears entirely. Her hair seems to darken, becoming a blood red that is not entirely natural. Those violet eyes that are almost impossible to see in that color shift to a brilliant purple as her skin becomes fairer and closer to marble. More, there's a palpable sense of danger coming from her now. Stupid whitens, his hand falling away as his jaw drops. Behind Lana, a waitress drops a tray, and nearby patrons shrink back in their seat.

Aura of the Red Queen Resisted.

Capstan lets out a low growl of approval while the other Yerick shrink back like the rest of the pub. Nelia's face tightens before she straightens, obviously fighting and winning against the Aura.

"Out," Lana says again, her voice a whisper that rings through the silence in the pub.

Stupid lets out a low whimper, frozen in space. Suddenly Lana steps back. The acrid smell of fresh urine reaches my nose a moment later. I have to hide a grin as Lana's face twists in disgust, Stupid still frozen in place.

"Oh god, you did not pee yourself!" Ali laughs, obviously not affected.

I stand up, grab Stupid by the arm, and lead the unresisting man out. At the door, I shove him slightly to send him sprawling onto the ground. His friends follow him quickly, shooting fearful glances back at the young lady who continues to dominate the pub. Once they're gone, Lana shuts off the Aura and sighs, directing one of the waitresses to clean up the new mess.

Lana walks up to me and touches my arm, smiling. "Thank you."

"You're welcome. Though you might consider being a little lighter on your touch next time." I chuckle. "Unless you like having Health & Safety get upset with you."

"No such thing anymore," Lana says. "I don't have a lot of opportunities to practice using the Skill anyway."

"Was that a Class Skill? Never seen Richard use it," I ask.

"No. Shop bought. Watching Roxley, well, it gave me the idea," she explains, smiling slightly. "It's been useful."

"I bet." I smile slightly, noting that she hasn't moved her hand as yet.

She catches my glance and flushes, dropping her hand to the side. "I should talk to the others."

"Yeah." I nod, watching her step away. I shake my head after a moment, smiling slightly as I walk back to the table. Surprises everywhere.

"Your mate is interesting," Aron says, nodding toward Lana. "Few Adventurers bother with such extravagant Skills."

"Lana's not my mate. Or an Adventurer."

"My apologies," Aron says, shaking his head. "The mating rituals of other cultures are difficult to understand at times. Even with purchased knowledge."

"We don't call it mating here," I point out.

"In John's case, it definitely isn't mating. Or dating. Or anything," Ali chimes in.

"It is a pity she is not…" Nelia adds from the side, pushing aside the last of the nachos she ordered. "She has the heart of one. More than some of your…"

"Adventurers," Capstan fills in after the silence lingers.

I grunt, shaking my head. "Don't tell Jim that."

"Of course not," Nelia replies, aggrieved.

As I open my mouth to apologize, Capstan adds, "We should go. Nelia and I have duties in the clan, and Aron and Tahar must ensure our equipment is ready for tomorrow."

I nod. "Tomorrow then. I'll lead you guys through the dungeon I cleared. Should be very simple, so we should check out the other monster lair too."

Capstan nods agreeably as his team quaffs their drinks. I watch them leave quietly, smiling slightly. Well, clearing dungeons with this team should be easy.

"The Minotaur was right, she was very impressive," Bill says, interrupting my thoughts.

I look the man over then flick my gaze to Luthien and the raven-haired female who accompanies him. Ali floats back from outside, having finished heckling the poor hunter, and he sniffs as he notes Luthien.

Getting no answer from me, Bill sticks out his hand. "I'm Bill. We haven't met yet, but I thought we should talk."

"Oh?" I glance at his hand then nod to him, not releasing the grip on my pint of beer.

"John, you can be polite!" Luthien snaps.

"Toots, why don't you take your skanky-ass back to your man?" Ali says before I can say anything. "Looks like you still haven't told him you're rubbing naughty bits with this guy, so perhaps it's time to do that?"

Luthien snarls, raising a hand to blast Ali, but he just smirks at her.

Bill doesn't even twitch, staring at me. "John, you should control your fairy. Accusations like that could get him hurt."

"Go ahead." I wave, leaning back and smiling slightly.

"What?"

"Go ahead and beat him," I clarify, gesturing to the smirking Spirit. "He deserves it."

"Hey! I'm helping here," Ali says, spinning to look at me. The backhand that sails through his body, thrown ever so casually by Bill, makes Ali stick out his tongue at him.

"I see," Bill says.

"I know something that will hurt!" Luthien smiles viciously, pulling a dark cloud into her hand.

"No fighting in the pub," Lana snaps as she strides over, glaring at the group.

Bill shoots Luthien a look, and she subsides, her lips curling up as Lana approaches.

"Thanks, Lana. At least someone appreciates me," Ali says.

"Ali, shut up." Lana glares around the group. "Now, will you all calm down? Or do I have to kick you out too so I can have an evening of peace?"

"Can it, Ali, she's not kidding," I send to Ali.

He thinks back, *"No shit. I'm not the one who doesn't understand women here."*

Gritting my teeth, I raise my glass to my lips while Bill speaks. "My apologies. We were just here to speak, peaceably, with John."

"About what?" Lana says, foot tapping.

"Oh, just the city. I was led to believe he and I might have something in common." Bill continues to smile at Lana, facing the redhead fully.

"Well, do it quietly." Lana casts a worried look at me then at Luthien before she walks away.

"So, John, are you working with the Minotaurs at this time?" Bill says.

"Yerick. And yes," I say, deciding that answering might be the fastest way to get rid of him.

"Oh God, you going PC on me now?" Luthien mutters, rolling her eyes.

For a moment, I wonder what the hell I saw in her. She was always biting about people being careful about terminology. After all, they just needed to grow thicker skin! I have to admit, I never said a thing, never objected or argued with her about how words can grate on you, chip away at your ego and control. How simple insults, delivered dozens, hundreds of times can get under your skin until even casual, non-vicious use can anger you. I should have said something. Could have. I stare at her then smile. All right then, if they want to underestimate the Yerick, they can.

"Interesting. Will you be partying with them for a while?" Bill says, brows furrowing as I smile at Luthien, who looks puzzled at my reaction.

"What's it to you?" I tilt my head, leaning back in my seat.

"Nothing at this time. I feel like you and I might have something in common. You do not suffer the fools on the Council, like I do. You've also gained in power outside of their silly rules," Bill says.

"Thanks, but you're not my type."

Bill's eyes tighten slightly though his lips don't shift from that smile of his. "May I ask why?"

"Her." I point at Luthien. "You can go now."

"Well, that is… unfortunate." Bill turns and gestures to Luthien, who has a snarl on her face. He grabs her arm, tugging on it as he walks and forces her to walk after him.

My eyes narrow as I read her lips. "*I told you so.*"

"*Yes, you did. I wanted to…*"

They're fully turned away and too far away to catch the rest, so I just watch the trio move away. I frown then look at Ali.

"*Do you remember what the third of the group was doing?*" I frown, racking my memories.

"*No. Hmmm…*" Ali frowns, staring into the distance as he accesses the System. After a moment, he lets out a low hiss. "*Right, she's a spy or rogue or assassin of some form. Data's entirely hidden in the System. Pretty sure she's got a Skill that makes you forget about her.*"

"Interesting." I grimace, watching the trio sit down at their table. Very, very interesting.

Chapter 8

"You need to make your motions even smaller," Mikito says as I groan, rotating my shoulder after our latest sparring match.

In terms of raw speed, I actually am faster than her these days. The problem is, she's got at least a Master's level of Skill and years of experience dueling humanoids and learning to move her body. I still have a tendency to make too large a motion, especially when I make my sword disappear, the shift in weight throwing my body off. Between that and smart positioning on her part, most of my attacks have to cover more ground than hers, allowing her to hit me more often than I do her. Good thing I have a lot more health than she does.

"Easier said than done." I eye her naginata. "Am I wrong or is that thing hitting harder?"

Mikito hugs the naginata, glaring at me as I speak so casually of her prized possession. "It is. It gained a new Skill."

"Your weapon got a Skill?" My jaw drops.

Mikito smiles, the coldness dropping off her face for a moment as she looks at the weapon lovingly and caresses the haft. "Yes."

I'd call her attachment to it weird except I know that the weapon is the last gift from her husband, his sacrifice of his Perk to give her a chance to survive. "Is it Leveling?"

She nods slightly.

Ali zips over, his eyes wide as we speak, and hovers next to her. "You got to be shitting me, girlie. You mean your boytoy got you a linked weapon?"

"Linked?"

"It levels every time you level," Ali explains.

"No. It levels over time after use," Mikito replies.

Ali's jaw drops. He moves to hover near the weapon, a hand held out but not touching. "May I?"

For a long moment, Mikito hesitates before she nods, offering the weapon to Ali. He doesn't take it, instead flying low to touch the weapon. After a moment, I see Mikito's eyes focus just in front of her face before she taps on the screen. The moment she does, information blooms in front of me.

Tier II Polearm (Hitoshi)

Base Damage: 94

Durability: 750/750

Special Abilities: Soul Drinker (Level 3), Armor Piercing (Level 1)

"Soul Drinker?" I cough. "That's not at all ominous. Not one bit."

"Oh, stop being a whiny baby," Ali says, rolling his eyes. "Some overly melodramatic idiot decided to translate it as that. It just means that Hitoshi over there can Level the more it gets used."

"Why is it only Level 3?"

"Don't think of its levels like your sword. It isn't." Ali lets the weapon go before floating up to Mikito's face to stare at her, his face utterly serious. "Don't ever let anyone do that again."

"Care to explain?" I have an inkling why, but better to be sure.

"Soul Drinker weapons are rare. Many of the most powerful weapons in the System are Soul Drinkers. Gods, you are right—that sounds so fucking pretentious," Ali grumbles. Mikito clears her throat and Ali sighs, switching back to the topic at hand. "Your sword is soulbound, so it'll level at the same rate as you do, but in a different way. It'll get more… swordy. Eventually, it might even get a new ability or two. Uncommon, but not rare. Hitoshi on the other hand will Level like a person. It'll get Skills, and unlike your sword, it won't ever disappear. Weapons like these are heirlooms—they grow stronger with each wielder."

"Is it alive?"

"No. Not yet," Ali replies immediately. "I've heard rumors that at high enough levels, these weapons might gain a personality, but I've never met one."

I nod and Mikito hugs her weapon once again. I have one more question. "Hitoshi—was that the name of your…?"

She shakes her head before she slowly looks up, her answer barely a whisper. "It was what we would have called our son."

I flinch, looking away, and she steps back too.

Ali just stares at the two of us before snorting. "Right, well, now we know why you hit so damn hard. Keep using it and don't tell anyone else. Got it?"

Mikito nods, then after a moment, she turns and flees back into the house. I watch her go, breathing slightly easier as the tension eases. I never know what to say to things like that.

***

I've got a day off from dungeoneering today, since the Yerick are busy with some internal issue in their compound. I guess when your party leader is also the leader of the community, you can't go out killing monsters every day. You have responsibilities that transcend simple leveling.

I don't, of course. I'm not responsible for anyone but me, which means I get to run around killing things for my pleasure. Okay, that just seems a bit psychotic. Then again, we kind of live in a psychotic world. I could lounge around at home but Lana is always busy and I only spot her in the evenings at best when I finally make my way back. Mikito and Richard are out as always and since the kids no longer need to rely on our house for electricity, we've mostly gotten the place back. That leaves sitting at home playing computer games or watching movies, something I used to love doing. Now, between the burbling pit of anger in my stomach and the ever-present sense of doom the System has brought, I can't sit still.

As I jog through the lower zones around Whitehorse, I dodge around the monsters that pop up. Most don't even attempt to attack me, hiding from the bigger predator. I've got a goal today—check out my fort then do some hunting.

As I pound through the forest, I find myself curious about my companion floating beside me, his eyes locked on an invisible screen in front of him. "What are you watching now?"

"*Island Hunters.*" Ali shakes his head. "It's… so strange. It's strangely addictive. Will they buy this piece of property or this one? Are the granite countertops of this residence worth the trade-off in space? Most importantly, why did you humans spend so much time caring about dumb shit like that?"

"Seriously, why are you obsessed with our TV?" I ask, pausing long enough to lop off the head of a snake-worm creature that pops out of the ground before I continue onward. "And don't tell me it's about the tits and ass, because you're watching house hunting."

"Research," Ali says, his face unusually serious. "I'm doing research on you humans."

"Through reality TV?" I stop and stare at Ali, my eyes wide. "You're shitting me. Please don't tell me you think we're like *Jersey Shore* or the *Real Housewives?*"

"Gods, that'd be fabulous. Even better if you were like *Queer Eye*. At least you'd have a fashion sense. 'What am I going to wear today? Oh, black. Black. More black!'" Ali says. "I'm a Spirit, boy-o, not stupid."

"Then why reality TV? Half of it is scripted."

"Have you ever tried watching a documentary? Trust me, if I've got to do research, I might as well be entertained while doing it. Your fictional TV is amusing, but your reality TV is useful."

"What are you trying to learn?"

"About humans of course." Ali stops, pointing at a monster in the distance that has spotted us.

I pull up my rifle, and a few moments later, it lies on the ground, smoking.

Before I can walk farther, Ali holds up a hand. "Let's talk first."

"Okay."

"When I was first summoned, I got a basic download of you people. I got to choose my sex and my general appearance. I threw together what you saw while I was nursing a headache, which by the way, isn't a lot of fun and is rather unique to you humans. My appearance, my body, the knowledge downloaded is what was set up by the System by some hackjob. While I'm not really human, I'm not really what I was—what I am—when I'm not here."

I nod. I'm not entirely surprised he doesn't look like a Middle Eastern man when he's banished. I kind of assumed his appearance was some random generation pulled from my mind, maybe something based off a twisted idea of what a Djinn should look like. It does make me wonder what he really looks like as a Spirit, and for that matter, why they recognized him immediately in the Shop. Questions, questions, questions.

"But in the Shop?" I ask, recalling how they knew who he was when he first went in.

"They recognized my Mana signature. As System-bound Spirit Companions, it's not unusual for us to change forms. My Mana Signature doesn't change though," Ali explains, and I nod. "Here's the thing. I still have a bunch of your urges and some really, really weird memories and experiences in my head. I mean, shoulder pads and queues?" Ali shakes his head. "On top of that, I've got you and all the data you humans are dumping into the System. The better I understand you humans, the better I understand you. The better I understand you, the more likely I can keep you from killing yourself."

"Almost sounds like you care," I tease.

"Funny. It's my job, boy-o."

"So how'd you get this job anyway? You applied to be a Spirit Companion or…?"

"Not exactly." Ali frowns, his lips tightening before he blows out a breath in a huff. "Right, well, I'm contracted to be here because I'm indentured to the System for a rather large debt."

"So you didn't have a choice?" I frown.

Ali waggles his hand slightly. "Not exactly. I could have done some other things, but being a Companion can be a pretty good-paying gig. Generally we get paid based off how long you survive. As a Linked Companion, my pay scale goes up based on your Level. The longer you stay alive and the higher your level, the more I earn, which means the faster my debt is paid off."

I nod slowly and wait. He doesn't say anything more, so I turn, finish looting the corpse, and take it into my Altered Space. I start jogging again and Ali floats alongside, keeping pace easily.

As the silence grows, he finally cracks. "So you're okay with that?"

"With what?"

"The fact that you're just a job."

"I don't know. It's nice to know that your motivations are kind of normal, you know? On the other hand, it was kind of nice thinking you were, you know… doing this because you were some System-gifted Companion, my very own Tinker Bell."

"Tinker Bell?"

"Spirit," I say, hiding my smile by ducking underneath a tree branch.

"Well, I'm System-bound to not harm you," Ali points out.

"You've mentioned." I fall silent again, letting my feet carry me deeper into the zone.

Seemingly satisfied, Ali turns back to his viewing.

After a time, I say softly, "You know, it was kind of nice."

"Not your Tinker Bell."

"Talking. We don't do much of that," I say.

"I take it back. Be less *Queer Eye*."

"Asshole."

***

The Carcross Cutoff is no different than the last time I was here. I look around the location once more, scratching my chin as I walk through the rooms. I pull a beer from the fridge as I think about what to do. I could upgrade the fort, make it even stronger and more defensible, but that makes no sense. I don't have the means or the people to take care of the place and really, no desire. A fort, at the end of the day, is a facility for an organization or a city, not a holding for one person. Costs that wouldn't even be a line-item for a larger organization are a major investment for me.

Looking around the place one last time, I mentally make myself give it up. I'll pick it up if it's available, I'll keep an eye on it, but at the end of the day, it just isn't for me. Learning to let things go, things that I can't affect or in the end don't matter, is important. It's not an easy thing to do and just saying you intend to do it isn't really a solution, but it's the best I can do.

Walking out of the fort, I leave it unlocked. Let someone else struggle for it. It's time for me to focus on what I can change, what I can affect.

"Ali, map," I call to the Spirit.

He flicks his hand and I look over the information he's given me, searching for clusters and Bosses. Mostly to avoid the last, but you never know. Charting my path for the day, I realize I'm going to be closing in on Carcross for the largest and most numerous clusters. They weren't joking when they said they needed help dealing with the growing monster population.

Well, thinking isn't going to get me there. One nice thing about the System is that I don't even have to start at a jog to warm up. So long as I keep an eye on my stamina consumption, I'm good. Slipping into high gear immediately, I run toward the closest dot. Time to go hunting.

***

"Go right," Ali says suddenly.

It's been a couple of hours of hunting and killing, moving from one monster to another, but the urgency in his voice has me perking up. I move automatically, scanning for dangers.

"I'll patch you in," he says.

"We need more people over at Wall 2. They won't stop coming…"

"Jason, marker 3. Ice storm."

"Autogun 3 is down. I repeat, Autogun 3 is down!"

"If anyone can hear us, please. We need your help!"

Quest received: Save Carcross!

Save the city from the monster swarm. Destroy or drive away the monster swarm before they kill all the survivors in Carcross. Note that experience during this event for monster kills will be reduced.

Reward: 50,000XP(shared)

Type: Unique

The voices cut off in my helmet and I find myself speeding up, going from a fast jog to a full sprint. I turn on Thousand Steps for the speed boost, feeling myself grow just slightly lighter. Faster. I have to get there faster.

"What's happening?"

"Monster swarm," Ali says. "Too many Bosses, too many monsters. The lower-level bosses and their kind finally get pushed out and swarm the next zone down. Those monsters then swarm the next one and so forth…"

"So not an attack?" I duck under a pine tree branch, wishing for once that running was easier. Even cutting a straight line and plowing through smaller obstacles, a forested hill isn't exactly fast running. Then again, maybe I should be glad it isn't a damn jungle.

"Not a direct attack," Ali confirms.

I grimace. Well, that's good, because the swarm of gray, yellow, and green dots is bad enough as it stands. Now that he's mentioned it, I can see the movement, the way the swarm is packed on one side and more dispersed in others. They're still attacking, probably because monsters are stupid and aggressive, but they aren't pressuring the walls in a coordinated maneuver.

"Time," I growl and Ali lets out a sigh.

A few seconds later, a timer appears in the top right of my heads-up-display in my helmet, counting down how long it'll take to arrive. Thirty-four minutes and change. That's an eternity in a fight.

For a time, the fight seems very one-sided. The shields must be holding, the defenders able to pick off and kill monsters without danger. It doesn't last though. At the nine-minute mark, blue dots, friendlies, flash out at the wall, one by one. I don't ask for the radio (or whatever they were) transmissions again. I don't need to hear it—the little dots tell their story more than sufficiently. At five minutes left, the swarm of monster dots suddenly appears behind the now-sparse blue line. The flood of colorful dots stops, frozen and boiling for a minute as more blue dots appear to face the tide, monster dots disappearing to be replaced by ever more. Then a blue dot disappears in the center and the tide floods the streets before they suddenly freeze again at another line.

Two minutes later, I realize that the timer is going to be off. I can't run in a straight line anymore, can't afford to completely dodge my attackers. I don't have time to shoot with my rifle, so I'm cutting at anything that gets close and shooting targets in front of me with my beam pistol. I cut off the Thousand Steps, conserving my Mana because I know I'm going to need it in a second—in fact, I grab a potion out of my inventory and down it to speed up my Mana regeneration. Best to get this going now when I have time.

The second, hastily improvised line breaks, and monster dots flood through the new gaps into the city proper. Ali is floating above me, flying back and forth and drawing attention to create the gaps I need to keep running. Cutting across the corner of the city to get to the break through, I feel my lips pull into a wolfish grin, blood pounding in my ears as adrenaline courses through my body.

Monsters in all shapes and sizes flash by me, most of them, but not all, mutated Earth creatures. A brown pod that travels on a trio of spiky legs rears up, facing me with its single eye that begins to glow. I duck low and slide as it unleashes a beam of fire at where I was. I cut off a leg as I slide pass, my sword sliding through muscle and bone without catching. Once past the monster, I push off and keep running.

I crest a small hill, shoulder-checking the Ice Elk in my way and sending it crashing down among the other monsters, giving myself a moment of peace to evaluate what I see before me. A giant, stone-encrusted Grizzly Bear lies in the breach in the wall, its corpse offering sufficient space for other monsters to scramble into the town. Only the corpse itself stops the swarming, squirming horde from entirely overrunning the town.

"Ali, Lightning Special!" I hold up my hand, summoning my magic.

The little Spirit flies to me, sliding in front of my arm to join hands seconds after my lightning bolt unleashes. As always, I feel the magic change when he joins me, his greater Elemental Affinity enhancing and twisting the lightning bolt I unleash.

This is where the Lightning Strike spell shines. The longer I channel the spell, the more monsters the spell strikes, jumping from monster to monster and spreading out. I sweep my hand from side to side, ensuring that the electricity catches the monsters swarming the walls. Most of them are under Level 20, but their sheer numbers have overwhelmed the defenses.

Dressed in my one-piece armored suit, full-faced helmet on and weapons holstered, I sling lightning like a crazed wizard on crack on the hill, burning through monsters without care about my Mana. Unfortunately, I can only face one direction at a time and that means my back is exposed. I get swarmed in a minute, a striped black-and-white ex-housecat clamping its jaws around my shoulder as a feral wolverine chews on my ankle. I crash into the ground and trigger the QSM, sliding away from the monsters.

I dance aside, firing my pistol into the housecat's head as I turn off the QSM. Point blank, the pistol burns the monster's eye away and blinds the other, though the creature continues to thrash around. I kick it away, sending the body sprawling amongst others, where it is torn apart.

Ali is no longer floating, sitting on the ground and panting as a Frost Raven attempts to peck him to death. I take off running, heading into the scorched earth and the gap in the wall. I duck, dodge, and fight my way through the few monsters that still live, racing against the tide to get to the gap before them, ignoring the pain and slowly accumulating injuries as stray spikes, bolts, and other projectiles rain down on me.

I leap onto the bear corpse and run forward to a relatively flat portion of its neck. Ahead of me, more monster corpses. Dozens of them are burnt, frozen, and smashed apart before the second improvised earth wall. Right in front of the wall is a series of all-too-human figures, including Jason's mom. Dead, holding the tide back for a few minutes. Just a few minutes for her son and her city.

I turn, taking station on the relatively flat portion of the bear's neck, and call forth my sword before downing a health regeneration potion. I watch as what looks like hundreds of monsters rush forward, all of them coming for the gap and me.

Her life, for a few minutes for others. I stand there, watching the horde come, and I find myself smiling, that sea of rage inside me churning. Time to buy a few more minutes.

***

A subjective lifetime later, I stand amidst a sea of corpses and blink the sweat out of my eyes. A swipe and my helmet retracts, letting me wipe the sweat away at last. Rage subsides, frenzy ended, and I find myself assaulted by pain. I collapse, hand on the ground as I breathe slowly, the glowing red of my lifebar in the corner of my eyes.

Minutes that seem like hours later, I have enough Mana to cast a healing spell. And then another before I can stand straight. I stare at the shredded pieces of my armor and pull it into my inventory before sliding on a new set of clothing as Gadsby limps over to me. Behind him, his hunting group spreads out to kill the last of the monsters, a pair standing watch over the breach.

"John. Thank God you were here." He claps me on the shoulder and I wince, feeling the newly healed bone creak in pain. Gadsby flushes slightly then looks at the corpses strewn about, whistling. "Damn, you did one hell of a job."

"Not me." I shake my head. "I got here late." *Like you,* a snide and vengeful part of my mind adds. Not the truth though—in fact, it was the arrival of Gadsby and his hunting group from outside the city that had finally broken the damn swarm, forcing them to flee. "Most of this was from the defenders."

"I should check inside," Gadsby says.

I nod, falling into step with him and heading into town, sword held loosely as I search for stragglers. *"Ali, loot please."*

"Oh, great. I get to do all the hard work now," Ali grumbles but sets to it, flying over to each body and looting it.

We don't bother with my Altered Space. It was two-thirds full before I got here, and Carcross has its own butchering yard after all. I do pause at the gap to touch the Grizzly, filling the rest of the storage with its body so that we can enter the town easier. Almost as soon as we step in, one of Gadsby's men casts an Earth Wall spell, filling the gap.

Inside, the town is buzzing with activity. Workers—freed from hiding—move corpses and work to fix the damage, eyes bleak when they come across the infrequent bodies of their protectors. In the crescent where Melissa made her last stand, the corpses are piled thicker. Jason stumbles forward from within the town, rushing over to the pile. He pulls aside his mother's corpse while Gadsby and I stand there, useless.

"Jason?" Gadsby says and gets no answer. He places a hand on Jason's shoulder and still gets no response. He tries calling his name again but still getting nothing. Looking up, he casts a worried glance deeper into the town.

"Go. I'll sit with him," I tell Mike.

He has other responsibilities after all. Me? I can spend the time watching over the kid. Gadsby nods in thanks before heading into town. Within a few steps, questions are already being called to him as others look to him for leadership. In the relative silence around us, I take a seat on the ground, content to let my body slowly heal.

"I had to do it," Jason breaks the silence with a whispered confession. "She told me to."

I glance at him then at the crescent of the earth wall and nod. No surprise that it was their most powerful mage who created their hasty line of defense. "Okay."

"We'd planned for it. Just in case you know, just because. Well, she was always planning, you know. She said if they ever got through the shield and the wall, we'd need to hold them. Keep them from coming in farther, throw up another wall. Mum knew about my spell, had me test it out once," he rambles as he stares at his mother, the numerous wounds across her body making it impossible to tell what eventually killed her. "When they were about to break in, she told me she'd be the one to hold it. Told me to do it, so I did. She was supposed to jump out after that. Get away. But they caught her, crippled her. I didn't have enough Mana. I couldn't save her."

I nod dumbly, uncertain of what to say. What can you say? Sorry your mom is dead? Sorry you had to put up a wall behind her and let her die? I don't know what there is to say, but I have to say something. "She knew the risks."

"I couldn't save her." He sobs, his voice growing strained as he attempts to hold back tears. "I should have saved her."

"You did your best."

"It wasn't good enough," Jason cries out, shaking his head as he stares at the body, tears flowing. "I screwed up. I couldn't..."

"You tried." My heart threatens to break watching him, but I push it aside. No time, not now. I squeeze his shoulder hard until he finally looks up at me. My voice grows hard as I stare at him. "It wasn't your fault."

He pushes at my arm, trying to budge it, and I let him. "Then whose it is?"

"The System. The Council." My voice trembles with the rage I always feel when I think of them. "You and your mom, you guys are just trying to survive. You didn't ask for this, you didn't choose it. This isn't your fault."

He closes his eyes, tears continuing to stream. He grabs his feet, hiding his face behind his knees as he sobs, "I didn't want her to die."

"I know." I fall silent, listening to him cry and shooing others off.

Gods, I hate this fucking System.

***

Later, when he's calmed down a little, we take her body out of the compound to their old house. Its windows are broken, the doors shattered and the garden churned up. Together, we place her in it, then we walk out and Jason sets the entire building on fire.

We watch it burn as others come by to spend some time with Jason, to offer their condolences and their support. Few spend much time with him though—his is not the only loss. We stay till the house is burnt down, then I walk him back and feed him Apocalypse Ale till he crashes. After that, I tuck him into bed. A part of me wonders where that blonde is, the one who grabbed him before, but another part of me figures it's not my business.

Outside, I find Gadsby and Elder Badger directing the group in cleanup. The wall is fixed, the shields back up for now, but there are more things that need to be done.

"How bad is it?" I ask as I walk up.

"We lost fourteen of our primary fighters, including Melissa. About another two dozen others. Her loss…" Gadsby shakes his head, brown eyes filled with grief. "I shouldn't say this, but losing her with her Levels—that was the worst."

I nod in understanding. A single high-level fighter can do significantly more damage than multiple low-level fighters. Worse, Carcross has a much lower population and they were particularly top heavy in their Levels, having over-relied on their main fighters for defense. Andrea looks back to where I came from, her face tense with concern that etches lines deeper into her face.

"How is he?" Andrea asks, her voice filled with concern and weariness.

"Asleep. He'll need someone to watch out for him."

They nod.

"We know. It's not as if we haven't had experience at this," Andrea says, her voice tinged with regret.

"It isn't safe out here. You need more fighters, more defenses," I say, feeling as if I'm stating the obvious. I probably am, but if I don't say it, I'll regret it later.

"Yes. We'll... talk about it," Andrea says, sharing a meaningful glance with Mike. I don't get it, but that's okay, so long as they're thinking about it. "Thank you, John. Again."

"Eh, it's fine." I wave away her gratitude, staring into the night.

I shut my eyes then open them again—an older blonde lying on dirt among blood and guts floats into my mind. Rage boils in me, warring with grief. I can't do this right now. Not the people, not the gratitude. I don't say anything as I walk away, heading for the exit.

There are monsters out there that still need killing.

Chapter 9

By the time I got back to Whitehorse, it was the evening of the next day. Even with my ridiculous Constitution, I'd crashed right after eating, resting up after pushing myself. I missed the funerals in Carcross, which was fine— I've been to enough of them to last me a lifetime. When I woke up, I found a small note of thanks and a big bar of chocolate from Rachel. Ali had already drunk through his gratitude. The only other thing I had was a note from Capstan to meet them at their compound.

Compound. Sounds like a such a defensive, scary word, doesn't it? Unfortunately, that's what we have forced the Yerick to build in their own portion of the city, after we burnt down the existing human buildings. A walled compound with watchtowers and a passive defensive shield that watched for intruders.

Perhaps most surprising are the buildings in the compound itself. Or maybe I should say building, since everything is connected via shaded walkways on the ground and in the air, broken up only by a series of open air, grassy courtyards. The buildings themselves are filled with graceful lines and have a tendency to make me feel a little small, what with their doorways being at least twelve feet high and ceilings a good twenty feet up, with a minimum of three stories in each portion. I let my eyes wander, drinking up the information while I consider how much to let the Hakarta know of this. I'm sure they'll be interested, but as always, I've got to balance my utility to them with the security of the city. Well, most of this looks pretty standard so it's likely nothing I can say here would be surprising.

The Yerick at the gates let me in without comment and direct me to wait in the square ahead. A cynical, paranoid part of me notes that this first square has a number of windows looking into it, windows which have armored shutters and what look like portable shield ports. There are also only two exits from this location, even if I can see the walkways ahead of me. I'd place good Credit on there being shield generators in front of those exits, ready to be triggered in the event of an attack.

Right now, the square is filled with Yerick children and a lone human child playing tag. Of course, the tagger is a Bounding Rabbit, a Level 1 monster that is certainly not playing in its attempts at child homicide. However, the adults who watch over the group look entirely relaxed, including, surprisingly, Miranda LaFollet, human councilor.

I frown, eventually deciding to speak with the only other human here. "Miranda?"

"Mr. Lee." LaFollet's French-Canadian accent makes it hard to understand her, as always.

"Is that safe?" I ask, and she shakes her head, lips twisting wryly. "Then…?"

"Why am I letting my son participate?" Miranda's lips thin, her eyes darkening with worry. "Do you know that the Yerick train their children from young? They play tag with monsters, play 'steal the eggs' with blinded cockatrices, and adults conduct weekly hunts with their children. They aren't the only ones too—a number of other Council races train their children from a young age. The Hakarta are very similar in their methods. The Truinnar are even more harsh."

"No CPS then?" I say.

"They do it because they believe, all of them do, that hiding their children from the realities of the System is tantamount to abuse," Miranda says, her hand clenching. "I lost his father because we weren't ready. We, I, hated violence. I thought it was barbaric to hit your child, to hunt for your meat. I still do. For the world before the System, it was wrong. But we don't live in that world anymore. And I won't lose my son."

As we speak, a Yerick child, a small ball of fluff and anger, slips as he dodges. The Rabbit smashes into him, and the sharp crack of a broken bone resounds through the square. I begin to move but am caught by Miranda, her head shaking slightly. Even as the Rabbit spins, getting ready to finish his downed opponent, another child darts forward and smacks it on the nose with a stick. While the Rabbit's attention is diverted, another pair of children, including Miranda's son, grab the fallen youngster who is gamely keeping his face straight. Working together, they drag him to the corner where a bored-looking teenager waits. In defiance of my expectation though, no healing spell is used. The child is forced to sit and wait for his System-assisted body to fix the damage.

"Harsh," I murmur, watching the scene, and Miranda nods.

"Not really. Kid's in no danger and the teenager has a healing spell. He'll be back playing in minutes," Ali says into my mind. *"The Yerick might be a bit more rustic in their approach, but she's right. Most races adopt some form of childhood training."*

"I'm going to push that we begin such training soon. That the Yerick help us with it," Miranda says, her eyes flashing in determination.

"What... what does Fred think of this? And Minion?"

"They think it's stupid. Foolish." She shakes her head, her voice growing firmer. "Fred wants us to go back to what the world was. Wants it to be safe again for his child. He wants everything back to what it was. Eric... Eric is single. He always has been."

I nod and fall silent. I have nothing to add. I have no power in the Council, no say in this. I am relieved of the duty of speaking further when Capstan exits a building, waving to me.

"Got to go."

"Yes. Goodbye, Mr. Lee." As I hurry off to join Capstan and his team for our next dungeon run, I hear her murmur, "Next time, finish the job."

I make sure not to let on that I heard her. I really don't need any encouragement.

***

"Nope. Not a chance. I'm out," I repeat, backing away from the ledge.

We're standing in Miles Canyon, a canyon carved by the Yukon River a few kilometers outside of Whitehorse and just a few hundred meters away from the pedestrian suspension bridge. It's one of the prettiest spots in the Yukon, a beautiful location that was quite popular with tourists due to its accessibility and the picturesque canyon walls and glacial water. Standing on the cliff edge, I feel the breeze on my skin, carrying the smell of fresh pine and clean, cold glacial water to me.

"It's not that bad," Aron says.

I look once more past our feet, where the river widens significantly into a nearly circular lake before narrowing again as it flows to Whitehorse. Right in the center, there's a new whirlpool, the water swirling deep into darkness. That's where they want me to jump.

"Not happening." I shake my head, stepping away. "I know your scouts found this dungeon recently, but I'm not doing it."

Capstan frowns, tilting his head, then gestures to the water again. "The dungeon is within a Level 20 zone. It is unlikely to be of significant difficulty."

Arms crossed, I say, "Don't care. Not going in."

"That is, of course, your choice." Capstan shrugs, gesturing to the others to get ready.

They move to the cliff's edge, strapping on their scuba gear while leaving the additional gear aside for me. My lips tighten as I watch them.

"So there is something you're scared of," Ali says.

"Fuck off. I just really don't like the water."

I shiver as a memory flashes through my mind. Water entering my mouth and chest as my friend and I claw at each other. Neither of us able to swim and both of us in the deep end of the pool by accident. No bottom that I could touch, no air that I could breathe. I shut my eyes, a sliver of fear escaping its coiled confines. I push it aside, forcing my breathing to settle, and I open my eyes again.

"Well, it's a good thing you aren't going in. It'll give me a new story to tell," Ali says, and I snort. Seeing his goading isn't working, Ali adds, *"To Luthien."*

"I know what you're doing and it isn't working. I know you don't talk to her."

"True, true. I do have Minion's contact information though. And Richard's. And Lana. And Roxley's," Ali continues, and I glare at him.

"Really? You think this is going to work? Threatening me with shame?" I growl, turning to face him as anger spills out.

"Why not? You don't like having your... face, was it? taken away. This should do quite well," Ali points out with that smirk that makes me want to beat him into a pulp.

"Fuck you, you spineless little twerp. I'm going to fucking banish you," I shout, my hands moving to dismiss him.

"Sure, boy-o. And while you're doing that, why don't you buckle on your gear and get going, you big baby," Ali adds.

Finger hovering over the dismiss button, I realize he's right. I'm way too angry to be scared. At least not right now, and not if I... if I stop thinking, making myself move and strap on the equipment. The Yerick stare at me as I slap on the facemask then take a running leap, jumping directly at the whirlpool before the rest of my brain catches up.

"I hate you!"

***

I hate the water. I hate the water. I hate the water. Even if I was taught to swim later, even if I know I won't drown, I still hate it. It's entirely irrational, and while I can fight through it, I still hate it. It makes my chest tighten, my breathing come shorter, and my adrenaline spike.

Funny thing though—you'd think that having razor-teeth fish and squid-humanoid hybrids trying to kill me would make this my worst nightmare. It's actually the opposite. At least fighting them, I have something to distract me. So what if one of them has pinned me in the side with a stinger? Or that the fish are swarming me, tearing chunks of flesh from my body? It's all good— I'm not thinking about how I'm not entirely sure where up is. Or where the Yerick are. Or why I'm doing this.

Also, something new and fun to note. Lightning Strike is very, very effective at clearing your surroundings in the water. Of course, you and your friends end up a little crispy too and you get shouted at a lot for doing it, but that's just details. If they didn't like me using the Spell, they shouldn't have invited me down here.

That's really all I'm going to say about underwater dungeons. I'm never, ever going back into one, no matter how good the loot is.

***

"John?" Richard finds me later that evening, sitting outside in the garden at home with a very large keg of beer and a big bowl of chocolates, ice cream, and braised short ribs.

"Richard!" I wave hi to him before refilling my mug. Yes, I'm indulging myself. No, I'm not getting piss-blind drunk. It'd take Apocalypse Ale to do that, and I've avoided drinking it because, well, my sense of control is shaky at best most days. On the other hand, this amount should get me a bit of a buzz.

"You okay?" He looks over my sprawled form and the various pets that have gathered around me, waiting for the bones I discard. While technically short ribs, the mutated pieces of beef are nearly a foot long each.

"Oh, I'm great. Just great. Just completed another dungeon. It was so much fun," I drawl while Ali snorts, busy on his own meal.

"Yeah… okay." Richard slowly sits down on a lawn chair next to me. "Which dungeon?"

"Miles Canyon. It's an underwater dungeon. Real pretty, you know, with all that freezing glacial water and carnivorous fish. Did you know that there are fucked up mermen in the dungeon?" I grin widely, waving a rib at Richard. "Want some?"

"No, I'm good," Richard says. "So… you partying with the Yerick now?"

"Why is everyone so interested in that?" I complain after I swallow, waving the rib around to make my point. "I like them. All they want to do is fight and kill and get sweet, sweet loot. It's real easy."

"I see."

"Yeah, we clear all the dungeons we find. We're getting a bunch of bonuses for completing them first too." I burp slightly. "But we're nearly done now. Then I guess I'll be back soloing… unless you guys know of any."

"A few," Richard answers. "We were hoping you'd come with us to try to clear them actually."

"Me? And you?" I frown, staring at Richard. "You sure you trust me not to go crazy?"

"John, you were strangling a man to death!" Richard snaps.

"Yeah, but he was an asshole."

"You still don't do that shit, man," Richard says, voice growing angry. "That's not what heroes do."

"Who says I'm a hero?"

"No one. But I'm not standing by watching you do that."

"Oooh, you're so fine and perfect, aren't you?" I snap, anger flaring.

"You asshole—"

"Enough already!" Ali shouts, waving. "Oh my god. You girls are worse than Sooki and JWOWW. Get over yourselves!"

"Shut up," we chant in unison at the Spirit.

"Bite me. You lost control, boy-o. You know it. And you, pretty boy, you could have tried something a little more useful than fighting. What's the point of all that Charisma if you aren't using it? Outside of bedding women," Ali says.

I glare at the Spirit, anger flashing in my eyes. On the other hand, he is right. I know he is. I just… ugh.

I finally say, "Are they in the water?"

"No, not at all," Richard mutters.

"I'm in then. Sure. No water dungeons though, nope. No water dungeons. Don't like them." I frown, touching my head with the hand that still clutches the stripped rib. "I'm feeling a bit… off."

"Yeah, funny thing about that. I can actually alter your Resistances a bit," Ali says and points at me.

"Oh… so I'm drunk?" I blink. I frown, raising my hand to cast a Healing Spell. I twitch my fingers, Mana flowing then shorting as I mess up the incantation, pain flaring. "Oops…"

"Maybe you shouldn't be casting a spell right now," Richard says. "Come on, let's get you into your bed."

"No. No," I snarl, anger spilling out, and I find myself shouting at Ali. "Don't do that. Don't ever do that. I don't like being drunk. I don't get drunk. I don't like losing control."

"Sorry." Ali shrinks back, a hand flickering slightly. "I thought I was helping. I've changed it back."

I nod, slumping back into the chair again, anger draining away as quickly as it came. Richard lets out a breath of relief next to me. The animals slowly relax too, fur no longer bristling as the threat passes.

"Just don't do that. I don't want to get drunk, I just want to relax, damn it."

"Okay." Ali stares at me for a moment longer before he slowly relaxes too.

"John," Richard starts again, concern etching his face, "are you really okay?"

"I'm good. I'm good." I exhale, tossing the bone aside and reaching for my mug. I pause and change directions to grab some chocolate from the bowl. "I just… it wasn't a good day. I'm fine though."

"Okay," Richard relents, staying seated. After a time, he grabs a rib and chews on it.

We eat in silence for a while, the fog in my brain slowly clearing.

"You know, these Dungeons have been appearing more and more often," he says.

"I know. Not much we can do about it. Clearing the Bosses helps reduce the incidence, but they're still going to appear. All we can do is try to contain them, clear them enough that they don't start spilling out and overrunning us."

Richard sighs then glances sideways at me, sipping on his own beer. "Sorry by the way. About, you know, all that shit."

"Whatever. Shit happens. That's our life now, isn't it? Shit happens." I stare at my hand, shaking my head slowly. "I'm over it. Have to be, don't I? We've got more shit to kill."

"That's…" Richard shakes his head as he decides not to tackle the giant signs of denial I've posted. "You going to join us for our dungeons then?"

"I said I would, didn't I?" I sigh. "I can't tackle them, not by myself. Some, sure. But most, especially the uncharted ones, the ones deeper—it's just not possible. Not at my Level anyway."

"All right then." Richard falls silent, and I join him in quiet contemplation and eating.

"Why do you do it?" I ask suddenly, tossing the latest bone into the distance to watch the puppies rush for it. "I mean, Mikito's all about revenge. Me, I'm just angry and stupid. You, you're a bit more, you know, normal. Yet you keep heading out just like the rest of us, killing and maiming."

"Thanks, I think." Richard pauses before saying, "It's stupid. You'll laugh."

"Yeah, probably. I've got a fucked up sense of humor. Ask Minion."

"Not funny."

"A little funny," Ali says.

"*Spider-Man,*" Richard finally says.

"Uhh…?"

"When I was a kid, my father used to have these old *Spider-Man* comics around. Read them from cover to cover. I, well... when this happened, I just wanted to get safe at first, get Lana safe. But then I started seeing that not everyone had a fighting class. Not everyone could go out, or would go out. I-I needed, I wanted to be better."

"With great power comes great responsibility?" I'm not a giant geek, but I lived with one and the movies were fun. And yeah, I've read a few comic books in my time.

"Yeah. Told you it was stupid." Richard shrugs.

I consider what he said for a moment, staring at the man before I smile slightly, guzzling down the last of the beer. "Yup, stupid."

"Asshole."

"Yup."

***

"Seriously?" I mutter the next day, walking behind Aron and Tahar as they tear through this newly discovered dungeon.

"Not all dungeons will be dangerous," Capstan points out as we walk along.

A hare manages to get past the pair in front and he casually flicks a stone at it. The empowered pebble rips a hole through the Level 5 monster and drops it to the ground. The creatures are no larger than a normal-sized animal, but they're faster with barbed fur. Their major mode of attack is to rush you and run across your body, their fur gripping and tearing off strips of flesh. I bend down and loot the corpse before tossing the body into my Altered Space.

"Ugh," I grumble as we continue through the giant burrow.

At least I find walking easier than the Yerick, who have to crouch as they walk. Ali's ahead of us all, guiding the front pair, his tiny orange-clad body shining with light.

After a time, I talk to just fill the silence. "Why'd you come here?"

"This dungeon probably would not last. Another monster would clear it for us. Best for us to do it and get the experience," Capstan points out, and I nod, accepting his point.

What will and won't be permanent is still very much in the air right now. I brighten up as I realize that might mean the dungeon in Miles Canyon could disappear. On the other hand…

"Not really what I meant. I mean, why Earth? Why Whitehorse?" I clarify.

"Dungeon Worlds are where we thrive," Capstan says, glancing at me. "You know of our history?"

"A bit," I say.

"The Yerick were introduced to the System five hundred or so of your years ago. We were always few in number and we had not progressed much in technology. Not like some of the other civilizations." Capstan absently grabs a hare that jumps at him, killing the creature before tossing the looted body to me to store. "We did not adapt well. Some of my people refused the System. Others fought the invaders. Eventually, all those who refused the System died. All that were left were those who embraced the System. By then, it was too late. We had lost our leaders, our builders, our artists. All we had left were our fighters.

"We needed Credits, we needed places of safety. All we could do was to hire ourselves out to work as Adventurers. We found we were good at it. In time, that's what we became. A world of Adventurers. At least, most of us."

I nod slowly, wondering if that was to be humanity's future. We've already lost so many—how long before we could grow again, live again?

"As for why Whitehorse…" Capstan looks me over. "I am unsure you will find the explanation satisfactory."

"Try me."

"We came because Lord Roxley asked," Capstan explains simply, and I frown. Seeing my expression, he continues. "There is much of this world, of this System you do not understand still. Lord Roxley is not what you consider a typical Truinnar. What he has done for the city, how he has managed it, is unusual. Among the Council or the Truinnar in particular."

"Oh?"

"Most others who have arrived have been much more… forceful in their acquisition. More direct in their introduction of Galactic Law." Capstan's placid brown eyes darken, his voice coming out as a low rumble. "The Yerick have experienced the yoke of Galactic Law before. Indentured service for many is no better than slavery."

I nod slowly. It doesn't take a genius to realize what Capstan means. It'd be a simple enough thing for Roxley to charge us for the use of his guards while Whitehorse was desperate. To charge us rent for the safe zones he's provided, increase the tax on the Shop until we were indebted to him constantly. Raise the interest rates on the loans he made to us, charge us late fees when we couldn't pay, and dictate all payments be made in Credits. Humanity had a ton of history with things like that. Still, I can see why he didn't. We've done slavery and it doesn't work, not when you need people with knowledge and skills. At least, not efficiently. Then again, sometimes efficiency isn't everything.

"Are you coming?" Nelia turns toward us, stamping her foot.

Realizing we've fallen behind, Capstan and I focus on picking up the loot. Still, what he said has left me with some serious food for thought.

Chapter 10

A week later, we're finally done with all the dungeons we've found. With the Yerick, I've cleared a total of five dungeons, of which at least three will be permanent. I've even managed to gain first clear bonuses for four of them, pushing my Level up another step. Working with the Yerick has been quite relaxing overall. Since I'm not a front-line fighter with them, I don't take as much damage and I need to replace my armor a lot less. About halfway through, I made enough Credits to fix Sabre up if I wanted to. However, on consideration, I've left her with Xev for a series of upgrades. A lot of the material we need will take a few months to arrive via "regular" delivery rather than picking it up direct from the Shop, so for now, Sabre just sits cooling her heels.

Interesting fact—while it's possible to teleport via the System, most commerce is actually done by spaceships. The cost of porting goods is significant, so using freighters and automated delivery ships helps reduce the cost of transportation. That's what makes people like Xev more competitive than getting the Shop to just "fix" everything. Paying through the Shop, amusingly enough, usually means hiring smart Shopkeepers using a combination of teleportation, rush contracts, and time dilation to allow products to be fixed. Or in a few cases, just swapped out entirely.

Finding ourselves done with the dungeons, the Yerick go back to "farming" the dungeons and hunting raid bosses. I am not invited along though. I have a feeling it's more because they want me to go hunting for more dungeons for them to raid than because they don't like me.

What I don't mention to them is that I'm going dungeon delving with Mikito and Richard instead. Which leads me to today, standing outside my house, waiting for Richard to detach his lips from his latest lady.

"We good to go?" I grumble, leaning against the truck. Damn it, it's been months since I've gotten laid. I know it's my fault but still…

"We're waiting—oh, there they are!" Richard nods down the street.

I blink as Aiden and Amelia drive up on a pair of quads. As usual, both quads make no noise at all since they run off the installed Mana engines and batteries, though I'm pretty sure their weaponry wasn't part of the dealer package. Amelia's quad has a pair of smaller rifles, each on their own mount, while Aiden has gone for a series of rocket tubes strapped to the side of his quad. I guess heavy weaponry is the new fad post-Apocalypse. I bet road rage has a whole new meaning.

"Hey, toots," Ali greets the pair, looking at Aiden and his manbun.

As always, Aiden just ignores Ali. I've never actually hunted seriously with Aiden though we've run into one another on the training sessions. Hopefully, he'll do fine – it's one thing to deal with the low-level monsters that surround Whitehorse, another to fight Dungeon monsters. Then again, Richard and Mikito trust him, so I guess I'm going to have to too.

"You guys coming?" I nod to the pair before glancing back at Richard.

"You have any objections?" Richard asks as he gestures his pets onto the truck bed before personally carrying Elsa the fire-breathing pet turtle on board.

The huskies don't bother the turtle as she settles into her usual spot. Mikito grips the edge of the truck bed before leaping in. Above us, Orel, Richard's mutated eagle, perches on a chimney, waiting.

"Not at all. Amelia would make a great tank." I grin.

"Your bike still not fixed?" Amelia asks.

"Not yet."

"Let's get going. It'll take us an hour to drive there and at least another hour to hike in," Richard says.

I nod, opening the passenger door and sliding in. Richard doesn't take long before he guns the truck, taking us out of Whitehorse and further north. A brief explanation later and I touch my helmet, pulling up the appropriate communication channel.

"Before we reach the dungeon, let's talk loot," I say over the channel while watching out for potential trouble.

"What's there to talk about?" Aiden's voice comes clearly over the channel, his West Coast accent tinged with doubt. "We split everything evenly."

"The Yerick actually use a different system. They give a bigger share to the tanks, the guys taking on the monsters directly, because they have to more stuff to replace. Seemed more fair, whether its potions or armor or just fixing up their weapons." I detail my recent experience. "I actually thought it was quite appropriate. What do you think?"

"What's the split?" Aiden asks, his tone doubtful.

I shrug. "I guess we should figure out who's tanking. Amelia?"

"That's what I do," she answers. "How about Richard's dogs?"

"Well, unless he's changed recently, they're mostly kept back a bit to hurt. They harass and deal with leakers so, like Mikito, they don't really count as tanks," I reply and get a confirming nod from Richard.

"Great, so we got Amelia as a tank and the rest of us dealing damage. Aiden, I'm assuming you're our main spellcaster and healer?"

"Yup," Aiden replies. "Most of my spells are actually support spells, so I'll be casting them on all of you before we enter. I have a couple of damage dealing spells, but not much."

I nod slightly, opening my mouth to clarify the split before Mikito speaks up. "John, you should tank too."

I grunt, rubbing my neck, and nod. "Yeah, I can do that. If you guys don't mind the pot being split three-fifths to the tanks and the rest among you three."

"Okay."

"Yes."

"Uhh… sure," Aiden adds last, his voice tinged with doubt.

"John's a good chew toy. Even without Sabre, he's very good at soaking up damage," Mikito clarifies.

Ali smacks his forehead as he listens in on the conversation.

"Why would the bike help?" Amelia asks, and Mikito shuts up, silence hanging in the air. "Guys?"

"Sabre has a few tricks up her sleeve," I finally answer, grimacing. Well, that cat is partly out of the bag.

"Look, lively people, we've got a pair of monkey-horses coming up," Richard says.

I smile. Good timing, monkey-horse creatures.

***

"This is a dungeon?" I whisper as we peek over the hill, staring at the encampment laid out before us. A simple wooden wall surrounds a dozen thatched huts, the material for the buildings obviously taken from the surrounding countryside.

"I know, right?" Richard mutters and shakes his head. "Orel found them a week ago, and when he flew over, he got the notification that it was a dungeon."

"What are those things?" I mutter to Ali, who's crouched down low too surprisingly.

Beneath us, a small swarm of thin, green, and barely dressed creatures with long ears and big noses scramble around, carrying an array of melee weapons and crude rifles.

"Closest translation I've got for you is Goblins. In this case, it actually suits them. They're... semi-sentient monsters created twenty thousand years ago by a rather mad individual. Give or take a few hundred years. They're the cockroaches of the Galaxy," Ali says. "Should be an easy job for you guys."

"About that..." I frown, shaking my head. "We should report this to the others."

Richard nods and we head back to where the group is hidden. At his command, the puppies spread out, watching over us as we talk.

Still, I keep my voice low. "So we've got a problem guys. Ali..."

I gesture for him to explain about the Goblins.

Amelia frowns, shaking her head. "They have houses?"

"And a wall and a town square. That's a village down there," I mutter.

"What's the problem?" Mikito says, leaning forward and pointing toward the hill. "They're monsters. We kill monsters because if we don't, they kill us."

"Ali said they're sentient. Maybe we can, you know, talk to them," I answer. "I'm pretty sure I saw kids."

"They're monsters," Richard says, shaking his head. "They might look human, but they're not really. Anyway, they're a dungeon, right, Ali? So they're not really real either. Just something the System created."

"Are any of us real anymore then? The System has changed me, you, your puppies drastically. What makes them any less real than you?" Aiden asks, growing intense.

"You siding with them now?" Richard says.

"No, but we should be clear that we are choosing to add to our karmic burden," Aiden says, lips twisting under his goatee. "We might have no choice to kill to survive, but we must do so with eyes open."

I do my best not to roll my eyes, though Ali doesn't bother hiding his snickering.

Amelia shakes her head, crossing her arms. "I came to kill monsters, not little green men."

"They're not men. They're Goblins. Little nasty fuckers who breed like rabbits and, if left unchecked, become a swarm. You don't want a Goblin swarm. Trust me on this," Ali says.

"I know what you're saying, but killing sentients…" My doubt shows in my voice. Ever since I actually talked to Labashi, I've been getting occasional nightmares about the Hakarta I killed. Nothing that I can remember, just vague, unsettling memories upon waking. "They haven't attacked us yet. They're just living out here peacefully."

"That's because they haven't seen you!" Ali growls. "Trust me, these guys will eat you, your mother, and your bike and ask for seconds."

Mikito nods firmly. I continue to frown while Amelia keeps her arms crossed in support of me.

Richard rolls his eyes before he finally sighs. "So why don't we have John try to talk to them then? Ali can translate, right?"

***

It isn't that easy of course. As much as I think we should try talking to them, going in dumb is stupid. We plot and plan for half an hour before I finally find myself walking down the hill with Ali floating alongside and grumbling. I understand his reluctance—I'm not entirely happy about the idea either—but since I'm one of the ones protesting genocide, we get the chance to establish peaceful communication.

"Hello, the settlement," I shout.

Thanks to Ali, my words come out as a weird clicking, grunting noise. Not that I needed to say anything to get their attention. A large number have already started clambering onto the walls, staring at me while wielding crude melee weapons. I shake my head, trying to imagine how anyone could be scared of a bunch of low-level monsters like these, even if they are sentient.

They say nothing, but since they see me, I figure the next step is theirs. Keeping my hands to the side, I walk forward and stop when I get the message.

Dungeon Located!

Warning! The current dungeon has not been categorized at this time due to System limitations. All XP rewards are doubled. Successful completion of the dungeon by a System-registered individual will generate additional rewards.

My nose can't help but wrinkle as an errant gust brings the smell of unwashed bodies tinged with lemon, rotting garbage, and feces to me. Okay, step one in on-going relations, teaching these guys about soap and water.

"*Boy-o,*" Ali says worriedly, and my minimap flashes.

I look up and blink as what were a few gray dots have become a flood. "*How the…*"

I never finish the thought because at an unspoken command, the Goblins open fire, launching a barrage of loud gunpowder slugs and arrows at me. As their attack arcs toward me, they splinter on an invisible barrier that flashes bright white. I snarl, dropping to a knee as I call forth a tower shield from my inventory. I drop it in front of my body as I channel a Lightning

Strike spell in my free hand. Aiden's single-use, short-lived spell, the Guardian's Embrace, will protect against anything short of a dragon's breath, but it only lasts a few seconds once activated. It's his most powerful protective spell but it costs a ton of Mana, which is why he doesn't use it often.

Even as the spell fades, I see gray dots rushing toward me, Goblins dropping over the wall in a wave. I ignore them, sticking my hand far enough around the shield to direct my spell at the range attackers. Lightning escapes my hand, its sudden appearance leaving behind the familiar pungent, almost chlorine smell of ozone. A blink of an eye and the lightning smashes into a Goblin on the wall. I continue to channel the spell, sweeping the wall and watching the lightning dance from body to body. As corpses fall, I cut off the spell and stand to meet the charging warriors. Now that they're actually trying to kill me, I'm done dithering over the morality of this.

Behind the warriors, the gate has opened and more Goblins flood out, their four-foot-tall bodies spilling out as they try to close on me. As the first Goblin gets within a few feet of me, they fall back, small holes appearing in their bodies, accompanied by the hiss of fast-moving pellets. Standing to my side, firing in a classic two-handed pose, Amelia guns down the attackers with her modified Gauss pistol. Even as fast as she can shoot, the Goblins make it to me, the first launching itself at my shield to pull it aside for his friends.

As the monster reaches the peak of his jump, I pull the shield back into my inventory and let the Goblin meet my fist. A sickening snap of its neck accompanies the body flying backward into its compatriots before I counter-charge, calling forth my sword. I find myself grinning, killing the very creatures I was attempting to speak with. Truth be told, I'm glad they decided not to talk to me. This is so much simpler. Kill or be killed.

I dance through the monsters, blade appearing and disappearing as swords, pistols, maces, and axes flash around me. I'm no legendary swordsman, no impossible anime character, so I get cut, stabbed, and shot, each blow sapping just a little of my health. Sadly, it's really hard to stack regeneration effects on an individual. Mostly, you can get away with a spell and a potion, or if you're really good, two spells. Of course, I've also got my Skill, which helps as the creatures keep coming and coming.

As I spin a Goblin around by its arm, using it to clear some space before tossing him into his friends, I spot Amelia. Unlike me, she's staying still in a single position, a sword in her off-hand. She continues to shoot and stab her enemies while a series of five glowing octagons swoop around her, blocking attacks with impunity. Her face is fixed with a look of grim determination as she fights, moving only when the bodies that pile up around her feet get too deep. Even with her Skill, attacks are sneaking in and she bleeds from a dozen different wounds. It won't be long before she goes down, just like me.

For once, my little Spirit friend seems to be getting his hands dirty. No nasty spells or just floating in front of monsters, incorporeal. He's swooping in and out, doling out Superman punches before swooping away. While he stays out of the majority of the fight, he still sports a bruise and a cut along one leg that bleeds blue light.

As good as we are, as high level as we are, the fact that we're literally getting swarmed is beginning to tell. I slice apart a Goblin who's latched onto my leg and backhand another trying to jump onto me, even as a third stabs into my collarbone with its dagger and hangs off my body while another drops a mace onto my foot. I snarl, spinning in a circle and loosing a Blade Strike that buys me a few moments, the blue cut of power ripping through Goblins. A few seconds to hear the screams and shouts from the other side of the field as the cavalry finally arrives.

The puppies and Mikito smash into the flank of the horde, their attacks ripping a giant hole into the swarm and relieving the pressure on us. Behind them, Richard fires his shotgun in pellet form, raking the archers and riflemen to keep their heads down. Aiden finishes casting a spell and the earth beneath the wall shifts, heaving and rippling in a mini-earthquake. The wall tears apart, its foundations turned to mud. I watch as he stands there, headphones on to drown out the noise, his face pained even as he begins casting another spell. Reluctant or not, Aiden is doing his job. Above, Orel swoops in to aid us, blades of wind slicing ahead of it as it banks.

"About damn time!" Ali shouts as he floats, finally letting go of the Goblin he hoisted into the air and dropping the monster onto its friends.

Freed for a moment to focus, I raise my hand and channel Lightning, playing it across the screaming Goblins. One after another they fall, twitching, then I'm running to help Amelia, hoping I'm not too late. The pile of Goblin bodies that mark where she fell erupts as I close in on it, reformed shields shoving aside Goblins. I breathe a sigh of relief, casting a quick healing spell on her as I absently cut another monster apart. Surprisingly, she isn't as badly injured as I thought she would be after seeing her go down.

As the horde flees back into their settlement, broken by the sudden attack on their flanks, I pant in relief, Stamina quickly recovering. At least fifty bodies lie on the field before me, even more fleeing back, and untold numbers hidden underneath the collapsed walls. The puppies rush through the rout, biting and tearing apart Goblins with savage ease. As the creatures reach the wall, Mikito and the puppies pull back, returning to where Richard and Aiden eye the wall, joined soon by Amelia and me.

"I thought you said there was around twenty!" Aiden points out, pulling his headphones off his ears to hear my reply.

"That's all we saw! What the hell, Ali?" I look at the Spirit, who blinks.

"What? We saw twenty, so of course there're about four hundred Goblins." At our incredulous expressions, Ali blinks. "My bad. I forgot you guys don't know that one. It's like your cockroaches—see a single cockroach, there's about another twenty hidden. Goblins live underground mostly, so there's always a lot more underneath."

"And what, the most dangerous Goblins live at the bottom?" Amelia says incredulously.

"Don't be stupid. Goblins like fresh air just like we do. The Chief and his guards live on the surface, the others beneath," Ali replies.

"Four hundred." Even Mikito looks a bit daunted by that number.

I can't help but agree with her. Looking at the carnage around us, as blood cools and adrenaline leaves, a part of me feels sick. Blood, entrails, and limbs lay scattered all around, the fallen already rotting. A part of me wonders what kind of loot we could even get from this.

"Richard, you said there were about four or so that Orel saw a week ago?" I ask, and he nods.

I can see everyone doing the math. Four Goblins equals about eighty monsters. That's another three hundred that appeared in a week. If left unchecked, these four hundred could become a few thousand in another week. No wonder they called them a horde.

"We started this. We need to finish it," Richard's voice grows firm as he gestures toward the settlement. "Ten minutes. We loot what we can, then we finish this."

I draw in a deep breath, pushing aside my doubts and my nausea. He's right. There's a job to finish, and whatever I feel, whatever I think, we need to finish it before the Goblins truly become a threat. I reach for that ocean of anger, letting it rise and bathe me in its cleansing clarity. I bend down, touch the nearest Goblin, and pull up its loot. I flinch slightly as I stare at the ear that hangs in my hand.

Yeah, fuck you too, System. Fuck you too.

***

Dark warrens with ceilings barely five feet high at times filled with smoke and screams. Flashes of pain as Goblins drop from ceilings or crawl from unseen holes. Fire, thrown in close confines, forcing us to switch to gas masks and helmets. Occasionally, very powerful wind spells by Aiden.

Goblins charging us, again and again, until even Amelia is out of pellets and we're all fighting hand-to-hand, death wherever we go. Monsters clambering over each other, swarming Mikito and bringing her down by the sheer weight of bodies to stab at her, again and again. The pain which I share with her during the attack as Richard punches, kicks, and smashes Goblins with his rifle, Shadow by his side.

Aiden, headset on to drown out the screams and cries, vomiting in the corner, none of us daring to ask if its Mana exhaustion or something else. A Goblin mother, clutching her child as an impromptu shield, using my moment's hesitation to plunge her blade into my stomach. Richard forced to call Max back from eating a Goblin's body.

Flashes of pain and death and brutality and finally, finally we're done.

***

One last look, then I give the command, none of the others wanting to do it. Cobbled together and real explosives we placed next to magically weakened supports throughout the dungeon go off. At first, nothing happens beyond a small dust cloud and a tremor. Both grow as the ground collapses beneath the dungeon, the burrows burying the corpses and our memories.

When we leave, the only sign of the dungeon is a deep depression and a few scattered bodies for the ravens and other scavengers. No one says anything, faces drawn and haggard as we walk away, blood dripping from our armor.

Gods, I hate this damn System some days.

Chapter 11

"Minion." My voice drips with scorn when I walk into the City Council's offices.

After yesterday's dungeon and today's hunt, I figured it was about time I updated the Council's map with my latest findings. I've been popping in every once in a while, letting them know of new monsters, new hazards, and the like. Most of the time, it's Miranda or one of the many other workers in here. This time, it's Minion.

"Mr. Lee." Eric's lips thin and a little part of me grins. Gods, but I really want to punch that face. Just seeing it makes my fist itchy. "What is your business today?"

"Map update." I walk over to the table and reach for some paper. At Minion's raised hands, I blink, then I remember a moment before the screen appears.

Eric Roth would like to share map data with you
(Y/N)

I really, really dislike Minion. Perhaps mostly because he's just so damn efficient at being a bureaucrat. I agree and watch as he blinks, staring into space from my viewpoint. It only takes him a few moments before he nods, swinging his hand up to dismiss the screen.

"This Goblin dungeon, it's gone?" he says.

"As gone as we can make it. Best to have someone swing by for the next little while, check it out. At least once every few days."

He nods, making a note in the air. "Then we are done. Unless there is something else?"

"No." I turn away then stop, turning back. "Why?"

"Why what, Mr. Lee?" Minion's voice is cool as he stares at me.

"You know what," I growl.

"And if I do not answer, you'll beat it out of me? That's the thing with you people, isn't it? It's all violence and anger, rage and destruction. You stomp through the city acting like you own it and maybe you do, but the rest of us have to pick up after you and your kind. You Adventurers, you're just waiting for a chance to pick on us, push us around. Damn you all," says Minion, his voice trembling. Catching himself at the end, he draws a deep breath.

I stare at the small man shouting at me, and I blink as it sinks in. "Adventurers... you hate the Yerick and me because we're Adventurers?"

"You may leave, Mr. Lee," Minion says.

"Wait a second. You hate me because I fight to survive? To keep all of us alive?" My voice rising, I stare at the man.

"Very well." Eric turns and walks to the other office door. He shuts it behind him, leaving me staring at him.

I could have stopped him of course, but then I'd just be using violence to get my way. I shake my head, staring at door. Yeesh... some people.

***

"Quiet tonight," I murmur, staring around the Nugget as I enter.

Ali nods and flits over to our usual table. We all needed a break after the Goblin dungeon, so the group split apart to do their own thing after we came back.

Richard, as far as I could tell, was in and around town, doing meetings and ladies in equal amounts. Aiden was back to his books, training and teaching, and I have a feeling he might not come out with us again. Amelia has her duties, and the stink eye I get from Vir tells me he doesn't approve of her jaunt with us. Or maybe it's just that he doesn't approve of me. Mikito, out at our shoddy training grounds, works with hunters and others who want to improve their melee skills. That leaves me as the only one dumb enough to go out hunting still. What can I say? There's a peace to fighting creatures that don't talk or scream or have babies.

Of course, that time alone also gives me a chance to check out the fort and speak with the Hakarta. It's my first visit with them since I've made the deal. We both have better things to do I'm sure, and it's not as if I can gather that much more detail in only a few months. Our talk was both interesting and profitable, though I make note of what they're asking. Numbers, Classes, defenses, and Roxley's whereabouts all are prominent in the questioning, but we touch on other matters too, like the number of buildings and the dungeons that have appeared and the food situation. I get the feeling that whatever they're hunting for or need is hidden in the mess of questions they ask. I'm still not sure if keeping secret the fact that they've been asking about us is a good idea, but I don't entirely trust the Council not to go off their rockers with this information. We're so busy doing our thing, I'm not entirely sure there is anything the Council could do even if they did know.

Resting against the chair, I nod in gratitude to the waitress who drops off the beer and the appetizers. After all the Credits and loot I've picked up, my latest visit to the Shop came with some significant purchases. A thought is all that's required to pull up my character sheet so I can survey my growth.

Status Screen			
Name	John Lee	Class	Erethran Honor Guard
Race	Human	Level	26

	(Male)		
Titles			
Monster's Bane, Redeemer of the Dead			
Health	1190	Stamina	1190
Mana	930	Mana Regeneration	65 / minute
Attributes			
Strength	72	Agility	114
Constitution	119	Perception	45
Intelligence	93	Willpower	100
Charisma	16	Luck	25
Class Skills			
Mana Blade	1	Blade Strike	2
Thousand Steps	1	Altered Space	2
Two are One	1	The Body's Resolve	1
Greater Detection	1	Instantaneous Inventory*	1
Cleave*	1	Frenzy*	1
Combat Spells			
Improved Minor Healing (II)		Greater Regeneration	
Improved Mana Dart (IV)		Enhanced Lightning Strike	

Fireball	Polar Zone

I'm still disappointed that there wasn't any particular bonus for crossing one hundred in any attribute. I'd considered it a possibility, and even though I had checked with Ali earlier, it felt as though it should be significant somehow. However, since the numbers themselves are rough approximations of the changes in my body, it does make sense that there's no benefit. For that matter, I'm being rather human-centric—there's no particular reason why it had to be a hundred.

"Hey, Ali, does the Council have 'special' numbers?" I ask the Spirit, who's staring at a screen.

"What, like the number eight or ten?" At my nod, he shrugs. "Depends on the race. The Tuinnar really like prime numbers. The Joxin revere the number fourteen. There's the Prixamars—giant rolling spheres—who find Pi extremely important."

I nod in thanks before returning to my screen. Interesting but irrelevant. Looking over my Status Screen, I smile slightly at how much better it looks now. I've adjusted the screen to display just my combat spells, since those are the ones I'm mostly concerned with. Utility spells like Tinder, Light Orb, Purify Water, Cleanse, and the like just aren't that interesting, even if they are useful for everyday life. They're so useful that Aiden now spends a good two thirds of his class time teaching those spells to others. After all, not everyone needs to throw a fireball, but everyone needs to do laundry and dishes.

Fireball is my new mass monster killer and follows along the line of the old Dungeons and Dragons spell—a small flaming orb that shoots forward before sending a sphere of heat and flame outward. Polar Zone, drops the temperature in a targeted location and slows monsters down. Size of location and temperature drop are dependent upon Mana and how big I make it—the bigger the area, the less of a drop. Of course, the minimum area I can target is about ten feet wide. It's a pretty good crowd control spell and does some minor damage, but mostly, it's my anti-forest fire spell. Throwing around fireballs in a dry forest is a bad, bad idea. It's also why I still prefer Lightning Strike.

One thing I'm holding off on is purchasing more direct protection Spells and Skills since at Level 30, I'll be able to access Soul Shield, my Class Shield Skill. I've fast come to realize that you're constantly trading off between acquiring passive Skills, which are powerful but reduce your regeneration rates, with active Skills and Spells that require Mana to operate. It's why even Mages wear armor in this world—after all, other than Credits, it costs nothing to purchase nano-woven armor that could stop a "normal" sword stab.

Of course, theoretically I could just spend the Credits and buy an active protection spell or Skill. The trade-off of purchasing something now is that if I could earn it later on, I'd be wasting Credits now that could be spent on upgrading my equipment. As it stands, I've begun to realize that having both the System Inventory and Altered Space abilities is quite broken.

Altered Space lets me ignore a whole series of knowledge areas that most professional Adventurers, like the Yerick, have to learn. For most Adventurers, picking up the basics of monster lore and anatomy is very important, along with basic Skills in skinning and harvesting. Most monster corpses have only a few parts that the Alchemists and Armorers want. Knowing what they are is an important secondary source of Credits and can add anywhere from ten to fifteen percent to your days earnings. Harvesting the bodies for parts with a Skill lets you place them in your inventory, so most Adventurers dedicate time or money to learning those Skills. I just ignore the problem by tossing entire bodies into my Altered Space and letting the butchering yard deal with it.

In addition, because I've got a secondary and significantly larger form of storage, I don't have to husband my inventory space. Working with the Yerick, I realized that many of them carry numerous other pieces of equipment with them on a "typical" Adventure. These range from extra sets of clothing, spare armor, weapons, and potions to more mundane equipment like ropes, living accommodations, food, water, and light sources. Then you get the specialized toys—directional explosives, mines, portable shield barriers, and drones for scouting to name a just few.

All of those things take up a ton of space but make dungeon delves and combat safer. Of course, the more you carry in inventory, the less space you have for Loot. Since I don't have to worry about space, I've been devoting surplus Credits to adding to my "normal" loadout in the hopes of giving myself more options in the future. I might never need a dozen Claymores and a half-dozen bounding mines or over fifty grenades in various forms, but if I ever do, at least I've got them.

I've been tempted repeatedly in the last few weeks to add more points into my Mana Imbue, increasing the damage output of my sword. Fighting at range is a nice idea, but between dungeons, where visibility is about five meters at most, and monsters that need multiple shots to kill, I've found myself in close combat more often than not. Compared to the Yerick, I'm just not hitting hard enough. On the other hand, my Mana Regeneration is already suffering from my numerous passive Skills and I'm really curious to see what a Thousand Blades is like in combat. After all, if I can hit a dozen times rather than once, a minor increase in damage will definitely be negated.

My thoughts about my build—and damn Jason for making me think of it in that way—is interrupted as Lana drops into a seat next to me, snagging a chicken wing as she does so.

"Hey, beautiful," Ali greets her. "You're looking tired."

"I am." Lana flashes him a smile that washes away her exhaustion for a brief moment. "John."

"Lana. You okay?" I look around once more, noting again that only a few tables are full.

"Just been a long day." Lana shakes her head, worry lines appearing between her eyebrows again. "Finding someone to run this place after the last manager quit has been a pain."

"Ah!" I nod slowly. That explains her absence in the evenings for the last week and her constant presence here. "Quiet today. There something going on that I missed?"

"Tons!" Ali quips while we both ignore him.

"The Cellar reopened today. They've got lower prices and a human-only policy," Lana says tiredly, looking around the Nugget. "A lot of the regulars decided to check it out."

"Who bought it?" I say.

"Bill." Lana's voice rises slightly at the mention of his name. "He picked up the motel next to it at the same time and put the same policies in place. I hear there's work being done on the restaurant that was located in the motel too."

"Huh." I look around the Nugget again, wondering if the lowered volume will affect the viability of the business. I frown, trying to recall Lana's ramblings about the business before I quickly realize that I don't have the details to make an educated assessment. "I guess that's what's stressing you out?"

"Mmm… not really. He's still buying most of his alcohol from the brewery, so either way, we win. And maybe this way the newcomers will start coming by more," Lana adds.

I nod. The Yerick, mostly led by Capstan, started showing up at the Nugget in the last few weeks, but the Truinnar continue to stay to themselves, preferring to live, sleep, and relax in their quarters in Roxley's building. Vir's about the only Truinnar we see in the Nugget, and his obsidian skin and white hair always get more than a few stares.

Looking at the plates before me, Lana says, "Are you okay?"

"Hmm…?" I answer as I chew on a mouthful of wontons.

"There are only four plates here. That's about half of what you normally eat." Lana points.

I look at the food before shrugging. "Huh. Funny story about that."

"I could use a laugh," Lana replies.

"Boy-o here gets hangry. The Yerick started feeding him every few hours and he stopped being as bitchy," Ali cuts in before I can say anything.

I growl at the Spirit, who just shoots me a wide smile.

"Oh," Lana says, her eyes twinkling as she tries not to laugh.

Yeah, yeah… so maybe part of my anger control issues are due to low blood sugar. Real funny.

"Hey, sis." Richard bends down to give the top of Lana's head a quick kiss.

She glares and swipes at him tiredly while he chuckles, taking a seat. Richard's latest girl flashes us a quick smile, dropping into a seat as well. Both of them have that weird, too clean look of someone who just got hit with a Cleanse spell. Useful spell, as I said, but it's particularly harsh on clothing and creates this weird dichotomy where the clothing itself looks factory fresh but any wear then shows through in stark contrast.

"Dick. Patti," Ali says, and I nod in welcome to both newcomers.

"The Cellar's busy. I saw a pair of Amelia's people standing nearby, keeping an eye on the crowd. Rumor has it that they don't intend to close at all," Richard says without preamble, waving to the waitress and holding up a pair of fingers.

"How did Fred take it?" Lana says.

"Kicked up a fuss at the meeting today. Of course, Bill's just ignoring him so far. Fred even mentioned maybe taking it up with Roxley." Richard shakes his head.

Fred must be at his wit's end if he's asking for Roxley's help—the alien interloper, as Fred likes to call him.

"Why is the Cellar being open all hours a problem?" Patti asks, her brow furrowed.

I smile at Richard's latest girl, who has managed to last three days so far. That's pretty surprising. Of course, the way Richard is eyeing the waitress as she bends over to serve him, Patti's days might be numbered. At this point, if a woman in town doesn't know about Richard's womanizing, she's either catatonic or completely socially inept.

"Because Fred is Mayor No Fun and wants us back to ten o'clock closings," Richard says.

"It's more complicated than that," Lana corrects, holding up a finger. "We've always had a problem with alcoholism. While a lot of the active alcoholics didn't make it, quite a few of those who were on the wagon have relapsed. Limiting the hours the Nugget was open helped reduce the temptation and the times they could drink, which gave us potential windows to help, well, sober them up."

"If they die off, isn't that better for us?" Patti asks, brown eyes glittering.

"Cold..." Ali grins. "I like you."

Richard looks startled as she says that. He opens his mouth then shuts it then tries again. "It's, well, shouldn't we try to help them?"

"Why?" Patti shakes her head. "They're just a drain on our resources. We don't have the, the space for them, you know."

"But they're humans, like us. We just can't discard them to the wayside," Richard protests.

"We're not discarding them, we're letting them choose," Patti points out. "I didn't put the bottle in their hands. They did. If they choose, isn't that better for us?"

"If they aren't useful now, we should just let them die if they want to?" Lana states, and when Patti turns to her and nods, Lana huffs out a breath. "You know, a lot of people have said that. A lot."

"Yeah, see? We should do that," Patti reiterates.

"Except if everyone did that, most of us would be dead," Lana points out. "John saved us when we couldn't fight off a Troll. Roxley put his guards into place to save the city when we couldn't fight off the spawns. Richard, Jim, John, and the rest, they've all taken the hunters out again and again to level them. Part of being human is that we all stumble sometimes. We all need help sometimes," the last is said while Lana faces me, her violet eyes somber.

"When is enough? When do we say that's it?" Patti says, hand clenching her pint glass. "When do the rest of us get to live our lives and stop sacrificing for the useless? We're dying out there. We go out, we kill the monsters, and we bring back the food, and the Council tells us it's not enough. Never enough. And then we go out again and we die because we're too damn tired or under-resourced. When do we get to stop?"

"Well, that is the question, isn't it?" Lana murmurs, seemingly unaffected by the anger Patti shows. Then again, she's dealt with me for months now. A little leaked frustration is small potatoes. "Who are you with?"

"I'm in Wigmore's group. That's how I met Richard."

Taking the opening, Lana adroitly steers the conversation to something a little less controversial, getting Patti to talk about how she and Richard met. I tune it out, focusing on my meal, and catch a glimpse of Richard staring at Patti with a bit of a shocked expression.

A large, stocky man trundles in. "Pearson!"

Both redheads look up and he points straight at Richard. Behind him, a young lady scrambles around the enraged man, calling for him to calm down.

"Uhhh…" Richard looks confused, his gaze flicking to the girl then back to the man.

"You slept with my wife!" The man stomps over, shoving a table aside and sending it crashing to the floor.

Richard stands up quickly, setting himself for a fight.

"No!" Lana snaps, her Red Queen Aura snapping on. Everyone freezes, dread kicking them in the stomach while she adds, "Take it outside. Both of you!"

Richard blanches at her words, casting an imploring gaze at his sister.

She snaps at him, "Now!"

Richard moves, staying outside of the man's reach, and when he's halfway to the door, Lana snaps off the Aura. The man has already turned, his feet happy to obey the instructions of "get away from the scary woman."

As Richard reaches the door, he's followed by one last instruction from his sister. "No pets!"

"Not helping him?" I say to Lana while Ali heads off to enjoy the show, already calling out for bets on the winner.

"I warned him this might happen. He's a big boy. The pain won't last long," Lana says, shaking her head. "Idiot."

"You not worried he's going to beat up the husband?"

Lana shakes her head. "He might be an idiot, but he's got a good heart. He'll take his beating."

I chuckle softly, and then remembering Patti, I shoot her a look.

She snorts, shrugging. "Before my time."

"Right," I add, voice doubtful.

She doesn't bother explaining herself, and after a moment, I let it go. None of my business after all. The table falls into an awkward silence, punctuated by shouts and cheers from outside as the beating draws a crowd.

Richard finally comes back, sporting a deep shiner and holding his side. "She told me he was dead."

Patti just shakes her head at him, though there's the ghost of a smile on her face.

Lana, on the other hand, props her head on a hand while asking, "How did he find out?"

"So about that…" Richard clears his nose, blowing clotted blood into a tissue. "Congratulations? You're going to be an aunt!"

"Didn't you fix that?" Lana almost shouts, and he winces.

"I thought so! I think the Beast's Vitality actually overrode the System fix. I guess going for the cheapest option might not have been the smartest thing," Richard says sheepishly.

"What are you going to do about it?" Lana's voice is calmer, though colder.

Patti's lips are thin and tight, the smile gone as she waits for Richard to answer.

"I don't think I'm wanted, you know? She's keeping it, but, yeah…"

"So you're going to leave her, them, alone?" Patti asks, her voice cold.

Richard looks away from his sister and pales even further. "No. Yes. They don't want me, I think. I…" Richard draws a deeper than normal breath, wincing. "I just let myself get beaten, damn it. Let me, you know, process this. Figure it out."

Patti's eyes flash, and she gets up. "Well, when you figure it out, don't bother calling me."

Richard opens his mouth to protest then shuts it with a clack.

Ali, who has finally returned, catches the last couple of sentences before Patti strides out. "I really like her. Can we keep her?"

Chapter 12

"Aiden!" I scream as I grab the stinger coming at my face and use it to throw the gray, eight-legged, bastardization of a scorpion at its friends. Three pairs of eyes and a mouth, with rows of needle sharp teeth, that take up the entire torso help complete the horror of a monster.

Mikito steps back, the naginata glowing with red light as it cuts through the claw targeting her head. Her movement opens up a space for another of the creatures to scramble past, but the monster is blocked by Max as the husky teleports in close enough to tear off a leg.

Aiden claps and the ground ahead of us rises up, earth turned to mud that swamps monsters that attempt to push past it and then hardens. The entrance before us blocked off, we turn our concentrated attention on the remaining monsters. I snarl, severing a stinger that pins Bella to a wall before booting the monster away from the puppy. As the monster rises, I throw my Mana Darts into its face before following up with a Blade Strike that kills the creature. Together, Max, Shadow, and Richard finish off a third while Aiden freezes a monster for Mikito to kill.

Frakin (Level 58)
HP: 980/980

As I dash over to tackle the last Frakin, the impromptu wall cracks.

I snap a command immediately. "Go! Ali, lead them out."

The group listens for once, fleeing for the exit as I dance back from a pincer strike and cast another group of Mana Darts into the monster's face. As it rears back, I channel a Blade Strike to rip off its legs, accidentally tearing down a part of the wall. Scrambling through a crack, one of the Frakin gets stuck and chitters angrily. All the monsters on this side are either crippled or dead, so I run for the exit too. It doesn't take long to reach the entrance to the cavern, where I slap down a pair of bounding mines. A short distance away, I chain together three of the modified claymores before adding the laser tripwire. I spin around, watching as the last of the wall breaks free and the monsters clamber over each to get to us. Bastards. I take the time to cast Polar Zone to slow them down further to give my friends a little more of head start.

Preparations complete, I run down the passage, headed for the dungeon's entrance. Gods, I hope I've bought us enough time.

***

I didn't. Thankfully, Aiden took the time to narrow the dungeon entrance before he ran for it. Made for an uncomfortable moment for me, but it was even harder for the damn Frakin to escape. We find ourselves regrouping a distance away, the monsters having decided to give up after circling the entrance for a bit.

"Bella okay?" I ask.

Richard nods grimly, running a hand over his dog. The wounds seem to have closed up pretty well, but he still spends some time looking her over carefully.

"We nearly died!" Aiden says, sounding half-panicked.

For a moment, I pity him. Second time out with me to a dungeon and it's the second time we've run into something outside of our league.

"Easy," Mikito says, placing a hand on Aiden's arm.

Aiden looks at it then draws a deep breath, actually saying, "Ommm," as he tries to center himself.

"He's right," Richard adds, standing up slowly. "Those things were tough."

"Level 55 to 60," I clarify, and the startled looks from the group makes me smile grimly.

"You can read levels?" Aiden says, pointing at me.

"Yes." I pause before looking at the others. "We can't tackle that dungeon alone. We're going to need more help if we want to do it."

"Can we smoke them out?" Mikito asks.

I contemplate the question. Last time, we basically poisoned a group of Crilik Shifters in their lair, choking them out with carbon dioxide and a lack of oxygen.

"No idea. It's a thought." I swallow to clear my throat once again. "So… another dungeon?"

"Uhh…" Aiden looks worried.

"I know one around here that's Level 20. The Yerick and I cleared it a few weeks ago. Should be ready for another group," I add.

The others nod slowly. As good as the bonuses for checking and clearing new dungeons are, we still have to deal with the existing ones too. Anyway, something a little easy would help settle Aiden's nerves.

After receiving agreement from everyone, we head out while I get Ali to bookmark this location. We'll be back, one way or the other.

***

"You okay?" I ask Aiden as he leans against a tree, breathing slowly and regularly.

The others are seated in a loose circle watching the dungeon entrance, slowly relaxing after coming out of the dungeon. A Level 20 dungeon with this group was a cakewalk and we blasted through the location within a few hours. The only thing that slowed us down was the mazelike corridors that had changed in configuration since the last time I was there.

Aiden looks up, pulling his headphones down as I repeat my question. He opens his mouth, glances to the side where the puppies are tearing happily into their lunch and our most recent nemesis—a creature that vaguely resembled a hippopotamus without its sunny disposition—and turns a little green again. Once more, Aiden shuts his eyes and forces himself to breathe. "I'll be fine. I just need a moment."

"You sure?" I ask, slightly concerned. I can't understand him, not really. Aiden did well in the dungeon and every time we've been attacked, but now, when things are quieter, he's panicking and looking like he's about to throw up.

"Yes. I just need to find my center. And stop looking at… that." He waves toward where the dogs are ripping into the body, tearing off chunks of flesh and gulping it down. The crunch of bones and the wet, tearing noises of their meal ripple through the clearing, making Aiden flinch every time. He's the only one who seems disturbed by it, probably because the three of us are much more used to this scene.

"Okay then." I pause, considering. "Mind if I ask a personal question?"

"Maybe. It depends on how personal," Aiden says.

"Why are you out here? You've got a pretty good gig in the city, teaching and training. You might not earn as much as a hunter, but I can't see you being poor."

"Don't want me here?"

I shake my head. "I'll take all the competent help I can get."

"I need to Level," Aiden replies. "It's, well, I need it. Leveling is the only way to be safe in this world. I need more Skills, more Spells, all of it. Being weak in this world, you die."

"Yeah, there's not much space for the weak." I look around us, at the corpse of the monster being torn to bits. "You going to be okay doing this then?"

"Yes. I have to be." Aiden slowly straightens up, exhaling one last time. "How about you? Why do you do it?"

I open my mouth then shut it, lips twisting wryly. "Well, I'm kind of stupid."

***

I'm running back through the evening summer sunlight, breathing in clear, clean air filled with fallen pine needles and the remaining spring flowers. I enjoy the fresh air, especially after having just escaped the twisted, poisoned air of the land behind me. The world is changing and so is our environment. The trees in that particular location have warped to become poisonous, releasing a nearly undetectable toxin that starts doing damage only after it hits a certain toxicity level. If it hadn't been for my Class Resistances and my greater than normal regeneration rates, I'd never have escaped. I've got the location mapped, and I'll need to come back at some point to work out how large and how dangerous a threat these new trees are.

At the least, after escaping the trees, hunting was good. I even found a relatively newly spawned Boss. I only needed to wade through a half-dozen of its minions before I got my chance to chop off its twisted, bulbous legs then carve its heart out. I know it sounds gruesome, but I couldn't figure out where its head was in the weird, knobby sphere that made up its body.

Cutting bits and bobs off it didn't seem to actually kill it, so heart it was. Sometimes, mass violence is the only answer.

Coming in from the wrong side of the river, I decide to dive in and swim across. I don't like the water, but considering it'll take me all of three strokes before I'm across, it's a lot better than running to the nearest bridge. One day perhaps I'll be able to bridge the distance with one solid jump.

Running through the industrial lands that make up this part of the city, I can't help but note how the buildings have begun to come apart. Wood rots, plants grow between cracks, and roofing sags under the onslaught of untamed Mana. Without being brought into the System, these buildings will eventually come apart at the seams—unless they get converted into something else of course.

First stop for today is the butchering yard, then the Shop. By the time I reach Whitehorse, even at the slow jog I'm moving at, I'm nearly dry. Love these high-tech one-piece suits, even if this one needs replacing soon. Somehow, a wild boar had made its way into the wild and doubled in size with some truly nasty tusks. I hadn't even heard it coming till it was on me, which was surprising in itself. Either way, the armor took most of the damage but would need fixing.

A crowd around the butchering yard isn't unusual. The size of this crowd is, and I find myself slowing down, checking for potential problems. I find it in the haggard-looking form of Rachel and another member of the Brothers of the Wolf. Jim stands next to them, speaking softly while the crowd mill around the trio.

"…not your fault…"

Reading Jim's lips from this distance is hard with the way the crowd keeps shifting, so I give up, instead threading my way through the group. My eyes narrow slightly as I note it's a mixture of First Nation civilians and hunters.

"You should rest," Jim murmurs, putting a hand on the shoulders of the pair.

Rachel flinches away from his hand, and the young First Nation teenager's face is filled with tears but obstinate.

"No. We have to go back, we have to help them!" Rachel cries, looking around desperately for help and latching on to me. "John! Please. You have to help me. Please!"

"Uhh…" I pause as the crowd parts. I step forward, looking between Rachel and Jim while the other teenager continues to shake.

"Please!" Rachel rushes up to me and grabs my hand. I let her take it, staring at her as she blurts out, "I couldn't… they told me to run. But they were stuck, we've got to save them. Please."

My eyes widen slightly and I look at Jim, who shakes his head ever so slightly. I draw a deep breath, looking at the distraught girl, then nod slowly. "Okay, I'll go. Ali, map projection."

When the map comes up, Ali shares it with Rachel. who bites her lip, staring at the map. She stares at it for so long that I have to clear my throat.

"I don't know. I… I'll just show you," Rachel blurts out.

"No. You're not going, Rachel," Jim says, his voice brooking no argument.

He glares at me, but I ignore him, focusing on the other kid, who has begun to stare at the map too. "Kid, do you know where you were?"

"I… maybe." He raises a hand then lowers it.

"If you tell me, I'll go. Alone," I urge him, holding out the carrot of rest.

He presses a hand to the map and I watch as a small blinking dot appears. I nod in thanks.

Rachel grabs at my arm again. "I'm coming." Her voice breathy and desperate, she digs her fingers into my arm.

"No." As she opens her mouth to protest, I cut her off. "You'll just slow me down."

She clamps her mouth shut, knowing that I can move faster than she can. Her goal complete, she deflates, tears refilling her eyes and running down her face. "Please, save them."

"I'll check out the spot." My voice soft, I make sure not to promise anything.

Another woman comes up, grabs Rachel by her arm, and pulls on her. The tired young lady gives in, letting herself be led away.

Jim looks at me, his eyes dark. "I'm coming. Unless you think I'll slow you down too."

"Got a truck?" I murmur, keeping my voice low to ensure Rachel can't hear.

He nods, and I gesture for him to get moving. Jim's lined face tightens as he turns and leads me to a nearby red pickup. A pair of hunters peel off to join us. As he puts his hand on the door, he's stopped by a toddler who rushes his legs, hugging his body.

He bends down, rubbing the child's head. "I'll be fine, Aya. I'll be fine. I got to go."

She hugs his leg again, refusing to let go, and finally has to be pried off by a harried-looking youngster.

I keep silent till we're out of the gates, following the map we've shared with Jim. "Your granddaughter?"

"Yes," Jim answers tartly. I nod as he puts his foot to the accelerator, taking corners a little faster than I'd like. After a time, he says what we both know. "They're dead, you know."

"I know. Do you have more details?"

Jim falls silent, chewing on his thoughts. "Not much. They were sweeping the area, looking for Boss monsters. It seems like they found one."

"Levels? Type? Strength?" I ask, and Jim shakes his head.

Joy.

"Ali, how far can you range now?" I ask my Spirit, watching as we slowly, ever so slowly, close in on the dot.

"About five kilometers from you in these Mana densities. You want me to check it out when I can?" Ali asks.

I just nod. It's better than nothing, and Greater Awareness should keep us safe enough while he's gone.

"Can do, boy-o," Ali says.

I close my eyes for a moment. There were six Brothers before Rachel joined, so if one came home with her, we lost five. And they were some of our most promising new hunters to come out from our training program.

***

I bite my lip, forcing myself not to curse as we make our way through the forest and carefully hike up the mountain. Jim and his hunters are so damn slow. I could have run to the marker by now! I push the anger down, knowing it isn't worth it. It took us nearly an hour and a half to drive out this far and Rachel would have taken just as long, if not longer, to come back. Whatever happened happened a long time ago, and rushing now would add nothing but four more bodies.

Still, I can't help my impatience. I've released my drone as well as Ali in the hopes of picking up more information, but unfortunately, the drone was smashed an hour after release. A massive bug launched itself from the treetop and landed on it, ripping fuselage and wings off before attempting to feast on my expensive piece of junk. Since Ali can only range a set distance from me, I'm stuck waiting as we hike the rest of the way in.

I grit my teeth, and to stop myself from killing anyone, I pull another chocolate bar from my inventory and chew on it. The taste, the motions, the sugar rush all help a little. Jim flicks a glance to me, his lips tightening, but he says nothing as the group sneaks forward. I wonder if he's more annoyed that I'm better than his group is at sneaking or that I'm eating. One of the benefits of my Subterfuge Perk is that I'm quite practiced at these stealth skills.

"Okay, boy-o, I need you to keep calm when I report," Ali states the moment he's back in range.

I can see him flying back as fast as his little body will take him even as we converse mentally. *"What?"* I feel the anger I've been repressing surge and I have to fight it back by breathing slowly and deeply to regain control. *"Just tell me. Please."*

"I found their bodies. They're all dead, and the monsters, well, they're doing what monsters do."

"They're eating the corpses," I say out loud, alerting Jim to Ali's information.

"Yes," Ali sends to me, concern in his mental voice.

I freeze in place, not saying a thing, not moving as I process this information. I can't move, because if I do, if I let my control go for even a second, I think I'll charge the monsters. I see Haines Junction again, the bodies of the townsfolk, the children torn apart, cooked and eaten. Bones and bodies, so many of them. I shudder, my body shaking with repressed rage.

In.

Out.

In.

Out.

Slowly, so slowly, my rage comes under control. I force it down, apply rigid control on myself. So many years of learning to accept that all I can control is myself. What is, is. I can't make them live again. I can't save them. They're already dead.

All I can do is kill their murderers and build a pyre from their bodies.

"Talk to me, Ali. Tell me what I'm facing."

***

Four Xu'dwg'hkkk Beasts left, including the Alpha. The Brothers left three of the Xuds as corpses. Unfortunately, each of these monsters has high 40s, low 50s levels and the Alpha is a mid-50 Alpha. The Yerick or my old team, we could have taken all four. I don't trust my chances with Jim and his friends, not in a straight fight.

The Xuds are each around thirty feet long, clad in blue scales, with an extremely long neck, a stub of a tail, and a horn that rises from its head. The scales absorb energy beams, redirecting any electrical energy they receive to their horns, making the monsters nearly impervious to energy weaponry. Not a problem for Jim, since his team still sticks to slug throwers, but since I wield a beam rifle, I'll either have to stick to magic or get in close. No puppies to aid me this time.

By the time Ali has finished explaining what we're facing and described the Xuds to Jim, he and his friends are looking a little worried.

"Can we?" Jim asks.

"Not directly," I answer, thinking furiously. I pull up the map, looking for an answer, but find no convenient gullies, caves, or terrain features to aid us. "Ali?"

"Nothing. Usual assortment of spike elms, sticky pine, and some new bladed asp leaves, but nothing that'll kill the Xuds," Ali answers, knowing what I want.

Jim looks grim for a moment before his gaze slips to his friends. At last, he shakes his head and I see his friends relax.

"You guys should get going," I say.

"You're not coming?"

"No. I've got a lesson to be teaching."

"John, you can't be serious," Jim says gruffly. "That's suicidal."

"Maybe. Don't worry about it. I'm not one of your charges, and this, this is what I do," I say, a smile pulling on my face. Oh yes, this is what I do.

Jim hesitates, looking conflicted before he shakes his head finally. "No. I'm staying."

"No. You're not. You've got a grandchild and others waiting on you. Go home. Take care of them. Do the right thing. The smart thing."

Jim's face hardens, getting mulish until his friend puts a hand on his arm and whispers something. Since I don't speak Southern Tutchone, I don't know what is said, but it's enough to make Jim relent.

"Don't die," he says.

"Not the plan." I point at his rifle. "I do want to borrow that though. And any ammunition you have."

Ali stays silent for a few minutes after Jim and the group depart, then he berates me. *Do we have to do this every Goblin's vomit time? And what kind of insanity have you thought of this time? Going to call a dragon to eat them? Or maybe a Troll?*

"No. I'm going to do this myself." I absently heft the weapon Jim has provided me. Nice little slug thrower, fully powered by a Mana engine with armor piercing rounds and a decent scope.

"Oooh, you going to stab them to death? Shoot them with your pea shooter?"

"No." I smile. *"Relax. I have a plan."*

"I really, really am growing to hate those words," Ali says out loud, and I grin at the little Spirit.

***

This is not a smart plan. This isn't even a particularly creative plan. It takes hours of setup, hours of backbreaking labor, most of which Ali spends telling me how wasteful an activity all this is. I eventually threaten him with banishment to shut him up. Finally, I'm ready.

I sneak up on the monsters, getting close enough that I can eyeball them from a distance.

Xu'dwg'hkkk Beast (Level 48)

HP: 2880/2880

Xu'dwg'hkkk Beast - Alpha (Level 55)

HP: 3780/3780

Get close enough to see them. Aim and fire, targeting the eyes, and hope to blind them. At the end of the day, the goal is to get their attention and make them chase me. Run, spin, and shoot when they get bored. Dodge the blasts of electricity and be grateful for the stupid Lightning Squirrels upping my resistance when I do get hit.

Run, duck, dodge, and fight, keep moving to the target location. Thankfully, it's not too far, and even more thankfully, unthinking aggression is something the System seems to favor in its monsters. X marks the spot and I'm finally here with a hundred-meter lead. Simple.

X is a steep cliff, about five meters above a small forested clearing. The cliff's not high enough for it to hurt if they fell off the edge normally, but it's high enough for my purpose. I leap off the cliff, slam into the ground, and spin, calling forth my sword and a Blade Strike at the same time. The Xuds follow, getting ready to jump, the Alpha already charging up another shot.

I'm not targeting them though—I'm targeting the cliff face. Or more specifically, I'm targeting the remaining columns of stone and earth that hold up the cliff. I hit them, one after the other, with my Blade Strikes as the creatures get ready to jump, their weight and the weakened structures giving way into a mini landslide.

That's when they get to learn about my second surprise underneath the ground of the clearing. I'd considered leaving the ground as an open pit, but I wasn't entirely sure the landslide would work. If it didn't, at least if the pit was covered, they might still jump. As it stands, the monsters, the remains of the cliff, and the light covering I placed over the pit all crash into the deep, deep hole I've dug.

I hate manual labor. I really do. I had to cut down a tree to make an improvised shovel just so that I could dig into the ground and the cliff before I could take the clumps of dirt into my Altered Space. Once that was filled, I had to dump the accumulated dirt a distance away and repeat the process. The good news is that my altered attributes made the manual labor tedious, not impossible. The bad news is that even with never-ending Stamina, just to make this happen before the end of the day, I had to add another point to my Altered Space. That gave me a much larger dimensional space and gave

Ali a higher degree of control over it too. It made the work much easier, especially since I needed a pit big enough to fit four thirty-foot-long monsters.

The dust-filled air when the landslide eventually stops is enough to make me cough. When I peer inside, the Xuds are still moving, attempting to climb up. I decide to put a stop to that.

"Ali?"

The Spirit flies up high into the air and concentrates, pulling open my Altered Space right next to himself and dropping its contents inside. Stone and chopped trees rain down, smashing into the monsters. The moment the space is empty, Ali flits off to collect more while I cast my Fireball Spell inside to distract the monsters.

We bury the Xuds alive, their bodies pounded under tons of earth and rock, unable to get enough of a purchase to climb out. When we finally get the last notification of their deaths, all that can be seen is a small depression filled with churned earth and stone. I mentally message Ali then turn back to collect the remains of the Brotherhood.

This wasn't a fight. This was an execution. I wish I could say that I'm happier, that I'm less angry, but all I feel is a caustic, churning sea of rage in my stomach. I almost wish I had fought them straight on—at least I'd have felt a little better.

Chapter 13

By the time I get back, its mid-afternoon of the next day. The guards at the wall nod at me, only one of them looking slightly startled. Halfway down the stretch of road to the city, I'm met by a hunter who drives me the rest of the way and drops me off at the reclaimed Kwanlin Dun Cultural Center. I leave the bodies to their people before I walk to the City Center and the Shop.

Gods, but I'm tired. I don't bother with haggling or arguing, instead sending the Spirit, who never seems tired, to deal with it. I crash on the lounge chair, eyes half closed, but soon enough I get bored. I pull out another of my books, happy enough to catch up on my "light" reading. Others might find window shopping in the Shop interesting, but I've never liked it. Tempting myself with what I can't afford just seems like a waste of time. Picking up Adventuring equipment, the Credits for fixing up Sabre and the Skills that I could use in the future, Ali and I have this mapped out. The rest—well, the rest is teasing.

"'Mana Allocation and the Development of Monsters in Dungeons.'" The voice is relaxed, cultured, and familiar.

As I look up, I see a pair of shapely legs in tight black pants with silver piping and a vest-and-tunic ensemble in the same design encasing a well-muscled, toned body. Dark skin, tipped ears, and silver hair complete the portrait of a very handsome Tuinnar noble.

"Not your regular reading," he says.

"Lord Roxley." My lips twist in a light smile, a part of me happy to see him. The last time we met, he was lecturing me on my many mistakes. Since then, he's been a no-show in the city. "Where have you been?"

"Away. I have had to deal with some of the issues from the Yerick's arrival in person," Roxley says, and I frown. "Our first major batch of colonists having their buildings destroyed has not been particularly good for my recruitment efforts. I have been attempting to attract others."

"Others…" I frown. "You're trying to bring in more people?"

"Of course. The City is not sustaining itself currently. Cannot sustain itself. Certainly not before the deadline. When the System is fully online, when the Dungeon World is created, we must be ready."

"You're talking in riddles again," I grumble as I stand, dropping the book back into my inventory.

"Perhaps if your reading was a little more practical," Roxley says, shaking his head. "Not so esoteric…"

"I like what I'm reading." My eyes narrow. "Anyway, I used to have someone who was willing to explain the more mundane."

"Used to." Roxley tilts his head and sighs, stepping forward to close the distance. "I was not the one who left first."

"I…" I open my mouth, suddenly finding it dry as he closes on me. I stare at his shoulders then upward, shaking my head. "Roxley… what's ready?"

A corner of his lips tug up in a well-remembered movement. Still, he answers me. "Whitehorse must have, at the very least, a stable safe zone. Without it, none but the desperate will visit us."

"Is that so bad? Seems like it's not a bad idea to have the tourists ignore us."

"You're so ignorant, John," Roxley says, heat rising in his voice. "Already Boss monsters and dungeons appear around the city constantly. My guards have had to deal with one swarm. Soon, the monster population will grow too great and the city will be overrun. Without a steady stream of Adventurers, the city will fall.

"Your people have been unable to stabilize the Mana flows through your own efforts. I have attempted, I am attempting, to draw others to us. But we are not the only city in need of immigrants, and the actions of your Council do not aid me in this."

"You're saying things are going to get worse," I murmur, and he nods.

"Have you not seen it already?"

"Yes," I sigh.

"We have an opportunity. The city has an opportunity. We have a large population and the most proximate locations to a series of high level zones. However, none of that will matter if we do not stabilize the city and upgrade the city itself." Roxley's voice softens as he continues. "If there is no improvement my efforts, my methods will be considered a failure."

"Then what?" I frown, hearing the thread of worry in his voice.

"Then others of my kind, or worse, will take over. Their methods will be harsher, more inclined to use the Galactic population than mine."

I blink at Roxley, my mind racing with the implications of his words. Hints from conversations with the Yerick and Ali give me a bleak picture of what "harsher" methods might be in store. Still… "Why tell me? Why now? Why here for that matter?"

"I am currently not on Earth. Accessing this particular Shop version allowed me to speak with you directly, now, here." Roxley sighs. "As for why you… perhaps I believe that you may affect some change in this city of yours. Mostly, I do not wish you to misunderstand my actions in the future."

I grunt, staring at him. "Why? What does it matter what I think?"

"You know why," Roxley says. His hand twitches at his side, almost as if he meant to do something with it then decided against it. Considering his control, I wonder what it was. "It has been good speaking with you, John. However, I have other things to attend to."

"That's it? Drop some information and go?"

"Yes. I am pressed for time now. I but grasped the opportunity that was presented to me." Roxley's voice is laced with meaning, one that I choose to ignore.

Damn pretty Elf. I will make up my own mind at my own pace. With one last mocking bow, Roxley turns and walks away. He isn't even two steps away before he fades, leaving me with new knowledge and an ache of loneliness.

Gods, but I'm tired.

***

It's easy to tell when Lana is back. The fox—Anna—always appears first, gliding into the backyard and its den. With Richard, it's Orel who makes his appearance first. Anna never pays any attention to me, always sliding into her den without a single sound. I would almost think that she dislikes me except that I haven't been burnt or bitten yet.

Lana follows with the puppies, finding me sprawled under a tree in the back of our house, staring at the dark, fluffy clouds. They suit my mood, cold and gloomy with a temperature probably hovering around zero.

"John?"

"Here." I move a hand to dump scattered candy wrappers into my inventory. No need for her to see me being a slob, not when it requires so little effort.

She comes around the corner, red hair bouncing on her shoulders and purple eyes tight with concern. I blink, tilting my head as I check my memory and realize, yes, she did get a haircut.

"John!" Lana's voice sharpens for a moment, and I blink, staring at her.

"Yes?"

"You weren't answering."

"Oh… just thinking. Did you get a haircut?"

The moment I say it, she preens slightly, puffing out her generous chest and smiling. "Yes, do you like it? No, wait. Are you okay?"

"I do, and I'm fine. All in one piece." I wave down at my body, smiling. "Didn't even need to get regenerated to make that true."

She frowns, squatting next to me. One of her puppies—Lexi—slides in underneath her hand to steady her while she speaks. "Jim told me about the Brothers. About Rachel. And you."

"Easy-peasy," I answer her unasked question, my eyes absently tracking down her figure before resting on her jeans-clad knees. There's a tear in one of them, showing off pale, smooth skin. I blink when her hand comes down on my arm, making me look up.

"Flattering as it might be another time, that's just creepy right now. Zombie eyes aren't sexy," Lana says, and I flush slightly. "You should go rest."

"I'm fine. Stamina's full."

Lana snorts, not at all feminine like, before sitting fully. "You know that isn't what I meant." Lana picks up a candy wrapper I missed, raising one graceful eyebrow.

"I'm just a little tired. Only so much the System can do," I finally relent, leaning back against the tree and staring at the sky.

Lana falls silent, waiting patiently.

"We keep dying. All the time. Melissa. Nicodemus. The Brothers. We keep dying."

"I know." There's sympathy in Lana's voice, in her eyes as she squeezes my arm.

I stare into her eyes and drown in them and realize how stupid I'm being. Stupid. I was the one doing the comforting a short time ago, and now here I am. I close my eyes, drawing a breath as I work on pushing it down, putting the emotions away. No. I'm not doing this. I can't do this…

"Owwww!" I glare at Lexi, who has nipped my hand. She must have put quite some force into it to get through my health points.

"Stop that." Lana waves a finger at my face before pointing at the sword I have in my hand without realizing it. "I told her to bite you."

"Why?" I huff, putting the sword away.

"Pinching you doesn't work. And you're being an idiot again. I can literally see you repressing your emotions."

This time I don't run or fight her. Maybe because I'm too tired, or maybe because I've gotten closer to accepting that repression all the damn time is a bad idea.

"I am not." Just because I'm closer doesn't mean I'm not going to argue.

"Right, right. Because that churning ball of rage and the gritted teeth are normal."

"It is for me." I sigh. "And I'm fine the way I am."

"The hell you are," Ali butts in. "You're about one good hit away from going on another run."

"He's right, you know. And we need you sane and healthy, you idiot," Lana says before squeezing my hand.

"Sane and healthy…" I shake my head. "I don't think any of us are that sane, not anymore."

"Speak for yourself, boy-o."

Lana shoots a look at Ali, who subsides, before she nods slowly. "Saner then."

I snort and fall silent before I exhale roughly. "I don't want to be needed. I don't want the responsibility."

"Then you can walk away," Lana points out. "But we… I'd… be disappointed. Do you want to?"

"I-I don't know," I answer truthfully. Gods, I wish I could say I wanted to be the hero, the man who stands up for everyone, who holds the line no matter the cost. Except it's easy to say you want to be that man. Easy maybe to do it the first time, until you see the cost, the lives you failed to save, the monsters you let escape. The failures that pile on you and whisper their regrets. In the end, I find myself saying, bitterly, "It doesn't matter anyway. I'm no Superman. Doesn't matter what happens, they keep dying. At this rate, we'll all be dead soon enough."

"You know I'm going to be an aunt right?" Lana says, and I nod slightly. "Three times over actually. But my brother hasn't been the only one trying to repopulate the earth. Nearly two-thirds of the women in town are pregnant."

"Two-thirds?" I blink, my mind going over my memories recently. Well, that'd explain the recent number of non-combat citizens wearing dresses and loose tops. Still, two-thirds?

"Oh yeah." Lana smiles slightly. "Less in the hunters of course, but they're mostly made up of men anyway. There is a future, John, and it's coming in about four months."

I nod slowly, eyes tracking over the clouds again. Four months and hundreds of mewling babies will appear in this world. In a city that isn't safe, that hasn't gotten itself organized. Where monsters swarm and Bosses and dungeons grow. I shudder and realize it has nothing to do with the cold. As I think that, the first snowflake drops in front of my eyes.

"Roxley says it'll get worse soon," I say.

Lana nods as more snow falls, faster and faster. "It always can. But it's getting better too. We're rebuilding. Slowly perhaps, but we're rebuilding," Lana squeezes my hand. "We just need a little more time."

"Time…" I watch a snowflake drop onto our hands and melt.

"Time for bed. Come on." Lana tugs on my hand, and I frown as she stands and leans back, pulling me off the ground. "You need some rest."

"I'm not sure I can sleep," I answer truthfully, and she smiles.

"Then I'll sit with you until you do. Inside and out of this snow." She drags me in while still holding my hand.

Behind us, the first snowfall of the autumn arrives.

***

"John…" Richard's eyes narrow as I walk in with Lana for breakfast the next morning. He blinks, looking between the two of us, probably searching for and not finding Ali.

Truth be told, I'm curious where the little Spirit has gone, but I'm mostly enjoying the peace and quiet. "What?"

"Finally!" Richard shakes his head and turns back to his cereal.

"Nothing happened!" I splutter, realizing what he's saying.

Mikito titters at my reaction while Lana just grabs a bowl, smacking her brother on the top of the head when she gets near him.

"Yeah, right. I can smell her on you and vice versa," Richard replies. "Perk of bonding with the Huskies."

I blink, staring at him then Lana. Oh… well that explains his level of awareness out there. Still… "We didn't do anything. She just slept with me. In bed. Asleep."

Mikito laughs as I splutter and Richard snorts, obviously not buying it.

"Just ignore him, John," Lana says, adding milk to her cereal. "He was always like this, even in school."

After a while of us working on our respective breakfasts, Richard says, "Snow didn't stick."

"When will it?" I ask, frowning. "Seems a bit early for snow really."

"Chokato." Lana chuckles, and Mikito and I share confused glances. "It's mid-October. We'll start getting snow regularly from now on, and it could stick at any time. About time for us to be changing tires really."

"Oh…" I blink then consider the gardens, the farms where plants are still growing. "How about the farms?"

"Shields," Mikito pipes up, shaking her head slightly in bemusement. "One of the hunters realized that if you use a low-grade shield, the shield blocks airflow but lets in light. Makes a great greenhouse."

Lana nods, lips thinning slightly. "The Council should have made the purchases already, but the decision has been held up in committee."

Richard makes a face and I find myself echoing it. Bureaucrats.

Lana sees our faces and rolls her eyes, putting the bowl aside as she stands. "I've got to go. Try to remember to go shopping for more food, will you?"

Those are her last words to us before heading out.

Richard stares at his sister before turning back to me. "You guys really didn't do anything, did you?"

"Not a thing," I say.

"Damn. Okay." He frowns, opening then shutting his mouth as decides better on commenting further.

Mikito snorts as she puts her chopsticks down on top of her bowl. "Dungeon. What's the plan?"

"More people. A lot more," I state firmly.

"Who?" Richard frowns, holding up his fingers. "We can ask Rachel, maybe the last Brother. Aiden will come, and if we schedule it right, Amelia too. That's seven."

"Not enough." I shake my head, remembering our ignoble retreat. "Mikito and I might be able to take two or three of those each, but the first room alone had over twenty."

"The Carcross group?" Richard asks.

I frown, shrugging. "Maybe, but they've got their hands full with the Bosses around Carcross."

"Jim," Mikito adds, fingers laced together in front of her. "His group can come."

"No. They'd be seriously out-leveled." Richard exchanges a glance with Mikito before he says, "There's the Circle of Ravens. Or well, Bill's group if you will."

"No. I don't trust them," I say firmly, and the pair nod.

"Just making sure I asked," Richard states. "How about the Yerick?"

"That might work." I nod slowly. "We could add your sister too. Between your pets and hers, we'd nearly double our front-line fighters."

Richard makes a face, shaking it slightly. "No. Too dangerous."

"You should ask," Mikito points out.

Richard's face scrunches up in distaste before he nods. "Fine, fine. So you going to ask the Yerick, John? I'll talk to Amelia and Aiden. Maybe we could visit Carcross today, help them out for a few days. Might make it viable for Jason and Gadsby to come."

"I want to ask Jim," Mikito adds, interrupting us.

"Mikito…"

"Hear me out. He's the strongest hunter among the non-grouped, and he's in his low 30s. If we bring him and maybe a couple of others, we could have them level with us," Mikito says. "It'd be like a training run, just at a higher level."

Richard looks at Mikito, seeing the mulish expression she has, and shrugs his acceptance.

"Only if the Yerick agree. More people means more of a split in Credits and experience," I add to help pacify Richard.

"Okay," Mikito accepts my codicil without complaint.

"Sounds like we've got a plan then." I stand up, stretching. "Give me a ride to Xev's? I want to check on Sabre first."

"Can do." Richard dumps his bowl into the sink with a clatter while Mikito gently places her aside. One quick Spell later, and we're on our way.

***

"Xev!" I wave to my mechanic as I walk in.

It scrambles away from the hulk of a Hummer it's busy converting to greet me. From beneath the Hummer, a pair of lizard feet are sticking out and muffled cursing can be heard. I ignore it for now, waiting for Xev to answer the unasked question.

"Mostly done, Adventurer John. Nanobots finished rewiring circuits, armor is mostly replaced. I've added two of the three weapon upgrades and was waiting on the third, but your Sabre can be taken out now. Has been good to take out for weeks," it adds, guiding me to where Sabre rests.

I touch my bike, my first real prized possession in this System world. I had outgrown it, the combination of the high-level areas in the Yukon and my high base stats making the mecha less and less useful. Yet I couldn't let it go. It was everything I needed when I first started, and just discarding it had seemed wrong.

So I put in more Credits than I should have upgrading it. I'd switched out the internal systems entirely. Along the way, we added a nanomachine upgrade for the base system. I'd used a hardpoint and softpoint for that, but now Sabre could self-repair anything but catastrophic damage. Xev had ripped out and replaced enough internal systems that we actually managed to create an additional hardpoint for the PAV, which meant I had space for a few new toys.

Specifically, I got myself a new portable shield generator that ran off its own Mana battery, and some heavy-hitting missile launchers. I'd considered getting beam weaponry, but since the Shield was also linked directly to Sabre's engine, in a pinch I could increase the shield regeneration. Of course, doing that meant we'd drain the battery faster, which is why I went with external ammunition that didn't need the Mana battery.

Armor, after our little tussle, had upgraded itself to add a twenty-five percent resistance to electrical damage. I was loath to swap the armor plates out entirely, knowing the nanomachines would eventually add even more resistances as we encountered tougher enemies. So long as the mecha lasted at least. I smile slightly, pulling up the stats for Sabre.

Omnitron III Class II Personal Assault Vehicle (Sabre)

Core: Class II Omnitron Mana Engine
CPU: Class D Xylik Core CPU
Armor Rating: Tier IV (Modified with Adaptive Resistance)
Hard Points: 5 (5 Used)
Soft Points: 3 (2 Used)
Requires: Neural Link for Advanced Configuration
Battery Capacity: 120/120
Attribute Bonuses: +35 Strength, +18 Agility, +10 Perception

Inlin Type II II Projectile Rifle
Base Damage: N/A (Dependent Upon Ammunition)
Ammo Capacity: 45/45
*   Available Ammunition: 250 Standard, 150 Armor Piercing, 200 High Explosive, 25 Luminescent*

Ares Type II Shield Generator
Base Shielding: 2,000 HP
Regeneration Rate: 50/second unlinked, 200/second linked

Mkylin Type IV Mini-Missile Launchers
Base Damage: N/A (dependent on missiles purchased)
Battery Capacity: 6/6
Reload rate from internal batteries: 10 seconds
Available Ammunition: 12 Standard, 12 High Explosive, 12 Armor Piercing, 4 Napalm

While I'm busy with the mecha, Xev skitters away to get back to fixing up the Hummer. After pushing out from underneath the vehicle, Tim stands and stretches, his dragon scales covered in oil and grease. He looks happier than he did the last time I saw him. For that matter, thinking about it, I haven't seen him at all.

"Tim." I nod absently to the ex-Raven's Circle member. I can't say I like him, but I don't dislike him either.

"John." He walks over, long tail swinging gently behind him. "Picking up Sabre?"

"Yeah." I smile and rest my hand on the bike again.

"She's one heck of a machine," Tim says.

Then I blink, realizing if he's been working here… I grow guarded, wondering what he might have told others. Then again, I wonder why I'm being so damn paranoid. Even if people do know about her, it's not as if we've not all gained numerous levels in the last few months. She's no longer an automatic trump card like before, so people stealing her should be significantly less of a worry.

Tim sees my face and works to reassure me immediately. "Don't worry. What happens in the shop, stays in the shop. Can't work here if you don't understand that rule. If I told you some of the things people have us fix—"

"You'd be fired," Xev chitters.

"Anyway, not as if I've got anyone to talk to these days," Tim says grumpily, and I raise my eyebrow. He gestures down his body. "Whitehorse has gotten a lot more speciesist since I left."

"Even to you?" I say.

"Yeah. Seems like if you aren't a vanilla-looking human now, well, you aren't good enough to be human." Tim growls, pointed lower and triangular upper teeth flashing in the light. "They didn't complain when we were saving their asses or fighting the monsters for them. Now that they think they're safe, it's 'you're scary,' 'you're not human,' 'you're a freak.'"

"Sorry, man," I say.

"It's just so messed up, you know? I always thought Dragons were cool, and when the System came, well, I got a chance to be a Dragon. Well, Dragonkin." Tim sighs. "We were the cool kids for once, you know? Nic and the rest of us, we were the heroes. But now I'm just a freak again."

"Do you regret it?" I ask.

Tim shakes his head firmly. "No. I still love being a Dragon." He grins. "But I'll be damned if I fight for them anymore. The idiots can go twist on a stick."

I nod. I can understand his feelings, the way the ingratitude can eat at you. I almost make the offer for him to come with us, but he seems happy here, working on the vehicles. We don't really need another person…

"Anyway, I got to get back to work. And, John, sorry about Luthien. We, I, knew about her and Kevin but… they were my friends then, you know," Tim says.

"I get it," I reply, waving him back to his work as I trace my hand down Sabre. Old grudges—they seem so distant now, so petty. I still don't want to deal with Luthien, but really, what's a little betrayal among all this blood and death? It just seems so… small. "See you, Tim."

The Dragonkin raises a hand in goodbye without turning around, and I sit on Sabre, smiling slightly. Right then. Time to talk to Capstan, then we're off to Carcross.

***

Capstan was gone by the time I managed to make my way to their compound, so I left a brief message for him to contact me. By the time I finally meet up with the group, Ali is back and refusing to answer questions about where he has been.

We make our way back to Carcross, taking the Klondike Highway and passing by the Cutoff as we drive down the highway. Autumn's certainly here, with many of the trees having shed their leaves and patches of snow on the mountains. Unfortunately, with the lack of upkeep of the highway, driving is fast becoming a pain. I wish I had the Credits to add in a hover mode for Sabre—it'd certainly make a less jarring ride. If we want to continue hunting in the Winter, it'll probably have to be our next major upgrade.

When we reach Carcross, I'm impressed by the changes. They've pushed back the forest by another kilometer and added a deep trench right in front of the wall. Along the walls, smaller beam rifles have been added, each of them tracking along a smaller axis while a few watchtowers watch over the entire wall with significantly larger weaponry. Behind the wall, a single squat building, where the old First Nation's community center was, towers over everything. Looks like they'd upgraded their city center to act as their final fallback point.

We're greeted by Jason, the teenager still dressed in jeans and a plaid shirt but looking older and more mature. He's even taken to growing a beard, which surprisingly suits him. Instead of greeting us with a usual smile and shout of joy, his greeting is much more subdued.

Richard takes over describing the dungeon and what we need while the rest of us take a moment to stretch our legs. I spot Mikito walking over to a group of hunters, and she makes carton after carton of cigarettes appear, to their delight. I guess someone decided that earning a little additional income by bringing nicotine over wasn't beneath her.

As I look over the city, I blink, staring as I finally get a good look at the guards on the wall. I'd noticed new faces, but I hadn't really twigged until now. They look pretty human for the most part, but from this side, we can see the rest of their bodies and the oddity of their height comes through pretty clear.

"*Ali, are those Dwarves?*" I try not to point, but I'm comfortable staring. After all, it's not as if they can see where I'm looking underneath my helmet.

"*Galactic term for them is Gimsar. But yes, it's your world's Dwarves,*" Ali replies. "*For once, the Mana translation didn't mess up too badly. Everything you know about them is correct—hard drinking, hard fighting short humanoids. On their home planet, they built their cities underground—mostly due to the much longer and colder nights. They aren't particularly well known as smiths though, not any more than any other sentients. The Clans hire out as mercenaries, like the Hakarta. And yeah, Gimsar and Hakarta don't like each other—mostly because they're always fighting over the same contracts.*"

By this time, Mikito has returned and is eyeing the group as well. She does so blatantly, but I figure that's fair—more than one Dwarf is giving her a look-over. Of course, their regard is much more lecherous, but I figure Mikito can handle these guys. They're all around our level after all.

"Dwarves?"

"Yup. Other than not being smiths and mostly acting as Mercenaries, Ali says the Mana translation worked," I reply, and Mikito nods.

Mana translation—the term that Ali has used to explain why so many creatures from our mythology are making an appearance. Basically put, because Mana often collects in small amounts in non-System worlds, the System can send packets of information into the consciousness of the sentients of those worlds to prepare them for eventual initiation. Unfortunately, due to the low level of Mana in those worlds, it's quite common for the data packets to be significantly corrupted. Thus the Mana translation problem and why certain myths only appear in certain parts of the world—most packets are too fragmented to be picked up by the entire populace.

Richard comes back, looks at the Dwarves, and I have to repeat the explanation.

He nods before gesturing out of the city. "Jason says he'll be happy for us to hunt around Carcross. We're, of course, welcome to stay. However, he and Gadsby won't be leaving the town. In fact, Gadsby is taking a page out of our book and is busy training up more people."

I frown. "So who do we have?"

"Rachel, Aiden, Amelia, and the three of us," Richard answers immediately. "We really need the Yerick."

I find myself nodding with Mikito. I almost consider going over to see if I can wheedle Jason a bit to come with, but that's probably a bad idea. He's stepping up, trying to fill in the gap left by his mother's death. Asking him to join us on a dungeon delve when he's turned us down already is just selfish.

"Okay. Let's hunt," Mikito says before suiting actions to words and climbing into the truck.

I blink, startling at the abrupt transition before I sigh and roll Sabre around. Lady's right. We might as well do what hunting we can.

***

After a brief discussion, we decide against hunting for meat and go for the kill—looting for System-generated items without picking up the corpses, outside a few bodies that I dump into my Altered Space because they're too good to leave aside. Instead, we focus on clearing as large an area as we can.

Funny thing—Lightning Squirrels are really easy to deal with when they aren't backed up by a Boss and you've got a trio of fast-moving, savage dogs. We even manage to track down a pair of other Bosses. The first Orel kills, dropping from the sky to latch his claws around the Boss's hairy, ape-like body and lifting it into the sky. The ape-creatures the Boss was directing become a lot easier to deal with without its leadership. We're in the midst of mopping them up when Orel drops their leader's body into the group, splattering them and us with its innards. I have a feeling we're not getting a Christmas card from Jane Goodall this year.

The second Boss fight is probably one Mikito never wants to be reminded of. Snow Geese are evil, nasty, vicious creatures and that was before they were evolved by the System. We end up standing back to back as they literally try to shit us to death, their waste being not only toxic to the touch but to the smell. I was fine in my Sabre, completely sealed away from the smell. Richard had a resistance he gained from his class—I guess when your puppies are the size of a pony, their excretions are spectacular too. Mikito spent the entire fight puking her guts out with Bella curled up next to her though.

Luckily, I could throw Sabre's shield over her body to ensure none of the waste landed on her directly while she was incapacitated. Richard and I spent the rest of the fight using our respective firearms to cripple the birds, bringing them down low enough for the puppies to finish them off.

Orel and Ali took care of the Boss in the air while we dealt with the minions. The aerial dogfight was rather amazing to watch, since we really couldn't do much to help. The Boss might be tough, poisonous, and fast, but it didn't stand a chance against Orel once its minions were whittled down.

All in all, it took us over a day and a half to get everything sorted and roll back into Whitehorse. When we get back, I find Capstan a bit grumpy with me. I guess leaving a note asking him to speak with me and not being in town for a few days could be considered bad manners, but he gets over it pretty fast when I tell him about the dungeon. When I explain how I found it and why, he gets grumpy again until I point out that Mikito and Richard were my original party. Yeesh! You'd think a guy who's nearly ten feet tall and can bench press a tank would be less sensitive.

At the end of the day though, he agrees to come along. I can understand that entirely—the experience bonus from completing a dungeon the first time, along with the first completion bonus, is significant. I understand that motivation; after all, I'm so close to hitting level 30.

After that, it's all about coordinating our schedules.

Chapter 14

"All right, listen up, people. I know you've all heard this before, but try to pay attention and hold your questions till the end." I find myself standing in front of the group, giving the last-minute briefing before we head into the dungeon a couple of days later. I'm fully armed and armored, including being in Sabre in full mecha mode. "We don't know how big this dungeon is. We don't know how many floors there are. We don't know what kind of monsters there are beyond the Frakin. We do know that the Frakin are mid-50s to low-60s and swarm."

When I stop, Ali takes over, waving. A small image appears in front of everyone with the Shop-purchased data on the Frakin, though he summarizes for the slow readers. "The Frakin are highly resistant to poison, extreme cold, and high temperatures, and yes, carbon dioxide poisoning. Fire and Ice spells will be less useful than normal, and their chitin requires significant force to pierce, so crushing attacks are best." He nods to the Yerick, who have switched out their usual axes for giant hammers. "Beam weapons work but are, again, resisted."

I wave at Capstan. "Capstan is leading this group. He's got the most experience at hitting dungeons, so he'll be in overall command. Nelia's second, then it's me, Tahar, Richard, Mikito, and Aron in that order. If you aren't out yet by the time Aron is dead, I'd recommend running like hell."

There are a few grim laughs at that. Rachel and Aiden look a bit green, while Amelia seems unperturbed to be left out of the list.

I wait for everyone to calm down before I look around the group, my voice hardening. "This is the toughest dungeon we've run across, and it's quite possible we might not be able to clear it yet. There's no shame about backing out, and if anyone feels like it's time to pull out, we'll do so. This isn't a game—we get no respawns."

The humans, of course, nod at that. The Yerick mostly look confused but nod along to the sentiment. I nod to Capstan, and he takes over.

"The Redeemer shall be on point with Tahar and Mikito behind him. The dogs and I shall be the second line while Nelia and the mages and Richard are behind. Lastly, Amelia and Aron are our rearguard. Listen to our orders. Keep your spells and weapons to individual targets unless we tell you otherwise. Questions?"

Amelia raises a hand. "Who's the Redeemer?"

"That'd be boy-o." Ali points at me, sniggering.

I sigh and add, "It's a Title."

"Oh." Amelia nods and falls silent.

Seeing no other questions, Capstan nods to me, and I turn and walk into the dungeon entrance. Walk into one limestone cave, you've walked into them all. This wasn't even that large a limestone cavern, about twenty feet by thirty. Stalagmites and stalactites abound, though most are pretty small, leaving the cave relatively barren-looking. At the end of the cave is an exit, which we'd explored and were run off from such a short time ago. On our right, halfway down the cave, is an as-yet-unexplored passageway.

Once I'm inside the first cavern, I open up with luminescent bullets to ensure everyone can see without a problem. We'd debated trying to sneak in, but with such a large group, there really wasn't a point. While the amount of light some of the bioluminescent moss in the caves provides is enough for the Frakin, it definitely isn't for us.

Capstan snaps an order to Aron, who moves immediately to the unexplored entrance and drops a small device in front of it. It's a mini-drone that acts as a combination alarm, weapon platform, and shield generator and will let us know if something tries to flank us. At least, that's the theory. Our rear secure, he waves me forward and I get moving.

I'm watchful but relaxed, Ali having headed deeper in Spirit mode to keep an eye out for potential trouble. I see the vast glow of red dots in the cave down the passageway, but there's no movement yet. I raise my hand, reporting in, and Capstan gives me a short nod as we set the first part of the plan into motion. We wait, since it takes time for the drones to get in position.

"John?"

I turn, looking down at the hand that rests lightly on my armor unnoticed.

Having gotten my attention, Rachel drops it. "Thank you. For trying."

I flinch slightly, glad she can't see my face beneath the helmet. I consider Rachel quietly for a moment, her eyes are still sunken and haunted. There's none of that self-assurance I saw in her when we first met months ago.

I have to ask, "You up for this?"

"I think so," she replies, her expression firming. "I have to be, don't I?"

I don't have time to reply. The drones are finally in place, waiting. Capstan gives a nod, and Aiden pulls an Earthen Wall into place around the entrance. It's enough to alert the Frakin, and the swarm begins to converge on us. Last time, we managed to make it about three quarters of the way down the first passageway before they swarmed us. If they'd waited till we were actually in the cave, we'd have been dead.

I watch the dots stream toward us on the minimap, wondering when Ali will talk and getting more and more nervous.

The first Frakin are already in the tunnel entrance, all of them clustering around and trying to get to us when he finally sends word. "*Now.*"

I trigger the drones with a savage grin. These are modified firefighting drones, and instead of water or fire-retardant foam, they're carrying acid. Nasty stuff that sprays out behind the drones and onto the horde of clustered monsters as they rush us. I almost believe I can hear them scream as the acid eats into their armor and skin. No real time for celebration though, because it's a short corridor and the first of the Frakin reach us quickly.

The Frakin can only fit three in a line, and that means their greater numbers aren't as useful. As the monsters rush us, I focus and swing my sword, using Blade Strike to send a screaming blue wave of destruction into my enemies. The Blade Strike shatters carapaces, forcing the monsters to pause long enough for the second Strike to injure and cripple. Their friends don't wait, clambering over the injured monsters and continuing their headlong rush.

Tahar lets loose a moment later with his beam rifle on full auto. Blueish-white energy plays across the fronts of the monsters, cutting apart shells and cooking exposed flesh. The monsters rushing us don't care, charging through the beams and my next Blade Strike as if they are nothing, intent on killing us.

"Wall!" roars Capstan.

The mages finally act. Rachel is faster, the ice wall she's held ready to cast slamming into existence ten meters ahead of us. Aiden backs her wall up with one made of earth, suddenly cutting the vanguard from the rest of the swarm.

"Charge!" Capstan barks, and Mikito moves.

One second she's next to us, the next she's ahead of Tahar, whose rifle has finally run out of charge, and stabbing her polearm into the first monster. The puppies flow without hesitation into the gap that she creates in the line, Max flickering ahead to join Mikito in her attack. Another monster attempts to flank her, and Max bites down, hard, and rips off a leg before flickering back and away from the stinger counterattack. Bella charges in, grabbing the stinger in her System-enhanced teeth and shattering the appendage before retreating backward. Shadow can't fit in behind the pair, but that's okay, since its shadow can. When a claw swings at Bella, it gets caught and held by the shadow as the puppy flexes its power.

Tahar rushes down his side, literally running up the side of the wall for a moment to get around the puppies and get to his own target. Capstan takes a much more direct route, launching himself over the frontline, his hammer held between both hands. Blocked, I have no target, so I step backward, letting others get a view while I check on my drones.

All three drones are undamaged, but their payload is empty now. They've taken to their secondary orders, which involve sticking as far up on the ceiling as possible at different locations through the cavern. This gives me a wide view of the cavern while drawing the angry Frakin to different spots. Sadly, none of the Frakin are dead from the acid alone, but many of those caught in the overlap of the acid sprays look much the worse for wear. Damn it! We were hoping to reduce their numbers significantly before we had to finish this.

Turning my attention back to the fight in front of me, I see Mikito caught in a claw and smashed into a wall. The monster is crushing her while Bella is kept back by the other claw. The only good news is that Mikito managed to lop off its stinger before it caught her. As I raise the Inlin's barrel on my arm, an earth spike shoves upward and spears the monster, forcing it to open its claw spasmodically. The distraction is all Bella needs to get in close and rip the offending claw away from its body, ending the monster as a threat.

As the earth spear retracts to give us room to fight, I rush forward, jumping to close the distance. There's not much clearance, so I've got only a moment to judge what is going on before I land. Capstan is fighting two of the monsters, easily holding his own, while Tahar is smashing apart another monster. The other puppies have taken a series of wounds, including a yellowish, deep gash down Max's side that I don't like the look of.

I land and open fire with the Inlin, switching to full auto for a moment to spray the monsters and those behind, projectiles drilling through armored carapaces and leaving gaping wounds. Unfortunately, it's only seconds before I run dry and have to get medieval.

After a sharp whistle, the huskies pull back, letting the mages land a series of fast, targeted spells at the remaining monsters. Their attacks give the melee fighters a moment's respite, enough for most of us to kill our remaining opponents. A healed Mikito flashes forward to back up Capstan, sliding underneath his swings with ease. We have a few seconds to savor our victory over the vanguard before a claw punches through the earth wall.

Here we go again.

***

A good thirty minutes later, we've had to retreat all the way into the original cavern. Not because we can't beat the damn Frakin but because the bodies keep piling up such that it gets difficult to fight. We got into a rhythm halfway in, getting comfortable trading people in and out so that no one ran out of Stamina. A lot less of a problem for me and Capstan, but the others had started to slow down as the monsters kept coming and coming.

I even had to light up the entire room once with a Lightning Strike, dumping nearly the entirety of my Mana into the monsters to give us a break. Beautiful thing about electricity—most creatures really can't move much when you're frying them.

In the end, no one died and we finally get back into the first cavern. We take the time to rest and loot while Ali and our drones are sent to scout out the exits we've found. He can't go far, not in a dungeon, but between him and the drones, we begin to build a map of the dungeon and the threats we face.

***

"Capstan?" I wave and send the slowly growing map out to him. I couldn't get the drones too far from Sabre—the high level of Mana in the dungeon meant that the signal broke down too fast. Technically, the drones all have on-board software that could map the entire dungeon for me, but that's assuming they don't run into anything particularly tricky.

The big Yerick stares at the map before he flicks his hand, sending it to Nelia and Richard, while I call the drones back. They're close to their limit, and if we're going to make a decision about what to do next, I want them here.

"We doing door number one, two, or three!" Ali intones, pointing at each dark passageway in turn. As he speaks, he lights them up with different colors, though I'm pretty sure that's only for me.

The large cavern that we rest in has been set up with additional lights by the Yerick and mages, giving us a base we can fall back on if necessary. Following my example from our previous escape, Richard has even taken the time to mine the exit with Claymores and an anti-gravity mine so that if we need to run, we've got a bloody distraction.

Capstan shoots the Spirit an annoyed look before he points at door number two. The moment he does so, Aron runs over to the passageway to pull the guard drone back into his inventory. I grunt, mentally making a note to pick some of those up when I can afford it.

As I walk over to the indicated passageway, I pass by where Amelia and Mikito quietly chat.

"Did Una get mad at you?" Mikito says.

"Yeah, she really hated me leaving. Says that policing is safer than Adventuring any day," Amelia says huffily. "She doesn't want to understand that I have to Level to stay ahead of the idiots."

"I know," Mikito replies.

Then I'm past the pair, staring into the darkness. I fire a single luminescent orb, watching it light up the passageway. I know why Capstan chose this one—for one thing, there's actually enough clearance for the Yerick to stand straight. Not much chance of that in Option 3, and Option 1 has a tendency to get tight across the shoulders. Still, I have a bad feeling about this.

***

"Why aren't they coming?" Aiden mutters nervously.

Aron hisses at the mage and he shuts up, but I don't blame Aiden at all. He's just saying what we're all thinking.

Where we stand a hundred meters from the next cavern, the Frakin should have heard us by now. They should know we're here and they should be charging us. Instead, they're doing nothing, just sitting there. I can't tell for sure, with the low-light vision of the drones, but there's something wrong with the way they look, something I can't exactly put my finger on.

"Redeemer, send Ali to roust them," Capstan growls finally and I nod, sending the mental request to Ali.

"You know, boy-o, I can get hurt. Goblins, other Spirits, spells, elementals... all those things can injure me," Ali grumbles, beginning to do his light trick.

"*Yeah, but not Frakin, right?*" I point out and wait for a few more seconds. "*Anything?*"

"*Well, a pair of the bastards looked at me and lobbed something, but none of them are moving,*" Ali says.

I report the results back to Capstan. He lets out a growl, his eyes tightening. I don't much like it either—when monsters stop being super-aggressive, it means they're smart. Smart monsters are bad. Smart monsters are dangerous.

Finally, Capstan taps Tahar's shoulder and waves him back. Capstan walks forward till he's shoulder to shoulder with me. "The Redeemer and I shall proceed first. The rest of you, stay back."

Great. Just great. I walk forward with Capstan, both of us doing our best to be quiet even though it's probably utterly useless. Just because I have the best armor and a ton of health, I get to be the guinea pig. At least Capstan is with me.

When we reach the entrance, the Frakin all turn toward us and my minimap blooms. Creatures that were hidden before, that ignored even Ali when he was doing his light show move, suddenly appear. Capstan and I just stare at the Frakin and they back at us, neither of us willing to move.

I'm wondering how the hell we missed this, how the monsters could avoid detection by Ali, when Capstan mutters, "Sixty-seven."

"Huh?"

"There are sixty-seven Frakin. Levels are the usual, but they are red," Capstan says, the Yerick seemingly perfectly calm. His tone, his professionalism pulls me back to the present, and I actually look.

"That's a lot..." I frown, then mutter to Ali, "Any data on the color?"

"Incendiary. Don't use fire," Ali says after a moment, shaking his head. "Sorry, boy-o, they fooled me. Something in here was hiding them from me."

"Why aren't they charging us?" I growl softly.

Capstan shakes his head. He jerks his head upward after a moment, his lips snarling. "They're flanking us. Aron just commed—two of our drones are under attack. We have to retreat." He steps backward and freezes as the Frakin rustle.

Jesus, these guys by themselves could probably rush us all and finish us—they have to flank us too?

"I don't think they want us to leave…" I eye the monsters, my mind flicking over options. We move, these guys light us up and charge us. We don't move, their friends sweep in behind us and take us and then these guys will light us up anyway. We need them frozen, held here which means… "Oh hell. On my word, Capstan, run."

"Redeemer," Capstan growls softly, and I shake my head.

"No time. You can get my friends out, and I've got the mecha. I'll light these guys up with everything I have and you get running. I've got a few tricks up my sleeve, so you just get my friends out," I say, my voice strangely calm. I'm not angry, surprisingly. What's there to be angry about? What is, is.

"Honor to your family," Capstan growls.

I nod, recalling Ali to me and dropping the drones back into my inventory. No need for them to get wrecked. From the corners of my eyes, I see the group already retreating, backing off to where we came from, but they're going to hit opposition any moment now. I mentally issue a command to the suit, letting it inject every single potion of regeneration into my system before I replace them via my Skill with instant heal potions. I'm as ready as I am going to get, which means…

Now. I trigger the missile launcher, dumping the full load in one wave. Twelve high explosive missiles sent direct into the cavern. The moment I make my move, I see Capstan sprinting away. I take a short hop backward again and again, even as the Frakin open fire, tiny balls of plasma flashing from their stingers.

Then my missiles land and explode and the blast wave is enough to pick me up and throw me backward onto my butt. Sabre's already cycling and reloading, but I don't have time for that because the Frakin are rushing the entrance. Seated, I bring my hand up and open up with the Inlin, lobbing armor piercing rounds downrange as fast as I can target a new monster. Five seconds and I'm dry.

Lightning next, a spell that I've used so often, the spell formations are second nature to me. I feel myself reaching into it, altering the structure of the spell in a way that has nothing to do with the System, enhancing it with my Affinity, even as Ali ducks overs and helps. We throw electricity and death down the cavern hallway. All the while, plasma lands around us, burning through armor and circuity in search of my flesh.

We bring death, and for a time, it's enough. The missiles killed a bunch. The electricity strikes stun and eventually kill the vanguard. When the vanguard dies, I wait a moment for the monsters to clump together again before I loose another wave of missiles, backing off a bit and hunkering under the blast wave before backing off further. I repeat the shoot-and-lightning process once more and start feeling light-headed, my Mana down to nearly fifteen percent.

Pain as plasma sears my skins, the temperature in the cavern so intense, it cuts through my battle haze. Without my Resistances, without Sabre, I'd be dead already. Sabre whines and cycles, attempting to fix itself and load my weapons, but there's only so much it can do. I reach into my inventory with a thought and drop a portable shield generator, activating it with a flick of a hand before I run away. It lasts for three seconds before it blows.

By then I've dropped a second generator. Outside of the punishing heat, the second generator lasts seven seconds before the plasma bolts tear the shielding apart. Five thousand Credits each time, all gone. I can't even mourn it as I hit the spot where the team planted the Chaos mines in the vain hope I could get there. Ali's zipped right ahead of those, not wanting to get caught when I release them. I don't want to be there either—Chaos mines are powerful but cheap. You never know what you'll get.

"John!" Ali screams and flashes the map up to me as we take the next corner.

I see it—the others are caught, stuck in a bottleneck, unable to push past the monsters that clog the exit. I stick my head around the corner, back the way we came.

The Chaos mines go off and maybe we're lucky, but they rip open a portal and tentacles of lurid yellow and pink stick out, grabbing and pulling in Frakin. There's something in there, something that even with my mental resistances, I can't see, can't comprehend. Or maybe it's because of the mental resistances that I can't comprehend what's in there.

"Shield up. NOW," snaps Ali.

I comply, then suddenly my eyes are filled with notifications.

Level Up!
You have reached Level 30 as an Erethran Honor Guard. Stat Points automatically distributed. You have 6 Free Attribute Points to distribute. You have 6 Class Skills to distribute.

I've been saving my points, my Class Skills for a rainy day and for Level 30. I might not have much time to use it, but I'll be damned if I don't see what I can do. I slam my points into my Class Skills and feel the ice cold rush of knowledge and pain that hammers into my body as the System grants my wish.

Chapter 15

I come back to my senses in time to see Sabre's shield fail. To see the damage icons, feel the heat radiating from the missed and blocked plasma bolts, to taste the dryness in my mouth and the smell of cooked flesh and ash. I come back to see the Frakin storming me, and I grin.

My friends are behind me, fighting their own battle in a desperate attempt to escape. I need to buy them time, time enough to break through, time enough to live. I find myself grinning, laughing as pain courses through my body, as new knowledge and abilities resolve themselves in my mind.

I flicker, one second crouched and the next behind my attacker, spinning to punch my sword through it. I step and kick out with Sabre, mecha- and System-enhanced strength picking up the Frakin and sending it bowling into its friends. Even as the monsters fire on me, their shots explode against my newly created Soul Shield. The translucent barrier of Mana absorbs the damage and covers both Sabre and me. I duck to the side, grabbing one of the Frakin by its tail and lifting it, using its body to shield me against more attacks while I wait.

Time. I'm fighting for time. I feel my Soul Shield flare, cutting off plasma blasts that slip around my improvised shield. When the Frakin stops twitching, I send it flying into its buddies, then I step sideways, giving myself a few moments to open up with the Inlin. I shoot to cripple even as the Soul Shield flares red.

"Corner," snaps Ali.

I trigger Blink Step and cut across the corner. I snap the Shield off the moment I'm away.

"Sticky grenades!"

I pull and throw. I bounce three around the edges, following the lines of power that Ali drops into my vision. The explosion is muted, and for a few moments, silence holds as the creatures struggle.

"Polar zone," is the next command from the diminutive olive-complexion Spirit who hovers and plays eyes for me.

I spin around the corner, raising my hand and casting the spell. The glue-cement mixture that makes up the grenades is already melting and burning in the residual heat. I let the spell loose, and the fires go out, the glue hardening again. Resistant to heat and cold or not, the Frakin aren't used to sudden temperature changes and their carapaces shatter, exposing yellow flesh to the cold.

A mental command and the barely regenerated shield in Sabre flickers to life before me. I open fire with the Inlin, each shot shattering frozen flesh and scattering limbs. Bodies pile up and monsters die, but the next wave is already here, firing plasma bolts at me. I spin back around the corner as a plasma bolt burns through Sabre's shield and its armor into my stomach. I groan, the fire quenched in my flesh, and I thank the vagaries of the System even as my health drops precariously. I trigger the potions, watching my health shoot up as my Mana refreshes itself. Unfortunately, the instantaneous potions only work a couple of times a day, after which they lose all effectiveness.

Between the initial health regeneration potion, my spell of Greater Regeneration, and my Skill Body's Resolve, I can literally see my body stitch itself together. It's a battle of attrition now, and even with all my Class Skills allocated and Ali watching and calculating, all I'm doing is buying seconds.

"Missiles!" Ali chants.

I snap around the corner, Soul Shield triggered. I open up with the missiles, my last full load, and watch as they fly out, shattering bodies and splintering rock. The dungeon's walls crack and shatter but they don't come down, and I snap back around my corner. The monsters are barely five feet away now. I skip back a few steps, wishing that the dungeon hadn't reinforced the structure of the walls. It'd be so easy if we could bring the walls down…

One, two, three seconds as the monsters recover and race across the ground, skimming over the dead bodies of their comrades. I pull out my sword and set myself, waiting. Health about a quarter, Mana nearly all gone. I have enough Mana to trigger Soul Shield one last time and then… and then it's over. I stop looking, knowing there's no point. I can buy them a few more seconds, so that's all that I can do.

"Incoming," Ali intones.

I meet the first Frakin as it skitters around the corner, its legs attempting to find purchase as it makes the turn. Time to finish this.

***

The sunlight of the exit is the best damn thing I've felt in ages. I walk out, helmet down as I soak in the liquid happiness, under-armor burnt to a crisp on my body. Sabre is stored in my Altered Space, so damaged that its actuators no longer work. I look around, the Frakin scrambling left and right as they sweep the exit and the surroundings, and I shake my head.

"Best get moving, boy-o, you've only got another minute left," Ali intones and I grunt.

"Give me a break," I mutter.

Then I lurch ahead, the burnt shell of my right leg barely wanting to move. It doesn't help that my balance is completely thrown off by the fact that I'm missing everything from my left arm down, the casualty of a too slow dodge. It's only some Adventure-strength painkillers and a hell of a lot of willpower that keeps me on my feet as my body works to stitch me together. I pass right through the Frakin in front of me, the counter in my left eye ticking down the time I have left on the QSM.

As I told Capstan, I've got a few tricks left up my sleeve.

***

Finding the group is easy—the rally point was the same spot we found ourselves the last time. I'm half-healed by the time I make my way to them, and as always, it's the puppies who note me first. Shadow hits me so hard, he knocks me over, and I find myself being assaulted by wet tongues. Trust me, a pony-sized puppy has a very big and wet tongue.

Eventually the Huskies are pulled away and I'm dragged to my feet by my friends, everyone looking a bit shocked. I let my eyes survey the group, assessing the damage.

"Again, Richard?" I blink, staring at his missing foot.

He nods slightly, glancing at the stump of my arm, which is slowly reforming. Amelia is seated next to him, a pale pink shroud covering her upper body as replacement skin. She seems unconcerned by the pain, drinking from a water bottle, but her slightly too large pupils tell me she's drugged out of her mind. Most of Mikito's armor and clothing has been burnt off, the shreds not even covering her dignity. The normally reserved Japanese lady is so tired, she doesn't even care. Rachel's missing most of her hair and is dressed in civilian clothing while Aiden... well, Aiden looks fine actually.

As bad as the humans look, the remaining Yerick are even worse for wear. None of the Yerick seems to have any fur left, most of it burnt to a crisp, and Nelia seem to be missing one of her horns. Aron lies on the ground, bare-chested as his flesh slowly knits over exposed bone, the side of his face bandaged. Capstan, on the other hand, looks to have been in the blender. There's so much blood, some of it still leaking from him, that I can't tell where the injuries start and his skin ends. That he's still standing is freaking impressive. When I raise an eyebrow at Capstan, he just shakes his head.

Thousand hells. I close my eyes for a second, feeling frustration boil out of me before I push it down. Not right now, we're still too close. Later, later, I can process my feelings about losing another.

On the way back, my body curled up against the puppies in the back of the truck, I take the time to review the piled up notifications.

Status Screen			
Name	John Lee	Class	Erethran Honor Guard
Race	Human (Male)	Level	30
Titles			
Monster's Bane, Redeemer of the Dead			
Health	1420	Stamina	1420
Mana	1100	Mana Regeneration	77 / minute
Attributes			
Strength	80	Agility	133

Constitution	142	Perception	45
Intelligence	110	Willpower	112
Charisma	16	Luck	25
Class Skills			
Mana Blade	1	Blade Strike	2
Thousand Steps	1	Altered Space	2
Two are One	1	The Body's Resolve	3
Greater Detection	1	Instantaneous Inventory*	1
Soul Shield	2	Blink Step	2
Cleave*	1	Frenzy*	1
Combat Spells			
Improved Minor Healing (II)		Greater Regeneration	
Improved Mana Dart (IV)		Enhanced Lightning Strike	
Fireball		Polar Zone	

The Body's Resolve (Level 3)

Effect: Increase natural health regeneration by 35%. On-going health status effects reduced by 33%. Honor Guard may now regenerate lost limbs. Mana regeneration reduced by 15 Mana per minute permanently.

Soul Shield (Level 2)

Effect: Creates a manipulatable shield to cover the caster's or target's body. Shield has 1,000 Hit Points.

Cost: 250 Mana

Blink Step (Level 2)

Effect: Instantaneous teleportation via line of sight. May include Spirit's line of sight. Maximum range—500 meters.

Cost: 100 Mana

I wince again at the low, low Mana regeneration rates. Gods, I'm going to have that get fixed at some point, but without increasing my passive healing, I'd be a lot deader. Thank the gods that the System has more than one way to get your body patched fully. I admit, I'm a little curious to see what Mana Shield is like, but I'll need to dedicate my Class Skill points to Thousand Blades before I have chance to check it out. For now though, I'm happy enough to just chill till we arrive home.

***

We are a sad and sorry lot by the time we get back to Whitehorse. Most of us have lost our armor, and there are more than few missing limbs in the group.

As we reach the Yerick's compound first, Capstan turns to each of us. "Tonight, we hold a memorial for Tahar. As blood companions, you are invited."

Nods and assurances of our presence are given in short order before the rest of us make our way farther into town. Amelia and Richard head directly for the Shop, Mikito helping them along. Aiden breaks away, begging off to his apartment, and suddenly, it's just Ali and me.

I stare at the buildings, watching people walk without seeing them. We lost. Again. Even with more people, even knowing what we were walking into, we lost.

"*John,*" Ali speaks, jerking me out of my morose brooding.

"*Yes?*"

"*I grabbed a body. I want you to drop it off with Sally,*" Ali sends to me, and I frown, looking at the Spirit. He doesn't mean for us to… "*Well, we moving or not?*"

I consider just walking into the Shop to sell it. Going back in was insane. There are other dungeons, other places to explore. We already lost one, why go again? But refusing to do so is a good way to get Ali to whine, and I just don't have the energy.

"John?" Sally turns from the counter as I walk in, looking at me then at Ali, sympathy etching her face. "Something I can do?"

"Yup, pint-size." Ali flies over and floats above the counter. "I need an autopsy."

"I'm an Alchemist not a Doctor. I wouldn't really know where to start."

Ali shrugs. "Yeah, yeah, I get it, and I'll buy it off the System if I need to, but there's something I need to know. Now, we good to go or not?"

I watch, bemused.

"Ugh… fine. Backroom, but I charge a hundred Credits an hour," Sally replies and walks toward the back counter, holding up a finger. "And I'm not negotiating on that, Spirit."

"Got it, pint-size. Just get me the information I need."

I watch him float away to deposit the body. I sigh, rubbing my temples. He's right, I know it. There's something weird going on in that dungeon and we need to know what. I know that, but I find it hard to care right this second.

Chapter 16

That evening, we gather in the Yerick's compound. A single brazier, no larger than an arm's length, dominates the square. A small fire burns in it. Strips of cloth, colored red, blue, and gray, are laid alongside brushes and chest-high tables. Yerick move to these tables, where they write on the cloths strips before depositing them beside the brazier.

As the humans gather, Nelia walks up, inclining her head to us. Amelia and Richard have regrown their limbs, and all of us washed and dressed for the ceremony.

"All we ask is that you write a memory of Tahar on a cloth strip, one that has meaning for you. As blood companions, you will use the red strips. Place them in the bowl set aside for such strips. Before the burning ceremony, we will be Gifting his possessions within the clan. In two hours, we will burn the strips to remind Tahar that he is not forgotten, though he resides in the fields of Heaven. Any questions?" When she receives none, Nelia moves away.

The others move ahead and pick up strips of cloth to write.

Ali stays behind, floating next to me, his voice soft. "The Yerick traditionally only used two colors—the blue for family and lovers, and the gray. Blood companions—those the Yerick fought with—would open their arms, bleeding on the gray strips till they turned red." I look at Ali, raising an eyebrow, and he shrugs. "I figured you'd be into it, boy-o. Being all melodramatic and all. Unless you're done brooding?"

"Fuck off," I answer.

"Guess not," Ali mutters as he floats away to a pile of cloth.

I watch them move around for a while before I make my way over and find a red cloth. I stare at it for a time, wondering what to write, what memory to share. So much blood, death, and pain that we had faced together. Yet it's not those memories that rise up the strongest.

Tahar, standing on a hillock, laughing as autumn sun pours down on him through a break in the clouds. Covered in mud, hands on his hips as he enjoys the absurdity of the situation—a powerful warrior covered in mud due to a simple misstep.

Three taps with a staff is all that is needed to bring silence to the soft-speaking crowd. The humans have mostly clustered together, though Yerick have come and spoken with us, drawing forth stories as we wait. It's not all about Tahar of course; conversations turn to the dungeons, to Whitehorse as it was, and the food that we are given. It's a wake, and there's only so much that you can say about the departed before you realize it's time to move on to different topic.

Nelia is standing beside the brazier, an older, gray-haired Yerick beside her. When we are all looking, Nelia speaks. "For Umbrak, a pair of throwing knives. May you learn to find your target."

A small Yerick child, barely above my hip, scurries forward at his mother's urging to take the pair of throwing knives that are offered by the older woman. He touches the knives to his forehead then scurries back, embarrassed by the attention.

"For Inunuk, the glow-lamps of Askana that she so admired. May it brighten her evenings with her family," Nelia says next with a slight gesture. The lamps appear, curving structures of crystal that glow with a pale purple-and-yellow light.

"For Logram, the training weights. Grow strong, brother."

"For Oranda, the Ares bi-focal pistol that she craved. Remember, seat the battery!"

And on and on it goes. Most gifts are weapons or training equipment, all with a small personalized message. So many gifts, so many messages. I see that I'm not the only human looking surprised. The thought and effort astounds to us. Ali offers little help.

Capstan finds us passing looks of confusion and admiration between us. "Every item we buy, every item we earn or are given, we attach a message or note to it in the System immediately. It is a small Skill, one that is purchased at the Shop for every Yerick at their third rotation. All Yerick do so to ensure that the gift may strengthen the herd. We update the information as and when we need to, but the gifts are our legacy. Our deaths are written in the stars, but even in death, we can strengthen our herd." Capstan's deep, grumbly voice is soft so as not to disturb the ceremony.

I see a few nods, even a few questions about what the Skill is called, from my friends. I say nothing, do nothing as I watch the gifts keep coming. I see it now that it's explained. I watch children given a new gift scurry away, murmuring to themselves. Watch as these children plan for their deaths, for the passing of these newly given items.

"For John Lee, a stash of chocolates. For his temper and our sanity."

It's only Ali's mental hiss that makes me move forward to grab the chocolate that Tahar always seemed to have on hand to offer me when I was grumpy or quiet. I take the product, bowing to his mother, and find myself back at my spot with no memory of the in-between. I find myself saying nothing still, a single chocolate held in hand.

Capstan points at it. "Eat." I look up and stare at Capstan, who nods at my hand. "Eat. Tahar would not want you angry at his wake."

I nod and find myself pulling the wrapper apart. The chocolate tastes like ash in my mouth. I eat though, because Capstan is right. My blood sugar is low, and there is more to watch.

Chapter 17

Sally came through for us. The next afternoon, she contacts me with her autopsy results and I rush to the Shop for more details. What she found out confirmed the hunch we had—the Frakin aren't smart enough, aren't sentient enough, to plan and plot a trap like that.

Onlivik Spores

A parasitic being, the Onlivik Spores attach to lesser beings and invade their cerebral and nervous system, taking control of conscious mental impulses. Onlivik Spores showcase a rare split-hive mind with a main controller host and varying levels of sophistication and sentience dependent on the number of additional host bodies.

Quest Received—The Onlivik Spores (Shareable)

Destroy the Onlivik Spores that have infected the Frakin in the Two-Horn Mountain Dungeon.

Rewards: 50,000 Credits, 20,000 XP

There's more, a lot more, in the information I purchased from the Shop, detailing everything from biological details to past encounters with the Spores. Thankfully, it seems that the Onlivik Spores can't invade System-protected host bodies—at least, not any with any decent amount of Willpower and Constitution. Still, I'm not going to take a chance that we're all clear, which is why perusing data at the Shop is kept to a minimum. I only stop long enough to get the details on the Spores and how to clear out an infection if there is one among us.

***

I come back to Earth amid turmoil. Outside the City Center building, the Yerick stand in a group. Capstan is in front, with Nelia standing next to him, and flanking them is Aron and another pair of Yerick I don't know. Surprisingly, Xev is here in all its glory, maneuvering around in its own powered armor. Sally stands to the side too, arms crossed in anger.

Facing the aliens is a group of humans, made up mostly of the City Council and members of the hunters and butchering yard. Between the group are a very worried Amelia, Vir, and two more of the guards.

"What will you do about this?" Capstan growls, his voice so low it reverberates in my chest. His fur is standing on end, and I can almost see the anger rolling off him.

"Your accusations are unfounded and insulting," Fred says, nodding to the butchering yard personnel, as he stands there in his pressed suit. He seems confident, standing tall as he opposes the aliens. However, he has his arms crossed and his grip on his upper arm is just a little too tight. "Our men would do no such thing."

"Lie," Nelia intones, her voice dispassionate.

"How dare you, you cow!" Eric snaps, his insult eliciting a series of growls from the Yerick.

I'm struck once again that when a Yerick growls, it's significantly more intimidating than a human's. Maybe it's the way they hit lower, deeper notes, or maybe it's the fact they tower over us mere humans. Either way, the human hunters shift the grips on their guns, which cranks up the tension further.

"Put the gun down," Amelia snaps when one of the hunters attempts to bring it to his shoulder. She steps in the way, putting her body in front of the barrel. "No one is getting shot today."

Vir, on the other hand, is speaking to Capstan, his voice low. "First Fist, this is not the way to do things."

"We have been insulted. Attacked. Disrespected, and now, cheated. We have died for these people. The Yerick will not take any more of this," Capstan snarls, his voice reverberating. "I demand these Goblin-children return the Credits they have stolen."

"We have stolen nothing!" Eric snaps.

"Truth," Nelia intones in that same cold, dispassionate voice.

"There! You see, even your woman knows we speak the truth," snaps Fred.

"Lie," Nelia says.

"What?" Eric yelps, eyes swinging between the two as something seems to cross his mind.

Capstan's lips curl up, a low rumble beginning in his chest.

"Tell your woman to shut up," Fred snaps.

Capstan moves, surging forward. It is only Vir who manages to make Capstan stop, his body braced against the larger Adventurer.

Fred's eyes glint in triumph as he adds, "It's all about violence with you aliens."

"*Enough!*" I roar, making my presence known. Gods, I wish I had an Aura or something to make my point, but maybe my reputation of being a complete psychopath will do. "Capstan, you need to stand down."

The First Fist turns to me, lips drawn as he snarls. "I expected more from you, Redeemer. You protect these humans?"

"If it'll stop you from attacking? Sure." I walk forward and watch as the non-human crowd parts around me. I see Sally standing there, arms crossed, and Xev watching me with its bifractal eyes, but my attention is focused on Capstan. "You are better than this."

"They cheated us," Capstan rumbles, eyes flaring.

"True," Nelia intones.

"I heard." I step forward, putting me in easy reach of the First Fist, and I look up, meeting large brown eyes. "Tell me what is going on and I'll see what I can do."

"True."

Before Capstan can speak, Fred injects, "You have no authority here!"

I hold up a finger for Capstan then turn to meet Fred's eyes. "Shut up. Or else I'll rip your tongue out and make you eat it."

"False," Nelia says.

"Hey, Truth-shitter, we're trying to help here!" Ali growls while Fred smirks.

"Fine, try this. If you don't shut up, I'll gag you and sit on you. I might even fart a little," I snap, irritated.

"And he had beans," Ali adds.

"True," Nelia says.

Fred shuts up and I grin, absently noting more than a few humans smiling slightly. Yes, my threat was childish, but it's effective.

"John…"

"You too, Amelia. I'm not going to kill him or hurt him. Just shut him up."

Her lips tighten, but I note she restrains herself from doing anything. Thank the gods she's predictable—so long as things stay verbal, she won't step in.

"Now, Capstan?" I ask.

"We have learnt that you humans have been short-changing us. Your butchering yard men have been taking parts of the kills and under-reporting what we have brought back. It was subtle at first, but it has grown extremely blatant."

"Truth," Nelia says.

Fred and more than a few humans shoot her a glare. I can't help but flick a glance at her then at Ali.

"*You got it, boy-o. She's channeling a Skill that lets her tell the truth of a statement. As the speaker knows it,*" Ali explains.

"Fred, your turn," I say.

"I don't answer to you," Fred says.

I consider my next steps quickly. I could beat the florid politician till he tells me what I want to know, but I'm trying to stop violence here. On the other hand…

"Okay. It was more out of courtesy anyway. I'll just buy it at the Shop." I glance at Capstan, who inclines his head in agreement.

Fred frowns, but it's Minion who speaks. "What do you mean, buy it at the Shop?"

"Everything's for sale, idiot. I've told you before. All you need to do is be willing to pay the System's price," I answer, turning back to Minion. "This little scheme of yours? Real dumb. You might not have broken any Galactic Law, but you've not gotten away with it either. There's no getting away with anything in this world—it's always, always recorded."

Eric snaps his mouth shut, blinking. When Nelia says, "Truth," he flinches before he points at her. "How do you know she's telling the truth?"

"Because that's her Skill, and Class too I'm guessing. She could be lying, but the Yerick aren't dumb. They know the System and know what an accusation like this could mean," I say.

Minion's lips firm even further. One thing about Eric, as annoying as he might be, he's also smart.

"Truth," Nelia says again.

I shoot her a glare. She's doing that each time we say something that isn't a question, which is actually becoming a little annoying. She must be a riot at parties when she does this.

Miranda's lips thin, her eyes hard before she jerks her head slightly. "You're saying we really cheated them?"

"You cannot be serious? You're willing to believe this rubbish? What is the System? An all-seeing God?" Fred says, waving. "Come on, if the System knew all this, why'd it take them so long to figure out who burned down the Yerick's buildings?"

"It didn't," Amelia says. "We knew who it was almost immediately. Hell, even with my own skills, I figured it out within a few days. We just wanted to make sure."

"Truth."

Fred sniffs. "Another damn alien lover. You all band together."

Amelia opens her mouth to speak but is cut off by Miranda, who says, "Assuming what you say is true, what is stopping the System from lying to us?"

"Never been a case that that's been proved," Ali pipes up. "And trust me, with the way we use the System, we'd know."

"Truth."

A dark worm of worry gnaws at my gut at that pronouncement, but Miranda nods slightly. "Very well. I'll go along with this. I had no hand in the cheating."

"Truth."

"Neither did I!" Eric spits out before anyone else can say anything.

"Truth."

That's not entirely surprising after all the protests before, but somehow, I'm still slightly shocked that Minion isn't part of Fred's little scheme.

While I'm dealing with my prejudices, Miranda continues. "Very well, First Fist, is it? Are you willing to discuss this matter in a more relaxed setting? Something a little less… aggressive?"

Capstan rumbles slowly, looking between Fred and Miranda and me, doubt on his face.

Vir speaks then. "May I offer my services in this mediation? I believe Lord Roxley would want this matter settled amicably."

Fred opens his mouth to say something and I reach into my inventory, making a piece of rope appear. I hold it in front of him, and he shuts his mouth with a clack.

Amelia, on the other hand, rolls her eyes, pushing my hand down. "I will take care of the mayor." She takes hold of Fred's arm, her face professional. "We'll be in my office."

I consider objecting then decide to let it go. Not my place. Anyway, interrogating Fred for what he knows is probably something I should leave to the professional. She might object to more violent measures, but the police have been worming confessions out of suspects for decades without resorting to thumbscrews.

"You know, Ali, the other thieves are going to run," I think to my friend, and I hear his mental snort.

"Where to?"

I consider his answer then smile grimly. He has a point. In an apocalypse, there really isn't anywhere to run. Sally prods me in the stomach while I'm thinking, and I remember why I came out from the Shop. A moment later, she has the same information I do, which has her hurrying back to her store to do a quick check.

"Ali…"

"Some of us can multi-task. Already scanned and the group here is clear. Once the others are in range, I'll scan them too."

Guess that means I need to hunt down Aiden. The crowd is breaking up—Vir, Capstan, Nelia, and the Councilors headed into the Council's offices, the hunters dispersing. Xev skitters up and over the buildings, probably back to its workshop. I sigh, rubbing my temples. At some point, we'll have to let the others know in more detail, but at least for now, we should be safe.

***

"Again."

Hours later, I'm in my living room in the dark, staring at glowing System screens of the battle. Thanks to the drones and Ali, I've got multiple recordings of the entire delve. I've been watching the recordings from start to finish, again and again, analyzing each moment, each interaction, looking for something, anything that can give us an advantage.

Sixty-seven Frakin stare at me from the screen, silent and eerie as when we first encountered them. They don't move, don't twitch, and yet, staring at the recording, I can see the marks of the spore infection on all of them.

"Pause."

The screen pauses and I reach out, swinging footage from my desperate fight with the Frakin in the tunnels. I watch as I duck and weave, jumping and twisting between the Frakin. I watch as I trigger Blink Step, flicking out of sight and reappearing in front of the horde that streamed pass me, plasma bolts flaring all around.

"Again."

I watch the fight, watch the dance of pain that I lay about me and the bolts of plasma that miss me by inches.

"Again."

I watch as I Blink, then I see it, what my subconscious mind picked up and what has been nagging me. I raise my hands, backing both screens up to where I want them to start, then I twitch my hands again, pulling up my minimap. I set up a pair of maps, then I set the timelines to play at the right time.

"Start."

It's there. Just a brief flicker of movement, so small I can barely see it, but it's there. A hesitation, a skip in the beat of attacks. When the Frakin are told to attack, the ripple happens at the back and flows outward to the front, the passage of the command so fast it's barely noticeable even with my enhanced attributes. At the same time, I spot a stutter in the movements on the map. It happens when I Blink, when I shift positions in an instant. That stutter happens when the Frakin are attempting to reacquire me.

"Weird," Ali says, and I nod slowly.

I stare at the screens in silence. I can see it—but I'm not even sure what I'm seeing.

"John?" Lana calls as she stomps down the stairs, sounding angry.

I look up from the windows, wondering what I did wrong. "Lana…?"

"Did you hear what Bill is doing?" she snaps, stalking in and throwing herself into a seat next to me.

"Uhh…"

"He's started a strip club!" she snarls, gesturing with her hands. "The old motel he took over, he turned it into a strip club. And he's selling drugs from it!"

"Oh." I absently pull out a chocolate bar.

Before I can eat it, she snatches it out of my hands. I stare at my empty hands for a moment before pulling out another.

"*Oh!* Is that all you can say?" Lana snaps, eyes cold in the dim light. "He's exploiting women! And selling drugs to everyone who goes in. We've been trying to keep that contained and he, he's just selling them!"

"Have you talked to him?"

"Of course I have. We have. He's saying he's doing nothing wrong! Since Roxley is the owner of the city, it's his laws that Bill's abiding by and there aren't any Galactic Laws against it. He says he's providing 'gainful employment' for women and that we should be happy he's contributing," she growls, snatching my half-eaten bar again from my hand and chewing on it. "He's... grumphff... such an... mmmm... ass. Is this nougat?"

"Yes."

"I hate nougat." She hands me back my mostly consumed bar and waits for me to deposit another in her outstretched hand.

"Well, it was mine," I point out, and she just shoots me a look that makes me smile.

"It's not funny," she snaps, though with less heat.

"No, but he is right. The City Council, well, it really isn't a real ruling body. Not in the System sense. And unless you guys are willing to physically force him to stop, there's not much you can do."

She nods, arms crossed. "I know. It's just... I hate strip clubs. They're so... so... demeaning!"

"And you don't mind the drugs?"

Lana grimaces, looking at her hands. "It's... not great. But it's been getting worse anyway. Amelia and Vir had to shut down a drug-making operation in one of the residences because they nearly blew up the block. At least Bill's is less… lethal. And he keeps rooms and places for them to use. We… I can't stop them. This world, it's just… it's just hard."

Hard. That's one way of putting it. She chews on her chocolate bar in silence after that. I don't break the silence, instead shooting a glance at the screens I was watching. Ali keeps silent, knowing better than to say anything.

"You know, the Council's reforming itself."

"Oh, really?"I don't even bother to hide my disinterest.

"Yeah. After Fred's… the incident, well, we're thinking we'll try, we will, involve the Yerick a little more. Maybe get them a seat or something."

"Uh huh."

"You want in?"

"In… what?" I sit up, staring at her.

"In the Council. I'm sure I could get you one." Lana says, rubbing her nose. "God knows, Jim will back me. And probably Miranda."

"No. Gods, no. I'd rather listen to Ali sing La Bamba, with his swings for a whole day than do that."

"Oh God, you love me. You really love me," Ali croons and I glare at him.

"Sorry. Sorry. I know, it isn't what you want," Lana says, slumping in the chair. She catches my glances to the side where my screens float unseen and frowns. "What are you doing?"

"Analyzing the delve." I gesture her over. "Come here, look at this."

She scoots over to my couch and sits next to me, leg pressed against mine.

For a moment, I just enjoy the closeness before I refocus on the task at hand. "Ali, share and show."

"I should never have told you I could do this. I'm not a damn AI. you know," Ali grumbles but he does as I ask.

"Oh, those things are disgusting," Lana says.

"Yeah. Again, Ali."

"Yes, master."

"Again."

"Again," Lana replies almost immediately after it stops this time. "Wait…" Lana falls back, staring at the ceiling, biting her lower lip. After a moment, she looks at Ali, who dutifully runs it again. When it's over, she nods firmly and looks at me. "There's a stutter, isn't there?"

"Yes."

"Huh. So…?" She tilts her head, obviously expecting me to say something brilliant.

"So. Yeah, a stutter." I shake my head and just talk because well, something might come from it. "The Spores are a hive mind, but they've got a single controlling host. It looks like that means they can't focus on more than a few things a time. The Frakin, they can act autonomously, but if they get out of… of… script, well, they need redirection. When they need to start a new program, they…."

"They…?"

I blink, looking at Lana, and grin. "They're a program. The Spores can't control all of the Frakin individually, and the Frakin don't really have conscious thoughts anymore. So they set up programs, certain behaviors. Break out of the program and the Frakin need to be reset."

Lana nods, trying to see what has me so excited.

"Don't you get it? It's a program! And what do you when you want to break a program?"

"Pull the power cord?"

Ali snorts while I continue to grin. "Introduce a virus."

***

It's only a couple of hours later that I find myself speaking with a thin, bespectacled man. Leonard worked in the hospital's analysis department before the System came, and he gained a rather weird Class called Bio-Technician. It's similar to Sally's Alchemist Class, except he specializes in the organic side of things. Like most people in the Yukon, when the System came into play, he had the choice of taking the System-generated "best" option or taking the hour to sort through and find something he could use. No big surprise that like most people, he went with the option offered to him. Few people had the time, ability, or desire to sort through the millions of options available. Mikito's husband and Jason were the only two that I knew of for sure, though I'm sure some of the Raven's Circle probably did too.

Sally was my first choice for this request, but it seems that small biological creatures are outside of her purview. Leonard was actually my third choice. My second—the Shop—turned out to be rather expensive. It seems I'm not the only one who has considered biological warfare, and the System Shop helpfully discourages that by pricing everything extremely high.

"Can you do it?" I ask Leonard as he peruses the biological information I've provided him on the Frakin.

"No," Leonard says, ignoring me and continuing to talk to Lana. He's been doing that the entire time we've been here. "I don't have the Skills to kill off the Spores. I don't even have the equipment to even start making something that could kill them."

I snarl then force myself to calm down. Shit. The Shop it would be except… well, let's just say Sabre cost less than the solution. By a few orders of magnitude.

"Isn't there something we can do?" Lana smiles at Leonard and, I swear, bats her eyelashes.

"Well… ahem… maybe. I could maybe give them a bit of a cold," Leonard replies, and I roll my eyes. He obviously picks it up, pointing at me. "A really bad flu. Something that would disorient, maybe even kill a few of them."

"That'd be helpful," Lana interjects, grabbing Leonard's hand and drawing his attention again. He smiles as she continues. "How long would it take?"

"Well, this isn't, you know, like hitting things. It's complicated. You've got to create a basic model then make multiple versions of each and run them all through a simulator. It'd be better if I had an actual creature to experiment on…"

"How long, four eyes?" Ali says.

Of course Leonard doesn't wear glasses anymore, but I have to agree he probably did wear them before the System.

"Two, maybe three weeks," Leonard snaps at Ali.

Lana nods, squeezing his hand again. "Thank you. I'll make sure to check in with you every few days." She smiles at Leonard, who bobs his head excitedly.

I watch Lana flirt with him a little more before we finally leave, Leonard promising to get us the first sample as soon as possible.

Outside, I thank Lana, who just shakes her head. "Don't. I'm just doing what I can to make sure you and my brother come back." I nod and she adds, "It's not enough, you know."

"I know." I exhale, staring at the setting sun. Disrupting them, making the Spores less effective will help, but there were still too many damn Frakin. We need something else, another edge. "I know."

Chapter 18

When the snow comes to stay, it does so without warning. Overnight, the clouds dumped over three feet of snow on the ground. No big surprise, no one has taken the time to fix up the snowplows or the salting trucks. On the other hand, who needs snowplows when you've got muscle-bound warriors and mages?

I stand outside on one of our watchtowers we've set up around the house, watching as the Hunter teams work together to clear the roads. Most of them are just walking around with appropriated bulldozer plows, sometimes singly, sometimes in pairs, and tossing the snow onto unused lawns. On other streets, mages work by channeling low-grade fire spells to just melt the snow off the roads, letting the water run into the sewers while they stand comfortably on dry porches. Occasionally, the lack of co-ordination between the two groups ends up with one group being buried in a house or a flood of lukewarm water running onto cleared streets while people are still working.

A smaller group of citizens run from unoccupied residence to residence, ensuring that the water mains are turned off and water tanks emptied. I'm guessing they're being managed by the newly-recreated General Council. Now, both the Yerick and Sally have seats at the table which should help matters. They've even finally added Lana to the table, though she's a lot unhappier about Bill being included too. Either way, the new General Council finally seems to include everyone. I hear Roxley's even given it his blessing by assigning Vir to mediate issues.

The more I see of Vir, the less inclined I am to believe that he's just a promising lieutenant under Roxley's service. I know, firsthand, how strong the First Fist is, and the fact that Vir managed to stop him was impressive. That Roxley is willing to give him free rein to chair the Council is another indicator that the Truinnar is more than he seems. I definitely need to keep a closer eye on the Lieutenant in the future.

Mayor-troublemaker Fred hasn't been seen in Whitehorse since the blowout. Amelia has no idea what happened to him, and all Vir will say that he has been "dealt with appropriately." When Richard heard that, he recommended we go look in the river. Myself, I think Roxley has better sense than to completely waste a resource. After all, I'm sure Fred could be sold for something in the Shop, even if it was just cheap parts. No surprise, there's some grumbling about the high-handed way Fred was dealt with, but it's been muted for the most part. Overall, while the Council hasn't fixed things between the races, at least it's a start.

In the distance, clear spaces in the schools have been turned into winter playgrounds with groups of children working to make the largest snowmen. Funny thing about System-enabled children—some of them are pretty damn strong and agile. Some of those snowmen have begun to top the buildings. Those never last long though, as children throw themselves off the roofs to knock the snowmen down amid screams of laughter and cries for more. I watch a kid, probably no older than five, pick up a snowball twice his size and toss it at another kid. The subsequent explosion and peals of laughter aren't enough to stop a minder from running over to chasten the kid. I barely need the magnification in my helmet to see the grin on the kid's face.

Overall, it's a tranquil-looking state of affairs a few weeks after we had our asses kicked so hard. Tranquil, yet I can't stop the worm of doubt in my gut.

Have you ever found something you're passionate about, then realized no one else gives a shit? Yeah, that's been my life for the last week. Outside of Ali and Lana, everyone else has given up on the dungeon.

When I brought up re-raiding the dungeon, Capstan said, "There are many more dungeons to clear. Sometimes, one must accept the limits of one's current level and move on. The Yerick do not fight unwinnable battles."

I'll admit, I was almost tempted to bring Tahar up right then and there. Almost. I do have a little bit of a sense of self preservation. I was still disappointed, especially when he also added that they'd be spending a few weeks breaking in a new party member.

Richard and Mikito both nodded agreeably when I brought up the matter, but beyond that, neither seemed particularly interested in my explanations and theories. I'm not sure if they just figure I'll do all the planning or that, like Capstan, they've already moved on. After the latest round of agreeable but non-productive discussions, I stopped talking with them about it.

Amelia has her work cut out keeping the peace, especially since Vir seems to be stuck in meetings half the time. The few times she and I have met up, she only complains about breaking in a new partner and mutters about "Rules of Force." I've started avoiding her myself since she shoots me a dirty glare whenever she gets onto that topic.

Aiden flatly told me to get out when I brought up going out again, and Rachel, well, Rachel's not much better. She's been hanging out with Aiden more and more, teaching and training others, but has pretty much stopped going out on even simple hunting missions. Even I'm not dumb enough to push her—losing another party member right after losing most of her group was probably not the best return to hunting. The only time we get her to come with us on our excursions is when we head in to Carcross.

Everyone's taken their eye off the dungeon, and I don't blame them. Not really. We tried it twice and we got our asses kicked both times. Yet something tells me that waiting will just make it worse.

"Boy-o?" Ali floats next to me as I finish my cup of coffee. "We doing this?"

"Just finishing my coffee." Sometimes, I hate being me.

***

Downstairs, I hold my hand and call her forth from my Altered Space. I can't keep her in my inventory or she wouldn't fix herself, so for the last little while, Sabre's been sitting in my Altered Space except when I'm busy hunting.

Omnitron III Class II Personal Assault Vehicle (Sabre)

Structural Integrity: 82%

System Integrity: 94%

Damn but that last fight kicked her ass. The good news is that the adaptive armor has added a twenty percent resistance to plasma and high heat effects. The bad news is that it'll take at least a few more weeks, assuming she doesn't get damaged further of course, before she's fully repaired. Thankfully, the only thing the repairs cost me this time was a whole bunch of materials, which I do have. Using Elementally-charged gold as a major component for replacements has added streaks of dark yellow to the armor plates. Thankfully, Elementally-altered gold isn't as soft as the real stuff or else the bike would really come apart in my next fight.

I stand there stroking my bike, and I know all I'm doing is procrastinating. Thinking of stupid shit because I know what I'm about to do is dumb. Everyone else has let this go—why can't I? I exhale, shaking my head, and glance at the bike one last time.

Hunii Dragonfly Drone (Scouting Type IV-Modified)

This dragonfly drone comes equipped with multiple visual and audio recording options and can update 3-D landscaping maps. Has been modified to carry additional storage items.

Operating time: 2 Hours

Storage: Bio-dispersal container

Leonard came through with the virus. Now the question is, will this work? There's really only one way to tell, and that way requires me to head back into the dungeon. Let's just hope they aren't waiting for me.

***

"Boy-o," Ali sends to me, flicking to me a video of what he's seeing.

I slow down then come to a stop, crouching behind an insufficiently large tree while I review the footage. It's a cat mutation of some form, a former housecat turned into a six-foot creature of spikes, scales, and fangs. I nod slightly as I stare at the monster just sitting there, watching the trail. Creepy but not surprising—cats are known to be ambush creatures after all.

"See it. Doesn't look too hard."

"Not that. That." Ali manipulates the System and the video floats higher as he does so, giving me a clearer view as he highlights the spots he sees. Right behind the head, a small yellowish-greenish bump that I'd missed.

"Is that…?" I gulp.

"Onlivik Spores, yes," Ali replies. *"It's spreading outside the dungeon."*

"How?"

"Don't know. My guess—either the Spores were never part of the dungeon initially, or they just escaped the System's controls because we're not fully integrated yet," Ali replies.

I find myself grunting. *"How fast?"*

"What am I? A silicone dummkopf? Fast. We're about two miles out from the dungeon and it's got scouts watching for problems," Ali says.

I sigh. Shit. *"All right, can we get a message back to the city? Package the video and send via one of the drones. We still need to get this virus into the dungeon."* If I die, the city needs to know.

"Do this, Ali. Do that, Ali," Ali mutters as he focuses, sending the appropriate commands to one of our last drones. *"Done."*

"Yeah, but it's more fun to listen to you whine."

I shut up after that, focusing on skimming around the cat. Better to find a way in that doesn't attract any attention if I can. I'll be making enough noise when I do get in.

***

Two weeks, and other than the snow, the area around the dungeon hadn't changed a bit. Snow-covered slopes, heavily laden trees, and the occasional set of tracks from a snowshoe hare or some weirder, unidentified creature is all that marks the terrain. As always, the Yukon is gorgeous and scenic, but this time round, I'm more concerned about leaving easy-to-follow tracks than how pretty everything is.

Unfortunately, there's not much I can do about the fact that each of my armor-clad steps is leaving a set of tracks a blind man could follow. The only thing that can fix that is a strong wind or another big snowfall, and the clear skies and dead air tell me I'm not in luck today. It makes my path into the dungeon a circuitous and slow route, but luckily, the Onlivik Spores seem more interested in setting up fixed guard positions rather than roving guards.

Interestingly enough, there aren't any guards at the actual dungeon entrance itself. I'm not sure if the Spores are just that confident or just that dumb, but I'll take it. Not that I expect my presence to be hidden very soon.

In the first chamber, I find nothing. It's rare to find monsters hanging out in the first chamber of most dungeons. At most, you get a trap. For a moment, I wonder why that is before I refocus. Right. Horde of mind-controlled Frakin ready to burn me to pieces.

Finding a place to hide is a tense, stomach-clenching affair even if I'm not heading much farther than the first cavern. I know I can run with the QSM, but its five-minute charge makes it a trump card I can only play with care. That means good old Stealth skills are more important in everyday use, and luckily, all that time hunting solo has leveled mine up significantly.

Once I'm hidden, I launch my last two drones. I wish I had all three, but getting word back to the city was more important. Curled up in a small rock outcropping halfway up the cavern, I remotely guide the drones in while letting Ali watch out for potential bad guys. I keep the drones high and quiet, edging in deeper and deeper along the paths I can see. I need to hit as many of these Frakin as I can, but there's only so far that I can guide them before the signal breaks down completely. After that, they'll have to run on their own on-board programming.

That's one of the reasons the Yerick don't use drones much. Not only do you have to have someone watching the drones consistently to get the data you need, it's often not as good as the information you could get from Skills. Add the fact that if you push them too far, they have a tendency to break down or get smashed by monsters and you can see why the Yerick just don't see them as a good use of their money. Overall, I can see their points but then you get a situation like this.

I grin as the first drone comes across the first group of Frakin. There's only a half dozen of them, most of them half-grown, which tells me they haven't recovered completely from our last encounter. That's pretty good news. I drop a quarter of one drone's payload and keep flying, passing my last stand before the signal finally shorts out.

I swear softly, hoping it's enough. Theoretically, all I need to do is ensure that the virus itself is spread around sufficiently, then it should propagate without a problem. According to Leonard, the virus is both airborne and System-borne—that is, the System helps the infection process. I'm not entirely sure what that means or why he gets grumpy when I call it a virus, but considering I never took biology and he insists on explaining everything in as many four-syllable words as he can, I'm okay with that. So long as it works, I'll even forgive him for asking Lana out.

Not that I have a right to get angry that he did. It's not as if Lana and I have done anything more than, well, talk. Irrational jealousy is irrational. So long as I realize it's irrational, I can keep it in check. However, I do wonder if I should be asking her out…

I grunt, shaking my head, and refocus on the feeds. I need to stop thinking about this. Sitting in the middle of a dungeon, waiting for my drones to either get caught or do their job, is not the right time or place to think about dating. Anyway, I don't have much to offer the lady—I'm a suicidal, hot-tempered mess of a man. She deserves better.

Thankfully, before I get even more morose and idiotic, the feed from one of my drones comes back. It's the one I sent on one of the side paths that the Frakin used to flank us before. The moment it connects, the map updates and I let out a low whistle. Jesus—the pathway leads down to a chamber beneath me, which seems to store a huge number of the Frakin. They're still doing that creepy, completely still thing, not even moving when the drone dumps its cargo.

I don't have time to watch further though because Ali hisses at me, making my minimap bloom. Looks like the Frakin around me are scuttling now, searching. I guess the other drone got caught. A quick command sends the drone I have in control into hiding and hibernation mode in the vague hope that I can retrieve it later before I drop to the ground and run. Time to go.

Running out of this dungeon with Ali floating beside me is beginning to get very old. A few of the infected monsters charge in, blips on my screen that flow toward me, but I ignore them. I've got too much of a head start on all but the cat I'm running toward. Really, it's stupid of the Spores to charge me—the cat doesn't stand a chance as I behead it. Then again, we've established that the Spores aren't that smart.

Yet.

Chapter 19

"A bigger, better man would take this opportunity to say I told you so pass him by," I say into the stunned silence of the gathered great and powerful of Whitehorse after Ali finished his presentation. I let the silence linger for a few more moments. "I told you so."

"John…" Lana says, her tone cool.

I flash her a smile, but I quiet down. Some are still pushing on their data screens, trying to make the information we presented say something, anything other than what it does. Others, having read it, turn to me or their respective leaders, waiting for an answer. No one provides one though, because there really isn't an easy answer.

"Very well, Redeemer. You were correct. I expect you have a solution?" Nelia finally breaks the silence, staring at me.

I smile grimly and shake my head. "No, I don't have a solution. I do have some suggestions. First, we send a team to wipe out the current scouts and guards the Spores have set up. That should slow the spread a bit since it takes a critical mass of the Spores to begin infection. Right, Leonard?"

Leonard twitches, obviously not used to being in this kind of company, before he jerkily nods.

"We'll still need to deal with the Spores eventually, but taking out the scouts will buy us time. Second, we need an answer from the System, and we need it sooner rather than later. Are the Spores part of the dungeon or are they an invader? The first means we'll constantly be dealing with their production, constantly having to destroy them as the System recreates the Spores. That means we'll need a much more permanent solution to their spread.

"The second, well, the second is simpler. We just kill everything that has the Spore and burn it all down."

"If you knew to ask that question, why didn't you get the answer?" Bill asks, hands steepled.

I flash him a grin. "Because the answer to that question is about fifty thousand Credits."

I see more than a few people suck in their breath at the price. No shit, it's expensive.

It's Jason, on the video-conference line, who asks the obvious question. "Why do we need to know? If we kill them all and keep them contained in the dungeon, won't that be enough, even if the dungeon is creating the Spores?"

Vir leans forward in his chair. "No. Infected dungeons are unusual, but they are not unique. An Infected dungeon cannot be contained by just killing the creatures within—eventually, the infection will spread. There are Galactic procedures to contain such dungeons, but they are expensive and require significant time investment. John is correct—understanding what we face is important."

I nod to Vir before looking at the group to see if there are any further questions. When there aren't, I add, "Lastly, we're going to have to clear that dungeon one way or the other. Like any dungeon, if we don't clear it regularly, it'll overpopulate and spill out. With an Overmind, that might happen sooner than we'd like, since there's no in-fighting. We've got a week before the Spores feel the effects of the virus, and it'll take a couple of days before it really gets going. Ten days, right, Leonard?" On confirmation, I continue. "Ten days, then we go in."

I watch as people grimly accept the deadline, slowly running the numbers through their mind.

Jim frowns, staring into space before he looks back at me, his voice husky from too many cigarettes. "I'll get a few hunting groups to the dungeon. We can't contribute much to the attack, not and keep the city safe, but my group and another could help man the area."

"That'll be great, Jim," Lana says, nodding for him to head out.

He gets up, offering a brief nod to everyone before he leaves to brief his people. I almost say something before I decide against it—Jim understands probably better than any of us how strong his hunting group really is. In the assault, they just won't be that much help.

"We're in, of course," Richard says. "We've got a couple of Credits saved up we can add to the pot."

Vir raises a hand, cutting Richard off. "The purchase will be handled by Lord Roxley."

I nod, grateful for that help. I don't know how deep his pockets are, though I've gotten the feeling they're not as deep as he'd like us to believe. Still, I'll take Vir's word for it. "Thanks."

Vir nods before looking at the ceiling. "While Lord Roxley is unable to arrive in time for the attack, I believe his guard may contribute a few additional men to the attack. I shall lead them myself."

Capstan speaks next, his voice a low rumble. "The Yerick can send three Adventuring parties."

"I'll speak with Xev to see what it can contribute, but I can outfit a lot of people with potions," Sally pipes up, her normally cheerful demeanor extremely serious now.

I watch this play out, and a part of me wilts at how mundane it all seems. A part of me expected orchestral music, grand speeches, and declarations of bravery. Instead, we get a boardroom with the clink of ice water and dry allocations of resources and studied consideration. On the other hand, as I look around, I have the feeling that this is a group I want to go to battle with. All but one…

"So, hillbilly, your crew coming?" Ali floats over to Bill, hands on his knees as he sits cross-legged.

Luthien snarls and I get more than a few looks that say the same thing—"control your Spirit." I ignore them.

"We have warned you before, Spirit," Bill says, raising a hand toward Ali, and a part of me wonders what he thinks he's going to do. My curiosity almost lets me watch Bill hurt Ali, but that won't get the answer I want.

"Ali, enough. Be quiet now." Ali shoots me the most horrified, betrayed look ever until I add, "Because Bill is about to answer your question."

Luthien turns to look at Bill, her lips parting slightly as she waits to see what he has to say.

Bill opens his mouth then glances around the suddenly quiet room before shutting it again. "We will not."

"Thought so." Ali smirks, floating back to me.

I sigh, sending him a thought. *"Enough, let the others handle it. You got the ball rolling."*

"Yeah, yeah. Knew he was trying to get out of it."

"Why am I not surprised?" Lana's voice comes out frosty as she leans forward. "Did the part that the Spores are a threat to all of us not get through that thick skull of yours?"

"Yes. I also note that there's more than sufficient numbers of you to deal with it." Bill shrugs. "I see no reason to risk myself or my people in addition."

"Except if we fail, we all die," Amelia adds.

"So you risk everything on a single throw of the dice," Bill says.

"Die," Ali mutters so softly only I hear him.

"You have a better suggestion?" Richard says.

"For myself? No. There is nothing to be gained by joining you or staying if you fail. My duty is to my people," Bill says.

Others begin to argue with him, all to be shut down by a light rap on the table by Vir. "Adventurer Cross," Vir says.

Bill's jaw clenches slightly, the muscles flexing as he readies himself for another attack.

"You own land in Lord Roxley's domain," Vir says. "You might not know this, but that ownership comes with certain obligations. One of which I will invoke now. You will join us in the attack, or you shall be declared *Mujinae.* I believe the closest human term is Outcast."

Bill leans forward. "You can't do that. This is a free country. There is no draft here."

"I believe you have, repeatedly, informed the Council that you are not breaking any Galactic Law, that we are under Galactic Law here in the city. As such, Canadian or the City's very own laws do not apply to you. Was that not what you said?" Vir's voice grows colder and colder with each word. "Now, do you refuse the call to arms?"

Bill jerks his head as if he's trying to get rid of a nasty crick in his neck but finally accedes to Vir's request. Lana's openly gloating, and even most of the human Council members seem quite happy. Of course, nothing compares to the smirk Amelia shoots Bill, obviously glad to see him finally dealt with. The non-humans ignore the entire interaction with aplomb though, obviously not wanting to get involved. Well, outside of Ali, who is grinning from ear to ear.

I stay silent—as does Bill, who sulks in his seat—as the others plan what we need. Names are thrown out—some familiar, some less so—as additional help for the fight is debated. All the while, I remember the hundreds of Frakin that wait for us.

"We don't have enough, do we, boy-o?" Ali sends to me as he spots my face.

"No, not yet." Not yet.

***

"It is unusual for a spy to request to speak with me directly," Labashi says as we sit down at my fort, the grounds nicely clear.

One good thing about the System—it certainly keeps its side of the bargain. I paid for clear fields of fire and an upgraded, well-kept yard, and even through the snowfalls and monster wanderings, it's done that.

"I'm an unusual spy." I pour him more tea before sitting back.

It's been a few days since the big meeting, and in the city, everyone is scrambling. Whether it's hunting to get more Credits, training to get ready, or planning the attack, the city is buzzing. I guess certain doom is a good way to get everyone's ass into gear.

Labashi sips on his newly filled cup. "This blackberry tea is quite good, as have been your reports thus far."

"Glad you like it. And the reports. I'm enjoying the Credits too." I smile at him, doing my best "innocent" look. Not that I even know if he can tell the difference, but you do what you can. "How'd you like to get information on the fighting groups—all the fighting groups—firsthand?"

"And how would you do that?" Labashi says, an eyebrow rising.

"Well, that's a funny story." I lean forward and fill him in on the last month or so. I drop all of it on him and end with our planned attack. "So we're going in. All of us. Except it won't be enough, I don't think."

"I know of this First Fist of yours, and Vir," Labashi says, finger tapping the edge of the cup. "I believe you might be surprised."

"Perhaps." I stare at my hands and shake my head. "But there's likely going to be more blood lost than I'd like. So I'm here. Asking to hire you."

"And what do you have to offer, Mr. Lee? Our services are expensive," Labashi adds.

I nod. "Yes. I figured as much. So let's talk."

I lean forward, meeting his gaze. This is a bad deal, a bad negotiation. I have no leverage, no way of making this come out good for me. On the other hand, if I'm dead, it won't really matter.

***

Hours later, I watch Labashi walk away. I shut my eyes, leaning back. The negotiation was...

"Horrible. This is a bad, bad idea," Ali finally speaks up, staring at me.

"Yeah, I know." I exhale, shaking my head. "But it's my choice. We need the bodies. Without more help, we're screwed. And the Dwarves aren't willing to help. Now come on, there's someone else we need to speak to."

Ali grumbles but says nothing as I climb aboard Sabre. I look back at the Fort. Gods, I actually enjoyed my time here—hunting, killing, being alone. No one to care about, no one to worry for. Just me and the Apocalypse.

"Oy! I thought you said we were going, boy-o."

I snort. Yeah, enough with the maudlin nonsense. There's work to do.

***

"Aiden." I walk in as he finishes class. I've been waiting outside for the last ten minutes, practicing my own Affinity.

"John," Aiden replies as he puts his notes on the table and turns to stare at me.

"Lana tells me you turned down joining us."

He nods firmly. "Yes. I'm sorry, I know you need everyone who can come. I just… I can't."

I take a seat next to him. "Because of what happened last time?"

He nods, fear clear in his eyes. "I… I don't want to die."

"Few of us do. I understand. Thank you. For coming out when you did. For teaching me what you can. If… well, if we don't come back, get the kids out. Head south. There might be something left back there."

"What do you mean?" Aiden says.

"Dawson's gone and Carcross won't last if—"

The mage cuts me off. "I mean, if you don't come back."

"Oh. This is our final toss," I answer, lips twisting. "We either win or we die. If we don't stop the Spores, they'll keep growing and growing, and eventually, they'll hit Whitehorse and swarm us. We have to win this. Now." He clasps his hands together, fingers shaking, as I continue. "So go south. If we don't come back, get everyone that you can out."

Aiden nods jerkily, looking at me before looking away, unable to meet my eyes. I give his shoulder a squeeze before I walk off, stopping only when he calls my name.

"How do you do it? I want to… I want to be braver, but I can't," he whispers.

"You're asking the wrong person." I don't turn around as I stop in the doorway, a hand on the doorframe. "From my viewpoint, you're plenty brave."

He laughs bitterly, and I leave before he can recover and realize I never answered his question. I don't have an answer for him, at least not the one he's looking for. How do I tell him that it's not because I'm brave but because I'm too fucking scared and angry to stop? How do I tell him that every time I stop and think, I see Haines Junction, or that damn village in the middle of nowhere, or Tahar?

I walk outside into the sunlight and shake my head. No, I have no answer for Aiden. His reaction is the sensible one. Mine—well, mine's certifiable.

***

"We don't have enough people," Jim states again, his fingers tapping the 3-D map of the dungeon and the surrounding areas.

We don't have a lot of the actual dungeon mapped, and all of what we do have comes from my drones which, frankly, is rather worrying. A major recent change to the area is the battlements and walls now surrounding the dungeon entrance, a hastily constructed series of defenses meant to contain any incursion. It won't hold against a major push, but it's sufficient to contain the occasional Frakin that wanders out and keep other monsters away.

"Even if we take my people off the walls, I see at least a half dozen different passages there. My people can't stand up to these Frakin," Jim adds.

"Yes," Vir answers, rubbing his chin. "We might have to hit and pull back, drawing small numbers out to us."

"Very dangerous work," Capstan adds, pointing at the entrance chamber and the chamber beneath. "The Frakin could attempt to overwhelm us at any time."

"What of the virus?" Richard asks.

The group shrugs.

"Might work, might not," I answer before sighing.

"We sure the Spores aren't part of the dungeon?" Richard says.

Vir answers that one for me. "Yes. We confirmed that via the Shop. The Spores are an invasive species, not dungeon owned. Of course, they eventually could be, but as of this time, they aren't. If we wipe the dungeon, we can always sweep it later to confirm."

Since the big meeting, a smaller group of us have been meeting more regularly, trying to work out a plan that will keep most of us alive. The group consists of Vir and Capstan, who have the most System-related battle planning experience, and Jim, who surprisingly is a former infantry sergeant in the army. Richard, Jason, and I drift into the conversation occasionally, throwing what help we can, but at the end of the day, we're civilians trying to plan a battle. We're mostly here so that we know what is going on.

The problem is, we're outnumbered and time isn't on our side. The longer we take, the more the Frakin will increase in numbers. While our people might upgrade in Levels in the meantime, the fact stands that it only takes a few Level 50 Frakin to overwhelm a single Level 40 Adventurer. Better weapons, better tactics, and better coordination can help tilt things in our favor, but the numbers still aren't on our side.

If the Frakin acted like normal monsters, they wouldn't swarm and cluster. We'd have a chance to fight them in smaller groups, whittling down their numbers in a series of battles. Unfortunately, the Spores are sentient and have shown a willingness to swarm us and lay traps.

"I have a partial solution to the number problem," I say. "The Hakarta have agreed to let us have three platoons of their men. Level 40 or so each, but they'll be coming with their full loadout."

Vir looks at me, startled, then his eyes narrow, "Hakarta. The same ones you fought before?"

"Yes."

"And how did you come in contact with them that you were able to arrange a contract?" Vir asks, his voice cold.

I just smile at him. His eyes narrow in suspicion until Capstan taps the table to get all our attention.

"Lieutenant, it is done. I assume there is a price involved?" Capstan says.

"Yes. We'll need to pay them ten thousand Credits per platoon for their involvement, and their share of the loot of course," I say.

People wince. Still, thirty thousand Credits isn't that much when you take into account a full platoon of five Hakarta will share it. Of course, I don't mention the favor I now owe Labashi, the one he can call in at any time. I hedged the favor to ensure that he can't make me use it against my friends or the City, but otherwise, it's pretty open-ended. That's on top of me needing to continue to feed him information of course.

Capstan nods, rubbing his chin. "With the three platoons, we should be able to keep the human hunters on the walls. That will give us enough men, barely, to cover the dungeon itself."

I stare at the map as Vir and Capstan hash out the details with occasional input from Jim, figuring out the best way to fit the Hakarta in our plans. All this talk and we've basically come up with three major strategies, dependent on what we find inside.

The first is simple—the virus reverts the Frakin and the dungeon back to its "normal" state. That means scattered groups without overall coordination. This is our best-case scenario, and if it happens, we can split the teams into smaller groups to clear the dungeon before we finally get to the Boss. It's also the least likely option, but we do have plans for it.

The second scenario is if there's no effect, or mild effects, and the Spores continue to act like the way they have before. In that case, the Frakin are likely to group together, attack in waves, and attempt ambushes. In such a scenario, the goal is to establish a beachhead in the first cavern, set up fortifications in it, and weather the attacks. That leaves us a fallback position in the tunnel where a secondary set of fortifications will be made, then the walls. We've also mined the entrance and the ground above it so, if necessary, we can cause a landslide that will give us enough time to vacate the dungeon's vicinity.

We'd decided against trying to bury the dungeon entrance entirely since there's no way to know if there's another exit. Or worse, if the Frakin are able to dig themselves out. Of course, if we do fail, Jim's men have orders to drop the entrance. As much as we'd like to know the layout of the dungeon, the cost of it in the Shop is exorbitant.

The third scenario is probably the most dangerous. If the Spores feel truly endangered, they might pull back, forcing us to come into the dungeon after them. As Jim's already noted, even after a few caverns, there are multiple passageways and potential entrances. Some, probably most of them, will peter out and dead-end. However, until we can verify that, we'll have to guard each. That means we'll have to move in slowly and carefully, checking each area. Worse, if there are multiple passageways that connect, we could be forced to split our force to cover each of those potential passages until we meet up again.

Depending on how deep and where the Spores decide to have their last stand, we could be extremely dispersed if we try to cover all the exits. If not, we run the risk of being flanked. It's not a great situation and why we're all hoping it's either one of the other scenarios. In either case, Xev's hard at work putting together multiple drones and signal repeaters for us so that we can scout out areas and keep in touch.

We've debated rolling in a couple of bombs and setting them off to clear the area before moving in deeper. Jim pointed out that the narrow corridors and their Mana-strengthened nature would ensure that the blast forces were more concentrated, giving us more bang for our buck.

Unfortunately, Vir and Capstan overruled him. For one thing, we have no idea how big the entire complex could be—we could be wasting Credits by purchasing bombs and setting them off without hurting anything. Even if we did manage to catch some Frakin in the explosions, if the dungeon has more than one floor, the blast wouldn't cross the floors. And of course, we just don't have the Credits to buy something powerful enough to ensure that all the monsters die. It was why most times, dungeons were still cleared the old-fashioned way—one floor at a time with small parties.

***

The night before the big day, the Nugget is hopping. I drive by on Sabre and almost go in but decide against it, stopping only long enough to visit the Shop and stock up on more grenades, missiles, and projectiles. I've loaded my Altered Space with as much of each as I can unreasonably see myself using already, so buying more is my version of fretting.

In the end, I head home. I might not need much sleep physically or mentally, but there's a calming emotional release in the emptiness that a good night's rest can bring. I drive slowly through Riverdale, knowing that icy patches lie hidden underneath the latest dusting of snow. We need a better solution for the roads, like so many other problems, but I push it out of my mind. I have other things to deal with.

At home, I find Lana and Richard seated around the dining room table that's connected to the open kitchen. For once, Richard is without a female companion. Instead, the two Pearsons are chatting quietly, accompanied by a single husky each. Even then, the large dining room is crowded.

Richard greets me, waving me to a chair. I take it after some maneuvering, seating myself and smacking Bella on the nose not too gently as she tries to lick me. Licky dog.

I greet the pair, looking around the kitchen. "No dinner?"

"It's nearly ten," Lana says, shaking her head. "There're leftovers in the fridge."

"Huh." I nod, eying the blocked off stovetop and fridge.

Seeing my predicament, the pair send the dogs out the door, freeing me to cook.

"You guys ready?" I ask.

"As much as we can be," Richard answers for them both. "I'm just glad that Leonard is certain the infected Frakin won't be poisonous for the dogs."

"Oh." I pause in heating up the stir-fried rice. I never even thought about how we'd be feeding their pets.

"And you, John?" Lana asks.

"This is what I do, babe." I turn around to flash her a cocky smile and a wink.

The redhead looks startled for a moment before bursting out laughing, Richard joining her.

"Please. Don't do that ever again," Richard says, shaking his head. "It really doesn't suit you."

I snort, face collapsing as I turn back to my leftovers. They're still chuckling behind me, and I find myself smiling slightly. As I'm busy and awkwardly placed to carry on the conversation, they end up recounting stories of their shared childhood and their dad's sense of humor. Really? Putting Lana's first set of car keys in Jell-O was meant to be funny?

When I'm ready, I walk back to the table with the plates of food and plop myself onto my seat before pushing a pair of plates out to them. I don't even have to ask if they'll be joining me—putting food in front of System-enhanced fighters is a guarantee of it being consumed.

As we eat, we talk, all of us avoiding the topic of our upcoming delve. Everything that needs to be said has been said or will be said. In time, Mikito joins us, pointing out that our increasingly loud conversation is keeping her up, before she snags a potato. For a time, we just talk and eat, worries about tomorrow pushed aside. The past is pain, the future uncertainty. The present is all we have, and staring at my friends, it's enough.

Chapter 20

"I really wish the weather would make up its mind," Richard grumbles as he stomps through the slush pile of mud and snow as we finally reach the dungeon.

Fun thing about being in the Yukon in mid-November—the temperature doesn't always stay beneath zero. So all that snow we received in the last few weeks—it's melting on its own, leaving the ground a mushy, slimy mess.

I duck my head to hide my smile as I walk easily on Sabre's armored legs, then I realize he can't see me beneath my helmet anyway. Tromping through the underbrush in the mecha is easy and doesn't involve getting my feet muddy. Of course, Richard could try riding one of his pets like Lana and Mikito are doing with hers, but Richard seems happier just grumbling.

When we finally reach the dungeon, I marvel at the changes since my last entry. A wall of concrete and earth has been thrown up around the entrance, and a pit faces the entrance. In a snaking path to the dungeon, stone spears stick out, making sure that no monster can get a running start to their jumps. Just outside the entrance, there's a clear area to allow our dungeon parties to gather. Of course, that ground has been heavily mined. Four watchtowers are set along the wall, mostly to allow the guards to watch for incoming threats from the wilderness. Each watchtower also holds one of the four shield generators and beam canons we've borrowed from the city defenses.

The entrance is as well guarded as we can make it. If things go to hell, we'll need to rely on these defenses to save our asses. I survey the area once more before I dump the drones and signal repeaters out from my Altered Space for everyone else to grab. People stream in in spurts over the next fifteen minutes, picking up their extra gear before grabbing some last-minute rest.

"Lana?" I murmur.

She looks up at me from where she works, stroking and petting her pets. "John." There's a hint of wariness in her voice.

"Be careful. Watch the sides and remember, your pets are there to keep you safe."

For a moment, her lips tighten before she smiles and kisses my cheek. "Yes, Dad."

I sigh, really wishing she didn't have to come. Really, I wish none of us was here, but that's the nature of our lives now. As Richard walks up, I nod to him and murmur, "Watch out for her, will you?"

"Of course." He shoots me a disdainful look and I accept it. She is, after all, his sister. "You're the one up front and center."

I nod then turn away, looking over the gathered group one last time. Arrayed before me are warriors and mages, fighters and healers, my allies and enemies, because I asked them to be here, because I said it was necessary.

To one side, Aiden leans against a nearby tree as he finishes throwing up. Mikito rubs the older man's back in an attempt to comfort him. Jim is walking among his people, talking softly and bolstering spirits. The Yerick squat, playing a game of stones that seems to consume their attention, but occasionally they glance at the dungeon entrance. There's a hush among the group, a stillness that makes people speak softly, as if speaking loudly would break the spell of peace and signal the start of what we all fear.

I spot Jason standing next to Rachel, their hands clasped. He sees me and mouths, "Not a game."

I nod. No, this isn't a game, and I wonder how many of these people will be dead before the day is over. As I think that, I note the new blips that have appeared on my minimap.

"Everyone, play nice. We've got incoming friendlies. Friendlies," I repeat, hitting the external mic to ensure that everyone hears me. Don't want anyone shooting the Hakarta as they make their way to us.

Twenty-five large infantry soldiers walk through the trees. They move in formation without thought, spread out in a way that screams organization even to me. Six and a half feet tall at the shortest, some going up to seven, and all broad across the shoulders. Their mottled green-and-brown camouflaged armor blends in with the surroundings as the group stomps forward, beam rifles and plasma grenades strapped to their bodies.

"John." A hand touches armor and strikingly intelligent eyes meet my gaze. "Sorry we're late. We had a small delay coming in."

I step forward, offering my hand to Labashi. "Not at all. Surprised you're here, and with so many others." Unspoken is the point that I can't afford him or the additions.

"Orcs? The Hakarta are orcs?" Jason splutters, staring at the group, and Rachel squeezes his hand to shut him up. He quiets down, though not without adding, "At least they're Uruk-hai."

"My employer decided he was not interested in having an infected dungeon in his territory," Labashi says, his eyes twinkling with amusement. "We are here at his request."

I consider that then shake my head. Well, seems like Labashi has figured out a way to get paid twice for this job. Vir stiffens slightly at the mention of Labashi's employer but says nothing. I really do wish someone would fill me in on the subtext here at some point.

Capstan walks forward, offering Labashi his hand. As Labashi grips Capstan's arm, I see Capstan's forearm muscles bunch before his eyes tighten, Labashi never losing that smile of his.

"First Fist, I am Labashi Ruka, Major of the Sixty-Third Division. I understand you are in command here?"

Hand released, Capstan surreptitiously flexes his fingers as he answers. "Yes, I am. Have you read the briefing notes? Do you have any last-minute recommendations?"

Labashi smiles slightly, nodding. "I might have a few."

I sigh as Vir moves forward to join the duo. Leaving the group to it, I climb the staircase to the top of the wall, surprised to find a pair of Hakarta up there already. They're releasing a series of small spider-like drones, sending them into the entrance and the dungeon without a word.

Well, this might go better than I thought.

***

Thankfully, the discussion takes less than an hour. Whether it's the fact that Labashi knows what he's doing or that the plans are already in place, it doesn't take long for the call to gather to come. I've sent out my own drones already, though the amount of data I'm getting pales in comparison to the constant data stream the Hakarta have. Tim's speaking softly to one of the Hakarta, working to get their equipment to sync up with our signal boosters.

There's a pair of Frakin in the main passageways and only scattered numbers farther in. Not enough to consider a threat and it's only on closer inspection that we realize why—these are dungeon-born Frakin that aren't infected yet. We've yet to see an infected Frakin, which is a bit worrying.

Everyone's a bit tense from the additional delay, but once we get moving, the tension ratchets up even further. A couple of Hakarta and Yerick, Bill's raven-haired friend, and Stupid from the bar play scouts, ghosting in ahead of us to eyeball for trouble that the drones might have missed. After all that talk of not being high enough level, Jim finally relented and is bringing in a pair of his hunting groups.

The rest of us move as a group at first, then parties split up, heading down each of the passageways. Signal boosters are added, providing us better and better coverage, but even the boosters can only do so much. At a certain point, we're going to lose contact. As the parties leave, I hear more than one happy comment that the dungeon is both dry and warm. While higher Constitutions might mean we can handle lower temperatures better, it's still not comfortable. At least, not for anyone who isn't fully covered in high-grade, temperature-controlling armor.

Bill, Vir, Labashi, Capstan and me are the heavy hitters and have to hang back, ready to hammer any resistance into the ground. That leaves Nelia and Aron under-powered, so Lana and Aiden join them while Richard and Mikito get Amelia, Rachel, and Jason. Gadsby couldn't come. Carcross needed at least one of their powerhouses in town and he drew the short straw.

In the end, the heavy hitters end up strolling along behind everyone else, watching the data and feeds while the others do all the work. We never hit more than a few Frakin at a time and those that we do fight aren't infected.

The longer this takes, the more antsy I get, and I eventually find myself chewing through chocolate bar after chocolate bar to find something to do. Labashi steals a few, though he, like the others, is focused on coordinating the search parties. Even Bill looks bored, though he mostly suffers in silence. I'm pretty sure he's just pissed that Vir dispatched a pair of guards to ensure he made it today.

***

Four and a half hours later, we're four main caverns in and finally taking a break. We've got three quarters of the groups deployed covering side passages, waiting for the Scouts to clear the passageways before they move on. While we rest, drones scurry around on their automated tasks, bringing more and more details about the dungeon back to us when they get back into sensor range.

"It seems the Spores have pulled back," Capstan says.

He doesn't look happy, and I completely agree. We're stretched thin already, covering the passages we've found, and it's been slow going since we try to keep sufficient coverage on each split group that they're able to pull back if they encounter resistance. The fact that they all have drones and scouts ahead of them helps. Still, our experience with the Frakin means we can't rely on that entirely.

We're pretty sure by now that there are at least three major passages leading farther in. The Frakin that holed up off the first branch are gone entirely, and that cavern eventually joins up with the main branch in main cavern number three. Now we're following one passage from cavern two and another from this cavern, not including the third that we've designated the main route. Each of these main passageways is so big, it'd take at least two groups to cover fully. Thus far, none of these passageways have shown to meet up, so we're stuck waiting for the drones to give us an idea of what it is we're looking for, while hoping they aren't completely destroyed.

"Yes," Labashi says. "Fall back to Cavern Two?"

"Yes," Capstan answers.

I sigh. Pushing ahead to this cavern was always a risk, since we haven't explored all the corridors fully, but it was a risk we were willing to take to see if we could find the Frakin faster. However, now that we've pretty much confirmed that we've got multiple main passageways, pushing ahead means leaving more area to guard. It's better to back off and finish checking the first branch fully before we do anything else.

Once we've dropped a few drones, we pull back and get back to waiting. For all the dreams of a slam-bang, balls-to-the-walls fight, all that has happened is a tense, slow, grinding wait.

***

Bored. I find myself next to Bill as we wait for something, anything to happen. I look the man over before I finally decide to say something. "You're a bit of a dick, aren't you?"

"Are you trying to start a fight?" Bill says, glaring at me.

Capstan shoots me a glare too, and I raise my hand in surrender.

"Sorry. Let's try that again. You're not much of a team player, are you?"

"I'm a very good team player. I'm just more selective about my team than some people," Bill states and turns to face me.

I grunt at his reply. Fine. Fine. So… "Enforcer, eh? Interesting Class."

"How…?" Bill's lips thin and I smile at him. He shrugs, answering the unasked question. "I was a bouncer before all this. I guess the System thought this was appropriate."

"Yeah…" I reply, not really meaning anything by it. I cudgel my brain for something else to say to fill the time, but I find nothing.

Bill snorts, shaking his head, and turns from me. I sigh. Fine. I guess we really don't have much to say to one another.

***

"Should we be thinking about calling it a day?" I wonder, staring at the glowing icons that make up our people in my map.

It's been another four hours and we're once again spread out across a wide distance. The Hakarta have reported losing over a quarter of their drones so far. We occasionally find the drones on the ground, shorted out from Mana overload or destroyed by the Frakin or one of the few other, smaller monsters that have begun to spawn in the absence of the Spore-dominated ecosystem.

After finding an extremely narrow, single-person corridor at the end of the second passageway in the first cavern, the First Fist decided to post a party and have us move forward with the search. Now, the majority of us are sitting in the fourth cavern with search parties headed down both passageways in an attempt to locate the Frakin. Hours of being on edge, of waiting for the other shoe to drop has made almost everyone tired. Only Capstan, Vir, Labashi, and I seem to be functioning at full capacity, probably due to our high mental resistances and Willpower. Everyone else is moving just a little slower.

As Capstan opens his mouth to answer me, a cackle comes through our communicators. "Frakin! We have Frakin!"

We don't need to ask who it is. Though of course Labashi does with a light growl. Since one party is filled with Yerick and humans and the other the professional Hakarta, the unprofessional report of trouble can only come from the humans.

I want to go, I want to fight, but Capstan shakes his head as he sees me edge toward the passageway. He stands there, arms crossed, waiting for more information to come in.

No surprise that more details come from his people. "Fifty Frakin hidden in a side cavern that the drones missed. We have them contained, First Fist. No aid required."

I find myself relaxing. Bill smirks, returning to the game of solitaire he's been playing for hours. Capstan asks for a little more information, but with things in hand, I find my mind drifting. I'm not entirely sure what the Spores' game plan is, but the fact that it's taken us nearly a whole day to make any form of substantial contact makes me lean toward scenario three. Not good, not good at all.

The battle doesn't take that long, probably only five minutes before it's all over. When the report comes in, we confirm it's infected Frakin, but nothing of unusual size. They do note that these aren't the plasma-wielding Frakin I fought before—these released caustic clouds of acid that ate through and damaged armor. Luckily, the mages were able to keep the gas mostly contained so it was only the melee fighters who suffered.

The side cavern dealt with, the group continues to search for trouble, obviously invigorated by the encounter. I wish I could say the same for us, stuck waiting as we are.

Capstan stands there, looking at the ceiling and presumably his system information. Coming to a decision, Capstan lowers that horned head of his and speaks into our communicators. "Pull back. Leave sensors. We're stopping for the night."

There's a rustle from those around us, but the professionals take action immediately. Even the humans don't actually object to packing it in. While we might not have been doing this for as long as the others, we've learnt a few lessons in the apocalypse.

***

Later that evening, I'm sitting next to Richard and Mikito, resting against the comfortable bulk of a puppy as I eat our rehydrated dinners. Not the tastiest form of sustenance, but I'll take it over the green goo that the Hakarta are busy squeezing out of their tubes. I guess ready meals the Galaxy over just aren't particularly tasty. Or I could be wrong and the green goo is a cultural delicacy. Certainly the Hakarta are taking to their meals with gusto. The Yerick in their own groups have set up small frying pans and are busy lightly frying up various vegetables, some recognizable and others significantly less so. Coming from a Chinese family, I've eaten a wider variety of foodstuff than most, but even I draw the line at lurid, neon-purple seaweed-like vegetables.

"Not what I was expecting," Richard says, gesturing around the group.

We've got Mana lights set up all around us, illuminating the bare cavern while shield generators and sensors cover all our entrances and the areas we've cleared. No reason to let the monsters sneak in on us while we're resting.

"What? Camping in the middle of a dungeon and waiting for a swarm of monsters to fall on you not to your liking?" Jason says sarcastically, Rachel snuggled between his legs.

Rachel playfully smacks his arm, and I smile slightly at the two teenagers, glad they've found something good among all this.

"Don't forget eating with orcs and Minotaurs," Aiden adds dryly.

Mikito smiles slightly at the banter, though she stays silent, working through a series of bento boxes of food. She gets more than a few longing stares at her packed dinners. For a moment, I wonder if it's a good thing that she's spending time doing more mundane things rather than constantly training or hunting monsters.

Once again, I wish I had a real psychotherapist on hand. It'd be nice to have someone trained to ask about how my friends are handling the stresses of the Apocalypse, whether Mikito's getting better or just about to jump off the cliff. We could use the Shop, but the problem with System-purchased information—it was information, not actual skill. For that matter, while a few skills are purchasable, they're all generic. I'm not entirely sure training to deal with Hakarta or an AI or whatever Xev's race is will translate to human psychology. Then again, I might be overthinking things. Trauma is trauma, right? Certainly the psychotherapy that Richard was taking worked. Is taking?

Coming back from watch, Lana flops down next to me, stretching out her long legs and prodding at the armored carapace of Sabre. "How can you stand sitting in that?"

"Surprisingly comfortable actually. I've slept in it before when I've been in the wild. Makes it hard for monsters to chomp on you."

She shakes her head. "Give." Lana holds out her hand, and I frown. "Chocolates."

"You know, you could buy your own," I grumble, handing her some.

Floating above me, Ali makes a whipping motion with his hand while I roll my eyes at him. A moment later, I'm dispensing chocolate all around to expectant hands. Lucky for me, I buy a ton. Labashi, noting what I'm doing, wanders over and holds out his giant green hand.

"You too?" I ask.

"Consider it part payment." Labashi grins.

I sigh, pulling out some of the Belgian chocolates he likes and passing it over. He gestures to a spot next to me and I nod, watching as the others scramble away a bit. Well, everyone but Jason, who is staring openly at the Hakarta.

"You did well out there," Labashi says, nodding to my group. A few people look startled then happy at his compliment. "It is impressive, considering how long the System has been in effect."

I nod slightly, but it's Richard who speaks. "So I heard you mention your employer. Who is he?"

"You do not expect me to actually answer that, do you?" Labashi says.

Richard looks disappointed.

"Her Grace Wuli Kangana, Duchess of the Pourquoi States," Vir says, having come up to join the group. He eyes everyone eating the chocolates but makes no request for any. "She also currently owns and controls both the Village of Fairbanks and the Town of Anchorage."

Seeing my brow furrow, Lana leans over and whispers, "Whitehorse is still a Village in the System's eyes."

I nod dumbly while Ali concentrates, staring into the distance. In a few seconds, I see a notification that I've got System windows waiting for me. At a guess, details about the duchess. I wonder how bad the translations are of her titles—something else to dig into at some point.

"Really?" Aiden frowns, rubbing his nose. "Are infected dungeons that dangerous?"

"Yes." Labashi nods. "A normal Spore infection is limited, the numbers forced to slowly grow. A dungeon gives the Spores a chance to continuously reproduce and grow, and on a dungeon world, it would be a simple matter to infect even more dungeons. It is much easier to deal with earlier than later."

Vir nods, letting his body relax as he stands there watching the group. I hear Jason ask another question about the Hakarta, which I find myself ignoring. I've always wondered why the Hakarta were checking us out, and while this sheds some light, it's not a lot.

As much as the explanation by Labashi makes some sense, I still don't believe that an infected dungeon could spread that fast to make it a threat to Fairbanks any time soon. Certainly not before the System stabilizes and Adventurers start pouring in. If I'm right, it means that she's got plans much closer to the dungeon. Vir meets my unfocused gaze and nods once, as if confirming my guesses. Great, we just settled City politics and now we've got Galactic politics to deal with. Somehow, I don't think shouting at them and threatening them with body odor will work as well.

Capstan walks up, grumbling at the group and sending us to bed down before the start of our shifts. The Yerick is right—we best get some rest. As it stands, we'll probably have a pretty nasty fight soon.

Chapter 21

"Contact!"

The word comes over the communicators, jerking us straight. Finally. We've spread out across three different openings, and down a side route, they've finally come into contact again.

"They haven't seen the drone," Aron says, watching the feed.

Ali has slaved a status screen to the drone, so I watch the hundreds of the Frakin packed into the cavern. Strangely, they aren't all staying still like before. Instead, some are skittering around in aimless circles. Occasionally a Frakin nears the entrance before it jerks to a stop and returns to its aimless movements.

"Going deeper," Aron says as he controls the drone.

Behind, barely a few hundred meters back, the teams that have been tasked to clear this passageway have stopped, waiting further orders.

Capstan stares at the information coming in before he turns to Labashi. "Send two of your parties to reinforce. We will hold here."

Labashi nods, barking out orders. His men split off and trot toward the opening at speed. I grit my teeth, frustrated at being forced to wait again.

"Incoming, boy-o," Ali says, flashing my screen for me, and I frown.

Everyone hears and turns, scanning their own screens as a lone Frakin totters down the main passageway toward us. It walks right past the drone without seeing, its movements erratic.

"Kill it?" I ask, gesturing down the way. Easy pickings.

"This feels wrong," Labashi says, eyes narrowed. "It's infected."

"Yeah…"

"It's a scout," Labashi clarifies for those of us who aren't following him.

Capstan nods and sends a Yerick to deal with the scout far from our position.

"More contacts," Ali reports, eyes narrowing as he sifts through the scattered data. We've got sensors spaced out even farther than the drones, but they aren't giving particularly good data, not with the amount of Mana interference we're getting this deep into the dungeon. "A lot more."

"Fall in," Capstan barks.

I walk forward to squat behind my assigned wall. Minor changes to the cavern have given us a raised stone wall that should slow down the Frakin. For a quarter second maybe. On the other hand, a quarter second at the speeds we fight can be a long time.

Bill joins me on my right, and I glance over. I note he's a left-hander, so I shuffle to the left a bit more to give us more space. Not that he's using a melee weapon yet, instead hefting a pair of modified futuristic beam pistols.

Ali floats over to my left and just above head, barely within my line of sight as he continues to stare at the screens. "Drone's broken into the second cavern. More Frakin." He frowns. "Feed's getting pretty jumpy, I don't think we'll get a proper count there…"

I nod, hefting my beam rifle as I watch the incoming dots on my minimap. Now that they're closer, the drone is picking them up on visual too, their lines staggered and jerky. The Frakin move forward, then occasionally, one or another Frakin will stop or turn around. They aren't the imposing wall of flesh that we encountered the last time.

"Looks like your virus is working," Bill says, watching the feed as well.

I nod and shoot a glance at the man, wondering how much I can trust him. There's no real way to fake Levels, so he's obviously got some skills. Doesn't mean he won't break if things get too hectic.

"They're moving," Capstan growls, his eyes locked on the screens.

I glance back. Vir and Labashi are standing next to the command group, heads turning slightly as they watch the feeds before they nod. A quick glance is all I need to confirm it—the Frakin on the other feeds are moving, heading straight for Lana and Richard. I grit my teeth, knowing Mikito has their back. All I can do is trust...

"You might want to focus here," Bill chides me, opening fire now that the Frakin are within range. His shots go into the darkness, but I hear flesh sizzling as beam weaponry punches through Frakin bodies. Those pistols are impressive.

My turn. I open fire, a second slower than everyone else on the front line, at the targets highlighted in my vision. A veritable rainbow of beam weaponry lights up the cavern, mixed with fast-moving projectiles that smash into the monsters before us, turning the monsters into so much slurry. We probably waste half our shots on already dead creatures.

"Who told you to shoot?" snaps Vir, striding up and shaking his head. "Wait until the order is given."

Shooting stops, more than a few of us looking sheepish. Vir just watches as the Frakin close the distance. When they're a hundred meters from us, he finally gives the order to resume shooting, staggering our fire so we don't waste our ammunition.

As I thought, the pistols Bill uses are special, upgraded up the wazoo by the Shop and then possibly augmented by Skills. Each of his shots does a significant chunk of damage, burning through Frakin defenses with ease. The rest of us don't have such spectacular results, but the sheer volume of fire and the lack of cohesion in their charge is enough to make this a cakewalk.

At least until we start running out of ammunition. I see the flickering numbers as my Mana battery runs down, my remaining shots dropping at a precipitous rate. Bill slows down his shooting too, and I see others along the line slap in new batteries. The gap in fire is small, the slowdown even smaller, but suddenly the Frakin aren't being held but are inching forward. Second by second, the line creeps forward, each new corpse a few feet closer to us.

"Hold."

The ending is ragged, a few last shots sent out after the command is given, but we eventually all stop shooting. The Frakin don't react much to the sudden cessation of fire, not until a few seconds have passed, then they're suddenly sprinting to us. I see a few hasty shots as hunters react to the danger, but I hold my fire, knowing what comes next.

"Ice spells," Vir commands.

Elemental spells fly over our heads, targeting the charging Frakin. Blizzard winds howl, dropping the temperature and coating monsters in snow and ice. Bolts of absolute zero impact carapaces, turning them into popsicles that break apart under their own momentum. Small motes of white dust float forward, landing on monsters and freezing them. Spears of ice pin Frakin to the ground or tear off limbs as they fly by us. All those spells and more rain down on the creatures at Vir's command.

"Fire," Vir commands, and the mages switch.

Previously frozen creatures are heated up as walls of flame erupt from the ground. Pellets of plasma fall from the cavern ceiling to smash into the monsters. Traditional fireballs are thrown, exploding in expanding spheres of superheated air. Whips of fire burst forth from the ground, catching Frakin and tearing through frozen shells. The chittering screams from the Frakin are drowned out in the roar of flames.

"This is easy." Bill smirks, and I almost hit him.

"These are the basic Frakin, idiot," Ali says. "Plasma Frakin coming in next…"

"Hold. Front line, get ready for incoming fire," Vir says.

I hear Vir step back. A quick glance shows that the mages are hunkered down beneath their own stone wall with additional coverage from portable shield generators.

Plasma Frakin push past normal Frakin, who refuse to enter the superheated passageway, closing on our line again. They totter over burning corpses, the bladed tips of their feet striking the ground as they rush forward.

Behind me, Vir finally gives the command. "Evens fire!"

The Plasma Frakin are dangerous, but they've got a shorter range than we do. We blow them up in the passageway, attempting to pile the bodies up to create an impromptu barrier from their corpses. The occasional extra fast or extra tough Frakin gets a bolt of plasma out before it's cut down, but a single bolt is nothing to the front-liners.

I even have time to glance at the drone feed from the other battle, enough time to tell that they're doing as well as we are. Things are going too easy. Way too easy.

"Ali…"

"I'm looking, boy-o, I'm looking," Ali replies, flicking his hands across his screens.

A quick glance tells me he's not the only one looking for the catch.

The Frakin stagger in at longer intervals, individual Frakin rather than the unorganized swarm. Vir designates shooters while the rest of us rest, checking over our ammunition. The short fight burnt through half of my Mana batteries, and I wonder how everyone else is doing. On the other hand, we probably stacked up over a hundred Frakin right.

It's not as if the Spores have shown extremely diverse tactics so far. Perhaps, just perhaps, all they're doing is trying to win a battle of attrition. For a moment, I let myself hope.

A snarl from Capstan gets my attention.

"They're behind us," Ali says, and I jerk my head up. He twitches a finger and I see the drone feed from behind us, showing the rushing monsters.

"How…?" Bill says. "We checked everything. There's no way they're back there."

"No idea," Ali replies, shaking his head.

Capstan is already calling out orders, splitting the teams to reinforce the back while the rest of us stay.

"They really like their pincer attacks," I grumble, and Ali nods.

In a moment, we don't have time to talk as the Frakin launch themselves at our defenses again. I find myself smiling grimly as I open fire. Tracking monsters and killing them has become so routine, I barely need to think about it. If the Spores think a simple pincer attack is enough to finish us, they're wrong.

The smell of ionized air, burnt flesh, and the excretions of the Frakin as they die clogs the air, and I mentally command the helmet to filter it all out. There's little I can do for the clatter of pincers on the ground and the screams of the Frakin as they die. We pile them up so high that the Frakin have to take time to pull down and shift bodies before they can come at us again.

Vir switches the attacks around more often, using the mages to hit the Frakin so we can husband our ammunition. Unlike many of the other front-line fighters, I'm carrying fewer Mana batteries, so I find myself switching over to throwing magic rather than shooting. I get a few raised eyebrows, but I've got the Mana to do so and I make sure not to let it drop below 80%. This is a marathon, not a sprint, especially with the numbers we've seen so far.

We hammer away at the Frakin. Plasma and normal Frakin are the majority, with the occasional acid-spitter, of the variations so far. It's a constant barrage of damage and spells, broken up only by Vir calling a rotation or when the bodies pile up so high that the Frakin have to pull them apart to continue their attack. In time, the drone feeding us information on our attackers stops sending us information, leaving us in the dark once again.

As the Frakin pull aside the next wall of bodies, I catch a glimpse of something new, a virulent purple, and I narrow my eyes, trying to spot it again. I only get a second before a new attack comes—blobs of barely-held-together purple sacs thrown from behind the wall of corpses. As they impact, the sacs split open. A greenish-purple liquid spills onto the ground and releases vapors. All around me, the humans begin choking and covering their faces. Bill slaps a hand outward, calling forth a gas mask, as do other humans. The fully armored Hakarta are safe in their suits and continue to fire. The Yerick just growl softly, fighting through the fumes without slacking off.

Even as gas masks protect against the primary effects, the secondary effects kick in, attacking any exposed body parts. The distraction is enough to make even the Yerick pause as they get proper armor on. The drop in fire means the Frakin surge ahead. I snarl, opening fire on full-auto with Sabre's projectile rifle, taking up the slack. Black lightning and fireballs surge past my head as mages behind me lend a hand.

Out of the corner of my eye, I see a hunter pop up, helmet down and gloves on, to receive a sac straight in the face. It splits on top of him, covering his entire body. I see the liquid eat away at his armor even as Vir grabs his body and tosses him into the backlines.

The combined fire by the mages and the humans quickly establishes a new deadlock. Unfortunately, the Spores aren't done with their surprises. Shouldering aside a pair of poisonous Frakin, a silver-steel creature charges forward. Beams of light bounce off its body, doing little damage and adding to the confusion of battle. Even as I target it, another of the oversized bugs appears, then another. Explosive projectiles do damage, splitting open the armored hide, but a single gun isn't enough. Even as the humans recover, the creatures bear down on us.

Almost, I trigger my missiles. Almost. Before I can, rock spears rise up, impaling monsters and hindering their approach. It buys us a few moments, enough time for the mages to send a breeze in to clear out some of the fumes and for the rest of the humans to get their gear on. Even the Yerick finally take the time to fully gear up, slapping on a small triangular patch that sets up a low-level repelling field. I make a mental note to look into that in the future as I lob a fireball into the cavern. Vir moves from group to group, shifting our fields of fire so that each section has a mix of firepower, beams, and projectiles smashing into whatever monster decides to show its face.

As the rock spears get broken down by the Behemoth Frakin, more are thrown up by the mages behind us. A few quick additions of fast-set glue grenades turns the new bodies into a new obstacle the Frakin have to fight through, which gives us time to rest and recover.

Our front covered, I glance at my map and screens to see how things are going in the other locations and flinch. I forcibly make myself hold still even as I watch the red dots overwhelm the friendly blues in the corridor. Not just any blues—those dots contain Lana, Richard, and Mikito. Behind us, Aron and Labashi's timely intervention has driven back the monsters long enough at least for the backline to recover.

"Trust in them, John," Ali says.

I nod dumbly. Even if I took off right this second, I'd be minutes away from the group, long minutes when the Frakin could finish them. I just have to trust that my friends can handle themselves. I watch the minimap and the sudden disappearance of a large number of red dots, then the reformation of the blue line farther back.

"They're retreating," I mutter, staring at the map.

Ali offers a nod of confirmation. The blue dots don't stop backing off even when the line reforms, the red dots surging forward constantly as my teammates lay down withering fire. I glance backward as Vir calls for the mages to take a break and give their Mana a rest. I have a moment to contemplate the sight of Capstan in huddled conversation with Labashi before I have to start shooting again. I've spent enough time with the Yerick by now to be able to tell that he's worried.

The introduction of the two new types of Frakin is forcing us to drain our ammo, stamina, and Mana at an even greater rate. Even with potions to increase the last two, strained and worried looks have begun to creep onto the human faces. The Hakarta are impossible to read under their masks, but even the Yerick occasionally seem nervous. We've been fighting nonstop for hours, and the monsters just keep coming.

Five, ten minutes and the Frakin shift tactics again. Instead of sending a single type of monster at us, the Spores mix it up, sending groups. This makes no difference really, as we concentrate on our firing lines, focusing on killing the ones in our fields of fire rather than what they are. A part of me is thankful for the experienced fighters here; otherwise, we might just have fallen for the change.

Equilibrium is achieved again, at least on the front lines. I've switched back to my rifle when I can, letting Sabre reload the projectile rifle during much-needed breaks and pulling additional ammunition from my Altered Space for Sabre. When I can, I flick my gaze back and forth between the front lines, my companions, and the map.

Equilibrium on the front lines, but not in our fast-draining Mana and ammunition.

The first cry comes from one of the Yerick, a snarling, "I'm out."

A moment later, his cry is echoed by a human. Then another, as guns fall silent. Vir snaps an order and the mages with earth spells throw up a temporary blockade, buying us more time at the cost of their Mana. We use it to reconfigure the front lines, staggering between melee and ranged fighters and the mages.

I can see the rearguard doing the same thing while my friends continue to retreat toward us at a glacially slow pace. They're still too far away to talk to them directly or view them via our drones.

"Ali, how are we doing?" I ask.

"Not good. Drones are mostly drained, but the few we've got around here aren't exactly seeing an end to these groups," he announces just before Capstan calls me over.

I follow and find Bill's raven-haired shadowy friend and Vir there too.

"They're pushing us too hard. Take a few minutes, then we're going with Plan F," Capstan announces.

I grimace. Plan F for Final Run. It's a Hail-Mary plan, one that we cooked up for use when and if the Spores and Frakin pushed us too hard. The three of us each have our own ways of getting through the hordes ahead. The plan is simple—while the others hold the monsters back, we'll rush in as far as we can, hoping to find and kill the Boss.

"That bad?"

"Yes. We're down to thirty percent of our reserves," Labashi clarifies, and I grimace.

I knew things were getting bad, but I hadn't realized it was that bad. That's the strange part of this fight. As hard as we're being pushed, no one has died on our lines so far and no one has stayed injured for long. Our unnatural healing and the Spells keep us in top fighting form—but that only lasts so long as we have enough ammo and Mana. Once we're out, the end comes soon after.

"We're uploading the latest scans from the drones to you now," Capstan adds. "May the stars guide your way."

Ali frowns, staring at the new information. He tilts his head as I walk to the side and pop open my helmet to scarf down some food. *"I'm heading out first. I can't get too far ahead of you, but if I push the edges, I might be able to lead you to the Boss."*

"Good idea," I reply, chewing rapidly.

Ali floats a bit away then stops, shifting on his feet a bit before he finally speaks. *"Take care, boy-o."*

Ali floats away before I can reply. I shake my head slightly, smiling grimly before glancing at the other two. They're getting ready—stretching in the lady's case and downing potion after potion in Vir's. I flicker a smile at that, his actions reminding me to take the potions I've reserved. These are the best regeneration boosters that Sally supplied.

"Ready?" Capstan rumbles.

We offer him a nod, standing up and facing the corridor. Last chance, last run. Damn…

***

"Plan F. Cover fire on three, two, one. Now!" roars Capstan. He raises his own axe-cannon, letting loose the blast he was charging while he was speaking.

His fire is joined by the mages', who have been holding back, vortex of destructive firepower ripping through the monsters that face us. The moment the fire slackens, the three of us are sprinting forward.

Covering fire from the sides flashes past us as guided weaponry and spells slam into still-living Frakin within the corridor, giving us a short, short few hundred meters of clear space. As we reach the first curve in the tunnel, we can see the Frakin boiling out of the corner. Vir's ahead of us all and he flashes forward, exploding into a white mist that floats through the group. His progress slows down significantly in that form, but they can't touch him.

Behind him, I jump and kick off a Frakin, my powered armor smashing the monster into the ground before I throw myself into a roll as I crash into the swarm. Even as I smash and bounce, I'm triggering the QSM and recovering on ultra-dimensional ground. A moment later, I watch as Bill's Assassin/Rogue friend turns into a literal shadow and disappear into the darkness.

On my minimap, I see Ali dashing ahead as fast as he can. As he spots new and interesting monsters and my map gets updated before they disappear again as he leaves their presence. Still, it's enough to let me know how much trouble we really are in—the swarm just doesn't seem to ever end.

I keep sprinting, my companions lost as we each make our way through the swarm. Powerful as these Skills or technological toys are, they all have their own timers. The moment they run out, if we're still in the swarm, we'll shrivel up like a plastic bag in flames. Our only hope is speed.

I thunder down the passageways, running through shadowy Frakin until I see something that makes me pause. I don't think, I just hammer the switch and flip back into reality, making sure I don't pop into anything too dense when I shift back. I'm already programming the drone, sending it winging back as I land and spin, using the built-up momentum to open up the Frakin

I spotted from abdomen to leg. It's a monster of a creature, three-quarters the size of the entire passageway itself, and its armor is so tough that without the added levels of my Soulbound sword, I probably couldn't even scratch it. The Frakin are slow to react, their senses scrambled by the illness, so I have a few moments to lay into the creature in peace. A few moments to tear a chunk into the creature's body and a few moments more to pull a grenade to plant in its body. The moment my hand is inside it and I've let go of the grenade, I trigger the QSM.

I run through the creature, three seconds barely enough time to get away before the explosion contained in the monster ripples outward. It buys the drone and my friends a few moments, since the Frakin will have to move the corpse. A few moments to get ready for the other three Titanic Frakin behind it. I don't have time to keep up this fight—in fact, draining the QSM to pop in and out like that might have been a bad idea.

Ahead, the tunnel splits and I take the right turn. It's the direction that Ali went. Even as I run, I unleash a lightning bolt, the energy from the Spell scarring the walls. I can only hope that it's a good enough indication for Vir and Shadow-girl to avoid this tunnel.

Four minutes into QSM with barely thirty seconds left and I finally pass the last of the Frakin. I dash past them all and the cavern they stream from, then I slide to a stop behind cover. Marginally hidden as I am, I kill the system, shifting over into my own dimension. I breathe raggedly, pulling in pure oxygen from Sabre's tanks as I recover, hoping that I'm hidden enough. I have to be—I don't have any other choice. Tucked in the corner as I am, the only sense I can rely on is my hearing. I find myself straining to hear something, anything that might tell me if I made it.

The drip of water, the skittering of insects and spiders, and the far-off tromp of Frakin are all that I sense. No sign of pursuit, no sign of my friends.

I slowly exhale, pushing away from my hiding spot, and head deeper, following the trail Ali blazed. I can only hope that the others are doing their job and searching for the Boss too.

"Boy-o, take the right. Dead end here."

I nod to Ali's instructions though he can't see me, doing as he says when I reach the split. I can see Ali flying back from the cavern that dead-ended on him, eager to catch up and take back his scouting duties. I can't wait for him, knowing that my friends are fighting with everything they've got behind me. I can't hear them or see them—even the updates to my map have stopped—but I know, I know, we're running out of time.

Time… I'm constantly fighting against it. I pick up the pace, dodging the occasional Frakin I spot curled up in a corner or wandering around, too sick to be controlled by the Spores. I'm moving so fast that I barely notice the immobile Frakin that comes alive the moment I bound over it.

Scouts. Or guards. Whatever the case, they know I'm here. On the other hand, guards probably mean I'm on the right track. I keep an eye out for more as I run, dodging from side to side as the Frakin behind me spits out bolts of destructive light. I turn the corner, finding myself hoping to run into more trouble. Trouble would be good.

My perverse desires rewarded in a few minutes with another sighting—a trio of Frakin that lie in wait. Their reactions are staggered, not coordinated, which is all that allows me to dodge through the barrage that opens up. The trick to actually dodging faster-than-sound attacks isn't to dodge the attacks themselves but to forecast and dodge around where they will fire. Bodies rise, mouths open, and glinting teeth reflect the building charge. I just make sure I'm never where they're pointing. It's a calculation I could never have made as a non-System-registered human—but with my upgraded abilities, it seems trivial. At least against three of these monsters.

I draw and send out a Blade Slash, the brilliant line of force slashing open the Frakin as I near them. I take a few moments to finish them off, figuring that I'd better deal with stragglers now rather than later. As it stands, I have a feeling I'm close.

"Ali, can you find the others?"

"Maybe. Don't you want me with you, boy-o?" the Spirit replies.

I shake my head. *"No, if you can get them or get close enough to get a message to them, that'd be better. Never know what kind of trouble I'll run into, and this looks like the way to the Boss."*

Left unsaid is the fact that if I fail, we need one of the others to succeed.

Down the hallway, as I close in on the upcoming cavern, my eyes widen. I guess they held back a couple dozen. I snarl, skidding to a stop. The sudden eruption of acid blobs, plasma bolts, and beams tell me that my arrival was expected. Crouching out of sight, I draw forth grenades and toss them in one after the other. I'm sure the Spores will send the Frakin to me eventually, once they realize what's happening, but it'll take time for them to figure it out and even more time to send the commands to the sick creatures. Time I can use to whittle down my opponents.

Explosions ripple outward from the cavern as I sling grenade after grenade, explosions and disappearing red dots telling the tale to me. Unfortunately, I can't kill enough of them before they're on me, trundling up the slight slope of the cavern to enter the passageway. I find myself fighting in the middle of a swarm again, sword spinning and cutting, moving from one hand to another as I cut, kick, and punch my way through the monsters. I know better than to hold still, so I dance into their midst. Blasts of plasma and globs of acid fly all around me. Pincers glance off my armor and add to my momentum. Don't stop—don't ever stop.

I find myself through the group, a pair of grenades in hand. I flip them into the center of the swarming mass, the resulting explosion barely muffled by the press of bodies. I hop backward, raising my rifle and spraying the remaining monsters on full-auto, dumping the entire magazine into them in a few seconds. I land, sword appearing in hand to deflect a spike of stone, as I scan my opponents. Only a half dozen left, most of them pretty damaged.

I flex my legs, dashing forward to finish this. Time to get rid of these minnows.

****

Finding the Boss Frakin and, hopefully, the core of the Spore mind is easy after that. There's only one passageway from here. As I sneak forward, I wonder how bad this is going to be.

Well, at least I know why the Spores haven't gotten much more active in spreading themselves—the Boss Frakin is so big, there's no way it could fit through the passageways. Of course, that also explains why the Spores have gotten so smart, if they've taken over that as their Overmind's body.

Eight legs, a double pair of pincers that fit over its bulbous body, three stingers, and more teeth than I have bullets make up the reddish-brown monster. Scrambling around it are more Frakin, maybe a dozen, that are each about double the size of a normal creature. And clustered around those are another score of smaller Frakin, a mix of glowing green, red, and purple stingers indicating a slew of nasty ranged options.

The fact that half the Frakin are watching my passageway and the other half are looking to my left has me giving the cavern a more thorough investigation. A moment later, I realize why—there's another entrance that way. Smaller, tighter, and more exposed than mine, but definitely another way in.

I draw a deep breath, exhaling as my mind runs. This is bad. This is more than I can handle. Certainly the Boss is a lot bigger than I ever expected. This—this is something I'd want my whole party to tackle.

On the other hand, it's not as if there's anyone else here to help me. If I want it dead, I'm going to have to do it. Biting my lip, I start planning.

Chapter 22

Five minutes later, I'm done. First step was to set up a few sensors down the way I came to ensure I have some warning when the monsters come for me. Sure, I could theoretically spot it in my minimap, but if I'm in the middle of a fight, I don't want to count on that.

Second step is to split their forces. No reason to try to fight all of them, not if I can help it. I tap into my Altered Space, grab the guns I stored there, and set them up quickly, along with more Claymore mines in two separate locations. I then push them outward and flick their targeting software on, watching as they spew fire at the monsters beneath me. I back off from the ledge and around cover as return fire comes in short order.

The guns last all of a few seconds before they get blown to pieces, which is the main reason why we didn't even bother setting them up for the swarm. However, they do what I wanted, which is attract attention and drag the Frakin to me. They come, but they come in force, nearly half the group that was watching my passageway rushing in.

I cast Polar Wind immediately, the Spell freezing and slowing the monsters as they trundle forward. It does very little damage, unlike the high explosive projectiles I unleash next, but it buys me time and, more importantly, bunches them up. When the vanguard is past the immediate blast area, I trigger the Claymores.

Only two thirds of the Claymores go off unfortunately—it seems they aren't rated to handle the intense cold brought about by my Spell. Pressurized air and thousands of ball bearings spin outward, confined in the passageways so that even those that miss on the first pass have a second, third, and even fourth chance to kill and damage. Of course, even backed off as I am, I get smashed by a few too, but Sabre's armor is more than sufficient to take the bouncebacks with little additional damage.

Once the explosion dies down a little, I wade into the group, cutting and chopping and firing into open wounds. Fun fact—screwed-up, System-enabled world or not, you can still do more damage by shooting into exposed wounds than you can just shooting indiscriminately. Of course, it isn't that easy—the Frakin Champions are true monsters, big and tough, and even injured, they put up a good fight. At the end of it, I'm limping and Sabre's down to eighty-two percent integrity. As my bullets get reloaded, I cast a quick Healing to speed up the recovery process for myself.

Stage two done, I poke my head around the corner carefully before pulling back as shots come within seconds. It's enough to let me know that not much has changed, other than a redistribution of the monsters inside. I scurry to the side then poke my head out again, noting they aren't coming up. My precautions are of little use as the Boss decides to let loose a blast from its stinger. The explosion throws me into the wall and backward down the corridor. I groan, seeing the flashing damage icons.

Stage three it is then.

I wish I could say I have a brilliant, mind-shatteringly smart idea. I don't. I don't even have a particularly good idea. All I have is a bunch of explosives, my Spells, and the need to finish this off. I take a running start, crossing the ground to the entrance of the cavern as Frakin continue to lob attacks at it occasionally. As I near, I Blink Step into the air, bypassing the additional reflexive fire that comes at where I should be if I exited normally. This gives me more than enough time to launch my first set of missiles into the gathered Frakin, and I watch the missiles throw up flame, dirt, and blood below me. Even as I land, I'm casting Polar Wind with one hand and snatching smoke grenades to toss onto the ground with the other.

As I sprint to the side, I keep my head swiveling, tagging monsters in my display with a thought as I keep dropping the temperature via Polar Wind. I have to keep them on their toes, keep rocking them with sudden changes and new tactics, so that I can fight them piecemeal and whittle them down. As the smoke grenades begin to fill the air, I add my last additional toy to the battle—high-tech white phosphorous grenades. I throw the self-propelled grenades into the air, where they split apart, each separate portion tracking their pre-selected targets. The portions attach before igniting the phosphorous and directing the burning substance into the creatures at 2760°C, or about half the surface temperature of the sun.

The Frakin go crazy, the incendiaries burning through their chitin and ticking down their health. Of course, the System does reduce the amount of actual physical damage based off their health points, but pain is the major goal here.

Instinct makes me trigger Blink Step and not a moment too soon, as the Boss's stinger smashes into the column of stone I was hiding behind. As I reappear, I spin around and trigger my rifle, going full-auto into the creature's side. The Boss is a weird image of wireframe outlines, infrared shading, and normal vision as my helmet compensates for reduced visibility. I'm targeting a single spot—just below the second pair of legs. where the creature's heart is. If I can chew through enough of its armor, I just might be able to do some real damage. My heart thuds faster, my breathing shortening slightly as I recall the stinger, but I don't have time.

I keep moving, opening fire with rifle and missiles, leaving my sword to cut and slice monsters as I dance through the cavern, always trying to keep my target in sight. Occasionally I toss a sticky grenade at a monster that nears me, capturing and locking it in place. Unfortunately, I forget I'm fighting a thinking creature and my movements are too predictable.

As I lop off the leg of a Champion Frakin, the Boss's pincer catches me and throws me into a wall. It's only the reduced visibility and its sickness that makes the Boss's next swing mostly miss, the pincer smashing into my upper left side and crushing Sabre's shield, sending me careening off in a different direction. Lucky for me—otherwise the follow-up blast from the other stinger might have finished me off.

My ears are ringing and I can taste blood as I slowly look up. The Frakin Boss isn't stopping though, rushing toward me as I stagger to my feet. I need time, so I slap on my Mana Shield just in time for one of the Plasma Frakin's blasts to be caught on it. I trigger Blink Step again, wincing as my Mana pool drops once more.

A glance at the Boss Frakin is all I need to tell me that this isn't working. Fighting a monster like this head-on was a vain hope, but it's not as if I had a choice. Somewhere back there, my friends are fighting, maybe dying. I have to finish this.

Of course, wishing something will happen doesn't mean that it will, and all I've got right now is a lot of wishes and dreams. Running to the side, sword slashing out against the monsters, I stare at the blinking icons indicating that I've loaded everything I have. Once I shoot this, I'm done— then I'm down to hacking and cutting at the Boss.

"Keep it busy for another minute, boy-o." Ali's dry tone almost makes me shout in joy.

I nod, thinking a confirmation as I switch directions, running straight into the incoming pair of Champion Frakin. I catch one of their stingers on the sword, spin around with its momentum to help me dodge the second, then Blink Step away as the blast from the Boss's stinger turns the Champions into so much crispy meat. A wavefront of the blast catches me, tossing me to the ground. I roll with it and spin up, loosing a short burst that tears open and ends the Acid Frakin rearing above me. Warning lights blink as the damn acid eats into Sabre, but I'm up and running again.

I trigger Blink Step, watching my Mana plunge as I flicker to a spot that gives me a view of the Boss monster. Or will, I hope, as I fire the missiles. The monster spins just like I figured it would. Or perhaps I should say its reactions to my previous actions are predictable. Either way, it puts itself perfectly in position to receive the full load of mini-missiles into its side, each tiny guided package impacting and ripping deeper and deeper into the Boss's torso.

In anger, the monster swings down a pincer to crush me and I don't have time to dodge. Instead, I conjure my sword and take the blow on it, gripping the blade with my other armored hand as the weight of the monster bears down on me. Power-assisted knees buckle and pain shoots up my thighs as I crumple, the too-sharp edge of my blade having cut through the monster's chitin such that the rest of the pincer smashes into me. Oops…

Warning lights shriek all around me and I whimper slightly, the ringing in my head having gotten so much worse. My sword, still embedded in the pincer gets taken into the air as the monster withdraws its appendage, leaving me in a crumpled camel pose. I watch in slow motion as the monster aims its glowing, beam-casting stinger at me even as I attempt to scramble away. The explosion of light and sound that comes from the side catches both of us by surprise.

A red beam of light with twisting green and white streams erupts from the second entrance, smashing into the creature with such force that its own beam is jerked aside and played across a trio of unlucky Frakin charging toward me. I stumble to my feet as the maelstrom of energy digs into the monster's side and tears off a stinger and two legs, ripping a giant hole in the Boss's body. The legs flop to the ground, still twitching, as blood spills in a waterfall, just like the Boss's health bar. The beam adjusts and continues to burn through the monster. A bare fifth of its health is all that's left when the beam finally stops, but the Boss is still standing.

I snarl, dodging to the side as a Champion Frakin staggers up to me. I recall my sword, cut at its pincers, and when a chance comes, I call up Cleave to help shear off a pincer entirely. I do all this while my brain switches to overdrive, trying to figure out what other options we have left.

"Ali, who was that? And can they do it again?" I find myself mentally shouting as I work to finish off this monster.

"Vir and no can do. He's tapped. Whoops! Sorry, those beams can hurt even me— got to do some dodging here. He's switching over to his guns, but that ain't going to cut it."

I grunt, stabbing my sword directly into the monster's mouth. *"Shadow-girl?"*

"The assassin? No idea—I haven't seen her."

Shit, if she doesn't find her way here herself, there's no way Ali can find her and make it back in time. It's a minor miracle he found Vir.

Too busy paying attention to my talk, I move just a little too slow and the damn Frakin chomps down on my arm. It compresses the armor around me, grinding away, and I snarl, summoning and casting Mana Darts directly down its guts. The Champion shudders, tossing me aside with a reflexive twitch that has me landing on my side and rolling for a few seconds.

I use a nearby stalagmite to pull myself up, grimacing as I flex my hand. Thankfully, the Boss, along with the majority of the surviving monsters, is busy making Vir's life miserable. The smoke has dissipated enough that the creatures are finding me faster and faster now. On the other hand, at least the bugger who decided to try to eat me is dead. Mana Darts down its throat was enough to make it choke to death.

I blink, staring at the Boss. I have a way to finish this. It just requires I do something utterly insane. Well… that's not new.

***

"Oy! Big boy!" I shout, using the mecha's inbuilt speakers to make sure I'm heard. The Boss hesitates, so I use a few Blade Strikes to drag its attention to me again, targeting the open wound I was working on. "That's right. Right here, stupid."

The Boss finally turns to me, beam stinger swinging around to aim at me. A targeted blast by Vir catches it as it begins to charge up, forcing it to aim higher. I don't waste any more time, dashing forward to the creature's body. One thing about it being so big, there are dead zones where its own pincers can't target—if you can get close enough.

I run ahead, letting loose with the last of my projectile ammo as I do so, and carefully watch for the attack I know will come. When the pincer swings, I Blink forward to where I should be safe. Then I open up with another Blade Strike, targeting the softer, less-armored underside.

Not good enough to kill it, but it certainly angers the monster. Anger is good—it lets you push through pain and obstacles that you couldn't otherwise, but it also blinds you, clouds your judgment, and makes you take the easiest, most instinctive choice. I can't be hit by the pincers, but I'm close enough to bite. So it does.

"*Noooo!*" Ali screams as I stand still, letting the mouth close in on me.

At the last minute, I kick off the ground and jump directly into its mouth, throwing myself as deep as I can get to bypass as much of the teeth as possible. I make it most of the way, my foot catching and ripping itself apart on the backrow of teeth.

It's very dark in here—dark and squishy. I'm entirely grateful that I can neither smell nor truly feel what is happening to me, thanks to Sabre and the

Soul Shield I've turned on. On the other hand, the Boss, having eaten me, has decided to swallow. I find myself thrown to the back of its throat, and only a hastily dug-in sword to its larynx stops me from sliding all the way in. It takes a little scrambling and a lot of hard pushing, but I find myself lodged just above the creature's esophagus.

Still, can't let it go hungry. I drop the first of the sticky grenades I have left down its throat, ignoring the screaming alarm bells and the increased pressure on me as the Boss swings its head around, trying to dislodge me. The grenade goes off, coating the insides of its throat. It explodes below where I wanted it to go off, but that's okay, I've got more coming.

Before I started this insane plan, I spent a few moments running around the cavern, grabbing bodies and rocks and stuffing it all into my Altered Space. Now I let it loose, along with everything else I've got stored in there. My tent, drone pieces, armor replacements for Sabre, tent pegs and hammocks, my dinner, everything in my Altered Space gets dropped down its throat, interspersed with the occasional sticky grenade. The Boss keeps reflexively swallowing, attempting to dislodge me and get its breathing back, but I refuse, continually working on clogging up its throat and thus its airway.

My Soul Shield finally blinks out and I don't have enough Mana to throw up another. The Boss swallows again and the muscles in its throat clench, sending pain through my body as Sabre compresses and begins to redline. That's it then. That's all I can do.

I rip downward with my sword, opening up the wound in its mouth, then I trigger the QSM for one final shift, dropping myself out of this reality and consequently its mouth. I hit the ground hard, as gravity still works on me, and am treated to the final death throes of the Boss. It tosses and turns, slamming its head against the ground and the wall in an attempt to dislodge and clear its throat.

As I get up to run, the Mana battery in the QSM beeps empty and it automatically kicks me back into "normal" reality. Without any additional Mana, the changeover is harsh and pulls a scream from me as muscles, bones, and nerves are thrown across the dimensional barrier. I whimper, lying on the ground in pain, unable to move as the Boss lashes out in a frenzy around me. A glancing blow from one of its legs sends me flying into a wall, and I black out finally.

***

I come to in blessed peace. Outside of the hiss of cooling stone and the drip of water, there is silence. Awake and without Sabre, I'm assaulted by the stench in the cavern. In its dying moments, the Boss Frakin voided its bowels, leaving a yellow-pink mixture all around that smells worse than two-week-old rotting meat and baby diapers. I heave and throw up, only managing to roll far enough to the side that only half of my vomit hits me.

I whimper, the sudden movement setting off a pair of screaming toddlers in my head. Mana drained, physically wiped, and with only a touch of health left, I wonder where Sabre is and why I'm unarmored, but mostly, I wonder when the pain will stop.

"Awake finally, eh?" The voice cuts across my misery, gloating amusement in its tone. "Well, rest five minutes, then we should get going. The Frakin are still around and some are beginning to come back."

I open my eyes, blurry spots slowly resolving into Shadow-girl. I've really got to remember her name sometime. Next to her, Ali floats, casually admiring her booty. I'd say something, but I'm pretty sure she knows—and has either given up on correcting the incorporeal Spirit or just doesn't care.

Next to the two is the split-open form of Sabre—the mecha must have ejected me after its Mana battery gave out.

"You are insane, boy-o. Effective but insane," Ali says, and I force a grin.

"Had you worried." I try to push myself up and find myself failing to do so. I just relax as my body, aided by the regeneration potions I downed earlier, works on putting me together. Already, my body is repairing the damage.

"I must concur with the Spirit," Vir adds from where he is seated, head resting on his arms. There's blood on his torso and one arm looks pretty shredded. He smiles at me though, probably to show he means no real disrespect. It looks creepy on the normally stern Guard, and I wish he'd stop. "That was not a tactic I would have considered."

"No shit," the woman says, eyes roving over the cavern.

I tilt my head upward, noting that her Status bar is still blank. Damn, but it's annoying not being able to read System data on her.

"What exactly did you do anyway? Poison it?" she asks.

I blink, then realize they would have no way to see into the monster's corpse. "Blocked its airway. Choked it to death."

"Huh." Shadow-girls frowns.

I see a slight shift in her body just before she disappears and closes in on the Frakin that wandered back into the cavern. A moment later, she walks back to us, cleaning her blade. Behind her, the Frakin screams and twitches, its legs on one side severed. It begins to froth from its mouth as the poison she used takes effect.

"You good yet?" she asks.

I glance at my bars and take stock of my own physical situation before I answer her. "Five minutes."

"Fine."

While I recover, Ali fills me in on what happened after I blacked out. Seems like Shadow-girl popped over to my body and dragged me out of the way of the frenzied Boss, then she protected Vir and me from the remnants of the Frakin guard while the Boss died. It didn't take long, and she mopped up the group soon after. Since then, they've been waiting for me to wake up. I guess I owe the lady one.

When they finish speaking, I read System notifications as a way to distract myself from the throbbing pain.

Congratulations! Dungeon Cleared

+10,000 XP

First Clear Bonus

Having cleared the dungeon for the first time, you have been rewarded an additional +5,000XP +1,000 Credits. Bonus for being the first explorer +5,000 XP +5,000 Credits.

Two-Horn Mountain Dungeon classified as Level 50+ and above.

System Quest Complete (Onlivik Spores)

Destroy the Onlivik Spores that have infected the Frakin in the Two-Horn Mountain Dungeon.

Rewards (shared): 50,000 Credits, 20,000 XP

Level Up! * 4

You have reached Level 34 as an Erethran Honor Guard. Stat Points automatically distributed. You have 12 Free Attribute Points and 3 Class Skills to distribute.

I blink, staring at the huge level gains. Between the completion bonuses and the kill bonuses, I jumped up a heck of a lot of Levels in one fight. I wish it'd been earlier, but beggars and choosers and all that.

"Next time you're on one of these jaunts, call me," Shadow-girl says as I look up. "The experience was pretty damn good."

I snort and glance at Vir, who is looking significantly better now.

He straightens, standing up and pulling a rifle from his inventory. "Shall we?"

***

The journey back is a slow one, only manageable because the Frakin are disorganized, damaged, and confused. The loss of the Boss must have wiped out their central intelligence, removing any last remnants of organization. Shadow-girl—whose name I finally learn is Ingrid Starling—makes sure to kill any Frakin we run into. Vir and I mostly offer verbal and moral encouragement.

Two thirds of the way back, we finally run into our first rescue party. They have been setting up signal boosters along the way, which lets us contact everyone else and confirm that we're alive. The news on their end is less than stellar and I find myself dragging my feet more than I need to as we return. Call me a coward, but I'd rather face another Boss than what is coming.

The air in the cavern is somber when we arrive, individuals clustered in silent groups around fallen comrades. Low sobbing and grunting can be heard, while others carry their loss with fixed expressions, unable or unwilling to grieve yet. We won, but we didn't get out of this unscathed. The Hakarta lost a third of their people, having borne the brunt of the attacks, while the Yerick lost another pair. On our side, Jim's lost half of those he brought in. However, to me, all that pales beside the drawn, haggard face that is swarmed by huskies in an attempt at comfort.

I walk over to Lana, gently pushing at the puppies to move them aside. My gut clenches and I feel tears threaten to take over, but I push them aside, walling away my feelings. Not now, not me. Lana is sobbing, clutching the unmoving body with a death grip, blood staining her clothing from the open wounds on his corpse. Rachel grips Jason's arm as they watch over the redhead, at a loss of words. Squatting beside her, I place a hand on her shoulder. Lana flinches slightly but doesn't pull away. I feel a lump in my throat, blocking any words I could say. In the end, I just squat next to her, a hand on her shoulder, and wait.

Damn it, Richard.

Chapter 23

It takes a day more to completely clear the dungeon. With Mana pools and beam weapons recharged and the Frakin no longer bunching up and coordinated, it's a simple matter for the teams to spread out and finish off the monsters. I stay behind, keeping watch over the camp and Lana, who has taken control of her brother's pets, replacing those she lost. The only pet of Richard's that survived but she doesn't manage to get is Orel, who is long gone when we exit. Their job done, the Hakarta take off immediately with promises to get paid. Labashi shoots me a look when he leaves which reminds me that I'm still indebted and under contract with him.

In typical post-System fashion, the moment we get back to Whitehorse, we end up having to man the walls and fight off a monster swarm. Thankfully, it hits us from the airport side of town, so all we have to do is hunker down and kill. A few monsters try going down the cliffs, but they're simple enough to kill that it's more of a bother than a serious threat. We'll never know if a party was planned because after the swarm, everyone pitches in on the cleanup. Even Bill, though I notice he spends about as much time looting as he does hauling.

The fallout from the delve comes in small portions. Rachel left Whitehorse permanently, joining Jason in Carcross. Aiden has vowed to never leave the classroom again. There're even rumors that we might get another batch of immigrants soon from the System.

When I find time to visit the Shop, I sell the System-generated loot from my inventory. The central-Spore mass and the Frakin plasma generators both bring in significant Credits. I don't have the heart to go shopping right then though.

Once she calms down, Lana has me take Richard's body into my Altered Space to preserve it. A week after he died, we finally manage to make the trip to their old farm to bury him, his body set to rest beneath the remnants of their old house. Lana says little during the entire process, though I think, I believe, she finds comfort in Mikito's and my presence.

I watch her stand with her menagerie of pets, staring at her brother's grave, and my mind returns to the first night we got back to Whitehorse after the dungeon. She entered my room, distraught, and pushed me down, straddling me and laying fevered kisses on my face. I have to admit, I returned them for a time before good sense came back to me and I pushed her away.

"Why? Am I not good enough for you?" She was crying, clutching her open blouse closed. I recall the flash of pale, smooth flesh and the intoxicating scent of her.

"No, but you're grieving. This… you aren't thinking right."

She slapped me then and left. Since then, there's been a wall between us. I don't know if I did the right thing, if I made the right choice. I want her, I care for her—but not like that. What she wanted and what she needed weren't the same thing—and if I took advantage of her at that time, perhaps it would have wrecked our relationship. Or at least changed it in a way that I don't want. Or maybe not. Maybe I was an idiot.

I don't know if I did the right thing for her, for us, for our future. All I know is that it was the right choice for me at that time. Whatever happens, happens.

Lana slowly steps away from the grave, which has already received a light dusting of snow. She turns toward us, nodding just once before she walks to the truck. Something in the way she moves, the way she looks at us keeps us from bothering her.

***

I stare one last time at the grave, just a plot of earth and a basic stone cross. My lips twist as I realize that this, a simple ceremony and a grave, is more than most on this planet have been offered. More than the majority of humanity has to indicate their passing.

I close my eyes and whisper to Ali, "How many?"

"Eleven point four percent," Ali answers, his voice as soft as mine.

I nod dumbly. Nearly ninety percent of humanity, countless millions, are dead. I can't do anything for them. I can't even stop the ones who are still alive from dying, can't stop the mass murder of millions by the System. We're not the only ones either. On all the planets of the System, more die every day.

Our heroes are dead. The smart, the brave, and the good lie in countless graves all over the world. I keep trying to be something I'm not, and I keep failing. I'm no hero, no Lancelot or Superman. I don't do this because it's the right thing to do or because I think there's an intrinsic value to human life. I do it because I can't let go, because I can't seem to choose anything else. I do it because I have a sea of rage that never ends and I need an outlet, a place to point it.

What is, is.

No more walking away, no more hiding. The dead howl and cry; the lost and forgotten souls of the world weep. I'll light a pyre for them—for the ones who have died, for the ones who will die, and for the ones who will come into this blasted world. I'll light a fire so bright that they'll see it all the way in their damn Council. And then, when I'm done, I'll burn their damn System to the ground.

Ali floats back to me, staring at my face, and he inclines his head slightly. Yes, it's time to get back to work.

###

The End

Follow John and Ali's continued Adventures in

The Cost of Survival (Book 3 of the System Apocalypse)

Author's Note

Thank you for continuing to read and support my writing. The System Apocalypse series is meant to be an on-going series that will span at least twelve books, potentially more. The Whitehorse portion of the series will come to a conclusion in the next book. I'd say more, but that'd be giving away the plot. ☺

If you enjoyed reading the book, please do leave a review and rating. Not only is it a big ego boost, it also helps sales and convinces me to write more in the series!

Continue reading on John's and co.'s adventures in:

- The Cost of Survival (Book 3)
    https://readerlinks.com/l/729247

In addition, please check out my other series, Adventures on Brad (a more traditional LitRPG fantasy), Hidden Wishes (an urban fantasy GameLit series), and A Thousand Li (a cultivation series inspired by Chinese wuxia and xianxia novels).

To support me directly, please go to my Patreon account:

- https://www.patreon.com/taowong

For more great information about LitRPG series, check out the Facebook groups:

- LitRPG Society
    https://www.facebook.com/groups/LitRPGsociety/
- LitRPG Books
    https://www.facebook.com/groups/LitRPG.books/

About the Author

Tao Wong is an avid fantasy and sci-fi reader who spends his time working and writing in the North of Canada. He's spent way too many years doing martial arts of many forms, and having broken himself too often, he now spends his time writing about fantasy worlds.

For updates on the series and other books written by Tao Wong (and special one-shot stories), please visit the author's website:

http://www.mylifemytao.com

Subscribers to Tao's mailing list will receive exclusive access to short stories in the Thousand Li and System Apocalypse universes.

Or visit his Facebook Page: https://www.facebook.com/taowongauthor/

About the Publisher

Starlit Publishing is wholly owned and operated by Tao Wong. It is a science fiction and fantasy publisher focused on the LitRPG & cultivation genres. Their focus is on promoting new, upcoming authors in the genre whose writing challenges the existing stereotypes while giving a rip-roaring good read.

For more information on Starlit Publishing, visit their website: https://www.starlitpublishing.com/

You can also join Starlit Publishing's mailing list to learn of new, exciting authors and book releases.

Glossary

Erethran Honor Guard Skill Tree

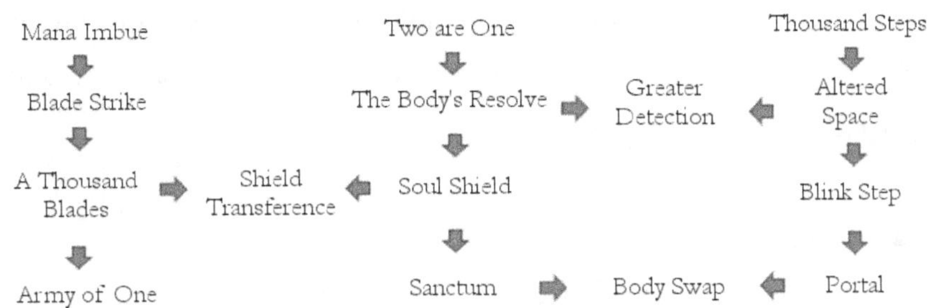

John's Skills

Mana Imbue (Level 1)

Soulbound weapon now permanently imbued with Mana to deal more damage on each hit. +10 Base Damage (Mana). Will ignore armor and resistances. Mana regeneration reduced by 5 Mana per minute permanently.

Blade Strike (Level 2)

By projecting additional Mana and stamina into a strike, the Erethran Honor Guard's Soulbound weapon may project a strike up to twenty feet away.

Cost: 35 Stamina + 35 Mana

Thousand Steps (Level 1)

Movement speed for the Honor Guard and allies are increased by 5% while skill is active. This ability is stackable with other movement-related skills.

Cost: 20 Stamina + 20 Mana per minute

Altered Space (Level 2)

The Honor Guard now has access to an extra-dimensional storage location of thirty feet cubed. Items stored must be touched to be willed in and may not include living creatures or items currently affected by auras that are not the Honor Guard's. Mana regeneration reduced by 10 Mana per minute permanently.

Two are One (Level 1)

Effect: Transfer 10% of all damage from Target to Self

Cost: 5 Mana per second

The Body's Resolve (Level 3)

Effect: Increase natural health regeneration by 35%. On-going health status effects reduced by 33%. Honor Guard may now regenerate lost limbs. Mana regeneration reduced by 15 Mana per minute permanently.

Greater Detection (Level 1)

Effect: User may now detect System creatures up to one kilometer away. General information about strength level is provided on detection. Stealth skills, Class skills, and ambient Mana density will influence the effectiveness of this skill. Mana regeneration reduced by 5 Mana per minute permanently.

Soul Shield (Level 2)

Effect: Creates a manipulatable shield to cover the caster's or target's body. Shield has 1,000 Hit Points.

Cost: 250 Mana

Blink Step (Level 2)

Effect: Instantaneous teleportation via line of sight. May include Spirit's line of sight. Maximum range—five hundred meters.

Cost: 100 Mana

Frenzy (Level 1)

Effect: When activated, pain is reduced by 80%, damage increased by 30%, stamina regeneration rate increased by 20%. Mana regeneration rate decreased by 10%.

Frenzy will not deactivate until all enemies have been slain. User may not retreat while Frenzy is active.

Cleave (Level 1)

Effect: Physical attacks deal 50% more damage. Effect may be combined with other Class Skills.

Cost: 25 Mana

Instantaneous Inventory (Maxed)

Allows user to place or remove any System-recognized item in Inventory if space allows. Includes the automatic arrangement of space in the inventory. User must touch item.

Cost: 5 Mana per item

Spells

Improved Minor Healing (III)

Effect: Heals 35 Health per casting. Target must be in contact during healing.

Cooldown 60 seconds.

Cost: 20 Mana

Improved Mana Dart (IV)

Effect: Creates four darts out of pure Mana, which can be directed to damage a target. Each dart does 15 damage. Cooldown 10 seconds

Cost: 25 Mana

Enhanced Lightning Strike

Effect: Call forth the power of the gods, casting lightning. Lightning strike may affect additional targets depending on proximity, charge and other conductive materials on-hand. Does 100 points of electrical damage.

Lightning Strike may be continuously channeled to increase damage for 10 additional damage per second.

Cost: 75 Mana.

Continuous cast cost: 5 Mana / second

Lightning Strike may be enhanced by using the Elemental Affinity of Electromagnetic Force. Damage increased by20% per level of affinity

Greater Regeneration

Effect: Increases natural health regeneration of target by 5%. Only single use of spell effective on a target at a time.

Duration: 10 minutes

Cost: 100 Mana

Fireball

Effect: Create an exploding sphere of fire. Deals 150 points of fire damage to those caught within. Sphere of fire expands to 5 feet radius (on average). Cooldown 60 seconds.

Cost: 100 Mana

Polar Zone

Effect: Create a thirty meter diameter blizzard that freezes all targets within one. Does 10 points of freezing damage per minute plus reduces effected individuals speed by 5%. Cooldown 60 seconds.

Cost: 200 Mana

Sabre's Load Out

Omnitron III Class II Personal Assault Vehicle (Sabre)

Core: Class II Omnitron Mana Engine

CPU: Class D Xylik Core CPU

Armor Rating: Tier IV (Modified with Adaptive Resistance)

Hard Points: 5 (5 Used)

Soft Points: 3 (2 Used)

Requires: Neural Link for Advanced Configuration

Battery Capacity: 120/120

Attribute Bonuses: +35 Strength, +18 Agility, +10 Perception

Inlin Type II II Projectile Rifle

Base Damage: N/A (Dependent Upon Ammunition)

Ammo Capacity: 45/45

Available Ammunition: 250 Standard, 150 Armor Piercing, 200 High Explosive, 25 Luminescent

Ares Type II Shield Generator

Base Shielding: 2,000 HP

Regeneration Rate: 50/second unlinked, 200/second linked

Mkylin Type IV Mini-Missile Launchers

Base Damage: N/A (dependent on missiles purchased)

Battery Capacity: 6/6

Reload rate from internal batteries: 10 seconds

Available Ammunition: 12 Standard, 12 High Explosive, 12 Armor Piercing, 4 Napalm

Other Equipment

Silversmith Mark II Beam Pistol (Upgradeable)

Base Damage: 18

Battery Capacity: 24/24

Recharge Rate: 2 per hour per GMU

Cost: 1,400 Credits

Tier IV Neural Link

Neural link may support up to 5 connections.

Current connections: Omnitron III Class II Personal Assault Vehicle

Software Installed: Rich'lki Firewall Class IV, Omnitron III Class IV Controller

Ferlix Type II Twinned-Beam Rifle (Modified)

Base Damage: 57

Battery Capacity: 17/17

Recharge rate: 1 per hour per GMU (currently 12)

Tier II Sword (Soulbound Personal Weapon of an Erethran Honor Guard)

Base Damage: 63

Durability: N/A (Personal Weapon)

Special Abilities: +10 Mana Damage, Blade Strike